With a great flapping of wings Reg launched herself from the ram skull and landed on his booted toes. Even through the polished leather he could feel her claws gripping.

"What job? With which organization? Saint Snodgrass and all her children defend me! Didn't you hear a word I said, Gerald? It takes *days* to choose a position properly! You have to check your prospective employer's references, his bank balance, his social standing, his pedigree! I don't believe this, it's the Department debacle all over again!"

Gerald peered down the length of his body at her. In the starlight from the open window her dark eyes gleamed, as did her long sharp beak. "Actually it's not. It's about as far from the Department as you can get. Didn't you say it was time I took a chance? Started walking the walk, not just talking the talk? Well, I've done it. This is me, walking. Reg, you are sitting on the feet of the next Royal Court Wizard to Lional the Forty-third, King of New Ottosland."

"New Ottosland?" she shrieked. "That obscure, sand-stranded, nothing little backwater?"

"Ah. You've been there," he said, pleased.

# Books by Karen Miller

*Kingmaker, Kingbreaker*

The Innocent Mage
The Awakened Mage

*The Godspeaker Trilogy*

Empress
The Riven Kingdom
Hammer of God

# Writing as K. E. Mills

*Rogue Agent*

The Accidental Sorcerer
Witches Incorporated

# THE accidental SORCERER

## ⇒ rogue agent book one ⇐

# K.E. MILLS

www.orbitbooks.net

New York London

Copyright © 2008 by Karen Miller
Excerpt from *Witches Incorporated* copyright © 2008 by Karen Miller
All rights reserved. Except as permitted under the U.S. Copyright Act of 1976, no part of this publication may be reproduced, distributed, or transmitted in any form or by any means, or stored in a data base or retrieval system, without the prior written permission of the publisher.

Orbit
Hachette Book Group
237 Park Avenue
New York, NY 10017
Visit our Web site at www.orbitbooks.net

Orbit is an imprint of Hachette Book Group, Inc. The Orbit name and logo is a trademark of Little, Brown Book Group Ltd.

Printed in the United States of America

Originally published in paperback by HarperCollins*Publishers* Australia Pty Limited: 2008
First Orbit edition in the USA: January 2009

10 9 8 7 6 5

With many many thanks to Russell T Davies,
who helped me rediscover my inner fangirl.

and

David Tennant, the 10th Doctor, because
he rocks and also, y'know . . . phwoar!

# THE accidental
# sorcerer

# CHAPTER ONE

The entrance to Stuttley's Superior Staff factory, Ottosland's premier staff manufacturer, was guarded by a glass-fronted booth and blocked by a red and blue boom gate. Inside the booth slumped a dyspeptic-looking security guard, dressed in a rumpled green and orange Stuttley's uniform. It didn't suit him. An ash-tipped cigarette drooped from the corner of his mouth and the half-eaten sardine sandwich in his hand leaked tomato sauce onto the floor. He was reading a crumpled, food-stained copy of the previous day's *Ottosland Times*.

After several long moments of not being noticed, Gerald fished out his official identification and pressed it flat to the window, right in front of the guard's face.

"Gerald Dunwoody. Department of Thaumaturgy. I'm here for a snap inspection."

The guard didn't look up. "Izzat right? Nobody tole me."

"Well, no," said Gerald, after another moment.

"That's why we call it a 'snap inspection'. On account of it being a surprise."

Reluctantly the guard lifted his rheumy gaze. "Ha ha. Sir."

Gerald smiled around gritted teeth. *It's a job, it's a job, and I'm lucky to have it.* "I understand Stuttley's production foreman is a Mister Harold Stuttley?"

"That's right," said the guard. His attention drifted back to the paper. "He's the owner's cousin. Mr Horace Stuttley's an old man now, don't hardly see him round here no more. Not since his little bit of trouble."

"Really? I'm sorry to hear it." The guard sniffed, inhaled on his cigarette and expelled the smoke in a disinterested cloud. Gerald resisted the urge to bang his head on the glass between them. "So where would I find Foreman Stuttley?"

"Search me," said the guard, shrugging. "On the factory floor, most like. They're doing a run of First Grade staffs today, if memory serves."

Gerald frowned. First Grade staffs were notoriously difficult to forge. Get the etheretic balances wrong in the split-second of alchemical transformation and what you were looking at afterwards, basically, was a huge smoking hole in the ground. And if this guard was any indication, standards at Stuttley's had slipped of late. He rapped his knuckles on the glass.

"I wish to see Harold Stuttley right now, please," he said, briskly official. "According to Department records this operation hasn't returned its signed and witnessed safety statements for two months. I'm afraid that's a clear breach of regulations. There'll be no First Grade staffs rolling off the production line today or any other day unless I'm fully satisfied that all proper precautions and procedures have been observed."

Sighing, the guard put down his soggy sandwich, stubbed out his cigarette, wiped his hands on his trousers and stood. "All right, sir. If you say so."

There was a battered black telephone on the wall of the security booth. The guard dialled a four digit number, receiver pressed to his ear, and waited. Waited some more. Dragged his sleeve across his moist nose, still waiting, then hung up with an exclamation of disgust. "No answer. Nobody there to hear it, or the bloody thing's on the blink again. Take your pick."

"I'd rather see Harold Stuttley."

The guard heaved another lugubrious sigh. "Right you are, then. Follow me."

Gerald followed, starting to feel a little dyspeptic himself. Honestly, these people! What kind of a business were they running? Security phones that didn't work, essential paperwork that wasn't completed. Didn't they realise they were playing with fire? Even the plainest Third Grade staff was capable of inflicting damage if it wasn't handled carefully in the production phase. Complacency, that was the trouble. Clearly Harold Stuttley had let the prestige and success of his family's world-famous business go to his head. Just because every wizard who was any wizard and could afford the exorbitant price tag wouldn't be caught dead without his Stuttley Staff (patented, copyrighted and limited edition) as part of his sartorial ensemble was no excuse to let safety standards slide.

*Bloody hell*, he thought, mildly appalled. *Somebody save me. I'm thinking like a civil servant . . .*

The unenthusiastic security guard was leading him down a tree-lined driveway towards a distant high brick wall with a red door in it. The door's paint was cracked and peeling. Above and behind the wall could be seen the slate-grey factory roof, with its chimney stacks belching pale puce smoke. A flock of pigeons wheeling through the blue sky plunged into the coloured effluvium and abruptly turned bright green.

Damn. Obviously Stuttley's thaumaturgical filtering system was on the blink: code violation number two. The unharmed birds flapped away, fading back to white even as he watched, but that wasn't the point. All thaumaturgical by-products were subject to strict legislation. Temporary colour changes were one thing. But what if the next violation resulted in a temporal dislocation? Or a quantifiable matter redistribution? Or worse? There'd be hell to pay. People might get hurt. What was Stuttley's playing at?

Even as he wondered, he felt a shiver like the touch of a thousand spider feet skitter across his skin. The mellow morning was suddenly charged with menace, strobed with shadows.

"Did you feel that?" he asked the guard.

"They don't pay me to feel things, sir," the guard replied over his shoulder.

A sense of unease, like a tiny butterfly, fluttered in the pit of Gerald's stomach. He glanced up, but the sky was still blue and the sun was still shining and birds continued to warble in the trees.

"No. Of course they don't," he replied, and shook

his head. It was nothing. Just his stupid over-active imagination getting out of hand again. If he could he'd have it surgically removed. It certainly hadn't done him any favours to date.

He glanced in passing at the nearest tree with its burden of trilling birds, but he couldn't see Reg amongst them. Of course he wouldn't, not if she didn't want to be seen. After yesterday morning's lively discussion about his apparent lack of ambition she'd taken herself off in a huff of ruffled feathers and a cloud of curses and he hadn't laid eyes on her since.

Not that he was worried. This wasn't the first hissy fit she'd thrown and it wouldn't be the last. She'd come back when it suited her. She always did. She just liked to make him squirm.

Well, he wasn't going to. Not this time. No, nor apologise either. For once in her ensorcelled life she was going to admit to being wrong, and that was that. He wasn't unambitious. He just knew his limitations.

Three paces ahead of him the guard stopped at the red door, unhooked a large brass key ring from his belt and fished through its assortment of keys. Finding the one he wanted he stuck it into the lock, jiggled, swore, kicked the door twice, and turned the handle.

"There you are, sir," he said, pushing the door wide then standing back. "I'll let you find your own way round if it's all the same to you. Can't leave my booth unattended for too long. Somebody important might turn up." He smiled, revealing tobacco-yellow teeth.

Gerald looked at him. "Indeed. I'll be sure to mention your enthusiasm in my official report."

The guard did a double take at that, his smile vanishing. With a surly grunt he hooked his bundle of keys back on his belt then folded his arms, radiating offended impatience.

Immediately, Gerald felt guilty. *Oh lord. Now I'm acting like a civil servant!*

Not that there was anything wrong, as such, with public employment. Many fine people were civil servants. Indeed, without them the world would be in a sorry state, he was sure. In fact, the civil service was an honourable institution and he was lucky to be part of it. Only . . . it had never been his ambition to be a wizard who inspected the work of other wizards for Departmental regulation violations. His ambition was to be an inspect*ee*, not an inspect*or*. Once upon a time he'd thought that dream was reachable.

Now he was a probationary compliance officer in the Minor Infringement Bureau of the Department of Thaumaturgy . . . and dreams were things you had at night after you turned out the lights.

He nodded at the waiting guard. "Thank you."

"Certainly, sir," the guard said sourly.

Well, his day was certainly getting off to a fine start. *And we wonder why people don't like bureaucrats . . .*

With an apologetic smile at the guard he hefted his official briefcase, straightened his official tie, rearranged his expression into one of official rectitude and walked through the open doorway.

And only flinched a little bit as the guard locked the red door behind him.

*It's a wizarding job, Gerald, and it's better than the alternative.*

Hopefully, if he reminded himself often enough, he'd start to believe that soon.

The factory lay dead ahead, down the end of a short paved pathway. It was a tall, red brick building blinded by a lack of windows. Along its front wall were plastered a plethora of signs: *Danger! Thaumaturgical Emissions! Keep Out! No Admittance Without Permission! All Visitors Report To Security Before Proceeding!*

As he stood there, reading, one of the building's four doors opened and a young woman wearing a singed lab coat and an expression of mild alarm came out.

He approached her, waving. "Excuse me! Excuse me! Can I have a word?"

The young woman saw him, took in his briefcase and the crossed staffs on his tie and moaned. "Oh, no. You're from the Department, aren't you?"

He tried to reassure her with a smile. "Yes, as a matter of fact. Gerald Dunwoody. And you are?"

Looking hunted, she shrank into herself. "Holly," she muttered. "Holly Devree."

He'd been with the Department for a shade under six months and in all that time had been allowed into the field only four times, but he'd worked out by the end of his first site inspection that when it came to the poor sods just following company orders, sympathy earned him far more co-operation than threats.

He sagged at the knees, let his shoulders droop and slid his voice into a more intimate, confiding tone.

"Well, Miss Devree—Holly—I can see you're feeling nervous. Please don't. All I need is for you to point me in the direction of your boss, Mr Harold Stuttley."

She cast a dark glance over her shoulder at the factory. "He's in there. And before you see him I want it understood that it's not my fault. It's not Eric's fault, either. Or Bob's. Or Lucius's. It's not any of our faults. We worked hard to get our transmogrifer's licence, okay? And it's not like we're earning squillions, either. The pay's rotten, if you must know. But Stuttley's—they're the best, aren't they?" Without warning, her thin, pale face crumpled. "At least, they used to be the best. When old Mr Horace was in charge. But now . . ."

Fat tears trembled on the ends of her sandy-coloured eyelashes. Gerald fished a handkerchief out of his pocket and handed it over. "Yes? Now?"

Blotting her eyes she said, "Everything's different, isn't it? Mr Harold's gone and implemented all these 'cost-cutting' initiatives. Laid off half the Transmogrify team. But the workload hasn't halved, has it? Oh, no. And it's not just us he's laid off, either. He's sacked people in Etheretics, Design, Purchasing, Research and Development—there's not one team hasn't lost folk. Except Sales." Her snubby nose wrinkled in distaste. "Seven new sales reps he's taken on, and they're promising the world, and we're expected to deliver it—except we can't! We're working round the clock and we're still three weeks behind on orders and now Mr Harold's threatening to dock us if we don't catch up!"

"Oh my," he said, and patted her awkwardly on the shoulder. "I'm very sorry to hear this. But at least it explains why the last eight safety reports weren't completed."

"But they were," she whispered, busily strangling her borrowed handkerchief. "Lucius is the most senior technician we've got left, and I know he's been doing them. *And* handing them over to Mr Harold. I've seen it. But what *he's* doing with them I don't know."

Filing them in the nearest waste paper bin, more than likely. "I don't suppose your friend Lucius discussed the reports with you? Or showed them to you?"

Holly Devree's confiding manner shifted suddenly to a cagey caution. The handkerchief disappeared into her lab coat pocket. "Safety reports are confidential."

"Of course, of course," Gerald soothed. "I'm not implying any inappropriate behaviour. But Lucius didn't happen to leave one lying out on a table, did he, where any innocent passer-by might catch a glimpse?"

"I'm sorry," she said, edging away. "I'm on my tea break. We only get ten minutes. Mr Harold's inside if you want to see him. Please don't tell him we talked."

He watched her scuttle like a spooked rabbit, and sighed. Clearly there was more amiss at Stuttley's than a bit of overlooked paperwork. He should get back to the office and tell Mr Scunthorpe. As a probationary compliance officer his duties lay within very strict guidelines. There were other, more senior inspectors for this kind of trouble.

On the other hand, his supervisor was allergic to incomplete reports. Unconfirmed tales out of school from disgruntled employees and nebulous sensations of misgiving from probationary compliance officers bore no resemblance to cold, hard facts. And Mr Scunthorpe was as married to cold, hard facts as he was to Mrs Scunthorpe. More, if Mr Scunthorpe's marital mutterings were anything to go by.

Turning, Gerald stared at the blank-faced factory. He could still feel his inexplicable unease simmering away beneath the surface of his mind. Whatever it was trying to tell him, the news wasn't good. But that wasn't enough. He had to find out exactly *what* had tickled his instincts. And he did have a legitimate place to start, after all: the noncompletion of mandatory safety statements. The infraction was enough to get his foot across the factory threshold. After that, well, it was just a case of following his intuition.

He resolutely ignored the whisper in the back of his mind that said, *Remember what happened the last time you followed your intuition?*

"Oh, bugger off!" he told it, and marched into the fray.

Another pallid employee answered his brisk banging on the nearest door. "Good afternoon," he said, flashing his identification and not giving the lab-coated man a chance to speak. "Gerald Dunwoody, Department of Thaumaturgy, here to see Mr Harold Stuttley on a matter of noncompliance. I'm told he's inside? Excellent. Don't let me keep you from your duties. I'll find my own way around."

The employee gave ground, helpless in the ruthlessly cheerful face of officialdom, and Gerald sailed in. Immediately his nose was clogged with the stink of partially discharged thaumaturgic energy. The air beneath the high factory ceiling was alive with it, crawling and spitting and sparking. The carefully caged lights hummed and buzzed, crackling as firefly filaments of power drifted against their heated bulbs to ignite in a brief, sunlike flare.

A dozen more lab-coated technicians scurried up and down the factory floor, focused on the task at hand. Directly opposite, running the full length of the wall, stood a five-deep row of benches, each one equipped with specially crafted staff cradles. Twenty-five per bench times five benches meant that, if the security guard was right, Stuttley's had one hundred and twenty-five new First Grade staffs ready for completion. The technicians, looking tense and preoccupied, fiddled and twiddled and realigned each uncharged staff in its cradle, assessing every minute adjustment with a hand-held thaumic register. All the muted ticking made the room sound like the demonstration area of a clockmakers' convention.

At either end of the benches towered the etheretic conductors, vast reservoirs of unprocessed thaumaturgic energy. Insulated cables connected them to each other and all the staff cradles, whose conductive surfaces waited patiently for the discharge of raw power that would transform one hundred and twenty-five gold-filigreed five-foot-long spindles of oak into the world's finest, most prestigious, expensive and potentially most dangerous First Grade staffs.

Despite his misgivings he heard himself whimper, just a little. Stuttley First Graders were works of art. Each wrapping of solid gold filigree was unique, its design template destroyed upon completion and never repeated. The rare wizards who could afford the extra astronomical cost had their filigrees designed specifically for them, taking into account personal strengths, family history and specific thaumaturgic signatures. Those staffs came with in-built security: it was immediate and spectacularly gruesome death for any wizard other than the rightful owner to attempt the use of them.

Once, a long long time ago, he'd dreamed of owning a First Grade staff. Even though he didn't come from a wizarding family. Even though he'd got his qualifications through a correspondence course. Wizardry cared nothing for family background or the name of the college where you were educated. Wizarding was of the blood and bone, indifferent to pedigrees and bank balances. Some of the world's finest wizards had come from humble origins.

Although . . . not lately. Lately, Ottosland's most powerful and influential wizards came from recognisable families whose names more often than not could also be heard whispered in the nation's corridors of power.

Still. *Technically*, anybody with sufficient aptitude and training could become a First Grade wizard. Social standing might influence your accent but it had nothing to do with raw power. *Technically*, even a tailor's son from Nether Wallop could earn the right to wield a First Grade staff.

Unbidden, his fingers touched his copper-ringed cherrywood Third Grade staff, tucked into its pocket on the inside of his overcoat. It was nothing to be ashamed of. He was the first wizard in the family for umpteen generations, after all. Plenty of people failed even to be awarded a Third Grade licence. For every ten hopefuls identified as potential wizards, only one or two actually survived the rigours of trial and training to receive their precious staff.

And even for Third Grades there was work to be had. Wasn't he living proof? Gerald Dunwoody, after a couple of totally understandable false starts, soon to be a fully qualified compliance officer with the internationally renowned Ottosland Department of Thaumaturgy? Yes, indeed. The sky was the limit. Provided there was a heavy cloud cover. And he was indoors. In a cellar, possibly.

*Oh lord*, he thought miserably, staring at all those magnificent First Grade staffs. It felt as though his official Departmental tie had tightened to throttling point. *There has to be more to wizarding than this*.

An irate shout rescued him from utter despair. "Oy! You! Who are you and what are you doing in my factory?"

He turned. Marching belligerently towards him, scattering lab coats like so many white mice, was a small persnickety man of sleek middle years, clutching a clipboard and looking so offended even his tea-stained moustache was bristling.

"Ah. Good afternoon," he said, producing his official smile. "Mr Harold Stuttley, I presume?"

The angry little man halted abruptly in front of him, clipboard pressed to his chest like a shield. "And if I am? What of it? Who wants to know?"

Gerald put down his briefcase and took out his identification. Stuttley snatched it from his fingers, glared as though at a mortal insult, then shoved it back. "What's all this bollocks? And who let you in here? We're about to do a run of First Grades. Unauthorised personnel aren't allowed in here when we're running First Grades! How do I know you're not here for a spot of industrial espionage?"

"Because I'm employed by the DoT," he said, pocketing his badge. "And I'm afraid you won't be running anything, Mr Stuttley, until I'm satisfied it's safe to do so. You've not submitted your safety statements for some time now, sir. I'm afraid the Department takes a dim view of that. Now I realise it's probably just an oversight on your part, but even so . . ." He shrugged. "Rules are rules."

Harold Stuttley's pebble-bright eyes bulged. "Want to know what you can do with your rules? You march in here uninvited and then have the hide to tell me when I can and can't conduct my own business? I'll have your job for this!"

Gerald considered him. *Too much bluster. What's he trying to hide?* He let his gaze slide sideways, away from Harold Stuttley's unattractively temper-mottled face. The thaumic emission gauge on the nearest etheretic conductor was stuttering, jittery as an icicle in an earthquake. Flick, flick, flick went the needle, each jump edging closer and closer to the bright red zone marked *Danger*. In his nostrils, the clogging stink of overheated thaumic energy was suddenly stifling.

"Mr Stuttley," he said, "I think you should shut down production right now. There's something wrong here, I can feel it."

Harold Stuttley's eyes nearly popped right out of his head. "Shut down? Are you raving? You're looking at over a million quid's worth of merchandise! All those staffs are bought and paid for, you meddling twit! I'm not about to disappoint my customers for some wet-behind-the-ears stooge from the DoT! Your superiors wouldn't know a safe bit of equipment if it bit them on the arse—and neither would you! Stuttley's has been in business two hundred and forty years, you cretin! We've been making staffs since before your great-grandad was a randy thought in his pa's trousers!"

Gerald winced. By now the air inside the factory was so charged with energy it felt like sandpaper abrading his skin. "Look. I realise it's inconvenient but—"

Harold Stuttley's pointing finger stabbed him in the chest. "It's not happening, son, *that's* what it is. *Inconvenient* is the lawsuit I'll bring against you, your bosses and the whole bleeding Department of Thaumaturgy, you mark my words, if you don't leg it out of here on the double! Interfering with the lawful conduct of business? This is political, this is. Too many wizards buying Stuttley's instead of the cheap muck your precious Department churns out! Well I won't have it, you hear me? Now hop it! Off my premises! Or I'll give you a personal demonstration why Stuttley's staffs are the best in the world!"

Gerald stared. Was the man mad? He couldn't throw out an official Department inspector. He'd have his manufacturing licence revoked. Be brought up on charges. Get sent to prison and be forced to pay a hefty fine.

Little rivers of sweat were pouring down Harold Stuttley's scarlet face and his hands were trembling with rage. Gerald looked more closely. No. Not rage. Terror. Harold Stuttley was beside himself with fear.

He turned and looked at the nearest etheretic conductor. It was sweating too, beads of dark blue moisture forming on its surface, dripping slowly down its sides. Even as he watched, one fat indigo drop of condensed thaumic energy plopped to the factory floor. There was a crack of light and sound. Two preoccupied technicians somersaulted through the air like circus performers, crashed into the wall opposite and collapsed in groaning heaps.

"*Stuttley!*" He grabbed Harold by his lapels and shook him. "Do you see that? Your etheretic containment field is leaking! You have to evacuate! *Now!*"

The rest of the lab coats were congregated about their fallen comrades, fussing and whispering and casting loathing looks in their employer's direction. The acrobatic technicians were both conscious, apparently unbroken, but seemed dazed. Harold Stuttley jumped backwards, tearing himself free of officialdom's grasp.

"Evacuate? Never! We've got a deadline to meet!" He rounded on his employees. "You lot! Back to work! Leave those malingerers where they are, they're all right, they're just winded! Be on their feet in no time—*if* they know what's good for them. Come on! You want to get paid this week or don't you?"

Aghast, Gerald stared at him. The man *was* mad. Even a mere Third Grade wizard like himself knew the dangers of improperly contained thaumic emissions. The entire first year of his correspondence course had dealt with the occupational hazards of wizarding. Some of the illustrations in his handbook had put him off minced meat for *weeks*.

He stepped closer to the factory foreman and lowered his voice. "Mr Stuttley, you're making a very big mistake. Falling behind in your safety statements is one thing. It's a minor infringement. Not worth so much as half a paragraph in *Wizard Weekly's* gossip column. But if you try to run this equipment when clearly it's not correctly calibrated, you could cause a scandal that will spread halfway round the world. You could ruin Stuttley's reputation for years. Maybe forever. Not to mention risk the lives of all your workers. Is that what you want?"

Harold Stuttley swiped his face with his sleeve. "What I want," he said hoarsely, "is for you to get out of here and let me do my job. There's nothing wrong with our equipment, I tell you, it—"

*"Quick, everyone! Run for your lives! The conductors are about to invert!"*

As the technician who'd shouted the warning led the stampede for the nearest door, Gerald spun on his heel and stared at the sweating etheretic conductors. The needles of each thaumic emission gauge were buried deep in the danger zone and the scattered drops of energy had coalesced into foaming indigo streams. They struck the factory floor like lances of fire, blowing holes, scattering splinters. The insulating cables linking the conductors to each other and the benches glowed virulent blue, shimmerings of power wafting off them like heat haze on a dangerous horizon.

Balanced in their cradles, the First Grade staffs began to dance.

"We have to turn off the conductors!" said Gerald. "Before all the staffs are charged at once or the conductors blow—or both! Where are the damper switches, Stuttley?"

But Harold Stuttley was halfway out of the door, his clipboard abandoned on the floor behind him.

Wonderful.

Now the etheretic conductors were humming, a rising song of warning. The air beneath the factory ceiling stirred. Thickened, like curdling cream, and took on a faintly blue cast. He felt every exposed hair on his body stand on end. His throat closed on a gasp as the etheretically burdened atmosphere turned almost unbreathable. Something warm was trickling from his nostrils.

He should run. Now. Without pausing to pick up his briefcase. Those conductors were going to invert any second now, and when they did—

"Bloody *hell*!" he shouted, and leapt for the nearest cable.

It wouldn't disengage. None of the cables would disengage. He ran up and down the benches, tugging and swearing, but the leaking power had fused the cables to the cradles and each other.

He'd have to get the staffs clear before they all got charged.

Stumbling, sweating, parched with terror, he started hauling the gold-filigreed oak spindles out of their cradles. Tossed them behind him like so much inferior firewood, even as the air continued to coalesce and the etheretic conductors juddered and sweated and discharged bolts of indiscriminate power.

In his pocket his modest little cherrywood staff began to glow. It got so hot he had to stop flinging the First Grade staffs around and drag off his coat, because it felt like his leg was burning. Moments after he threw the coat to the floor the wool burst into flames and disintegrated into charred flakes, revealing his smoking staff with its copper bands glowing bright as a furnace.

The First Grade staffs he'd released from confinement leapt about the floor like popcorn on a hotplate. Those still in their cradles began to buzz. On a sobbing breath he continued tearing them free of the benches.

Ten—twenty—thirty: oh lord, he'd never finish in time—

And then the staffs were simply too hot for flesh to touch. As he fell back, scorched and panting, the power's song became a scream. Both thaumic emission gauges exploded, the top of the conductors peeled open like soup cans . . . and a torrent of unprocessed, uncontrolled etheretic energy poured out of the reservoirs and into the remaining First Grade staffs.

The thaumic boom blasted him against the nearest wall so hard he thought for a moment he was dead, but seconds later his blackened vision cleared.

He wished it hadn't.

Terrible arcing lines of indigo power surged around and through the staffs he'd failed to pull free of their conductive cradles. The emptied conductors, ripped apart from the inside out, lay fallen on their sides. Two ragged gaping holes in the ceiling directly overhead spilled sunlight onto the dreadful aftermath of undisciplined thaumic energies. Through them spiralled two thin columns of unfiltered emissions: the leftover power not captured by the staffs escaping into the wider world beyond the factory.

Groaning, Gerald staggered to his feet. If he didn't shut down that self-perpetuating loop of energy pouring through the First Grade staffs it would continue to build and build until it exploded . . . most likely taking half the suburb of Stuttley with it. It wasn't a job for a lowly probationary compliance officer, or a Third Grade wizard who'd received his qualifications from a barely recognised correspondence course. He doubted it was even a job for a First Grade wizard . . . at least, not one working solo. A whole squadron might manage it, at a pinch.

But that was wishful thinking. There wasn't time to contact Mr Scunthorpe and get him to send out a flying squad of Departmental troubleshooters. There was just him. Gerald Dunwoody, wizard Third Grade. Twenty-three years old and scared to death.

*So long, life. I hardly lived you . . .*

Looming large before him, the howling, writhing mass of thaumaturgically linked First Grade staffs, bathed in unholy indigo fire. Abandoned on the floor at his feet, his pathetic little cherrywood staff, as useful now as a piece of straw.

And scattered around him, four of the First Grade

staffs he'd managed to rescue before the massive conductor inversion. Rolling idly to and fro they glowed a gentle gold, their filigree activated. They must have been caught in the nimbus of exploding thaumic energy.

Everybody knew that Third Grade wizards didn't have the etheretic chops to handle a First Grade staff. Even using a Second Grader was to risk life, limb and sanity. Attempting to use one of those erratically charged First Graders was proof positive that sanity had left the building.

But he had no choice. This was an emergency and he was the only Department official in sight. Instincts shrieking, fear a gibbering demon on his back, he reached for the nearest activated First Grade staff. If it was one of the special orders, keyed to a specific wizard, then he really was about to breathe his last—

A shock of power slammed through his body. The world pulsed violet, then crimson, then bright and blinding blue, spinning wildly on its axis. Something deep inside his mind torqued. Twisted. Tore. His vision cleared, the mad giddiness stopped, and he was himself again. More or less. *Something* was different, but there was no time to worry or work out what.

Bucking and flailing like a live thing, the staff struggled to join its brethren in the heart of the magical maelstrom. Gerald got his other hand onto it, battling to contain the energy. It felt like standing inside the world's largest waterfall. The staff was channelling the excess energies from the atmosphere, attracting them like a magnet. Pummelled, battered, he wrestled with the flux and flow of power. Poured everything he had into taming the beast in his fists.

But the beast didn't want to be tamed.

Gasping, fighting against being pulled into the maelstrom, he opened his slitted eyes. The etheretic conductors were empty now, their spiralling columns of power collapsed. But the trapped staffs within the indigo firestorm continued to blaze, amplifying and distorting the energies they'd consumed. Only minutes remained, surely, before they exploded.

And he had no idea how to stop them.

# CHAPTER TWO

Desperate, Gerald tipped back his head and stared through the nearest hole in the factory ceiling. This was no time for pride; he'd take help from anywhere.

"Reg? *Reg*! Are you out there? Can you hear me?"

No reply. Did that mean she was just refusing to answer or was she really not there? Was this the one time she'd actually done what he asked and was keeping her beak out of his business?

*Typical.*

"Reg, if you're out there I'm sorry, all right? I apologise. I *grovel*. Just—*help*!"

Still no answer. Breathing like a runner on his last legs he ignored the howling pain in his shoulders and wrists and battled the gold-filigreed staff to a temporary standstill. Like a wilful child it fretted and tugged, still trying to join its blazing siblings.

A glimmer of an idea appeared, then, an iceberg emerging out of a fogbank. Staffs were both conduits and reservoirs of power. They were attracted to it like flies to honey. Yes, this staff was already charged—but not completely. And everybody knew that Stuttley's staffs absorbed higher levels of raw thaumic energy than any other brand in the world. So if he could just coax some more of that untamed pulsing power into this activated staff and perhaps one or two others—maybe he could prevent the imminent enormous explosion.

Summoning the last skerricks of his strength, he inched closer to the indigo firestorm. Immediately the staff began to fight him again. He hung on grimly: letting go would be the worst, last mistake of his life. When he was as close to the writhing thaumic energy as he could get without being sucked in, he stopped. Raised the staff above his head. Focused his will, and plunged it end-first into the factory floor.

Where it stuck, quivering.

A questing tendril of thaumic energy licked towards it and, amidst a sizzling crackle, fused with the staff's intricate gold fretwork. More power poured into the tall oak spindle. Gerald watched, the stinking air caught in his throat. If it held . . . if it held . . .

The transfer held.

Staggering, he picked up another partially activated staff and plunged it into the floor two feet along from the first. Within moments it too was siphoning off the lethal, undirected thaumic energy. He did the same to a third staff, then a fourth. A fifth. A sixth. By the time he'd finished, he was looking at a whole row of crackling, power-hazed First Grade staffs and his legs could barely hold him upright. His lungs were a pair of deflated balloons. Indigo spots danced before his eyes. But he'd done it. He'd averted disaster. The suburb of Stuttley and its famous staff factory were saved.

Holly Devree had kept his handkerchief, so he smeared the sweat from his face with one shirt-sleeve and watched, exhausted, as the ferocious thaumic firestorm faded. Smiled, shaking, as the car-battering roar of untrammelled power abated.

Saint Snodgrass's trousers. Had anything like this ever happened before? A Third Grade wizard managing to successfully stymie a major thaumaturgical inversion? He'd never heard of it. As he stood there, gently panting, he let his imagination off its tight leash.

*This could be it, Dunwoody. This could be your big chance, finally.*

Mr Scunthorpe would have to take him seriously now. Let him off probation early. Possibly even approve a transfer to a different department altogether. Even— miracle of miracles—Research and Development.

The thought of reaching such an exalted height made him dizzy all over again.

With a final whimpering sputter the last randomly dissipated etheretic energies discharged into the staffs he'd plunged into the floor. The benches and staffs still trapped in their conductive cradles disintegrated in a choking cloud of indigo ash.

Despite his exhaustion and his myriad aches and pains, Gerald did a little victory dance.

"Yes! Yes! R and D boys, here I come!"

Then he stopped dancing, because it was that or fall over. Instead he just stood there, eyes closed, heart pounding, revelling in his moment of unexpected triumph.

Breaking the blessed silence, a sound. Thin. Sharp. Dangerous—and escalating. Nervously he opened his eyes. Stared at the militarily upright staffs plunged into the floor. Before he had time to blink, the first one transformed into a narrow blue column of fire. Moments later the second followed suit. Then the rest, one by one, like a row of falling dominoes. The air began to sparkle. The factory floor began to smoke.

He frowned. "Oh." Apparently he'd found the thaumaturgical limit of a Stuttley Superior Staff. *How clever of me*. Research and Development, indeed. "Right. So this would be a good time to run away, yes?"

His wobbly legs answered for him. He had just enough time and wit to grab up his poor little cherry-wood staff and reach the nearest door. The blast wave caught him with his fingers still on the handle, tumbled him through the air like so much leaf litter and dropped him from a great height into the middle of an ornamental rose garden.

The last thing he saw, before darkness claimed him, was the irate face of Harold Stuttley.

"You bastard! You *bastard!* I'll have your job for this!"

Mr Scunthorpe folded his hands on top of his desk and shook his head. "Gerald . . . Gerald . . . Gerald . . ."

Gerald winced. "I know. Mr Scunthorpe," he said contritely. "And I'm very sorry. But it wasn't my fault. Honestly."

It was much later. The ambulance officers from the district hospital had fished him out of the rose garden then transported him, over his objections, to the emergency room, where an unsympathetic doctor extracted all the rose thorns from various and delicate parts of his anatomy and pronounced him sound in wind and limb, if deficient in intelligence. Which meant he was free to catch a taxi back to Stuttley's and drive at not much above snail's pace home to the Department of Thaumaturgy so he could make his report.

Unfortunately, Harold Stuttley's tongue had travelled a damned sight faster.

"Not your fault, Gerald?" echoed Mr Scunthorpe, and looked down at the paperwork in front of him. "That's not what the people at Stuttley's are saying. According to them you barged into the middle of a highly sensitive First Grade thaumaturgical transfer, ignored all reasonable warnings and pleas to leave before there was an accident, used your Departmental authority to evict the personnel from their lawful premises and then caused a massive explosion which only by a miracle failed to kill someone, or reduce everything within a radius of three miles to rubble. As it is you totally destroyed the factory, which is going to put back staff production by months. I have to tell you Lord Attaby is profoundly unamused. One of the staffs you blew up had his nephew's name on it."

It took a moment for Gerald's brain to catch up with his ears. When it did, he almost choked. "What? But that's rubbish! Yes, all right, the factory did blow up, but I'm telling you, Mr Scunthorpe, that wasn't my fault! Harold Stuttley caused that! The etheretic conductors failed due to a lack of proper maintenance. They were on the brink of inversion when I got there! Ask the technicians! They'll tell you!"

Mr Scunthorpe tapped his fingernails on the open file. "What I just told you. Gerald, is a summary of their testimony. Theirs and, of course, Mr Harold Stuttley's. He's threatening all kinds of trouble. Lord Attaby is very unhappy."

"But—but—" He clenched his fingers into fists. "I *went* there in the first place because there was a protocol violation. Overdue safety statements. That proves they—"

Mr Scunthorpe's round face was suffused with temper. "All it proves, Mr Dunwoody, is that even the best of companies can fall behind with their paperwork. You were sent to Stuttley's to deliver a polite reminder to this nation's most valuable and prestigious staff manufacturer that the Department of Thaumaturgy looked forward to their prompt provision of all relevant documentation. You were *not* sent there to cause international headlines!"

*Mr Dumvoody*. Gerald leaned forward, feeling desperate. "But there was a woman! I spoke to her! She said things weren't being done right, she said there was trouble." He scrabbled around in his post-explosion memory. "Devree! That was her name! Find her. *Ask* her. She'll tell you."

Mr Scunthorpe rifled through the sheets of paper in front of him. "Holly Devree?" He extracted a statement, picked up his glasses on their chain around his neck, placed them on his nose and read out loud: "I don't know what happened. I was on my tea break. I never saw the man from the Department. This means my job, doesn't it? What am I going to do now? I've got a sick mother to support. Signed: Holly Devree."

"No," he whispered. "That's not how it happened, Mr Scunthorpe. My word as a compliance officer."

"*Probationary* compliance officer," said Mr Scunthorpe, still frowning. "Very well then, Gerald. What's your version of today's unfortunate events?"

Haltingly, feeling as though he'd wandered into somebody else's insane dream, Gerald told him. When he was finished he sat back in his chair again. "And that's the truth, sir. I swear it."

Mr Scunthorpe closed his mouth with a snap. "The truth?"

"Yes, sir."

Mr Scunthorpe's face was so red he could have found work as a traffic light. "You expect me to believe that a Third Grade wizard from Nether Wallop, who got his qualifications from some fourth-rate correspondence course, who got fired from his first job for insubordination and his second for incompetence, not only managed to single-handedly prevent a Level Nine thaumaturgical inversion but did so, moreover, by using the most expensive, the most finely calibrated, the most *lethal* First Grade staffs in the *world*? Is *that* what you expect me to believe?"

"Well," he said, after a moment. "When you put it like that . . ." Then he rallied. "But sir, far-fetched or not that's exactly what happened. I can't explain how, or why, but that's precisely what I did."

"Dunwoody, what you're saying is impossible!" said Mr Scunthorpe, and pounded a fist on his desk. "No Third Grade wizard in history has ever used a First Grade staff without frying himself like bacon.

To suggest *you* managed it is to stretch the bounds of credulity across five alternate dimensions!"

The urge to punch Scunthorpe in the nose was almost irresistible. "Are you calling me a liar?"

"I'm calling you a walking disaster!" Scunthorpe retorted. "A carbuncle on the arse of this Department! Do you have any idea of the phone calls I've been getting? Lord Attaby! The Wizard General! *Seven* prime ministers and *two* presidents! And don't get me started on the press!"

Gerald stopped breathing. Scunthorpe was going to fire him. The intention was in the man's glazed eyes and furious, scarlet face. If he was fired from another job it'd be the end of his wizarding career. No-one would touch him with a forty-foot barge pole after that. He'd have to go home to Nether Wallop. Beg his cousins for a job in the tailor's shop his father had sold them. They'd give him one, he was family after all, but he'd never hear the end of it.

*I'd rather die.*

"Let me prove it, Mr Scunthorpe," he said. "Fetch me a First Grade staff and I'll prove I can use one."

"Are you *mad*?" shouted Scunthorpe. "After this afternoon's little exhibition do you think there's a wizard anywhere in the world who'd risk letting you even *look* at his First Grader, let alone touch it? And do you think I'd risk *my* job to ask them?"

"Then how am I supposed to show you I'm telling the truth?"

It was a fair question and Scunthorpe knew it. He snatched a pencil from his desktop and twisted it between his fingers. "I'm telling you, Dunwoody, you won't be let anywhere near a First Grade staff. But—" The pencil snapped. With enormous forbearance, Scunthorpe placed the two pieces on the blotter. "—*if* you can use a First Grader then a Second Grader shouldn't pose the slightest difficulty." He stood and crossed to the closet in the corner of his office. From it he withdrew four feet of slender, silver-bound Second Grade staff. Holding it reverently, he turned. "Lord Attaby gave me this staff with his own hands, Dunwoody. In recognition of my twenty-five years impeccable service to the Department. If I give it to you, here and now, will you promise not to break it?"

Gerald swallowed, feeling ill. "I can't do that, sir. But I can promise I'll try."

Pale now, and sweating, Scunthorpe nodded. "All right then."

"What do you want me to do?"

"Nothing spectacular!" said Mr Scunthorpe, darkly. "Something simple. Noncombustible." He nodded at the painting on the wall beside him, an insipid rendition of the first opening of Parliament in 1142. "Animate that."

He swallowed a protest. Animation might be noncombustible but it was hardly simple. All right, for a First Grade wizard it was child's play and for a Second it was unlikely to cause a sweat. For a Third Grade wizard, though, animation required a command of etheretic balances that tended to induce piles in the unprepared.

Scunthorpe bared his teeth in a smile. "I take it you do know an appropriate incantation?"

Sarcastic bugger. Yes. As it happened he knew all

kinds of high-level incantations, and not all of them entirely . . . legal. Reg had insisted on teaching him dozens, even though his cherrywood staff was totally inadequate when it came to channelling them. Even though he, apparently, was equally inadequate. *Learn them*, she'd insisted. *You never know when one might come in handy*.

Maybe she'd been right after all. Maybe this was one of those times. And anyway, what did he have to lose?

He held out his hand for Scunthorpe's staff. Reluctantly Scunthorpe gave it to him. Closing his eyes, he took a moment to centre himself. To rummage through his collection of interesting but hitherto irrelevant charms and incantations until he found the one that would rescue him from his current predicament.

"Hurry up, Dunwoody," said Scunthorpe. "I've an appointment to see Lord Attaby. Somehow I've got to *explain* all this."

"Yes, sir," he said, still rummaging. Then he recalled a small but effective binding that would set the picture's painted crowd politely clapping.

The silver-chased staff in his hands felt heavy and cool. He couldn't detect the smallest sense of latent power from it. When was the last time Scunthorpe had used it? Or sent it out to be thaumically recharged? God help him if the damned thing had a flat battery—

"Hurry *up*, Dunwoody!" snapped Scunthorpe. "I'm running out of patience!"

"Right," he said, and settled his shoulders. Extended the staff until its tip touched the painting's frame, closed his eyes and in the privacy of his mind uttered the animation binding.

Nothing happened. No burning surge of power through the staff, no giddy-making roil of First Grade thaumic energy in his veins or repeat of that strange torqueing tearing sensation he'd felt in Stuttley's factory. Not even his usual Third Grade tingling. And no sound of tiny painted hands, clapping. No sound at all except for Scunthorpe's stertorous breathing.

He cleared his throat. "Um. Why don't I just try that again?"

Before Scunthorpe could refuse he attempted to animate the painting a second time. Nothing. A third time. Nothing. A fourth ti—

"Forget it!" shouted Scunthorpe, and snatched back his precious silver-filigreed staff. "You're a fraud, Dunwoody! After a performance like that I'm at a loss to understand how you even got your *Third* Grade licence! My Aunt Hildegarde's geriatric cat has more wizarding talent than you!"

Stunned, Gerald stared at the uncooperative painting. Then he fished inside his overcoat and pulled out his slightly singed cherrywood staff. Turning, he snatched the broken pencil pieces from Scunthorpe's desk, tapped them with his staff and uttered a joining incant, a task so simple it wasn't even included in the Third Grade examination.

The pencil stayed stubbornly broken.

*Oh God.* "I don't understand it," he muttered. "I've got nothing. *Nothing.* How can that be? Unless—" Horrified, he stared at Scunthorpe. "Do you think I burned myself out when I short-circuited the inversion? Do you think channelling all that raw thaumic energy through those First Grade staffs somehow used up all my power?"

"All *what* power?" roared Scunthorpe. "You don't *have* any power, Dunwoody! You're the worst excuse for a wizard I ever met! I must've been *mad* the day I took pity and gave you a job! I must've been *raving*! Get out! You're fired!"

Gerald felt his throat close. *Fired.* Again. His stomach heaved. "Mr Scunthorpe, I protest. I didn't do anything wrong. Harold Stuttley's the criminal here, not me. I don't care what he says, I contained that thaumic inversion, I didn't cause it. The resulting explosion was unfortunate but—"

"*Unfortunate?*" Scunthorpe wheezed. "You mean catastrophic! Are you really this naive, Dunwoody? Stuttley's is demanding a parliamentary enquiry! They're threatening to sue the government! They want this entire Department disbanded!"

"But—but that's ridiculous—"

"Of course it's ridiculous!" snapped Scunthorpe. "But that's not the point! The point is that if your head's not rolling down the Department staircase in the next five minutes we will lose control of this situation!"

"And then what? Harold Stuttley gets off scot-free?"

"Never you mind about Harold Stuttley! Forget you ever heard of Harold Stuttley! This isn't about Harold Stuttley. Dunwoody, it's about *you*. Don't you *understand*? You've embarrassed the Department and disgraced your staff. You're finished, do you hear me? *Finished*! So don't stand there staring like a poleaxed bullock! Get out of my office. Get out of the *building*.

So that when Lord Attaby demands the privilege of personally kicking you into the street I can put my hand on my heart and say I don't know where you are!"

Gerald shook his head. "This isn't right. I'm not going to take this lying down, Mr Scunthorpe. I'm going to—"

"What?" sneered Scunthorpe. "Demand an enquiry of your own? Go on record claiming you're a better wizard than the likes of Lord Attaby himself? *You*? A correspondence course Third Grader? Well, I suppose you can. If you insist. But you'll never work as a wizard again, Dunwoody. That much I can promise you."

Stung, he looked at his red-faced superior. "I thought I was already finished!"

Abruptly Scunthorpe's manner softened. "You are, son. At least around here. But if you go quietly, no fuss, no indignant, outlandish claims and accusations, lay low for a while, well, I'm sure once the dust has settled, in a few months, a year maybe, some little locum agency somewhere will take you on."

"A year?" He almost laughed. "And what am I supposed to do in the meantime?"

Scunthorpe shook his head. "Sorry. That's not my problem. You should have thought of that before you blew up Stuttley's. Now if I could just have your official badge . . ."

Fingers numb, Gerald pulled his identification wallet out of his pocket and handed it over. In a final act of petulant defiance, he undid his official tie and thrust that at Scunthorpe as well. Then, with as much dignity as his tattered pride could muster, he turned on his heel and marched out of Mr Scunthorpe's pokey office.

Mr Scunthorpe slammed the door closed behind him.

Braving the gauntlet of eyes beyond it, the secretaries and the other inspectors, the visiting bodies from elsewhere in the DoT, he felt as insignificant as a beetle and as conspicuous as an elephant. Not one of his former colleagues said a word, just watched him walk past desk after desk to the lifts in hot, humiliating silence.

Life in the street outside the DoT building continued in blissful ignorance of his latest wizarding debacle. Well-dressed, affluent citizens of the city were smiling, laughing even, as they bustled about their lives, the insensitive bastards. How could they? Didn't they know his lifelong dream had just gone up in smoke right along with Stuttley's bloody staff factory?

No. They didn't. And even if they did, would they care? Probably not. Nobody cared. Not even Reg. She'd flown off and left him. He was all alone. Alone, disgraced and unemployed.

*Stop snivelling, Dunwoody,* he told himself derisively. *Self-pity doesn't suit you.*

Maybe not, but wasn't he entitled? After three failed attempts at wizarding hadn't he earned himself at least one small snivel?

*All I wanted was to be a wizard. Is that so damned much to ask?*

Yes. Apparently it was.

The motor he'd driven out to Stuttley's belonged to the DoT carpool. When he wasn't on official business he caught the bus. Well, he couldn't afford to do that any more. He'd have to watch every last penny now until he somehow managed to find another job. Street-sweeping, probably, if he decided he really couldn't face his revolting cousins and the tailor shop his father had loved and toiled in for most of his working life.

With his spirits sloshing about his ankles he headed for home, the Wizards' Club, where he rented a room.

But for how much longer he had no idea.

At the time of its official opening—October 19, 1274, according to the tarnished plaque by the front doors—the Wizards' Club had been brand spanking new. The wrought iron gates were shiny and silent, the brass-bound front doors undented and scratchless, the windows unwarped, the roof tiles gleaming, and its sandstone bricks clean and creamy white like newly churned butter.

But down the long centuries the club's pale sandstone bricks had acquired a patina of soot and ivy; exotic weeds began a ceaseless war for equal squatting rights amongst the flowerbeds; and a tangled jungle of briars, blackberries and tigerteeth grew up to flourish like living barbed wire around the property's perimeter, guaranteeing privacy without the tedium of having to regularly renew unfriendly incantations.

Now, nearly six hundred years later, all that could be said of the club was that it was still there, defiant in its grimy and time-twisted old age like an ancient relative who refuses to be decently shuffled off to the Sunshine Home for Old Wizards.

Dusk was dragging slow fingers through the tops of the ornamental amber trees as Gerald dawdled his disconsolate, chilly and blistered way along the quiet street. Even the starlings settling in for the night sounded derisive as they commented on his reluctant progress towards the club's now rusty and slightly mangled front gates.

His heart sank as he scanned the visitors' car park. Errol Haythwaite's gleaming silver Orion. James Kirkby-Hackett's scarlet Chariot. Edward Cobcroft Minor's black Zephyr. Oh lord. They were *all* here? So soon?

Well, of course they were. Haythwaite and Co had probably rushed right over as soon as the news about Stuttley's hit the streets.

He perused the residents' car park, hoping to see Monk Markham's battered blue Invincible, but it wasn't there. Hardly surprising. Monk's current secret project for the Department's Research and Development division had swallowed him alive, metaphorically speaking. He hadn't been home for three days.

Gerald sighed. A pity. Monk was his best friend, and such a genius not even the likes of Haythwaite and Co dared to offend him. What he was doing renting rooms at the club and slaving away as a civil servant when he could name his price anywhere in the world and have his pick of palaces to live in was a mystery.

The lowering sun sank a little further behind the trees. He shivered.

*Come on, Dunwoody, you gutless worm. You can't loiter out here on the footpath all night. Might as well get it over with.*

He stared at the gates. They were shut. To open them, all he had to do was wave his hand and say the word.

Except . . .

What if it didn't work? Walking home he'd steadfastly refused to let himself dwell on that heartstopping moment in Scunthorpe's office when the thaumatic ether wouldn't obey him. But now he had to think of it. What if he really was finished? What if that insane stunt with the First Grade staffs had burned out his meagre talent? What if the only thing in the world he was good for now was tailoring?

Please, no. *No.* Heart thumping, he scrabbled for his cherrywood staff and waved it at the closed club gates. "Open! *Open!*"

A spurting fizzle of power. A momentary pause that lasted forever. Then, with a complaining groan and a flaking of rust, the wrought iron gates dragged sluggishly apart. He fell against them, panting. *Thank you, thank you, thank you.*

His abilities, such as they were, had returned.

Straight ahead, at the end of a long brickwork path, squatted six wide stone steps. Above them loomed the club's ancient, imposing front doors. And behind those doors waited Haythwaite and Co, doubtless primed with Bellringer's best brandy and salivating at the thought of dragging that upstart nobody Dunwoody down a peg or two. Because the idea of discretion or sympathy was as foreign to them as a delegation of ambassadors from Katzwandaland. Errol and his friends had tongues like well-sharpened knives and there was nothing they enjoyed more than carving up their social inferiors. Especially when those inferiors made spectacularly public blunders.

*On the other hand, perhaps loitering isn't such a bad idea after all.*

"Bloody hell," he said to the fading sky. "When did I turn into such a coward?"

Heart colliding painfully with his ribs, he walked through the gates.

The club's parquet reception area was blessedly deserted. Blinking in the carefully cultivated gloom Gerald checked his pigeonhole and found a letter from his globe-trotting parents. This one was post-marked *Darsheppe*. He had to think for a moment where that was. Oh, yes. Capital city of Hortopia. Halfway round the world. Suddenly that seemed even further away than it actually was.

As he stared at his mother's sprawling scrawl he found himself torn between relief that they weren't here to witness his latest disaster, and sharp sorrow that he'd disappointed them again. That was the trouble with being the only offspring: no sibling shoulders to help carry the burden of familial expectations.

Mr Pinchgut, the club's retainer and general fac-totum, emerged from his tiny office set underneath the grand staircase that led up to the private apart-ments. He saw Gerald and stopped. From the angle of his bushy eyebrows and the particular stiffness of his tail-coated spine it was clear he'd heard all about Stuttley's. Gerald tucked the letter into his pocket and nodded at him.

"Mr Pinchgut."

The retainer favoured him with a frosty bow. "Mr Dunwoody."

He sighed. "Would it help if I said it wasn't my fault?"

Mr Pinchgut thawed, ever so slightly. "I'm sure it's not for me to comment, sir."

"Even so. It wasn't."

Another bow. "Yes, sir. May I say I hope that's a comforting thought?"

"You may," he said, heading for the stairs. "But we both know you'd be wasting your breath."

It was tucked away at the rear of the club's top floor. Squashed cheek-to-jowl inside were a saggy-mattressed single bed, a lopsided wardrobe, a narrow cupboard, a three-legged card table, a rickety chair, a very skinny bookcase and a single temperamental gas ring. Mysterious plumbing groaned and gurgled at all hours of the day and night. The bathroom he shared with six other wizards was on the next floor down. This meant a chamber-pot, which added a certain piquancy to the atmosphere. There was one miserly window with a fine view of the noisome compost heap and only two places where he could stand completely upright without cracking his head on an exposed roof beam.

"Reg?" he called softly as he kicked the bedsit door unstuck and shoehorned himself inside. "Reg, are you here?"

A resounding silence was the only reply. He flicked on the light-switch and looked around, but the room was empty.

*Dammit.* Where the hell *was* she? He'd left the window open, just in case. She should *be* here, all broody and complaining on the tacky, revolting old ram skull she insisted on using for a perch. Eating a mouse and leaving the tail on the floor because tails always get stuck halfway down. Why wasn't she here? They'd quarrelled before. Hell, they quarrelled practically every day. Just because he'd lost his temper and called her a moulting feather duster with the manners of a brain-damaged hen, was that any reason to fly off in high dudgeon and not come back?

Had she gone for *good*?

Scrunching down to avoid the rafters, he crossed to the window and stuck his head out. The last of the daylight was almost gone and the first faint stars were starting to sparkle. A thin rind of moon teetered low on the distant horizon. All in all, it was a beautiful evening.

He couldn't have cared less.

"Reg!" he called in the loudest stage whisper he could manage. "Reg, are you out here?"

Nothing.

"Don't be an idiot," he told himself sternly. "She's fine. She's only a bird on the outside. Anybody who tries to mess with Reg is making their last mistake. She'll be back. She's just trying to wind you up."

And it was working, dammit.

Defeated, Gerald pulled his head back into the room and slumped on the edge of his horrible bed. Two more springs died, noisily.

His stomach grumbled. Lunch had been hours ago and he'd been a bit busy since then, one way and another. But steak and chips in the club's dining room was an expense he could no longer afford and anyway . . . Errol Haythwaite and his ghastly friends were downstairs.

He didn't have the heart to face them. Not without

Monk Markham as back up, at least. And if that made him a coward then fine. He was a coward.

There was a tin of baked beans in the cupboard, and a can opener, and a spoon, for emergencies. If this didn't qualify as an emergency he didn't know what did.

*Bloody hell. I hate baked beans.*

Morose, disconsolate and feeling more alone than he'd ever felt in his life, he went about eating his pathetic, solitary supper.

# CHAPTER THREE

Melissande heard the commotion when she was still one dingy corridor away from the palace's Large Audience Chamber. Raised voices. Indignant expostulations. The *rat-a-tat-tat* of ebony canes on marble-tiled flooring. She felt her insides clench. Her brisk footsteps slowed, and her heart suddenly felt too large for her chest.

Someone was arguing with Lional.

She started hurrying again, breath caught in her throat. More than likely it was the Council. Oh, how could they be so *stupid*? Didn't they understand her brother yet? When were they going to realise that Lional wasn't his father? The late king had been a kind, mostly ineffectual man who was more than happy to let the Council run the kingdom on his be-half. Leave him alone to potter in his gardens and trundle out once or twice a year for public display and he was perfectly content.

Lional wasn't. For a start, he didn't like gardens. Even less did he like being told what to do by a bunch of nattering old men. The only thing Lional and the late king had in common was the name. And in the last few months, as kingship took its toll, Lional's temper had grown markedly short.

Fearing the worst she sprinted the final eight yards and skidded around the corner to the audience chamber's reception area. Now she could make out actual words in the shouting. Words like "foolish" and "ridiculous" and "misguided".

Saint Snodgrass preserve them.

Her other brother was sitting in a plush red velvet chair, his bony nose stuck in a book as usual. From the ratty state of his britches and jacket he'd come straight from his butterfly house. It was possible he'd even slept there last night; half a green butterfly wing was caught in his hair and he had a rumpled, unbedlike look. Ignoring the shouting and the two discomfited attendants on either side of the open chamber doors, she rushed up to him and snatched the book from his hands.

"Rupert! What's going on? What are they yelling about now, do you know?"

Rupert blinked at her myopically. "What are who yelling about? Oh! You mean Lional and the Council?" He shrugged. "Haven't a clue, Melly. Sorry. I was engrossed in a particularly fascinating chapter about the mating habits of the Larger Crested Swamp Butterfly of Lower Limpopo." A gleam of passion shone in his faded blue eyes. "I'd give just about anything to have one in my collection but the Lower Limpopo government is so unreasonable when it comes to exporting their native fauna. I've even asked Court Wizard

Greenfeather to help, since he's from Lower Limpopo and seems to know everybody important, but—"

"*Rupert!*" Confiscated book pinned between her knees, Melissande clapped her hands sharply in front of his face. "Are you sure you don't know what they're yelling about?"

"Positive," said Rupert cheerfully. He wiggled his fingers at her. "Can I have my book back, please?"

Swallowing an impatient sigh she shoved it at him. There was no point getting angry with Rupert. He was a darling man, a sweet and thoughtful brother, but not even an adoring sister could call him the brightest candle in the palace chandelier.

Inside the audience chamber the shouting stopped. She heard Lional say, "Raise your voices to me one more time, gentlemen, and there will be consequences, is that clear?"

There was a moment's silence and then the voices resumed. This time they were pitched at a respectful murmur.

"Whoops," said Rupert, wincing. "I think they've really made him cross this time."

Melissande slumped into the chair beside him. "They always do, the silly old fools. You'd think they'd learn." With a sigh, she patted Rupert's threadbare knee. "What brings you here, anyway?"

He brightened. "I need permission to leave the country. There's a terribly important symposium in Aframbigi I want to attend. 'Natural Mutations Arising From Captive Lepidoptery Breeding Programs'. It's being chaired by Professor Sunyi herself!" He released a tiny, ecstatic sigh. "I've read every book and pamphlet she's ever written. The idea of *meeting* her—"

"Is pretty much out of the question," she said, as gently as she could. "Balloon season's over and the Kallarapi are still refusing nonessential camel-train passage."

Rupert's expression turned mulish. "There's still the portal."

"The *portal*? Don't be silly, Rupert. Lional will never let you use it. Not for a butterfly symposium."

"He might. If I ask him nicely."

Dear Rupert. Deluded, ever-hopeful Rupert. There was no point arguing, either. The only trait he and their older brother had in common was a streak of stubbornness as wide as the Kallarapi Desert. She patted his knee again. Sometimes she felt like Rupert's mother, not his little sister.

"Yes, Rupe. You can always ask."

"Don't worry, I will." He sniffed. "Why do you want to see him?"

"I don't. I was summoned." She chewed at a fingernail. "I hope it's not about finishing school again. How many more times can I say no? For pity's sake, I'm nearly twenty-one! Finishing school would finish me all right, but not in the way *he* thinks. And anyway, I don't have time."

"Because of your correspondence course with Madame—"

"*Shhh!*" she hissed, and glanced at the po-faced chamber attendants. They never looked as though they were listening but one couldn't be too careful. She lowered her voice. "Partly. And I have a feeling I should be here."

"But Mel . . ." said Rupert anxiously, "you might not have a choice. After all, Lional's the king now. Father didn't much mind what any of us did so long as we weren't running all over his flowerbeds. But Lional's got *views*. Especially about being contradicted."

She waved a dismissive hand. "I'm his little sister. Putting me in prison wouldn't look good. Besides, Lional's bark is far worse than his bite, you know that." She patted his knee again. "Don't worry."

Rupert smoothed his thin fingers over the cover of his precious book. "Well, I hope you're right, Mel. But I still think you should reconsider. You never know, finishing school might be fun and at least it'd get you away from here for a—"

"*Dismissed?*" roared a voice from inside the audience chamber. "The entire Council? Is Your Majesty quite *mad?*"

"Mad? No!" was Lional's cold reply. "But I am sorely tempted to serve you your liver fried with onions for daring to take that tone with *me*, your *king!*"

Melissande and Rupert leapt to their feet. Even the diplomatically deaf, dumb and blind chamber attendants quivered. "That sounded like Lord Billingsley," Rupert whispered hoarsely. "He always was a bit tactless."

"There's tactless and then there's suicidal," Melissande whispered back. She felt Rupert's cold hand groping for hers and wrapped her fingers round it. "I'm sorry, Rupe, but I think asking Lional for permission to leave the country will have to wait."

Rupert nodded. "Yes. D'you want me to stay anyway? You know, for moral support?"

A fresh babble of angry voices rose within the audience chamber. "No, I'll be fine. You go. We both know Lional in a temper gives you hives."

He let go of her hand. "Well," he said, sounding relieved. "If you're sure . . ."

She was certain. Rupert got on Lional's nerves even more than Lord Billingsley and the rest of the Council. All her life she'd pushed herself between them like a wodge of cotton wool, preventing unfortunate breakages.

"Positive." She stretched up and kissed his stubbly cheek. "I'll see you at dinner, all right? Say hello to the butterflies for me—and don't forget to shave. Lional's got views about that too, remember?"

Rupert departed, clutching his book. A moment later Lional's Council—his *former* Council—filed out of the audience chamber. Their expressions were identically thunderous. Ebony cane tips rapping the floor, they muttered to one another under their wheezing breaths as they limped and shuffled into the chamber's reception area, a group of old men whose aggregate age approached a staggering one thousand years.

No wonder Lional was tired of them.

Lord Billingsley, the youngest at seventy-six, paused to look down his bulbous nose at her. Like his colleagues he was dressed in the height of courtly fashion: striped trousers, tail coat and boiled shirt, with half a diamond mine's worth of stick pins and gewgaws thrust into his polka-dot silk cravat.

"Your Highness."

She nodded. "Lord Billingsley."

"Here to see the king?"

"That's right."

"Then I suggest you take a moment to talk some sense into him!" Billingsley snapped. His left eye twitched uncontrollably, threatening to shoot his monocle clear across the room. "He seems to have completely lost his reason!"

What could she say? The stuffy old man might well be right. It did seem crazy for Lional to dismiss the Council. He might be the king but he could hardly run the country on his own. However, agreeing with Billingsley meant disagreeing with Lional and that was treason. Technically, anyway. If Lional overheard he might ship her off to finishing school out of pique, no matter how old she was or how many times she declined the offer.

She graced Lord Billingsley with her most imperious smile. "Like you, my lord, I am His Majesty's loyal and obedient subject. If, during our audience, he asks me to talk some sense into him I will certainly attempt to do so. Was there anything else?"

Lord Billingsley cast a glance towards his colleagues, huddling like elderly sheep at the reception entrance, and made a great show of harrumphing and pretending he'd got the answer he wanted. Then he bowed, creakily.

"Not at this moment, Your Highness. Doubtless this is but a temporary state of affairs. I'm sure His Majesty will soon come to regret this decision. We will return to our estates now and await our recall. Good day."

Watching the offended Council members retreat, she almost felt sorry for them. All those years running the show behind the scenes while her father the cabbage king played figurehead . . . and now here was Lional. At nearly thirty he was less than half Lord Billingsley's age, and to the Council's mind scarcely old enough to shave unassisted. Throwing his weight around. Inconveniently insisting that kings had more important things to do than poison aphids and peruse seed catalogues.

"Melissande!" a deceptively sweet voice called from within the audience chamber. "I'm *waiting*!"

She sighed and looked to the rigidly noncommital chamber attendants. The one on the right banged his ceremonial pikestaff on the floor and said, unnecessarily, "His Majesty will see you now, Your Highness."

"Apparently. Don't bother announcing me, Willis." She poked a couple of escaping hairpins back into her slapdash bun, squared her shoulders and marched into the enormous, echoing audience chamber.

Lional was down off his throne, standing instead by the large leadlight windows in the grandiose room's far wall. Shafting sunlight turned his wavy hair to burnished gold and sparkled the rubies and emeralds in his crown. Long and lean, he wore his dark green silks like a second skin. His thickly lashed blue eyes were luminous, his wide cheekbones sharp enough to cut glass. His skin was lightly golden, and blooming fresh like a child's. Every inch of him shrieked athletic elegance and grace. He looked like a living legend.

It was hard to believe they were related.

A fat orange cat wove complicated patterns around his booted ankles. Tavistock. She didn't like Lional's pet, but the fact that he loved it without reservation gave her heart when his casual inconsiderations drove her to swearing and sometimes to tears.

It was a long walk up the thin strip of crimson carpet to reach him, and he didn't acknowledge her presence until she came to a stop a few feet from him. Tavistock eyed her with a slitted green gaze, smirking. Dratted animal.

Ignoring it, she sniffed. "Good morning. What was all that business with the Council? Surely you haven't—"

He raised a finger and both eyebrows. "Ah ah ah! What are we forgetting, Melissande?"

She frowned. "I don't know."

The finger wagged, admonishing. "I think you do."

"No, I really don't."

He sighed. "You're supposed to curtsey. I *am* the king, though sometimes I think the fact escapes you."

She looked around the otherwise deserted chamber. "Lional, we're the only ones in here."

"Nevertheless . . ."

"Oh, please! I'm wearing trousers!"

His glance was disapproving. "Put on a dress, then. You should wear a dress anyway. One with lace. And flounces. It's more princessly."

"You know perfectly well I don't wear dresses," she said, rolling her eyes. "They make me look like a badly sewn-up sack of wheat. Lional, have you really dismissed the Council?"

He turned away from the window and returned to his throne on its crimson-carpeted dais. Tavistock leapt into his lap with a grunt, turned around twice and settled on his knees. Claws like tiny scimitars paddled green silk, pulling threads. Lional tickled under the cat's chin. "You don't approve?"

No, she didn't, but wasn't stupid enough to say so. "I don't understand. I know Lord Billingsley and his cronies are tedious, but they—"

"Refuse to accept reality. The old regime is dead and buried, just like Father. *I* am king now. *I* make the decisions. Not them."

"Lional . . ." She stepped closer. "Be fair. They're old men, set in their ways, and you've been king for less than a year. I'm sure you'll get used to them once—"

"It's not for me to get used to them!" snapped Lional. "Like all my subjects they exist to serve, Melissande. And if they won't I have no use for them."

"But Lional, you need a Council," she said. "This kingdom's like a duck on a mill pond, you know. There's you sitting serenely on the surface and underneath there are all these other people working like demented grasshoppers to keep things moving. Believe me, I do understand if you don't want *those* councillors, but traditionally it's an hereditary position. Billingsley and the rest of them all have sons, they'll assume—"

"Assumptions," said Lional, dangerously, "are unwise. I have suspended Council activity for now. Billingsley, his cronies and their encroaching sons are forbidden the palace until further notice. I need time to think without them bleating in my ear, wanting this, demanding that, all under the mistaken impression that I'm here to *give* them things. Besides, they were costing an absolute fortune to feed and house here at court. It's about time they fed themselves and all their hangers-on, too. Last time I looked this was my palace, not a hotel."

She shook her head. "Gosh, Lional. They're not going to like that."

He smiled, his ring-laden fingers now buried in Tavistock's extravagant fur. "Behold me not heartbroken at the prospect."

It was true, the cost of keeping councillors, courtiers and their servants around the place was ruinous. But even so . . . "All right, you've stood down the Council for a while. So what will you do in the meantime? *Somebody* has to keep the wheels of government turning."

Another smile. "In the meantime, Melly, I have you."

She nearly swallowed her tongue. "*Me*? Lional, are you ma—" No, no, no. Don't say it. Dungeons were rumoured to be uncomfortable places. "—making a mistake?"

"Are kings capable of making mistakes?" her beautiful brother mused. "No, I don't believe they are. Melissande, my darling little sister, you cannot refuse me. The kingdom needs you."

"It needs a council more. Look, Lional, I appreciate your thinking of me but you need to think again. I'm not cut out for—"

"Oh, but you are. Intellectually you are as a giant to my former councillors' antish, ancient little minds," said Lional blithely. "And you're terribly organised. It used to irritate me, you know, the way you sat your dolls alphabetically by name along your toy shelf, but I see now I misjudged you. You're a born pettifogging administrator, Melly. And as New Ottosland's inaugural prime minister you'll—"

"Prime minister? You want to make me *prime minister*?" She knew her voice was squeaking but she couldn't help it. "Lional, you can't! It's against tradition! *And* I'm a girl!"

Lional's lips pursed. "Are you sure? I thought girls wore dresses."

"Oh, ha ha," she said, feeling desperate. "Lional, seriously, you can't make me prime minister."

"I'm the king, Melly," snapped Lional. "I can do whatever I want. And what I want is to drag us into the modern era and onto the international stage, kicking and screaming if necessary."

She folded her arms. "Not to mention foaming at the mouth. Lional—"

Ignoring her, he traced the edge of Tavistock's ear with a fingertip. His perfectly sculptured lips were curved in a dreaming smile. "I have such plans for this kingdom. A splendid vision."

"Then you need to get your eyes checked, because if you're really seeing me as prime minister then—"

The smile vanished. "*Silence!*"

She flinched and shut her mouth. Scowling, Lional shoved Tavistock off his lap, heedless of the cat's indignant yowling, and leapt lightly down from the dais.

"Save your breath, sister dear, for I'll entertain no further debate," he said, pacing. "You are henceforth Her Royal Highness Princess Melissande, Prime Minister of New Ottosland. Feel free to choose an office of your own, provided it's not too large, and decorate it however you like except expensively, because in case you hadn't noticed Father left us virtually *bankrupt*, the old coot. And after that make sure the kingdom continues to run like clockwork. That's all I ask."

Dazed, she sat heavily on the edge of the dais. "That's *all?*"

"Well, it is a very *small* kingdom, Mel. I can't imagine it'll be *that* hard."

She felt like tearing her hair out. "And I suppose in my spare time you'd like me to whip you up a plate of meringues?"

"I don't like meringues," said Lional, and leaned against the wall. "I'd not say no to half a dozen éclairs, though. With extra chocolate and cream."

She nearly threw Tavistock at him. "*Lional . . . !*"

Joining her on the dais, he slung his arm around her shoulders and squeezed. "Oh, come on, Melly. It's not like you won't have help. I'm sure I saw dozens of minions loitering about the place somewhere. It's about time they earned their keep. You'll love it. Giving orders from dawn till dusk. Bullying entire government departments into shape. You'll think you've died and gone to heaven."

She let herself slump against him. "Only if I can come back and haunt you. Lional . . ."

Another rallying squeeze. "You can do this, Mel. I know you can. I meant what I said about having a vision. We could be a great country, you know. Influential. Powerful. A major player on the world stage."

"I know you think that," she said carefully, after a moment. "And it's a nice idea, Lional, really, but please be serious for a moment. You said it yourself: the treasury's practically empty. What's more, we're hogtied and shackled by outdated traditions that'll get us laughed right off the world stage. Face it. We're a backwater colonial collection of rustics living in the middle of a bloody great desert and nobody cares what we do, or think, or say. Even the old mother country's almost forgotten we exist!" She pulled a face. "If you really want me to be your prime minister then fine. I'll be your prime minister. But as for the rest . . ."

Lional dropped a kiss on the top of her head and stood. "You let me worry about the rest, Mel. I'll make it happen, you'll see. And a lot sooner than you think. Tradition?" He snapped his fingers. "*That* for tradition! Right now, though, we need to concern ourselves with an important new development."

Groaning, Melissande got up and shoved her hands into her trousers' capacious pockets. "I'm almost afraid to ask."

Lional grinned. "The Kallarapi are coming."

She looked out of the nearest window, alarmed. "Now?"

Tavistock had curled up on the throne with his tail wrapped round his nose. Lional pushed him off and sat again, right leg slung negligently over its padded arm. The cat jumped back up to his lap, disgruntled.

"Not quite. According to the message I received this morning they should be here in a day or two."

"Which Kallarapi, do you know?"

"The holy man and the useless younger brother," he said, examining his manicured fingernails.

"And are they coming with or without accessories?"

Lional's eyebrows lifted. "I beg your pardon?"

She folded her arms again, glaring. "Are they bringing their army?"

He snorted. "Oh, come along now, Mel. We don't owe them *that* much. Strictly speaking we don't owe them anything at all."

"That's not how they see it."

"I don't particularly care how they see it," he said, admiring the way his ruby rings caught the sunlight.

She gave him a look. "I know. I expect that's why they're coming."

Typically, he ignored the look and the comment. "As my prime minister, Melissande, it'll be your job to entertain them while they're here. Naturally it won't do for *me* to see them. An audience with *me* will give them entirely the wrong idea. You'll show them the sights of a civilised society. Remind them of our blood ties to the oldest nation in the world. And after that you can show them the relevant records proving that when it comes to trade tariffs *we're* the ones who've been robbed, not them. In short, I expect you to make our culturally challenged neighbours lift their ridiculous camel-train embargo. It's not helping our financial position *at all*."

"That would be the point of it, Lional," she said, and heaved a sigh. "The thing is . . . I know you're convinced we're in the right but I wish you'd reconsider. Our trading treaty with the Kallarapi has been in place for nearly four centuries and there's never been any dispute over who owes what to whom until now."

"Meaning what, pray?" demanded Lional. "That somehow *I'm* to blame for their rapacious greed?

Why? Because I'm newly come to the throne? Must I remind you, Melissande, that the Kallarapi have also recently acquired a new ruler? And that all this trouble just happens to coincide with Zazoor's ascension to the throne, or the stuffed camel-hump, or whatever it is he sits on?"

She pressed her fingertips to her temples. "I know. And that's the problem, isn't it? You and Zazoor have hated one another from your first day at boarding school. Now, instead of behaving like sober, responsible potentates, you're treating this disagreement like just one more of your playground scuffles! And it's not! People's livelihoods are at stake here, Lional. Our very kingdom is at stake! Don't you understand? *Now* when you punch Zazoor *everybody* gets a nosebleed!"

Tavistock yowled, lashing his tail. Lional patted his head. "My sentiments exactly, Tav. Have a care, Melissande. There are ways and ways one may talk to a king. Some of them lead to unfortunate consequences."

"Like being fired, you mean?" she retorted. "Oh, please. You'd be doing me a favour. All I'm saying, Lional, is that like it or not they've got the advantage over us. The terms of the treaty are specific and binding and there's nothing we can do to change them!"

Lional's immaculate fingernails drummed the arm of his throne. "I suppose you have a point," he admitted at last, grudgingly.

"Yes. I have a point. I have lots of points, but not as many as the Kallarapi army. They've got thousands, each one at the end of a sword!" Feeling pressured,

Melissande shoved her hairpins back in her bun again. "I'll take a good long look at the tariff books myself, Lional, and I'll talk to the Kallarapi delegation when it gets here. But you have to be prepared to give some ground. Forget it's Zazoor you're dealing with. Remember you have a responsibility to your subjects. That's all I ask."

Lional smiled, revealing his perfect white teeth. "There. Didn't I say you'd make a splendid prime minister?" Scooping Tavistock into his arms, he stood. "Very well. I'll do as you suggest—this time. But be warned, Mel. There's giving ground and then there's surrender . . . and I'll see this verdant oasis of ours a charred and stinking ruin before I surrender it to anybody . . . least of all Zazoor."

Melissande felt her heart sink. He meant it. When it came to Sultan Zazoor, Lional wasn't entirely rational. He never had been, even as a child. What a shame the old sultan's heir had fallen into quicksand, leaving his second son to rule. She could foresee nothing but tantrums and fisticuffs for the next five decades or so.

It was a depressing vista.

"All right, Lional," she said, and dredged up a smile. "I'll consider myself duly warned. Now is there anything else? Only it seems I've suddenly got a lot of reading to do."

"In fact there is," said Lional. "I'm in need of a new court wizard."

She stared. "*Another* one? Why? What happened to Bondaningo?"

"Wizard Greenfeather resigned in a huff late last night and returned home via the portal just before

dawn," said Lional, shrugging. "I did my best to dis-
suade him but he was a most recalcitrant fellow.
Refused point-blank to reconsider. I don't mind
telling you, Mel: my feelings are hurt."

"I don't believe it," she said. "He didn't even say
goodbye. And I *liked* Bondaningo. Much more than
any of the others. He wasn't as ancient as most of
them and didn't talk to me as though I were six. Why
did he resign?"

Lional waved a hand. "I don't recall and it doesn't
matter. He's gone. Find me another one, will you?
Same specifications as before."

She shoved her fists in her pockets. "I've already
found you five, Lional. At the rate you're going every
wizard in the world is going to have 'Former advisor
to the King of New Ottosland' on his credentials."
Then, as Lional's face collapsed into displeasure, she
added, "All right, all *right*! I'll find you another one!"

"And quickly. It's very important."

"Yes, quickly, I promise. But for the love of Saint
Snodgrass, *please* don't fire or offend him until I've
finished dealing with the Kallarapi!"

Lional smiled. It was like watching the sun break
free of lowering storm clouds. "For you, sister dear,
whom I love as life itself? Of course. *Anything* for
you."

She'd never been able to resist Lional's smile, not
even after he'd decapitated one of her dolls or torn
the ears off her favourite stuffed donkey. "Thank you.
Now can I go?"

"You are excused, Prime Minister," Lional said
grandly, still smiling, and waggled his fingers. "Ta ta!"

Marching out of the audience chamber, head

whirling with dread premonitions of lurking obstacles yet to be discovered, Melissande throttled a shriek of frustration.

Prime minister? Prime *minister*? Whatever had she done to deserve this? And what had possessed her to accept the appointment? She'd only had the job five minutes and already she had a migraine.

If only she'd said yes to finishing school . . .

But it was too late now and regrets were pointless. She was Princess Melissande, Prime Minister of New Ottosland, and the Kallarapi were coming.

Time to get to work.

# CHAPTER FOUR

For two endless days Gerald lurked in his cramped bedsit, trying to work out what *exactly* had happened at Stuttley's. Trying to recreate that incredible sensation of transformation, of incandescent power welling up and thundering through him. All he did was give himself an incipient hernia. He couldn't even trust his Third Grade incants to work reliably. His power trickled, it sputtered, it sulked and wouldn't play.

Depressed, defeated, he gave up trying to recreate the miracle and instead fretted about Reg's continued absence. He'd gone from worry to anger and back again so many times he was permanently dizzy. She'd never stayed away this long before. Something must have happened. She was lying in a ditch somewhere, injured and delirious. Dying. Or she'd been captured by a travelling circus and imprisoned in a cage, forced to do tricks for food.

*Or she just got sick of your ineptitude and flew off to greener pastures.*

Whatever the reason, the result was the same. Reg was gone, he had no way of finding her, and he was turning into a crazy person staying cooped up in his tiny room. He needed to get out. Needed fresh air. A change of scenery.

And after that he needed to look his current predicament square in the face, accept it, and start the disheartening business of finding yet another job. Somewhere that had never even heard of Stuttley's Staff Factory.

If there was such a place.

*Oh lord*, he thought, sitting on the edge of his horrible bed with his head in his hands. *What I need is a drink. Two drinks. Lots and lots of drinks, and sod the dwindling bank balance . . .*

He went down to the club's public gallery. One glance through the doors and he nearly ran back upstairs. At the far end of the genteely shabby room, gathered around the sooty fireplace toasting crumpets and scoffing pastries, sat the appalling Errol Haythwaite and his equally appalling friends.

Thanks to the good fortune of being born into the stratosphere of wizarding society, the ineffably smug little group had risen swiftly to the top of the profession, leaving their less-favoured colleagues behind like so much skim milk. Like cream, they were smooth and lumpless and rich.

*Like cream*, he reminded himself, *they cause bloat, spots and apoplexy.*

Excruciatingly aware that to this group he wasn't so much the skim milk as the nasty bits at the bottom of the bottle once the skim milk had been fed to the cat, Gerald sidled further into the gallery, hoping to be overlooked. But just as he took his first step towards the solace of alcohol a hearty cry nailed his feet to the floor.

"I say, *look* who's finally crawled out of hiding! *Dunny*wood!"

Damn. Haythwaite was never going to tire of that stupid play on words. Whose bright idea was it anyway to nickname any outside toilet a *dunny*? And why wasn't toilet humour beneath Errol, along with servants, Third Grade wizards and anybody who couldn't trace his family tree back to the packet the seed came in?

If only he could ignore the man . . . but that, sadly, was out of the question. Third Grade wizards did *not* snub First Graders in public, with witnesses. Not if they ever wanted to work as a wizard again.

He turned, grittily polite. "Good evening, Errol. What a surprise to find you here. And it's Dun*woody*."

Errol Haythwaite, tall, thin and elegantly saturnine, waved a negligent hand. "Of course it is," he drawled nasally. "I say, come and join us why don't you, old bean?"

"Thanks, Errol, but—"

"No, really," said Haythwaite. Even from a distance it was clear the smile on his lips wasn't touching his eyes. "I insist."

Of course he did. Reluctantly Gerald joined the gruesome trio at the fireplace. "Yes?"

Typically perverse, Haythwaite ignored him. As though he was a butler, or Mr Pinchgut. "—*how* many times I have to say no. I mean, it's all very well the Potentate of Aframbigi offering me the position of Wizard at Large, but the old boy's put a few noses out of joint down at the Department and there's a whisper of sanctions."

"Then of course you can't accept," said Cobcroft Minor, reaching to the cake cart for a jammy doughnut. "Once you've fallen foul of the Department it's all over. One might as well shut up shop and find a job in the provinces as a tailor, or something equally menial!"

As Haythwaite and Co chortled merrily, carefully not looking at him, Gerald swallowed a string of expletives. "Well, it's been wonderful catching up with you, Errol, but—"

"Not so fast," said Haythwaite, whose cut-glass accent had acquired a new and sharper edge. "I've a little something to say to you."

Sarkiness was unwise but he couldn't help it. The remnants of his self-respect demanded he not play the doormat. "Sometime this century, I hope."

Despite the leaping flames in the fireplace and the general air of warm crony camaraderie, the ambient temperature dropped ten degrees. Haythwaite's pale green eyes narrowed. "I wouldn't go trying to be clever, Gerald. Not if I were you. Not after your recent debacle."

"It was an accident, Errol."

Kirkby-Hackett snorted. There was a gobbet of chocolate sauce on his receding chin. "So was granting you a wizard's licence, Dunnywood."

This time he bit his tongue. Seriously antagonising these three would be . . . unhelpful. Between them, their prestigious families had fingers in every last one of Ottosland's wizardly pies . . . and at least a half-dozen more abroad. If he didn't endure the insults he really would be headed home for a life of provincial tailoring.

Haythwaite leaned back in his chair and steepled his fingers. "Next week, Gerald, I'm to be inducted into the Masterful Company of Wizards."

"I know, Errol. Didn't you receive my note of congratulations?"

The note was waved away like so much grubby scrap paper. "The Masterful Company, Gerald, is the most exclusive wizarding organisation in the country, if not the world." Haythwaite's expression was mild, his voice mellow, but even so Gerald flinched; Errol's impeccably well-bred urbanity never quite managed to hide the pirate within. "Membership is restricted to First Class wizards, naturally, and is achieved by invitation after nomination by an existing member, a rigorous selection process and personal scrutiny by the committee. Presidents and prime ministers have been known not to make the cut. An invitation to join the Masterful Company of Wizards, Gerald, is an honour to which few may aspire." The look on his face added, *And you're not one of them.*

Somehow, he managed to keep his own expression apologetic. "I know that, too."

Still piratically smiling, Haythwaite continued. "Central to the induction ceremony is the presentation of one's especially commissioned and crafted First Grade staff, Gerald. I was due to take delivery of mine tomorrow. Sadly, according to a somewhat hysterical missive from one Mr Harold Stuttley, my new staff is little more than a melted thimbleful of slag spread thinly over the charred remains of his ruined factory. What have you to say to that, Gerald?"

Any number of things, none of which he could utter. From the looks on Kirkby-Hackett and Cobcroft Minor's faces anyone would think he'd murdered Haythwaite's firstborn son. Bitterly regretting the impulse to set foot outside his bedsit for at least the next ten years, Gerald shook his head.

"What can I say? I'm truly sorry, Errol."

Haythwaite blinked. "That's *it*? That's *all*? You're *sorry*? By God, Dunwoody, if you think you're sorry now, just you wait until I'm done with you! There won't be a hole small enough for you to crawl into here or—"

"Oh Errol, put a sock in it," said a cheerful voice. "If your family can't rustle you up a new First Grade staff for the ceremony you can borrow one of mine. I must have three I've never so much as breathed on and I'm pretty sure one of 'em's a Stuttley. Bloody manufacturers keep on sending them to me for gratis, hoping I'll give 'em a public endorsement. And since I'm a Masterful Companion myself of course, there'll be no questions asked."

Haythwaite closed his mouth, his expression curdled. Gerald turned round.

Monk Markham, released at last from the bowels of Research and Development. As usual, his friend's long dark hair was falling over his face in unkempt disarray and there were smudges of something dubious on the end of his aquiline nose and down the front of his shabby blue corduroy jacket. Behind the aggressive cheer he looked bone-tired. Fragrant smells wafted from the brown paper bag he carried in one hand. The other clutched the handle of his battered, bulging briefcase.

Composure recovered. Errol stared at him coldly. "Markham. Too kind, I'm sure, but it won't be necessary."

"Suit yourself," said Monk, grinning, then turned. "So Gerald, I picked up some Yoktok curry and rice on the way home. Fancy sharing?"

For the last two days Gerald had existed on coffee and toast. He had to swallow a bucketful of saliva before he could answer. "Uh—yes."

"Excellent! Catch you later, Errol. Give me a shout if you change your mind about the staff. Come on, Gerald. My octopus is getting cold."

Monk being Monk he occupied a plush apartment on the club's second floor with three rooms, several windows, ample headspace and no smelly chamber-pot or nightly serenade from the plumbing. Not that Monk ever really noticed his surroundings. He'd have been perfectly happy in one of the shoeboxes under the roof, except for the lack of space to continue his incomprehensible mucking about with things metaphysical.

"Careful," he said, dropping his briefcase as Gerald tripped over an oscillating octogram spinning hysterically between the living room's sofa and bookcase. "It took me three days to get that bloody thing to hold its axis properly."

Gerald pushed himself off the wall and rubbed his banged elbow. "What are you trying to measure?"

"Ambient tetrothaumicles in the fourteenth dimension," said Monk, cat-stepping around a tangle of test tubes.

He swallowed an unworthy lump of envy. "Of course you are. Isn't everyone?"

Squashed into his kitchenette, Monk grinned over his shoulder as he started unpacking the bag of food. "Hope not. *If* it comes off it means an article in *The Golden Staff*.

*The Golden Staff?* Good God. To date, the youngest person ever permitted to publish in *The Staff* had been forty-eight. The idea of a twenty-four-year-old wizard getting the nod from *The Golden Staff* was unthinkable.

Unless, of course, you knew Monk Markham.

"Well, good luck."

Monk rummaged in a drawer for cutlery. "Thanks. I need it."

No, he didn't. He was just being typically Monkish: modest, unpretentious and sensitive to the limitations of his less fortunate friend. Stinging only a little bit, Gerald edged his way around a set of hiccuping test tubes, sidestepped something that looked like a cross between a mouse and a dandelion doing somersaults in its cage, and sat at the gate-leg dining table. On the nearby windowsill sat Monk's crystal ball. It was pulsing a gentle red.

"You've got incoming here."

Monk had his head in the crockery cupboard under the sink-and-hotplate arrangement in the corner. "Play 'em back for me, would you?" he said, muffled. "New password's *confabulation*."

A hand wave over the crystal ball and the muttering of Monk's password unlocked its warding. The crystal ball hummed, the red swirl cleared, and the image of a face formed within its depths. It bore a spurious resemblance to Monk but was a year or so older and graced with an immaculately barbered beard, drop-pearl earrings and a starched neck ruff of outrageous proportions.

"*Monk, you wart-ridden little toad,*" the scowling face growled, "*why aren't you there, it's so early it's practically midnight. Are you there? Answer the ball, runt, I don't have all morning.*"

Gerald paused the message, grinning. At times like this being an only child was a positive advantage. "It's your brother."

Monk finished sharing out almond rice into two chipped bowls and started on what smelled like chicken in green sauce. "Prat. What does he want? Turn up the volume, I can't hear."

He increased the ball's volume, unpaused the message and sat back, prepared to be entertained. Aylesbury Markham's peevish grumble boomed. "*All right then. Listen up, you, because I'm not calling back. The olds are hosting a flash dinner party this weekend for some visiting foreign muckety-muck. Attendance is non-negotiable. So for the love of witchcraft get a sodding haircut, scrub the ink stains off your fingers and make sure you've got something halfway decent to wear, 'cos I'll be buggered if you embarrass me by turning up looking like something a paralytic cat dragged in backwards through a gorse bush, right? Right. I'm warning you, toadstool. Ignore me at your peril.*"

"Pillock," said Monk, squashing empty cartons into the rubbish bin. "Anything else?"

Aylesbury's elegantly menacing face faded away, leaving the crystal ball as innocuous as a lump of glass. "Doesn't look like it."

Monk stuck a fork in each steaming bowl and carried them over to the table. "Good. Dig in."

Gerald practically inhaled the food. After two days of charcoaled and barely buttered stale bread, the savoury chicken and rice was almost enough to make him cry. "This is great, Monk. Thanks."

"Uh huh," said Monk, and sat back. "So. You going to tell me what happened at Stuttley's?"

Damn. Couldn't Monk leave sleeping dogs lie? As soon as he could trust himself not to spit rice everywhere he said, "I thought you'd have heard by now."

"I'm interested in what really happened, not a garbled fourth-hand gossip-raddled version flavoured with malice."

He avoided answering by filling his mouth with more chicken.

Monk said, "Is it true Scunthorpe booted you?"

He nodded. Suddenly his masticated mouthful couldn't get past the lump in his throat. "Mmm."

"Pillock," said Monk, and speared another piece of curried octopus. "If they handed out medals for covering your arse, Scunthorpe'd be world champion ten years on the trot. Still . . . I'm a bit surprised you went. At least without a fight."

Gerald threw down his fork. "Really?"

"Yeah. I mean, there must've been *something* you could do."

"Says the certified genius and golden boy of the R and D division whose family entertains visiting heads of state every other night!" he retorted. "Well, here's a newsflash, Monk! I'm not you, I'm a barely qualified Third Grade wizard from a long and distinguished line of men's tailors! Don't you think I *wanted* to fight Scunthorpe? Don't you think I *know* when I'm being railroaded? I *couldn't* fight him. He made it damned clear what would happen if I caused any more trouble. I had no choice but to sneak away with my tail between my legs. And if you think I'm *happy* about that, well—"

"No," said Monk. "Sorry. Wasn't thinking."

His brief spurt of self-righteous anger fizzled and died. Slumping, he picked up his fork and stabbed another piece of chicken. "It's all right," he muttered.

"So," Monk said after a moment. "What happened?"

In a strange way it was a relief to tell his friend everything, right down to the final humiliation of his magic not working at all in Scunthorpe's office.

By the time he was finished Monk was struggling not to laugh. "I'm sorry, I'm sorry! It's not funny, I know. But Gerald, in trying to stop Stuttley's from blowing up you blew it up. Admit it, that's a bit bloody ironic."

"It's not ironic, it's typical," he retorted. "Every job I touch turns from gold to shit. I'm a jinx, Monk."

"Well, I wouldn't go *that* far . . ."

"*I* would."

Monk poked thoughtfully at his dinner. "It is strange. I mean, there's no way you should've been able to handle that much raw thaumic energy or those First Grade staffs. No offence, mate, but Third Grade wizards . . ."

"None taken," he said, shrugging. "And it doesn't matter anyway. My wizarding career's over."

"Who says?"

"Come off it, Monk. Who in Ottosland's going to hire me now? Even if I do what Scunthorpe said, lay low for a while, even for a whole year, it won't make any difference. I'll go to my grave as the idiot who blew up Stuttley's." He shook his head. "I was a fool to think that a tailor's son from Nether Wallop could amount to anything in wizardry."

Scowling as ferociously as his unpleasant brother, Monk shoved his chair away from the table and started pacing, automatically avoiding his various and scattered experiments. "Bollocks! Who was it conducted your thaumaturgical aptitude test?"

He blinked. "What?"

"Your aptitude test, the test that—"

"I know what it is! Drableys tested me. The correspondence school people."

Monk dropped back into his chair, eyes alight with a feverish enthusiasm that boded no good. "Well, don't you see? They got it wrong. No genuine Third Grade wizard would've survived depolarising that inversion. You'll have to get tested again to find out what your grading should be. On decent equipment this time. Department equipment, it's the best there is. It'll explain that weird feeling you had in the factory and give us an accurate reading of your potential. And if you don't test as a top-rate First Grader I'll eat Errol Haythwaite's underwear."

*A First Grade wizard.* Ha! "Nice thought, Monk, but after Stuttley's I wouldn't get one foot inside the Department's front door. And no, you're not smuggling me in there. Or the Department's equipment out. Bad enough I've scuppered my own career. I won't be responsible for scuppering yours too. And how much do I owe you for the takeaway?"

"Bollocks to the takeaway," said Monk. "I'm not

going to sit back and let you chuck your career down the boghole."

Gerald choked. "What career? I told you. It's scuppered. Nobody—"

"In Ottosland will hire you. I know," said Monk, impatiently. "I heard you. And much as I hate to agree, you're right. You won't get another job here, at least not until the fuss dies down."

"In other words, never. They'll be talking about Stuttley's into the middle of next century. They'll put me in textbooks under 'Stupid Things No Wizard Should Attempt'."

"You're exaggerating . . . but not by much." Monk drummed his fingers on the table. Nobody took no for an answer less willingly than Monk Markham. "Fine," he said after a moment's racing thought. "So you can't work here for the next little while. But Ottosland's not the only country that employs wizards. You'll just have to go overseas until the coast is clear. A year or two at the most. Trust me, Gerald, sooner or later there'll be another stupendous arse-up and Stuttley's will be yesterday's news. The minute you're off the hook you can come back, I'll retest your aptitudes myself and you can start again. Clean slate. Brand-new leaf."

Gerald tried not to resent 'another stupendous arse-up'. "Overseas where, Monk? I'm not multilingual. I'm not even *bi*lingual. And if you take the other day into account I don't speak wizard very well, either."

"Yes, but I don't take the other day into account," Monk said briskly. "And you don't need to be multilingual. Practically everyone speaks Ottish these days, and the people who don't aren't the kind of people you need to worry about." He was looking demonically cheerful: a dangerous sign.

Gerald watched him leap up from the table again and rummage through his briefcase. "What are you doing?"

"Getting this week's *Orb*," said Monk. "Catch!"

He snatched the magazine out of the air. Errol Haythwaite was on the cover, smirking about his invitation to join the Masterful Company. His fingers itched for a pen so he could indulge in some juvenile disfiguring . . .

Monk flopped back into his chair. "You haven't read it yet?"

In the never-ending struggle to make ends meet he'd stopped buying the *Wizarding Orb* as soon as he'd started working for the Department. There'd always been a copy floating round the tea room. "No."

"Well don't just sit there admiring Errol's haircut. What jobs are on offer?"

He flipped to the Positions Vacant section and quickly scanned it. "None that'll suit me, I'll guarantee you. Face it, Monk, there's not exactly a huge demand for Third Grade wizards. Especially ones with a talent for blowing things up."

"Stop being so defeatist. Here. Let me look." Monk grabbed the magazine. "Bloody hell," he muttered after a quick perusal. "They don't want much, do they? Second Grade or above, with a minimum ten years' experience—demonstrated talent for cloud manipulations and seed propagation—good with children—"

The familiar tide of despair was rising again. "See?

I told you. It's hopeless. I mean, good with children? Ha! Five minutes after I met the Brierly twins I wanted to strangle them."

Monk looked at him. "Gerald, five minutes after she met the Brierly twins my *mother* wanted to strangle them. And coming from the woman who gave birth to Aylesbury that's saying something." Scowling, he kept on reading. "What's this one? 'Prefer someone with connections to royalty.' Well, I trod on a visiting prince regent's toes at a ball last Wizard Eve, does that count?"

Disconsolate, Gerald poked his fork into his now lukewarm dinner and half-heartedly tried another mouthful. "It's no use. I just have to face facts, Monk. It was fun while it lasted but—"

"Ah *ha*!" Monk stabbed the *Orb* with his finger. "Here we go! This one's got your name written all over it!"

He dropped his fork, treacherous hope flaring. "What? Which one? Where? Show me."

Ignoring him, Monk began to read. "'Wanted: Wizard. His Most Esteemed and Sovereign Majesty King Lional the Forty-third—'"

Hope died. "Markham! Have you completely lost your mind? What king is going to want me?"

Monk lifted his gaze for a brief glower then kept on reading. "'—the Forty-third, sovereign ruler of New Ottosland, requires the services of an honest and upright wizard. Grading irrelevant and no experience necessary. Personality more important than pedigree. Must be flexible, adaptable and willing to muck in. Fondness for butterflies an advantage. To apply call crystal ball vibration blah blah blah'."

Gerald snorted. "Very funny, Monk. Kick a bloke while he's down, why don't you. Fondness for butterflies? That's low, that's really low."

"Here," said Monk, offended, and threw the *Orb* at him. "Read it yourself if you don't believe me."

After a moment's undignified hunting and pecking through the columns he found the advertised position. Monk hadn't been kicking him when he was down. The ridiculous job was right there in black and white. He looked up. "*New* Ottosland?"

"Our one and only colony. You must've heard of it. Established four or five centuries ago. In the good old days, when dashing about the world nicking other people's real estate was considered a suitable occupation for gentlemen and kings."

"Oh yes. Now I remember. Isn't it in the middle of a desert?"

"Is it? Geography was never my thing," said Monk, supremely indifferent. "But even if it is, who cares? At least it'll be warm. And it's a *job*, Gerald. A job with a *king*. Think of the snob value. Once you've got 'royal court wizard' on your résumé you'll be beating 'em off with a stick, Stuttley's or no Stuttley's. *Trust* me. *Call* them."

"Right," he said, with a glower of his own. "*Trust me*. This from a man trying to measure ambient tetrothaumicles in the fourteenth dimension. Does the Department know you're mucking about with the fourteenth dimension, Monk? I'll bet it doesn't. I'll bet if they knew you were—"

"*Gerald*! Make the bloody call!"

"Stop shouting! For all we know it's the middle of the night in New Ottosland!"

"It's not."

"How do you know?"

"Because it's night-time here," said Monk, triumphant. "They're halfway round the world, so it's daytime there. More or less."

"More or *less*? That's your idea of accuracy? And they call you a thaumatological genius?"

"They'll be calling me a homicidal maniac if you don't make that bloody call."

He picked up the *Orb* again and re-read the ad. "*Fondness for butterflies*? What does that *mean*?"

Monk shrugged. "Search me. Call and ask."

"The position's probably filled by now."

"Yeah? Know a lot of inexperienced wizards in love with insects, do you?"

He almost smiled at that but stopped himself just in time. The last thing Monk needed was encouragement. The man was a runaway tram with a brake problem. "And what about this?" he said, returning to the advertisement. "'Personality more important than pedigree.' What does *that* mean?"

His friend hooted. "It means they've had a bellyful of honking old wizards who blather on and on about their illustrious ancestors and demand ten times the going rate on the strength of 'em."

"And that's *another* thing. There's no mention of the salary."

"Gerald," Monk sighed, "right now you're unemployed. Your salary is nothing. So whatever old King Lional's willing to cough up, you win. Now make the bloody call. You know you want to."

Ha. What he wanted was to snap his fingers, turn back time and do the last week over minus the exploding staff factory and Reg flying off in a huff, never to return.

*Reg.* He felt his guts twist.

"Well, what about this 'apply by crystal ball' business?" he said, belligerent, distracting himself from that disaster. "If they've got someone on staff who can use a crystal ball what do they need a wizard for?"

"Now you're being ridiculous," said Monk. "Lots of civilians have enough sparkle to use a ball. That stopped being part of the aptitude test years ago and you know it."

"Yes, but—"

Monk sat back in his chair, disgusted. "Look, mate. Just *call* them. Or don't. Go back to Nether Wallop and spend your life as a pin cushion. Makes no difference to me. Just make sure to warn me before you tell Reg you passed up this chance so that *I* can get out of the country."

He looked away. "Reg is gone. She left me."

"*What?*"

"We had a fight, she—"

"Oh, like *that's* never happened before," said Monk. "Don't worry, Gerald. She'll come back. She always does."

"No. No. This time was different."

Monk rolled his eyes. "Look, Gerald. All external evidence to the contrary she's a woman. And you know what women are like."

Yes, but Reg was no ordinary woman. "Look, I'm worried about her, Monk, all right? It's a big bad world out there and—"

"And she's survived in it for a long, long time," said Monk, and slapped the table. "Reg can take care of herself. You're the one in trouble at the moment. You need to make a decision. The wild adventure and solemn glory of wizardry . . . or slaving for your cousins in Nether Wallop where the most exciting thing you'll see in a month is a pair of men's polka-dot underpants."

Yes, well, when you put it like *that* . . . Heart uncomfortably thudding, Gerald retrieved the *Orb*. Stared at the address listed at the end of the advertisement. Ever helpful, Monk lifted his crystal ball from the windowsill and plonked it on the table.

"Go on. Quick. Before somebody else gets the job."

He made the call.

# CHAPTER FIVE

As he waited for the etheretic vibrations to connect, Gerald frowned at Monk. "You know, if this doesn't work I won't have a choice. I'll have to go back to the Wallop and start tailoring. Maybe I should rethink this prejudice against polka-dots, they—"

"Excuse me," said a harried young female voice from the crystal ball. "Sorry if I'm interrupting your sartorial crisis but you're the one who called me."

Waving "shut up" at Monk's snorting laughter he stared into the depths of the crystal ball. Due to the voluminous black veil draped over her face it was impossible to tell what the speaker looked like. Her voice, however, left very little to the imagination. It was crisp and educated and very unamused.

"Yes! Sorry. Yes, I did call you! You're right."

The shrouded woman nodded. "More often than not. About the job?"

His mind went blank. "What job?"

Across the table Monk had his hand around an

invisible noose and was industriously hanging himself.

"Oh, the *job*," he said, gathering his wits. "You mean the position's still vacant?"

"If I say yes," said the mystery woman in the crystal ball, after a considering moment, "will I regret it?"

"Possibly. But then again so might I. Really, employing someone, being employed—it's all a bit like a blind date, isn't it, when you get right down to it?"

"Is it? I wouldn't know," said the woman. "What's your name?"

"Gerald Dunwoody. *Professor* Gerald Dunwoody."

"And you're a wizard, are you?"

She sounded sceptical. "Yes," he said firmly. "I am. May I ask with whom I'm speaking?"

"Her Royal Highness Princess Melissande," said the veiled woman. "Prime Minister of New Ottosland. I take it, Mr Dunwoody, that you've all the proper qualifications and credentials? Diplomas with fancy seals on them and so forth? Proof, in other words, of your exalted wizarding status?"

"Yes, indeed, Your Highness. Or should that be Madam Prime Minister?"

From under the veil came an inelegant snort. "Your Highness will suffice. Now tell me, Mr Dunwoody. Why should *you* be given the honour of serving my brother the king as New Ottosland's royal court wizard?"

He risked a glance at Monk, who nodded and made little "go on, go on" gestures like a stage mother at her child's school play.

"Well," he said, on a deep breath, "because I have loads of personality, no pedigree whatsoever, practically no experience and after working in the Ottosland Department of Thaumaturgy the mucking out of any substances at all won't be a problem."

Another snort. "It was mucking *in*, actually, but never mind. How do you feel about butterflies?"

"Honestly, Your Highness? I can take them or leave them."

"So can I," said the princess mordantly. "And you're from Ottosland, you say? Hmm. We've already had a—" She stopped, as from somewhere beyond the crystal ball's field of focus came a bang, the sound of books crashing to the floor and an anguished cry of pain. Her veiled face turned sharply. "*Rupert!*"

From more or less the same direction a plaintive male voice cried, "Sorry! Sorry! I didn't think—"

"You never do, that's the problem! Don't expect me to divert limited portal access to you again if this—"

"Never again, Melly, never again, I promise! Look, just hire the poor chap and come help me, would you? They're getting awfully stroppy and you know how delicate vampire butterflies are, not to mention expensive. And I simply *can't* catch them all by myself, I'll get bitten to death!"

Princess Melissande sighed. "Excuse me, Mr Dunwoody. My other brother Prince Rupert has just received a new delivery of butterflies and he's very excited about it." She looked again in the direction of the complainer. "Yes, all *right*, Rupert, I'm *coming*! Honestly, I don't know *why* you had to ignore the packing instructions and open the box now in the first place! And in my *office*."

Neither did Gerald. *Vampire butterflies?* Accosted by a vision of pretty flying insects with fangs and a penchant for haemoglobin, he stared at Monk. Monk shook his head vehemently and crossed his eyes, one pointed finger spinning circles round his temple.

And of course Monk was right. Prince Rupert did sound mad. The whole set-up sounded mad. Not the kind of place in which to serve out a hopefully brief exile. Bad enough he had to leave home. The least he deserved was a place where the natives weren't stark staring cuckoo.

On the other hand . . .

Across the table, Monk was shaking his head so hard it looked in danger of falling off, and waving his arms in giant "Stop! No! Go back!" semaphore signals.

He bit his lip. How did the clichés go? Beggars can't be choosers? If wishes were horses, beggars would ride? The word "beggar" was distressingly prominent. How long before it could reasonably be applied to him? His savings were negligible, his chances of re-employment here nil . . .

"Your Highness," he said, "if I ask you something will you answer me honestly?"

Her veiled chin shot up. "I am a princess, sir. We are *always* honest."

That wasn't what Reg had told him but this wasn't the time to quibble. "How many other wizards do you have in the running?"

"Why?"

Because if he had stiff competition for the post he'd retire gracefully from the field. He didn't have time to waste on round-robin interviewing. He needed a new job fast. "Oh," he said. "You know. Just curious."

A long silence, punctuated by yelps and squeals in the background. Then: "None. You're the only one."

"I see."

Now Monk had an invisible knife in one hand, a neck-stretching bunch of hair in the other, and was busily cutting his own throat.

He took a deep breath. Crazy or not, escapologist vampire butterflies or not, it was a wizarding position. It was out of the country. And there was a very good chance that as a royal court wizard he'd never lay eyes on a pair of polka-dot underpants. What had Reg shrieked at him during their most recent, calamitous argument? *You're too timid, Gerald. You're unadventurous and unwilling to take a chance. You're always talking the talk but you never walk the walk.*

"All right, Your Highness," he said. "I'm in. I'll be your new court wizard."

Monk threw up his arms in despair. In the crystal ball, New Ottosland's prime minister jumped as though she'd just been bitten by a butterfly. "You will? I mean, excellent. How soon can you start?"

"Soon. Within a couple of days, I should think. Just a few loose ends to sort out."

"Really? How fortuitous. Er . . . do you have portal access?"

Good question. Surely Mr Scunthorpe wouldn't be so petty as to have revoked his portal privileges? He crossed his fingers. "Yes, Your Highness."

"Excellent. I'm sending you our coordinates . . . now. Have you received them?"

The green recording crystal in the ball's base was blinking. "Yes, Your Highness."

"Then on behalf of His Majesty King Lional the Forty-third, allow me to congratulate you on your appointment. I'm sure he'll be thrilled to have you join him in implementing his plans for the kingdom."

"And please inform His Majesty that *I'm* thrilled to—" He stopped. An enormous red and black butterfly had landed on the princess's veiled face. "Er— Your Highness? There's a vampire butterfly on your nose."

"Yes," said the princess. "I can see that, Professor." She took a deep breath. "*Rupert!*"

And then the connection was cut, and Monk's crystal ball was a lump of empty glass again. Bemused, Gerald sat back in his chair.

*I'm still a wizard. In fact I'm more than a wizard. I'm a royal court wizard. To a king. Take that, Scunthorpe!*

"You're mad," said Monk. "Certifiable. You need your head examined. Vampire butterflies! Insane princes! A king with plans! Kings aren't supposed to have plans, Gerald, they're supposed to sit on their thrones and make new kings and that's *all* they're supposed to do. History is littered with the corpses of fools who got tangled up with kings who have plans!"

He shrugged. "History, maybe. But we live in the modern era, Monk. And anyway this was all your idea. You're the one who insisted I apply for the position."

"Apply, yes! Accept, no!"

Strangely, he was feeling exhilarated. All his life he'd been sensible. Conservative. Hoping for great things but never quite believing they'd happen, at least not to him. Dreaming of grand achievements, heroic accomplishments, but always being brought back to reality with a shuddering thud by a seemingly inescapable fact: tailors' sons from Nether Wallop were not the cloth from which heroes are cut.

So. Perhaps he wasn't ever going to be a hero but he *was* about to become court wizard to a king. And *that*, at least, was a grand achievement. Of a sort.

He smiled. "Monk, I'll be fine."

"You don't know that! And what about the salary? You didn't even ask how much they're paying you!"

"Like you said, the salary's not important. What's important is this job is my express ticket out of town. If I have to hang around here listening to Haythwaite and Co and everyone else going on and on about Stuttley's I think I *will* cut my throat. Don't you see? This is the answer to a prayer. And you were right: with *Royal Court Wizard* written on my résumé nobody will care about Stuttley's. Not after I've been gone for a while, anyway. So thank you. I think we can officially say you've saved my bacon. Again."

Monk shook his head. "I'm not so sure. The court of New Ottosland looks more like a three-ring circus from where I'm sitting. And what about Reg?"

"If the court's a three-ringed circus she'll fit right in." He sighed. "Look. If she comes back before I leave, we'll talk about it. If she comes back after, will you tell her where I've gone? She can make up her own mind whether she wants to join me or not. And if she doesn't come back—"

"I'll do everything I can to find her. But Gerald—"

"No. I'm going. We both know it's my only choice."

Reluctantly Monk nodded. "Yeah. But I still think you should get yourself tested again. There has to be some explanation for what happened. Maybe in a couple of months, once you've settled in at court, you can portal back for a day and we'll see what the Department equipment has to say about you. The dust over Stuttley's will be settled by then. Deal?"

Gerald laughed, the gloom of recent events abruptly vanished. He felt light enough to fly. "Deal! Now let's go back downstairs to the bar so I can buy you a drink."

"No, let's go back downstairs to the bar so *I* can buy *you* a drink," said Monk. "With luck Haythwaite and his little friends will still be there. I really want to see their faces when I call for a toast to the next Royal Court Wizard of New Ottosland!"

Sadly, Haythwaite and Co had departed. But that didn't stop Gerald and Monk from downing a prodigious number of colourful and highly alcoholic drinks in honour of the occasion. By the time Upjohn the barkeep called "Time!" they were definitely the worse for wear. Mr Pinchgut, gloomily inured to the excesses of young wizardry, helped them up the stairs, poured Monk into his bed then saw Gerald poured safely into his own.

"Good night, sir," he said, just before pulling the bedsit door closed. "I'll be sure to have the kitchen prepare a little something for your headache in the morning."

Sprawled face-up on his slowly expiring mattress, Gerald listened to the latch click shut and watched the ceiling spin lazy circles overhead. He felt warm and fuzzy and delightfully disconnected. Stuttley's exploding staff factory was a long, long way away.

A feathered shadow swooped through the open window and landed with a click of nails on the ram skull above the bed. He struggled onto his elbows and squinted into the darkness.

"Reg? Is that you?"

"No," said a snippy voice. "It's your fairy godmother."

He thudded back to the sagging bed. "Thank God! Where have you *been*? I've been worried out of my mind!"

"Must have been a short trip."

"Oh come on, don't be like that."

"I'll be any way I like, thank you very much." A censorious sniff. "You're drunk."

He folded his arms behind his head. "And you're a bird, but I shall be sober in the morning."

A short, sharp silence. Then, "That was unkind," said Reg, subdued.

"And true."

A cosily familiar ruffling sound as she fluffed out all her feathers. "I hear you blew up Stuttley's staff factory and lost your job," she observed, rallying. "How enterprising of you."

Of course she'd heard. Reg heard everything. It was one of her more irritating habits. "Yes, I did. But that's not why I'm drunk."

"Really? Don't tell me there's more. I'm an extremely senior citizen, Gerald, I'm not sure my heart can take it."

Slowly, carefully, mindful of his spinning head, he sat up and swung his feet to the floor. "Look. I'm sorry about the other day. You said a lot of things I didn't want to hear and I lost my temper."

Another feather-ruffling pause. "Your apology's accepted, Gerald. I'm sure I don't like to be scathing with you but sometimes things need to be said no matter how uncomfortable they are or how little one doesn't wish to hear them. I've only your best interests at heart, you know, and I—"

"Yes, Reg, I know. I do. Which is why I think you'll be pleased when you hear my news."

Reg heaved a sigh. "What news?"

"I found another job."

"Already?"

Sitting up was proving to be a bad idea. He lowered himself by inches back to the mattress and winced as another spring expired, stabbing his backside in its death throes. "Yes."

"When?"

"This evening. Over dinner, actually. With Monk."

"Oh, yes, well, I might've known *that* young reprobate would be involved!"

"He's not a reprobate, he's a lifesaver. I was all set to give up and go back to Nether Wallop. Monk convinced me otherwise."

More furious feather-rattling. "I can't believe what I'm hearing, Gerald! You actually accepted another wizarding position? Without consulting me? After everything I said the other day?"

Another wince. "Well, you weren't here to consult, Reg. You'd flown off in a huff, remember?"

With a great flapping of wings Reg launched herself from the ram skull and landed on his booted toes. Even through the polished leather he could feel her claws gripping.

"What job? With which organisation? Saint Snodgrass and all her children defend me! Didn't you hear a word I said, Gerald? It takes *days* to choose a position properly! You have to check your prospective employer's references, his bank balance, his social standing, his pedigree! I don't believe this, it's the Department debacle all over again!"

Gerald peered down the length of his body at her. In the starlight from the open window her dark eyes gleamed, and her long sharp beak. "Actually it's not. It's about as far from the Department as you can get. Didn't you say it was time I took a chance? Started walking the walk, not just talking the talk? Well, I've done it. This is me, walking. Reg, you are sitting on the feet of the next Royal Court Wizard to Lional the Forty-third, King of New Ottosland."

"New Ottosland?" she shrieked. "That obscure, sand-stranded, *nothing* little backwater?"

"Ah. You've been there," he said, pleased. "I rather thought you might."

"Not recently. And not on purpose. My hot-air balloon sprang a leak and we had to drop in for repairs."

"How long ago?"

"Three hundred years, more or less." She shuddered. "And I remember it as though it were yesterday."

"Well, three hundred years is a long time. Perhaps things have changed."

"One can only hope so," Reg said darkly. "One can also hope that Lional the Forty-third has better manners than Lional the Thirty-Second. *He* dropped a cocktail onion down my décolletage and then tried to retrieve it with his nose." Another shudder. "Disgusting. Of course, if he'd been thirty years younger and five stone lighter it might have been a different story."

He laughed, and immediately regretted it. His Bearhugger's glow was fading and he was starting to feel distinctly fragile. "I had to take the position, Reg. Things are just too hot for me here after what happened at Stuttley's."

She hopped from his toes to his knees then waddled up to his chest where she settled herself like a broody hen. "So what happened at Stuttley's?"

He told her. Miraculously she refrained from comment until the entire sorry story was finished. "Well," she said, her head tipped to one side. "That Markham boy's right about one thing, anyway: you can't be a common or garden variety Third Grade wizard, Gerald. Not if you can pull off a stunt like that. Haven't I always said there's more to you than meets the eye?"

"Yes, Reg, you have."

She clicked her beak thoughtfully. "So perhaps this mad move to New Ottosland might prove useful after all. As royal court wizard you won't be hamstrung by all those tiresome Departmental regulations, for a start. Without the likes of Scunthorpe breathing down your neck we might actually have a chance of finding out what you're really made of." She made a pleased little sound deep in her throat. "Yes. Indeed we might. Gerald, I take back everything I said. This is a *brilliant* move. A strategy worthy of me. I congratulate you."

"Hang about," he said. "I may have been kicked out of the Department but there's still my oath of office, Reg. My wizardly vows. I'm not about to break those. Not even for you."

She bounced to her feet, impatient, then kept on bouncing as though he were a trampoline. "Did I ask you to? Of course I didn't! I took vows too, you know, just as binding as yours and a damned sight older to boot! No. We're not going to violate our sacred sacraments, Gerald. But we *are* going to find out once and for all just how good a wizard you can be."

One more bounce and he was going to throw up all the Bearhugger's brandy still sloshing inside his stomach. He grabbed her with gentle hands and held her close to his face, squinting. "We? Does that mean you're coming with me?"

"Well of *course* I'm coming with you!" she snapped. "Five minutes out of my sight and you're blowing up staff factories! If I turn you loose unchaperoned on the other side of the world Saint Snodgrass alone knows the calamity that would follow!"

He grinned, and kissed the tip of her beak. "*Excellent*. I was hoping you'd say that!"

As he'd suspected, he was able to wrap up his affairs in two days. On reflection, he wasn't sure if that was a good thing or a bad. With his Portal slot booked, all his worldly possessions packed, his shoebox of a bedsit vacated, his mail forwarding sorted out with Mr Pinchgut, and Princess Melissande warned of his imminent arrival, all that remained was to lounge about the club library until it was time to leave, checking every five minutes that he still had the New Ottosland portal address safe in his pocket and worrying that his taxi wouldn't arrive.

He and Monk had said their farewells over lunch near Department headquarters. "Stay in touch, won't you, Dunnywood," Monk told him. "You've got my crystal ball vibration."

"And you've got mine," he replied. "Good luck with your ambient tetrothaumicles, Monk. I look forward to reading all about them in *The Staff*."

Monk grinned his irrepressible grin. "And I look forward to seeing you back here. Soon. There's some Departmental testing equipment with your name on it, remember?"

He decided not to tell Monk about Reg's plan: what his friend didn't know wouldn't worry him. They'd hugged, clumsily, then Monk dashed back to work and he'd returned to the club feeling ridiculously bereft.

Now, waiting for the taxi and contemplating the upheaval of his life, he couldn't help a certain amount of trepidation.

*It's an adventure, Dunwoody*, he kept telling himself. *You know you've always wanted an adventure.*

Yes. He had. Absolutely. He'd just never expected adventure to feel so . . . disconcerting.

In due course the summoned taxi arrived. He piled himself, Reg and his pitifully meagre collection of luggage into the cab, gave the driver his instructions, then turned and looked through the rear window at his home of the last three years as it dwindled, dwindled and finally disappeared in the fast-falling dusk.

*     *     *

The portal station was crowded with arriving and departing wizards and their luggage. Gerald found a trolley, loaded it up with his suitcases, deposited Reg on the handle and whispered, "Mind this while I get our coupon and find out which portal they've assigned us. And from hereon out no talking, all right? Remember what we agreed."

Reg rolled her eyes. "Yes, yes, I remember," she muttered. "I'm ancient, not addled. And I still think you're making a mistake. Royal wizard or not, you'll need all the advantages you can get. Gerald, and—"

"And a talking bird could chatter us both into trouble. Let's just see which way the New Ottosland wind is blowing before we start amazing the locals, shall we?"

"Pishwash," said Reg, and subsided into disgruntled silence.

There was quite a queue at the confirmation booth. By the time he'd shuffled his way to the attendant, picked up his travelling chit and fought his way back to where Reg was waiting like a martyr with the luggage it was perilously close to their allotted departure time. Naturally, the portal he'd been assigned was on the very far side of the concourse. He was forced to run with Reg and the luggage trolley, shouting "look out" and "so sorry" as he barrelled through the milling throng.

"Mister Dunwoody!" the supervisor was shouting as he arrived in a panting stagger at Portal 32, where a long line of other travellers waited. "Third and final call for Mister Dunwoody!"

"Here! Here! I'm here!"

The portal supervisor looked him up and down.

"Cutting it fine, there, Mister Dunwoody." He held out a white-gloved hand. "Chit, please."

The next person in line was looking disappointed that he'd turned up in the nick of time. He spared her an apologetic grimace and handed his travel coupon to the disapproving supervisor. "Here it is. Sorry. There's such a crowd."

With a grunt that might've meant anything, the supervisor punched the coupon into a small box on a table beside him, examined the result, nodded, and dropped it into a waiting tray. "Wait a minute, wait a minute, not so fast," he snapped as Gerald turned to decant Reg and his luggage from the trolley. "Contraband inspection first."

Oh. Of course. Ignoring Reg's snicker he stood still as the supervisor ran a slender bronze truncheon over him, Reg and his suitcases. Attached to each collar point of the supervisor's plain blue uniform was a small green button. So. The portal supervisor was a fellow Third Grader. Doomed to a life of coupon-punching, truncheon-waving and petty bureaucratic pettifogging.

*Poor bastard. And there but for the grace of Monk Markham go I.*

"Right you are, sir," said the supervisor, clipping the truncheon back to his belt. "All clear." He snapped his fingers at a hovering porter, who leapt forward and began transferring Gerald's battered suitcases from the trolley into the waiting portal. Then he took a bottle of pills from the table and held it out. "Need a suppressative, sir? Only Portal travel does take some folk poorly."

"No, no. We'll—I'll—be fine."

"Very good sir," said the supervisor. "In that case,

you're all clear to depart. If you'd kindly step into the Portal . . ."

With Reg perched firmly on his shoulder, Gerald stepped.

"Excellent. Have a pleasant journey, sir, mind now, I'm closing the door . . ."

. . . and he was spinning through time and space in a kaleidoscope of colour and sound. Then came the feeling that he was falling very slowly—or was it very quickly, he could never quite decide—down a long dark tunnel towards a bright light . . .

. . . which turned into a door, which opened onto an enormous, well-lit, unfurnished chamber decorated in various shades of gold. Head whirling, he stepped over his various bits of luggage and out of the portal.

"Hell's bells," said Reg, hauling herself back into place on his shoulder. "I *hate* that bloody contraption."

"My sentiments exactly," said a coolly familiar voice. "Good morning. Mister Dunwoody. Or should that be Professor? I confess the niceties of your profession leave me somewhat perplexed."

Still giddy and somewhat disoriented—he'd never portalled so far in his life—he staggered in a circle until he found the woman attached to the voice.

She was young. Well, youngish. His own age or thereabouts. Vertically challenged, horizontally overcompensated, clad in baggy brown tweed trousers and a plain blue cotton shirt and crowned with a thick braid of rust-red hair that sagged on top of her head like an úncooked doughnut. Her face was round and splattered with freckles, her chin determined, her eyes green and calculating behind wire-rimmed glasses. At her feet languished a long black exclamation mark of a cat, whose eyes were equally green and calculating.

"Bugger," said Reg.

The cat smiled and licked its lips.

"Now, now, Boris," said the woman. "Manners."

"Ah," Gerald said, standing straighter. "Princess Melissande?"

She smiled, revealing a hint of teeth. "Correct."

*Really?* This was a *princess*? Granted he'd never been this close to one before, but all the same . . . 'I'm sorry," he said. "I wasn't expecting you to meet me yourself, Your Highness. I thought you'd send a— a—minion."

"They were all busy," said the princess. "Minioning." Then she sighed. "Don't tell me, let me guess. You were expecting someone taller, blonder and thinner, yes? Well, it breaks my heart to disappoint you, Mister Professor Dunwoody, but we ran out of that model around here about four generations ago. When it comes to New Ottosland royal princesses, what you see is what you get." She smiled again, sweetly. "Deal with it."

Appalled, he stumbled forward and bowed. "No— Your Highness—you misunderstand—"

"I expect I don't, you know. But it doesn't matter. I'm more than used to it." She tipped her head to one side and considered Reg with narrowed eyes. "That's a most unusual bird you have there, Professor. I don't think I've ever seen one quite like it before. And it talks?"

He spat a silent curse in Reg's direction. "Ah— yes. She's—she's—a parrot. Very rare. One of a kind, actually. And you know what parrots are for meaningless chatter, Your Highness. I strongly suggest you don't take any notice of her. At all. Ever."

"A parrot?" said the princess thoughtfully. "Interesting. I was under the impression that parrots are generally noted for the curviness of their beaks and the brightness of their plumage . . . but there you are. If you say it's a parrot then by all means. It's a parrot. Does Polly want a cracker, by any chance?"

"Thank you, no," he said, fingers clamping tight about Reg's uncurved beak. "And her name's Reg, actually. Not Polly. I'm afraid she's a bit sensitive about—"

"How quaint," said Princess Melissande. She turned on her heel and headed at a determined rate towards a closed door at the far end of the golden chamber. The long black cat yawned and followed. He stared after her.

"Ah, Your Highness—my luggage—"

"Don't worry, Mister Professor Dunwoody," said the princess over her shoulder. "A spare minion will be along presently to see to it. I'd bring my personal effects, though, if I were you. Qualifications and what not. His Majesty might well ask to see them. And if he doesn't I certainly will."

He turned back, snatched his carpet-bag and hurried to catch up with her. "Actually, just Mister will do, Your Highness. Or Gerald. I'm not really one to stand on ceremony."

"Really?" she said, and spared him another glance. "I am."

They reached the golden chamber's vast double doors. The princess halted in front of them and waited, an impatient look on her face.

"Ouch," he said, as Reg nipped him on the ear. "What was that for?"

Reg sighed. "Open the doors. Blockhead."

He bit his tongue and opened the doors.

"What an interesting vocabulary you've taught your . . . parrot," said the princess as she marched past him, the cat smirking at her heels. "I can hardly wait to hear what it comes out with next. Incidentally, I hope it doesn't have lice. Birds do, you know."

Reg squawked.

The cat bared its sharp teeth in a grin.

"Oh yes, and by the way, Professor . . ." the princess added, already halfway down the corridor. "Welcome to New Ottosland."

# CHAPTER SIX

**W**ell don't just stand here like a ninny," said Reg. "Go after her!"

Since the princess showed no sign of slowing, he had to run. For a short person she moved along at quite a clip.

"Ah, there you are," she said as he and Reg joined her. "You must learn to keep up, Mister Dunwoody. His Majesty is impatient of laggards, as you'll soon see."

"I will?"

She glanced at him sidelong, her expression gently malicious. "In about five minutes, as it happens."

He slammed on the brakes. Reg sank her claws into his shoulder, swearing and flapping. "You mean we're off to see the king *now*?"

"Of course now," she said, spinning about to walk backwards just as quickly. Her cat leapt clear, spitting. "He's waiting for you in the Small Audience Chamber. Why? Where did you think we were going?"

"But—but—Your Highness—I can't see the king

*now*. I need to freshen up—change into my best attire! I can't appear before a king looking like—"

The princess stopped. "You can and you will. I've got strict instructions to escort you to His Majesty's presence the moment you arrive so let's just get it over with, shall we? You've got the rest of the day to stand in front of mirrors primping. Provided, of course, His Majesty doesn't send you packing back to Ottosland."

"Send me packing?" he said faintly. "I don't understand—I thought—"

"Ha," said Reg, under her breath. "Didn't I tell you? Not that I'm one to gloat, of course, or say 'I told you so', but if you'd just listened to me and—"

He twitched his shoulder, hard. "Shut up, Reg."

Hands shoved into her pockets, Princess Melissande had the grace to look uncomfortable. "All right. Look. Here's the thing. You're not the first court wizard Lional's hired, all right? But the others didn't work out, so—"

"How many others?" he interrupted, and to hell with protocol. "And why didn't they work out?"

She sighed, shoulders slumping. "It's complicated."

*Complicated*. The story of his bloody life. He took a deep breath, subduing angry panic. The woman standing in front of him might look like a badly dressed shop assistant but she was in fact royalty and had to be treated as such. Let appearances lull him into a false sense of security and he'd be portalling back to Ottosland faster than Reg could find something to complain about.

"I see," he said, with extreme care. "And if I may

be so bold as to ask, Your Highness, complicated *how*, exactly?"

She let out a short, sharp breath. "My brother—His Majesty—is a young and energetic man, Mister Dunwoody. He has views. Plans. A vision for the future. Our kingdom isn't the most progressive country in the world. In fact some might say—and perhaps not without cause—New Ottosland has become moribund. His Majesty intends to . . . stir things up a bit."

"Well, that seems reasonable. Only I don't see—"

The princess held up a finger. "The thing is, not all of the king's plans are what you might call *practical*. Daring, yes. Ambitious, absolutely. But practical? Not so much." Her gaze lost focus, as though she were staring into the past. "Practicality's never been Lional's strong suit, bless him. And there are other considerations as well. Matters geographical and political about which His Majesty is . . . sensitive. That's where I, as prime minister, come in."

"I'm sure you do," he said. "But I *still* don't understand why my predecessors—"

"Mister Dunwoody, have you ever worked for royalty before?"

"Worked for?" He resisted the urge to look at Reg. "No, Your Highness. I haven't."

"Then allow me to give you a little advice. His Majesty doesn't care for being contradicted. Or being told his requests are silly, frivolous and beneath the dignity of any self-respecting wizard. To be honest I would've thought that'd be obvious, he is a king, after all, but your predecessors had different ideas. To be blunt, Mister Dunwoody, your predecessors made it clear they thought Lional should defer to them and not the other way around. Well, obviously, he couldn't put up with *that*."

"Well, no, of course not, Your Highness. But—"

"*Excellent*," she said, smiling fiercely. "So, really it's very simple. Just remember that even though you're the wizard, it's *Lional* who wears the crown. Do what he asks with a song and a smile and the two of you will get along splendidly."

He didn't have to look at Reg to know she wasn't impressed. He cleared his throat cautiously. "Yes. Well. Only I should warn you that I'm bound by certain sacred oaths, Your Highness. Oaths that transcend national borders and the loyalty one owes an employer, that must take precedence over—"

She flapped a hand at him. "Yes, yes, I know all about that. And you needn't worry. Of course you won't be asked to violate your wizard's code. Lional—His Majesty—can get a trifle overexcited at times but he's a *king*, not a *criminal*."

Right. A king who'd already sacked who knew how many royal wizards. Who had plans and visions and was inclined to be overexcitable. All of a sudden his hasty decision to take the job was looking very suspect . . . What was it Monk had said?

"*History is littered with the corpses of fools who got tangled up with kings who have plans!*"

His sudden attack of doubt must have shown, because the princess's irritated expression collapsed into something close to entreaty. "Look, Professor, I know it sounds impossible but truly, it's not so bad as that. Lional's just . . . highly strung. Massively intelligent people often are, you know. And he's sensitive, too, that he's accorded the respect due to his position. As a wizard, I'm sure you can understand that."

"Well, yes, of course, but—"

"Please." She said the word stiffly, as though it was completely unfamiliar. And probably it was; royalty wasn't in the habit of begging. Her clear green eyes—rather nice eyes, actually, now that he came to look more closely—were suspiciously shiny. And her hands were caught together in a gesture that used by anyone else would surely be called wringing. In short, she looked desperate. Dangling on the end of a very short tether. "The thing is, you see, I could really use your help."

"Oh, lord," Reg muttered. "That's torn it."

The princess blushed, making all her freckles disappear, and shoved her hands back in her pockets. "The king's getting a bit impatient with me, you see, taking so long to find him the right wizard. If you change your mind and leave before even *meeting* him, well, it's bound to make him tetchy. And I've got so much on my plate as it is, I am the prime minister, you know. I don't just sit around painting my nails, Mister Dunwoody, I work very hard around here and, to be perfectly frank, the last thing I need is to have to go scouring the globe for *another* wizard, really, it's a most prestigious appointment, I would've thought you'd jump at the chance to serve as a royal court wizard and—"

"*All right!*" he said, before she dropped dead at his feet from asphyxiation. "I'll stay!"

"You will?" The words came out in a disbelieving squeak. "Oh. Well—good." She cleared her throat, and with a visible effort banished all signs of vulnerability. "Then let's go. Boris, heel!"

And off she marched again, the long thin cat undulating in her wake.

Gerald, with Reg muttering on his shoulder and his carpet-bag banging against his leg, hurried after them.

Endless corridors and staircases later—blimey, the palace was worse than a rabbit warren, he'd get lost five times a day—they arrived at an antechamber occupied by a single attendant, standing at attention before a pair of open double doors. Over the man's uniformed shoulder Gerald caught a glimpse of a larger room beyond, full of windows, plush gold carpet and a great deal of gilt.

"The prime minister and Professor Dunwoody to see His Majesty," announced the princess. "Professor Dunwoody is His Majesty's new wizard."

The attendant bowed; only the extreme rigidity of his spine betrayed his surprise. "Certainly, Your Highness." His gaze flickered to the black cat at her heels. "Er . . ."

"I know, I know!" She plopped the cat on the nearest velvet-covered chair. "Wait out here, Boris."

The cat crossed its eyes in displeasure but condescended to stay put. After another flickering glance the attendant rapped his pikestaff smartly onto the scuffed parquetry floor. "Her Royal Highness the Princess Melissande, Prime Minister of New Ottosland, and Professor Dunwoody, Wizard!"

Gerald's first thought, as he and Reg followed the princess into the king's presence, was that if this was the Small Audience Chamber he didn't want to see the Large one.

The room was huge and opulent in the extreme. Chandeliers like exploded diamonds dripped light onto every surface. Stained glass windows framed with silk curtains admitted shafts of stained glass sunshine. The walls were striped blue and gold and crammed with oil paintings of well-fed, self-satisfied aristocrats astride unlikely horses, or patting blockish cattle, or presiding over flocks of sulky children.

Apparently oblivious to the surrounding magnificence and his choked amazement at it, Princess Melissande led Gerald and Reg along a narrow strip of crimson carpet towards a dais at the far end of the chamber. Upon it loomed an extraordinary confection of wrought gold and rubies: the throne. And on the throne, with a fat orange cat puddled in his lap, sat a man.

Gerald swallowed. No. Not a man. A king. And if he was going to survive here, let alone thrive here, he musn't ever forget it.

"Cor," said Reg in an undertone. "This is all gone a bit upmarket compared to last time. Last time the throne was wood with a bit of gold paint slapped on and even then it was peeling. That one's got to be giving him piles." She let loose an admiring whistle. "And *he's* an improvement on last time, too! Phwoar! What a looker! If *he'd* been king then instead of the old fat one, history'd have a different story to tell and no mistake!"

Three paces ahead of them, the princess's fingers curled into fists and her head jerked sideways, just a fraction. Anguished, Gerald joggled his shoulder as hard as he could. "Reg! Shut *up*!"

Reg subsided, complaining under her breath.

She was right, though. Lional the Forty-third possessed the kind of astonishing male beauty generally found only on the cover of a romance novel. He even made Errol Haythwaite look plain, and that was an achievement. Gerald, more or less resigned to the face that looked back at him from his mirror every morning, suppressed a stab of envy. He had a lot more to worry about here than coming a distant last in an unlikely beauty contest.

Aside from himself and Reg, the princess, the king and his cat, the chamber was empty. Was that usual? According to Reg, kings and queens habitually surrounded themselves with advisors, fawners, toadies and any number of extraneous personnel designed to remind the monarch of his or her importance, wit, intelligence and general indispensability to the welfare of the kingdom.

So . . . where was everyone?

They reached the dais, eventually, and the narrow crimson pathway widened into a square. Princess Melissande stopped and cracked her knees in a brief, trouser-legged curtsey. "Here's the new wizard, Your Majesty. Professor Gerald Dunwoody, lately of Ottosland." She stepped aside. "Professor, you have the honour of addressing my brother, His Sovereign Majesty King Lional the Forty-third."

Nakedly revealed to royalty's stringent perusal Gerald dropped his carpet-bag and bowed, but not too deeply. He didn't want Reg to fall off his shoulder. "Your Majesty. It is indeed an honour."

From atop his lofty perch, Princess Melissande's brother stared down his architecturally perfect nose. In his lap, the fat orange cat favoured Reg with a slit-eyed glare and rumbled deep in its throat.

"Now, now, Tavistock," the king reproved. "You've already had lunch." He glanced at his sister. "Where's your horrible beast, by the way?"

The princess sighed. "Outside."

"Good. See that it stays there." One kingly finger, graced with an eyeball-sized emerald, tickled the orange cat under its chin. "So. This is my new wizard. He looks a bit young, Melissande."

The princess's expression became a trifle fixed. "Does he?"

"Yes," said King Lional, frowning. "Very young, in fact, when you consider the others. They were old enough to be this one's father—or possibly an uncle."

Gerald looked from king to princess, not certain whether to be annoyed, amused or apprehensive. Was royalty generally in the habit of discussing people as though they were in another room when in fact they were standing right next to them?

"Oh, I don't know," said the princess valiantly. "He's not *that* young. And anyway, lots of people don't look their age."

Apparently royalty was. At least around here.

The king's elegant fingers were drumming the arm of his throne. "That may be so, but unless this one's discovered an incant to knock twenty years off his face, I think I may be right in suspecting he lacks the requisite minimum fifteen years' wizarding experience. Well?"

It took Gerald a moment to realise the comment

was aimed at him. "What? Fifteen years experience? But the Positions Vacant piece said 'no experience necessary', Your Majesty."

"I can explain, Lional," the princess said as her brother's expression frosted over.

"I certainly hope so, Melissande," said the king. "For your sake."

Princess Melissande flinched, but she stood her ground. "I thought we needed a different approach. All the other wizards met your specifications to the last full stop but none of them worked out, did they? So I thought perhaps we'd have more success if I found you a wizard who was slightly less . . . set in his ways. One who could more easily adapt to the way we do things here in New Ottosland. A wizard who'd be grateful for the opportunity to serve a king instead of always banging on about how much better old Emperor Whosiewhatsit from Somewhere Else ran *his* country back in the day. You see? I was just thinking of you, Lional."

The king was not amused. "And I'm sure that's very touching, Melissande, but if you'd just gone on thinking for a moment or two *longer* perhaps you might've realised that there is such a thing as *appearances*! What will other realms and sovereignties think of me, Melissande, when they see I am being counselled by a beardless escapee from the nursery?"

Princess Melissande snorted. "Well, Lional, seeing as how you refuse to meet with any other realms and sovereignties, I don't see how they're going to think anything at all!"

The king leaned forward, which made the orange cat hiss. "And what is *that* supposed to mean?"

"You know perfectly well what it means! It means when are you going to give an audience to the Kallarapi delegation? This tariff business is *serious*, Lional! It's only a matter of time before they widen the camel-train ban to include essential imports! You can't ignore—"

"I've already told you, Melissande, it is beneath my dignity to treat with a mere younger brother. If Sultan Zazoor is serious about resolving this situation he can come and talk to me himself."

"And what am I supposed to do with his delegation?"

"I told you before! Show them the sights!"

"I *have*, Lional," said his sister, sounding pressed to her limit. "I've shown them the Royal Capital, the Royal Art Gallery, the Royal Gardens, the Royal Zoo and the Royal Duck Pond. I have taken them riding in the Glen and boating on the Zigzag and I'm afraid there's nothing left to do with them short of putting them in the post and sending them home. *Which*—" and she held up a finger as he opened his mouth "—goes without saying is out of the question."

"But you're the prime minister!" said the king, affronted. "I told *you* to deal with this!"

"And I've tried, Lional, but the delegation doesn't want to be dealt with. Not by *me*, at any rate," Princess Melissande pointed out. "Apparently *they* don't treat with mere younger sisters. Prince Nerim seems to think he should be speaking with *you*, seeing as how you're the king and he's the sultan's brother. And the holy man agrees. It's an odd notion, I know, but there you are. They're foreigners, so what can you expect? Of course, since they've got us surrounded and our economic survival depends on keeping their good-will, I've always found it prudent to humour them but then that's just me. I suppose as you're the king you can do what you like, but on the whole I'd rather not push them any further than we have already because you and I both know that—"

"Yes, yes, I know!" the king snapped pettishly. "All right. I'll see them."

"Today?"

"No. Tomorrow. I'll not have them thinking I'm a pushover!"

The princess frowned, apparently consulting an inner diary. "In the afternoon? Say three o'clock?"

"If I must," the king said with a martyred sigh. "But I'll not see them without a wizard!"

"You've *got* a wizard, Lional! He's standing right in front of you!"

Lional the Forty-third threw up his hands. "Well, *something* is standing in front of me, I grant you! But I'm yet to be convinced it's a *wizard*. Good God, Melissande, *look* at him! He's even younger than that daft idiot Rupert! He's almost as young as *you*!"

"So? What's age got to do with it?" the princess replied. "You sacked your entire privy council because they refused to accept that anybody under the age of sixty can rule a kingdom *then* turned round and made me prime minister, so how can you say that Gerald's too young to be a wizard? What would you know about it anyway? *You're* not a wizard!"

The king's eyes narrowed. "Oh, so it's *Gerald* now, is it?"

"Professor Dunwoody, I mean," said the princess. She was blushing. "And he absolutely is a wizard. Aren't you, Professor?"

"What?" said Gerald. It'd been so long since they'd noticed him *he'd* almost forgotten he was standing there. "I mean, yes, Your Highness! I absolutely am a wizard."

"A deaf one, from the looks of it," the king snapped. "You've brought your qualifications, I take it?"

He nudged the carpet-bag at his feet. "Yes, Your Majesty."

King Lional held out a hand, his expression long-suffering. Gerald dropped to one knee, rummaged inside the carpet-bag and pulled out his certificate of registration, complete with its impressive Department of Thaumaturgy crimson seal. Straightening, he proffered it to the king.

New Ottosland's monarch inspected the certificate. Then he looked up, frowning. "Is this your idea of a joke?"

He blinked. "Joke? Ah—no, Your Majesty."

"You're a *Third* Grade wizard?"

"Yes, Your Majesty."

"*Third* Grade? *Not* First—or even Second? *Third*?"

He risked a nervous glance at the princess, who was chewing on her lip. "Yes, Your Majesty. I'm sorry. Is that a problem? Only the Positions Vacant piece said grading wasn't relevant. But as it happens I do have a little First Grade experience. Sort of. If that helps."

King Lional stared, his golden eyebrows shooting

up. The orange cat yowled. "No, it does not! *Melissande—*"

"He's the only one who answered the ad, Lional!" the princess cried. "Nobody else was interested!"

"What do you mean, *nobody*," the king said, after an awful silence. "There must be hundreds of wizards in the world."

"Thousands," said his sister. "But not one of them put his hand up to be your new royal court wizard. And can you blame them, after all the ads we've placed lately? Did you think nobody would *notice* we've got a revolving door exclusively for royal court wizards in New Ottosland?"

"But a *Third* Grader?" the king shouted, and threw the certificate onto the floor. "You might as well have hired me a *toy* wizard! One of those silly wind-up dolls with the battery-operated staff!"

Gerald looked up from retrieving his qualifications. "I assure you, Your Majesty, I'm a trifle more magical than a doll!"

"Oh, bugger," muttered Reg. "Now you've done it."

King Lional the Forty-third sat back on his throne, smiling. His teeth were ice-white and immaculately even. "Really?" he drawled.

To hell with being intimidated by good dentistry. "Really."

The king's smile widened. "How exciting. Prove it."

Without meaning to, Gerald took a backwards step. Oh, hell. He really had done it, hadn't he? Prove it? Prove it *how*?

Still smiling, the king continued. "You have sixty seconds, Professor, by the end of which you'll have demonstrated one of two things: why I should keep you here as my royal court wizard, or why you'll be discovering first hand the joys of traversing the Kallarapi Desert on foot. Do I make myself clear?"

Horrified, he looked at Princess Melissande. She lifted her shoulders in a tiny shrug, mute.

The king cleared his throat. "Tick tock, tick tock, Professor."

"Yes, Your Majesty!" he said. "Please—if I might have a moment to think?"

"You have fifty moments, Professor," said King Lional. "What you do with them is entirely your own affair."

Gerald shoved the certificate back in his carpetbag and turned away, hunching his shoulder. "Okay, Reg," he whispered. "What do I do now? I can't walk across a desert! I'll *fry*!"

"Calm down," Reg whispered back. "This won't be solved by panicking."

"It won't be solved by magic, either! A simple Third Grade incant won't save me! You heard him, he wants a First Grade wizard!"

"Then a First Grade wizard's what you'd better give him. Gerald," hissed Reg. "And quick!"

"Professor," said the king, "am I imagining things or are you consulting with that fusty heap of feathers on your shoulder?"

He spun around, struggling not to glance guiltily at the princess. "Consulting? With Reg? Oh, no, Your Majesty. Why would I do that? Reg is a bird. No. I was just—thinking out loud."

"Then I suggest you think more quietly," said the king. "And faster."

The royal smile was by this time unsettling. "Yes, Your Majesty. Sorry, Your Majesty."

But it was easier said than done. His mind felt like cold molasses. All the incantations he'd ever learned whether he was supposed to or not stirred sluggishly, unwilling to be examined, and he couldn't feel so much as a *twinkle* of the power that had burst from him at Stuttley's.

*A dream, a dream, it was all a mad dream.*

Obdurately immune to King Lional's menace, Reg leaned close. "Come on, Gerald, you're running out of time! For the love of serendipity *do* something! *Anything!*"

With a fire-flashing of jewels in the bright chandelier light the king stood, tossing his fat orange cat unceremoniously to the floor. It dived beneath the throne and crouched there, swearing gruesomely under its breath.

"Well, Professor, this has been somewhat less than entertaining," he said briskly. "Such a pity you've come all this way for nothing but you can blame my sister for that. Melissande, do be sure to meet me in my privy chamber an hour from now so that we can discuss this little contretemps in delightful, private and uninterrupted detail. As for you, Professor, I'll have someone provide you with a map and a little bottle of water and show you the way to the kingdom's border. Such a pity but—"

As Princess Melissande leapt forward, protesting, Gerald threw caution to the winds and shouted at royalty. "No, Your Majesty! Wait!"

Encouraged by the pin-dropping silence, Lional's cat inched itself out from under the throne and began washing one chubby leg, still grumbling. Astonished, the king stared.

"You raised your voice to me," he said, wonderingly. "Are you *deranged*?"

Gerald winced. "No, Your Majesty. Just desperate. You see I really, really want this job." Well. Needed it. But want sounded better.

The king's eyebrows shot up. "Of course you do. But *your* desires are hardly relevant. What is *relevant*, Mister Third Grade Wizard, is whether *I* want *you*."

The cat snickered in the back of its throat. Hating it, Gerald felt his fingers itch to conjure a resounding case of feline scabby-arse. Feeling his hot gaze the cat looked up and smirked.

A nugget of an idea rolled to the surface of his stunned mind and glinted, briefly.

The fat, obnoxious cat. King Lional's ego. The memory of a First Grade wizard's power coursing through his veins. All those mysterious, forbidden incantations Reg had bullied him into learning . . . and one in particular . . .

"Yes, Your Majesty," he said. "You do. And if you'll give me a moment to prepare, I'll show you why."

# CHAPTER SEVEN

"Gerald?" Reg whispered. "I don't trust that look. Just say goodbye to the nice king and back out of the chamber, slowly. You don't need this job, there are other jobs. Whatever you're thinking, stop thinking it. At once."

He ignored her. Ignored too the pleading look he could feel from Princess Melissande. All his attention was focused on King Lional's cat.

*Can I do it? On the strength of one anomalous, out of character First Grade achievement, do I even dare try? I'm a Third Grade wizard, with the certificate to prove it. I must be deranged to be considering a Level Twelve transmogrification.*

More than deranged. To be thinking of this he was certifiably bonkers. Rowing up shit creek without any oars. Off his tiny rocker. Stark staring doolally.

*Desperate.*

A Level Twelve transmogrification was the most complex and convoluted incantation of its kind. Moreover it was a highly guarded government secret; how Reg had got hold of it was a mystery she had steadfastly refused to solve. *And* performing it was illegal without an Ottosland Department of Thaumaturgy Special Licence.

*When you're in Ottosland. But I'm not in Ottosland any more.*

No, he was far far out in unknown territory and he didn't have anything approaching a map. He was utterly mapless. Making things up as he went along.

*If this doesn't work...*

He wouldn't have to worry about being unemployed because he'd most likely be dead. Wizards who mucked around with a Level Twelve transmog and got it wrong weren't noted for their longevity, they were noted for the footnotes that got written about them in textbooks and medical journals.

*But if this does work then I'm set for life. I'll be able to write my own ticket. I'll never be in danger of polka-dots again.*

He had to try. *Had* to. Because the alternative wasn't anything he wanted to contemplate. Not sober. Not sane.

Time to find out what he was really made of.

*Let's hope it's not lots of squishy red stuff and a few mysterious tubes...*

Heart pounding, Gerald plucked Reg from his shoulder and thrust her at the princess. "Here, Your Highness. Just in case."

Princess Melissande stared at dangling Reg. "Just in case what? Professor—"

"It's simply a precaution. You're not in any danger, I assure you." As the princess hesitated he added, "Don't worry. She doesn't peck."

The gleam in Reg's eye belied that assertion but the princess took her anyway. Gingerly perching Reg on her shoulder she said crossly, "If I'd known you were going to be *this* much trouble, Professor . . ."

He spared her a swift smile. "Sorry."

On his dais, the king heaved a theatrical sigh. "You will be, I promise, if you don't do something magical *right now*."

Blimey, the man was *such* a pillock. *Do I really want to work for him?* The answer was swift and certain. *No, but I want the job.*

He nodded at Lional the Forty-third, handsome and spoilt and the answer to his prayers. "Yes, Your Majesty. Sorry, Your Majesty."

The king's horrible cat was now washing its face. Gerald pulled his Stuttley's-scarred cherrywood staff from its pocket inside his coat. It was nowhere near strong enough to contain the energies of a Level Twelve transmog but with luck it'd get him started, at least. After that . . .

*Saint Snodgrass, patron of wizards, deliver me.*

Raising the staff above his head he took a deep breath. Let the air out slowly and summoned the words of the transmog incantation to his tongue, adjusting them to the specifics at hand.

"*Innocuasi cumbadalarum. Amina desporato animali contradicta rexori!*"

Deep within him something powerful stirred from slumber. No pyrotechnics this time, no twisting and tearing. Just a flash like a firefly in the darkness of his mind. A tease, a hint, a whispered promise . . .

"Yes?" said King Lional, arms tightly folded. "And? Well? Was that *it*?"

Gerald shivered. His skin was crawling, the firefly flash stronger now, sustained and growing. As though the first words of the incant were some kind of trigger, punching a tiny hole into a reservoir of raw power hiding somewhere inside him.

"No," he said. "Wait."

"Wait?" echoed the king, impatient and offended. "I have *been* waiting, Professor, and as yet nothing has—"

"Don't interrupt, Lional, you might make something go wrong," said Princess Melissande. "Get *on* with it, Professor, quickly!"

Barely aware of her presence, of the king's temper, of Reg gurgling in alarm on the princess's shoulder, he bowed his head. The tiny hole was widening, he could feel the power pouring out of that hidden reservoir and into his blood, bolder and faster and increasing in urgency with every staccato heartbeat.

He had to keep going or the incant would collapse and with it any chance of his staying in New Ottosland as King Lional's court wizard.

"*Incantata magicata spellorantum infinatum! Enlargiosa lionara expellecta domesticia!*"

In a single slashing move he pointed his staff directly at the king's hissing cat. Incandescent power poured out of him like a river in full flood, transfixing the animal where it crouched on the dais. He felt as though he were being emptied, as though all his insides had melted and were streaming through his outstretched arm, into the staff and out again. The copper-banded cherrywood began to glow, hotter and brighter with each passing second. Surely his hand should be burning, but no. It was cool. Whole. Dimly he was aware of Reg's hysterical squawking, Princess Melissande's attempts to calm her, the king's shouted questions. He couldn't respond to any of them, could only stand there and let the incredible power do what it willed and hope it didn't kill him before it was done.

Overcome at last, the cherrywood staff crumbled into cinders and drops of melted copper. Gerald watched its charred remains fall piecemeal to the carpet, vaguely aware of sorrow, regret. The staff had been a present from his mother.

Its destruction didn't stop the power pouring from his body. On and on, lighting him up from the inside out like a firework. At last, though, it ran dry. As his knees buckled and his body swayed like a drunken sailor's, the air around the fat orange cat began to thicken like fog. Then it started to shimmer, suffusing with green and purple light. There came a sense of relentless pressure, as though an invisible fist was tightening itself around the room, squeezing, squeezing. Then the pressure released in a blinding flash and an eardrum-popping soundless explosion.

When the coloured fog cleared moments later, King Lional's fat orange cat was gone and in its place sat an enormous tawny lion wearing an expression of extreme apprehension.

"Saint Snodgrass preserve me," said the princess, breaking the stunned silence. "Professor Dunwoody, what have you *done*?"

"Kept my job," he said, dazed. *It worked, it worked, I can't believe it, it worked.* "I hope. Your Highness."

With an hysterical flapping of wings Reg launched

herself from the princess's shoulder to fly dizzy circles round his head. "A lion? A *lion*? You're *mad*, sunshine! Stark staring crazy bonkers! Off your bloody trolley with *bells* on! That was a *Level Twelve transmog*!"

He snatched her out of the air and shoved her under his arm. "Sorry, Your Majesty," he said to the king. "Terrible vocabulary her previous owner taught her. I've done my best but I can't seem to fix her."

King Lional ignored him. His gaze was trained on the lion. and in his eyes a bold bright burning. "Tavistock?"

The lion mewled, hauled itself to its feet and butted its head against him.

With an effort, Gerald stood to attention. When he'd recovered from the shock he was going to do some *serious* celebrating. *It wasn't a fluke, Stuttley's wasn't a fluke. I am a First Grader, no matter what my certificate says.* How it was possible he didn't know, didn't care. It was a pettifogging detail, he'd worry about it later. *There's a First Grade staff out there with my name on it! Pity it won't be a Stuttley's . . .*

"Your cat is quite unharmed, Your Majesty. And he's still Tavistock on the inside. Of course I can reverse the transmogrification if you—"

King Lional lowered his sharply raised hand. Shifting his burning gaze he said, softly, "Why a lion, Professor?"

He opened his mouth. Closed it. Frowned. "Well . . . I suppose because Tavistock is a cat. And your name, well, it's very suggestive. And—if you'll forgive the familiarity—a lion is a far more regal creature, isn't it? Not that cats aren't perfectly pleasant," he added hastily. "But. Well. They're not lions, are they?"

"No," the king said, his voice still soft. "Cats aren't lions at all. Professor, I am impressed. Not one of your predecessors, experts all, exhibited such power. And you say you're a mere *Third* Grade practitioner?"

"Well, Your Majesty, it is possible that in the matter of my grading there was a slight . . . clerical error."

King Lional threw back his head and laughed in abandoned delight. "A clerical error? Oh, Professor. You are exceedingly droll."

He bowed. "Thank you, Your Majesty. But if I may be so bold—am I also your next royal court wizard?"

Still chuckling, one hand now tangled in Tavistock's lavish mane, the king revealed all his teeth in a wide, wide smile. "Actually, Gerald, you're better than that. You are, officially, my *last* royal court wizard."

"So, Professor," said Princess Melissande, considering Gerald sideways as they left the royal audience chamber in their wake. "*That* was different. Quite the audition piece."

Clutching his carpet-bag, he managed a tired shrug. "I just wanted to make a good impression, Your Highness."

She gave him another considering look. "I think it's safe to say you succeeded." With a glance at the black cat padding at her side she added, "I hope you're not getting any ideas about Boris, now."

"No! No, of course not. Not unless you—"

"Because I like Boris just the way he is." The princess rubbed her nose. "You know, Professor, I'm no expert but it seems to me that little stunt you just pulled was—how shall I put it—insanely dangerous?"

"You can say that again," said Reg, rousing from her sulks.

"I'd rather not," said the princess. Gerald twitched his shoulder hard and hoped Reg would take the hint. "I admit," he said carefully, "transmogrification's one of the trickier feats in the wizarding lexicon."

She snorted. "That's quite a talent for understatement you've got there. Clearly, Professor, you're something out of the ordinary. Not at all like any other wizard the king has employed. Of course, whether or not that's a *good* thing remains to be seen." She surged ahead down the dimly lit corridor, heels thumping the musty carpet, Boris leaping in her wake.

"Well done," muttered Reg. "Get the boss's sister offside. That's always a good plan. Almost as good as doing a *Level Twelve transmogrification* without so much as consulting me first! You *idiot!* You *blockhead!* Don't you know you could have been *killed?*"

"Yes, but I wasn't, so stop fussing."

"Well excuse *me* for giving a tinker's cuss what happens to you!" Reg snapped. "You just about scared the feathers off me, sunshine! I haven't felt that much power rolling off you since—since—Gerald, I've *never* felt that much power rolling off you! What's going on?"

With that first giddy flush of triumph well and truly faded he was starting to feel apprehensive. Unsettled. Ever so slightly *spooked.* A nasty headache was brewing behind his eyes. "I don't know," he muttered. "And I don't want to talk about it now. I need some time to think, to—"

Reg chattered her beak. "You need to get a move on, that's what you need. Madam's getting away from us, in case you haven't noticed." She took a big breath. *"Oy, you! Princess Tearaway! What's the bleeding rush?"*

The corridor was so dimly lit and the princess stopped so fast that Gerald ran straight up the back of her, skittling her like an indoor bowling champion. The princess cursed, inventively and at length, Boris yowled and Reg shrieked as she fell off Gerald's shoulder.

He groaned, and sagged against the nearest wall. With a couple of well-placed pokes of her beak Reg had Boris totally preoccupied with matters reproductive, so she relocated and turned her attention to the princess.

"Language, woman!" she snapped from her strategic position on top of Gerald's head. "Pull yourself together. You're royalty, you've got no business rushing about like a lackey. Where's your pomp and circumstance, madam? Royalty doesn't *bustle*, it *glides*! Slowly, gracefully, as though it has got all the time in the world and more servants than a blind man can poke a stick at! Thirty hours, a staircase and a good thick book on your head, that's what *you* need, my girl."

Still on the floor and rigid with offence, the princess opened her mouth to respond but Reg rolled on, regardless. "And another thing. Why are all these corridors so damned dark? D'you *want* people flying into the walls and spraining their beaks?"

"I've got better things to spend my budget on than candles!" the princess retorted.

"You certainly have! Decent clothes, for a start, but you've been skimping there, too. It's a disgrace. Since when do royal highnesses tromp about in trousers, shirts and sensible shoes? Silk, satin, chiffon, floaty bits of gauze and the right amount of décolletage, *that's* the Princess Dress Code. Not to mention a nice set of diamond-studded high heels, peekaboo toe optional. And *who*, exactly, is the hairdresser responsible for that *jackdaw* nest I'm sure you're pleased to call a hair-do? I've met combine harvesters that could do a better job!"

Throughout this pithy homily on princessly personal grooming, Her Highness's expression faded from furious outrage to mild anger and came to rest at disbelief. Tearing her wide-eyed gaze away from Reg she turned to Gerald.

"I'm sorry. This is not a parrot. I'm not even sure it's a real bird. I don't suppose you'd care to explain, would you, Professor?"

He winced. "No. Not really."

"Do you mind?" Reg demanded, as the princess glared. "I'd rather you didn't discuss me as though I wasn't here. Contrary to popular opinion having feathers doesn't mean I don't have feelings."

"Maybe not," said the princess, "but I'm reasonably sure it *does* mean your conversations shouldn't be polysyllabic."

Hell. So much for keeping Reg under wraps. *I should have known.* "I'm sorry, Your Highness. It's just that—it's a long story."

"And an interesting one," added Reg. "Full of magic and mystery, not to mention beautiful queens, dastardly sorcerers and—"

"Fascinating," said the princess, ignoring Gerald's outstretched hand and picking herself up off the floor. "But I'm far too busy for fairy tales. I have to get you settled, Professor, then I have to deal with the Kallarapi and—" She swallowed the rest of the sentence as though the words hurt her throat. "But I digress. Shall we continue?" Bending over, she scooped the still-shaken Boris into her arms, flung him backwards over her shoulder and continued her brisk way along the corridor. The cat flopped bonelessly down her back, pulling hideous faces.

"You could at least *try* to glide!" Reg screeched after her. "You look like the goal keeper on an all-girl hockey team!"

Gerald snatched her from atop his head and shoved her under his arm. "Do you *mind*? What are you trying to do, get me arrested?"

"Of course not," said Reg, in a squashed voice. "But someone's got to tell her, she's obviously got no mother to do it and she's letting the side down."

He heaved a long-suffering sigh, picked up his carpet-bag and started after the princess. "Reg, how many times do I have to say this? Like it or not, you are a *bird* now. The rest of it—well, it's all gone. I know you don't want to accept that but honestly, don't you think it's time you did?"

"No, I don't," retorted Reg. "I'll never accept it, not if I live to be a thousand, which isn't going to happen if you keep on shoving me into your armpit! Phew!"

"Oh! Sorry." He stuck her back on his shoulder. "Look, you suit yourself. But *please* Reg, would you for once think before you speak? The last thing I need is to get fired from this job, at least not before I've figured out what's going on with me and my sudden upgrade."

"Well, I can't promise anything," said Reg grudgingly. "But I'll try. Now get a move on, would you? I want to get all the bureaucratic claptrap out of the way and put my feet up. I don't know about you but after all this excitement I could kill for a cup of tea and a nice fat mouse."

Several corridors and a couple of staircases later, the princess led them into a small room crowded ceiling to floor with overburdened bookcases and crammed wall to wall with a desk, filing cabinet, two chairs and several wilting pot plants. The only painting in sight was of a terminally pathetic kitten sitting on a dustbin, with its billiard-ball eyes cast mournfully to the heavens. It bore a faded resemblance to Boris.

"Oh, please," Reg muttered. "Spare me."

"My office," said Princess Melissande, and waved at the battered visitor's chair. "Have a seat, Professor. There's just some paperwork to sort out, then I'll show you to your suite." She deposited Boris on top of the nearest bookcase and slid in behind the desk, which was covered with files, papers, pens, inkpots, an antiquated telephone and some heavy leatherbound books. The crystal ball was there, too, doing double duty as a paperweight.

"Um . . . Your Highness . . . can I beg a favour?" he said as he sat in the proffered chair and settled Reg on its right-hand arm.

"By all means you can *beg*," she said, discouragingly.

"It's about Reg. I realise it's pointless trying to go on pretending that she's just a trained parrot . . ."

"Certainly it's pointless trying to pretend that she's *trained*. But?"

"But," he continued, willing Reg to silence, "if you don't mind I'd rather it didn't get about that she's . . . unusual. There might be unfortunate consequences."

The princess smiled thinly. "Trust me, Professor, I'm quite happy for your bird to remain silent. Whether your bird will be happy is another matter entirely."

"She will be," he said, and closed a hasty thumb and forefinger around Reg's beak.

"If you say so. Now, to get down to business—" The phone rang, and with an apologetically impatient glance at him she answered it. "Yes?"

As he waited, Gerald sat back and considered his surroundings more closely. They were positively . . . shabby. Which didn't seem right, seeing as how the princess was not only a princess but a prime minister to boot. Granted, New Ottosland wasn't a very big country, nor an important one, but even so. The second most important person in *any* country should warrant an office larger and more attractively decorated than a broom closet.

Without appearing to, he shifted his attention to the princess. Reg was right. Compared to the lavish sartorial display that was her glorious golden brother, she really did look dowdy. And then he realised *no*, it was more than that. She looked *beleaguered*. As though she were being slowly pressed flat to the floor by a weight too heavy for her to bear. Of course it could just be the strain of dealing with the king. On short acquaintance Lional did seem like a handful. But glancing around the drab office, and remembering the dilapidated state of everything except Lional and the audience chamber, he had the nasty feeling it wasn't quite as simple as that.

"Very well, Swithins," the princess said, bringing her conversation to an end. "Make the arrangements. I'll see the costs are covered somehow. The Kallarapi might be making things a trifle—challenging—just now but I'll be damned if the mailroom staff have to forgo their annual picnic on top of everything else."

So. His suspicion was correct. New Ottosland was running out of money. Unbelievable. *Can I pick them or can I pick them?*

The princess replaced the receiver. "Now . . . where were we?"

"Starting to wonder if you lot can afford a royal court wizard, actually," said Reg, her eyes bright with suspicion.

Which was true, but even so . . . "No we weren't!" he said hastily. "But if you don't mind me asking—"

This time the princess's smile was resigned. "Well, you were always going to find out sooner or later. New Ottosland is currently experiencing a minor and *temporary* cash-flow problem."

Yes, yes, *just* what he needed: continued penury. *When Monk hears this he's going to piss himself laughing.* "Because of the Kallarapi?"

"That's right."

"May I ask why?"

She fidgeted with a pen, avoiding his gaze. "If

you're worrying about being paid, Professor, don't. Lional always comes up with money for the things that matter to him."

"Oh, I wasn't worried."

"Speak for yourself," said Reg.

"*Reg*!"

"No," the princess sighed. "I suppose I do owe you an explanation. So: New Ottosland Economics, A Beginner's Primer. Pay attention, you will be quizzed at the end of the lesson."

"I already know that New Ottosland sits smack dab in the middle of a desert," he said helpfully.

"That's right," she said, nodding. "The Kallarapi Desert. Which explains everything, really. You see, when the Kallarapi ceded the territory which in due course became New Ottosland—"

"Why did they do that, incidentally?" he interrupted. "You'd think anybody who lived in a desert would *welcome* lots of grass and water."

She grimaced. "The best I've been able to figure out is that it's something religious. But since they don't discuss their religion with outsiders, that's as much as I can tell you. And anyway it doesn't much matter why, does it? It happened and now I have to live with it. So. As I was saying. When they ceded the territory a treaty-in-perpetuity was signed. We fly our balloons through Kallarapi airspace and drive camel trains across their deserts with our imports and exports and travellers and so forth, and they charge us a tariff for the privilege. And until five months ago the arrangement worked perfectly."

"So who put the fly in the ointment?" said Reg, scratching behind her head. "As if I didn't know."

"Weeeell," said the princess at length, "to be absolutely fair it's not *completely* Lional's fault."

"Just mostly?" said Reg sweetly.

The princess ignored that. "A month after Lional became king the old Sultan of Kallarap died and his heir Zazoor took over. Lional and Zazoor were at boarding school together in Ottosland and I'm afraid they didn't get along. They started competing with each other from the day they met, in everything from Algebra to Famous Ancestors, not to mention rugby, tennis, diving, cricket, polo and every other stupid game you can think of, and they didn't stop until the day they graduated." She pulled a face. "*Men.*"

"So," said Gerald, slowly, "the minute Zazoor came to power he started up the old piss—er—*conflict*—by hiking up the tariff rates?"

"Not . . . exactly," said the princess, with a look that suggested she was perfectly familiar with the original choice of phrase, thank you very much. "Yes, he started hiking up the tariffs but only after Lional started sending him snarky little notes implying some kind of financial double-dealing on his part."

"And was there?"

"No. At least, not that I or Treasury have managed to discover, but that's neither here nor there. The accusation's been made now, there's no way Lional is ever going to *un*make it, and after all the insults that have flown back and forth between him and Zazoor I think our friendly neighbourhood sultan would rather peel himself with a blunt bread-and-butter knife than admit there might be an error with the Kallarapi bookkeeping. And now the whole thing's come to a head because Lional's withholding the latest tariff payment altogether and Zazoor is threatening a total embargo of New Ottosland in retaliation. There's a Kallarapi delegation here now, being stiff-necked and difficult and demanding their money immediately or else."

Ah. Politics. Gerald pulled a sympathetic face. "A sticky situation, then."

She rolled her eyes. "More like syrupy. I've tried to sort things out myself but it's no good, the delegation won't even *begin* to discuss the crisis with me. So basically our entire future is riding on this meeting between them and Lional and to be perfectly honest I don't know that I can trust him to keep his temper. And that's where *you* come in."

"*Me*, Your Highness?" He sat up. "What's this got to do with me?"

"Everything. I need you to be my eyes and ears in that meeting tomorrow, Professor."

"But—you're the prime minister! Isn't international diplomacy *your* job?"

She slouched in her chair, sighing. "Ordinarily. The trouble is, I'm not invited."

"Not *invited*?"

"The Kallarapi government is one big boys' club," the princess said sourly. "No girls allowed. And with the entire privy council sacked—"

"You want Gerald to be your spy!" said Reg.

He glared at her. "Don't be ridiculous, Reg! Her Highness doesn't expect anything of the sort!"

Reg cocked her head. "Really? Then why is she blushing?"

It was true: the princess's face was distinctly pink. "Your Highness?"

Princess Melissande gave Reg a daggered look, then cleared her throat. "The term 'spying' is a gross exaggeration. Of course you musn't *spy* on His Majesty. But since I can't be there it would be extremely useful if I were to receive a report on what transpires between the king and the Kallarapi. Matters have reached a delicate crossroads, Professor. If I'm to avert disaster I need all the help I can get!'

# CHAPTER EIGHT

S orry," said Reg, before Gerald could answer. "I'm afraid that's out of the question. In fact, you'll have to find yourself another court patsy—sorry, wizard—altogether. We're leaving. Come along, Gerald."

"I don't think so," he said as she launched herself into the air. "You can go if you want. But I'm staying."

"*What*?" she shrieked, hovering haphazardly in front of the closed office door. "Gerald, are you cracked? This place is an international incident waiting to happen, and the closest you want to be to an international incident is reading about it in the newspaper over breakfast on another continent! Now let's *go*! I'm not a hummingbird, in case you hadn't noticed, and if you don't open this door in the next five seconds my wings are going to fall off!"

He sighed. She meant well, she really did, but it was long past time she stopped treating him like her wayward little brother. "Sorry, Reg. As New

Ottosland's royal court wizard it's my duty to assist His Majesty—and Her Highness—in resolving this unfortunate impasse with the Kallarapi. As for your wings, if you don't want them to fall off I suggest you stop flapping them."

Panting like a bellows, Reg lurched to the nearest bookcase that didn't contain a cat and landed with a thud. "But didn't you hear what she *said*? Things are going to get ugly around here! And you know my feelings about unattractive situations!"

"Yes, I do," he agreed. "And you know mine about conduct unbecoming to wizards. Running away at the first sign of trouble is pretty unbecoming, don't you think?" Not to mention a shortcut to career suicide.

*I am not giving up five minutes after getting here. I don't care how many camel pats this Zazoor starts lobbing over the border, I am staying put. And if I end up having to flush His Majesty's head down the bog to get him seeing sense, well, I'm practically a First Grade wizard. What can he do to me?*

Reg slumped against the row of books behind her and draped a wing across her eyes. "Gerald, Gerald, Gerald . . ." she moaned. "You've been reading romantic adventure novels again, haven't you? What have I told you about romantic adventure novels? They're *codswallop*! The only reason the heroes get out of those ridiculous dilemmas is because the writer is on their side!"

Peripherally aware of the princess's ill-concealed sardonic amusement, he fixed Reg with his severest stare. "You're being unnecessarily melodramatic. I have every confidence we'll be able to sort out this international misunderstanding. His Majesty and the sultan may be a bit at odds, but I'm sure the last thing they want is a lot of mess they have to clean up."

"Oh, *pishwash!*" gasped Reg, and flew heavily from the bookcase to her original perch on his chair. "Didn't you learn *anything* from your ill-advised sojourn at the DoT? The Lionals and Zazoors of this world *never* clean up their own messes. That's left up to the poor fools who don't know when it's time to head for the hills!"

A slow smile was spreading across the princess's face. "Well, don't look now, Reg, but I think your friend Gerald has misplaced his watch."

He smiled back at her. "Seems to me, Your Highness, you're a trifle watchless yourself."

"Oh, *please!*" said Reg, flinging both wings over her eyes. "Any second now an invisible orchestra is going to strike up a jaunty, never-say-die little tune with lovey-dovey undertones and I'll have to be sick!"

Magnificently unmoved by Reg's histrionics, Princess Melissande sat back in her chair and fixed her no-nonsense gaze on him. "Trust me, Professor, there's not going to be an international incident over this. Or if there is, it'll be over my dead body."

"That's what I'm talking about!" moaned Reg.

Gerald patted her on the head. "You missed your calling, Reg. You should've been on the stage." He looked back at the princess. "There is one thing. What if the king commands me not to repeat anything I see or hear during the negotiations?"

She blinked. "Oh—well—a stricture like that wouldn't apply to me. I'm his sister *and* his prime minister. He'll expect you to tell me so I can make the problem go away. That's what I'm for, you see. Making problems go away."

It sounded a daunting kind of life. "Well. If you're sure . . ."

"Positive, Professor."

"Then I'll do whatever I can, Your Highness."

Was it his imagination or did he see the merest shimmer of a tear in the princess's eyes? "Thank you," she said. "I'm grateful."

Marginally recovered, Reg sat up. "How grateful?"

"I'm sorry?" said the princess, frowning.

"What's the going rate for gratitude around here?"

For a moment the princess was perplexed. Then her frown cleared. "Ah! You mean salary? Good lord. You know, I'd quite forgotten about that."

Reg snorted. "I hadn't."

"Behold me not shocked beyond the power of speech," said the princess, staring over the tops of her glasses. "Actually, now that I think about it we never did discuss remuneration, did we, Professor?"

Scandalised, Reg whacked him with her wing. "Never *discussed*?" she screeched. "Have you *completely* lost your marbles?"

He rubbed his arm. "Calm *down*, Reg. The last time you got this excited it led to a spontaneous moulting and I don't want to go through that again! Do you?"

Reg's beak closed with a snap.

"As it happens," said Princess Melissande, "we can offer you a package deal, Professor." She opened a desk drawer. "Here are two copies of our agreement, which I need you to sign." She handed them over then gave him a pen. "Basically we—that is to say, the

Kingdom of New Ottosland—undertake to provide you with a palace suite in keeping with your august position, plus all meals, plus one day off duty per week, plus a horse from the royal stables or a carriage if you don't ride, but if you don't ride *and* hunt Lional will be displeased so I suggest you learn fast, plus fifty goldtroons a month from the royal Treasury. And you, Professor, in accepting the position of royal court wizard, become an honorary citizen of New Ottosland with all the rights and obligations thereto attached and undertake the performance of any and all wizardly tasks His Majesty might require."

He handed back the pen and her copy of the signed contract. "Provided, as we discussed, there's no conflict with my oaths of office."

"Yes, yes, I *know*!" she snapped. "Is my word on the matter sufficient or did you want it in writing?"

He swallowed. "Your word is perfectly sufficient, Your Highness."

"Good! Because while we're embattled, Professor, we're hardly unprincipled!"

"Of course you aren't," Reg muttered. "You just don't pay your bills."

"*Reg!*"

The princess stood. "And now I'll show you to your apartment."

"You don't need to do that, Your Highness," he said, scrambling to his feet. "Surely there's a servant who can direct us? I don't want to hold you up—"

"Too late," she said. "Besides. Your suite is on the way to the guest quarters for the Kallarapi delegation and I still have to tell them about their audience with the king. Come on . . ." She squeezed out from behind her desk and crossed to the office door with a finger snap at Boris. Grinning, the cat leapt lightly from its bookcase perch and joined her at the door. "I don't have all day."

"Of course not, Your Highness," said Gerald. He shoved his employment terms into his pocket, picked up his carpet-bag, waited for Reg to hop onto his shoulder, then followed the princess out of the cluttered room.

"And here we have Ancestors' Walk," she said as they turned yet another corner to be confronted by a long, wide, high-ceilinged corridor whose walls were covered with slightly tatty flocked wallpaper and crowded with ornately framed portraits. "Or, as I prefer to call it, the Rogues' Gallery. All the kings and princess consorts since New Ottosland was settled."

"It's very impressive," he said, slowing his pace to examine the faces.

She spared him a wry glance, for once matching his speed. "Oppressive, you mean."

"And which ones are your parents?"

The princess pulled a face. "Oh . . . well, actually, they're the only ones not here. Lional didn't get along with them so he refuses to hang their portraits. I'm hoping to sneak them in when I can be sure he won't notice."

"Oh," he said, and thought of the casual camaraderie and genuine affection he shared with his own parents. "I'm sorry to hear that."

She shrugged. "Don't be. I can't say I was overfond of them myself. Well, of my father. I sometimes think he'd have taken more interest in us if we'd had petals and stamens instead of arms and legs. As for my mother, I never really knew her. She died when I was very small."

"What did I say?" Reg whispered in his ear. "Practically motherless. I can always tell. Before you know it she'll be thanking me for my excellent grooming advice, just you wait."

Reg's buzzing tickled; Gerald rubbed his ear and said, "I really am sorry to hear that, Your Highness."

"Goodness," the princess said briskly. "Don't waste your sympathy on me, Professor. One quickly learns not to pine after the unattainable." She picked up her pace again. "Shall we get on?"

"You certainly have a lot of ancestors, Your Highness," he said, as the array of portraits continued. "Do you remember all their names?"

"Of course. On the left we have the Lionals and on the right, the Melissandes."

"I beg your pardon?"

She pulled a face. "Welcome to New Ottosland, Professor. A kingdom of Tradition."

He considered her. "You said that with a capital T."

"I did, didn't I?" She came to an abrupt halt, halting him, and looked him square in the eye. "Do yourself a favour, Professor, and don't ever forget it. Lional's doing his best to modernise us but I'm sorry to say it's an uphill battle. Here in New Ottosland we live and die by Tradition. You might think the horse-and-carriage look is quaint but trust me, it palls very quickly. However, since horses and carriages are what they had in colonial times that's what we still have today. No cars allowed. For the same stupid reason we don't have electricity, mass public transport, a stock exchange or any number of other modern conveniences which I'm sure you've taken for granted your whole life. Here in traditional New Ottosland we have candles and gaslight and an erratic hot-air balloon service, at least when the Kallarapi let us, and carriage post and exorbitantly expensive horseback couriers."

"What about your telephone? That's modern, isn't it?"

"The only reason we've got telephones is because I argued myself practically into asphyxiation to get them after there was an incident at the Mint, and only then in the palace and public institutions. That, Professor, is the sole concession to modernity you'll find around here. Oh, and me not having to wear crinoline and hoops." She shuddered. "And if you only knew what I went through to win *that* argument . . ."

"It's one you'd have been better losing," said Reg. "Hoops would do wonders for your posture, my girl."

The princess looked at him. "Tell me it gets better."

"Sorry," he said, shrugging. Then he stared again at the crowded wall of portraits. "So let me see if I've got this right. All the kings are called Lional because the very first king of New Ottosland was a Lional?"

"Exactly," she said, pleased. "And since his princess consort was called Melissande, *all* princesses, consorts or otherwise, are called Melissande." She marched off again, adding over her shoulder, "Whether it suits them or not."

"Well," he said, catching up to her, "I suppose it prevents unpleasant arguments at naming day celebrations. What about the queens of New Ottosland, then? What are they known as?"

"They're not. Women," said the princess in a studiously neutral tone of voice, "are unfit to rule, by virtue of their emotional natures and the woolliness of their wits."

"Oh," he said. "What an extraordinary thing to say."

"I thought so. Unfortunately, since those particularly inane words were uttered by Lional the First and tradition being what it is . . ."

He grinned. "Say no more. Still. At least it means New Ottosland and Kallarap have *something* in common. Perhaps the king and the sultan could build on that?"

The princess spared him a withering glance. "I'll be sure to mention it."

"So where do you display the Rupert portraits?" he asked as they reached the end of the corridor.

"We don't. There aren't any," she said. "Second and third and fourth etcetera sons, and daughters for that matter, are named whatever takes their parents' fancy and they're not important enough to rate a portrait. Not unless they're bumped up the ladder of succession into the top job, in which case they automatically become the next Lional. Or Melissande. It's all very *tidy*."

"Tidy," he said. "Yes. I suppose that's one word for it. I could possibly think of one more."

"Just one?" said Princess Melissande. "Live here as long as I have, Professor, and trust me: you'll expand your vocabulary. Now let's get a move on, shall we? All this talk of tradition gives me hives."

The walk to his living quarters was slowed considerably by constant interruptions, as various palace staff members popped out of offices and adjacent corridors to stop the princess with requests for advice and decisions. She seemed to know everyone by name, and dealt with their problems efficiently and with a smile. They in turn were respectful but relaxed, not the least bit intimidated.

"I'll say this much for her," Reg muttered. "She's got the common touch."

Gerald nodded, grateful. If she'd been a female version of her kingly brother, life here wouldn't be worth living.

Eventually, despite all the interruptions, they reached an ornately carved set of double doors. "Your suite," the princess announced, stopping. "I won't bother giving you a key since I expect you'll want to put in place your own wards or passwords or whatever it is you wizards use for locks. Your luggage should have been delivered by now. If it hasn't just pull on any one of the bell ropes and someone will attend you. Likewise if you have any questions, although I have prepared a handy little 'Guide to New Ottosland' you'll doubtless find helpful. Now I'll bid you good afternoon. Ordinarily I'd see you inside and give you a tour but I really must go and soothe the Kallarapi before they implode."

"Yes, of course, Your Highness. Don't let me hold you up," he said to her departing rear view. "Although—"

She turned back. "Yes?"

"I was just wondering . . . what time is it, exactly? I don't seem to have worked out the difference yet."

"A quarter to two," she said, after consulting a dented old pocket watch. "Past lunchtime. Which reminds me. Your predecessors usually ate meals in their suite unless they were summoned to sup with the king. If you don't hear from him just tell the kitchens what you want whenever you're feeling peckish."

Oh. It all sounded very . . . solitary. And haphazard. "What about you, Your Highness?"

"Me?" She looked surprised. "I usually grab a bite at my desk or in my suite unless I've been summoned too. Why?"

"Well, perhaps you'd care to dine with me tonight. If we're not required to be in His Majesty's presence."

Her cheeks tinged pink. "Oh. I see. That's very kind of you, Professor. Another time, perhaps. I'm rather drowning in paperwork just now."

He bowed. "Of course, Your Highness."

"One last thing," she said, darting a glance up and down the momentarily empty corridor. "That business we discussed. You know. With the Kallarapi."

"Yes, Your Highness?"

"I'd rather that stayed just between us, Professor. Consider it . . . a matter of state."

Who did she think he was going to tell? "Your Highness, as far as I'm concerned all our conversations are privileged."

She sniffed. "Does that go for the bird, too?"

"Do you *mind*?" said Reg, before he could answer. "I'll have you know, madam, that I was conducting matters of state long before your great-great-grandfather was a tickle in his daddy's britches!"

Another sniff. "I'll take that as a yes. Now, if there's nothing else?"

"Ha," said Reg, fuming, as the princess marched away with Boris. "'Does that go for the bird?' Who does she think she is?"

Gerald rolled his eyes. "Call it a wild guess but . . . the boss?"

"Her? The boss?" Reg hooted. "Ha! *Bossy*, I'll grant you. Definitely *that*."

"Oh, give it a rest, Reg," he sighed. "And let's inspect our accommodation."

"*Cor!*" said Reg admiringly as he closed the suite's front doors behind them. "Paint me pink and call me a flamingo! Would you get a load of this?"

"*This*" was the most luxurious, incredible decor Gerald had ever seen. After his drab shoebox at the Wizards' Club it made his eyes ache. Black marble floors scattered with kaleidoscope rugs. Chandeliers like glittering beehives. A skylight framed in solid gold. An enormous fountain-and-pond arrangement complete with vacuous goldfish. Exotic birds in gilded cages. A carved sideboard groaning beneath crystal bowls of fresh fruit and decanters of mellow amber nectars, two enormous armchairs and a gilded table and chairs. On the table a pink cardboard folder, neatly stencilled "A Guide to New Ottosland". Set into the back wall a gilded door inlaid with mirrors.

And that was just the foyer.

Forlorn in the middle of a rug shaded like a rainbow, his luggage looked embarrassingly decrepit.

Reg took a gliding turn about the room, pausing briefly to insult the real parrots. "Looks like New Ottosland really *has* gone up-market!" she declared, settling onto the back of a blue velvet armchair. "Say what you like, Gerald, this king knows how to treat his wizards. He's really got style!"

"Is that what you call it?" he retorted. "I'd have said more money than taste. *Look* at this place!"

Reg was grinning. "Posh, eh? Somebody's tax goldtroons at work with a vengeance." She flipped a wing at the mirrored door. "Let's have a gander at the rest of the apartment, shall we?"

Beyond the foyer was a sumptuously furnished salon complete with dining table and lounge suite. It had three more doors leading elsewhere, one on the left, one in the middle, one on the right.

Behind the left-hand door was his bedroom.

"This is ridiculous," he said, confronted by a curtained expanse of pillow-laden bed. "I'll need a compass just to reach the other side!"

"Wheee!" said Reg, trampolining merrily.

The opaline carpet under foot sank a good three inches beneath his weight. It was going to take something hydraulic to lift him out of the armchair by the window. There was a walk-in wardrobe, an ensuite bathroom containing a bathtub big enough to drown a herd of elephants, with gold taps and knobs and soap holders fashioned to look like terminally cheerful dolphins, and too many full length mirrors that reflected back to him the distinctly wild look lurking in his eyes.

The salon's middle door opened onto a library with bare shelves, and the right-hand door led to a wizarding workshop complete with benches, stools, cupboards, more mirrors, crucibles, mortars, pestles, herb racks, bookshelves, cages of various sizes, a specially designed crystal-ball holder, a globe and a few bits and pieces he'd never seen before.

He looked around, impressed. "Reg! Come in here!"

She flew in from the bedroom and landed on top of a cupboard beside the window. "Very nice. Gerald, we have to talk. This suite might be the bee's knees when it comes to prestigous comfort but you *can't* seriously want to stay in New Ottosland!"

He leaned against the nearest bench. "Why not?"

Boggled, she stared at him. "I think that trick with the cat must have melted your marbles, my boy. Why don't I start with the most obvious reason: His Majesty King Pillock."

Despite the brewing headache, which was threatening to erupt full force behind his eyes, and all his dark unanswered questions, he had to grin. "Pretty bloody awful, isn't he?"

"No, actually, he's pretty bog standard as far as royalty goes," said Reg. "But that's no reason to hang about. I don't like him, Gerald, and I certainly don't trust him. You've got to watch out for the smooth blond ones, they're always the worst."

"Reg . . ." He sighed. "You can't make this personal. The fact that the king is blond and handsome does *not* mean he's a villain. This is *my* story, not yours. We're agreed he's a pillock, but that's all. As for why I'm staying, I'd think it was obvious. Not only do I need the money, I have to find out how it is I'm suddenly able to do things like contain Level Nine inversions and turn cats into lions."

"Simple," said Reg. "You're a late bloomer."

He shook his head. "No. It's more than that. I'm

*different*, Reg. I can feel it. That massive jolt of raw thaumic energy in Stuttley's has done something to me. And until I've worked out what that is and what it means I'm staying as far as I can get from Ottosland and the Department of Thaumaturgy. All right?"

She fluffed up all her feathers, brooding. "All right," she said at last, reluctantly. "On one condition. Whatever else happens you are *not* to go falling in love with that sartorial disaster of a princess, is that clear? Because I won't have it, Gerald. If she was an orphaned only child I could possibly bear it. But she's a package deal with that pillock brother of hers so my foot *is* down. *No falling in love.*"

Blimey, that was the *last* thing on his mind. "Me fall in love, Reg? Now whose marbles are melted? I'm going to unpack."

The first thing he did was unearth his medicine tin and swallow three painkillers to eliminate the headache. Then he tackled the meagre belongings in his tatty luggage. It didn't take long. The walk-in wardrobe still looked tragically empty by the time he'd finished, and the workshop's shelves were barely half-full of texts. The last item he unwrapped was his crystal ball. Surprisingly, it was pulsing a frantic red. Incoming? Already? It could only be Markham, surely. *But why? I've only been gone a few hours. Unless . . .*

He went cold. Snatched up the crystal ball, rushed into his workshop and slammed it into the specially crafted receptacle on the bench.

"What's the matter *now*?" Reg demanded, startled out of a doze. She hopped off the ram skull, which he'd put on top of the cupboard by the window for her, and onto the workbench. "Are the Kallarapi invading?"

"Who knows? Who cares?" he muttered.

As anticipated, the first message was from Markham. "*Gerald, call me as soon as you get this.*" That was it. No explanation or mention of a parental touring catastrophe. Monk's slightly wavering face, distorted due to the cheapness of the ball's crystal, looked strained but not distraught. That had to be a good sign.

He triggered the next message. Monk again. Now his friend did look a little perturbed, and his voice was clipped. "*Gerald, I really need to speak to you. Call me.*" The third and final message was Monk, too. This time he was shouting. "*For the love of metaphysics, Dunwoody, stop playing with your bloody princess and call me! Do you have any idea what—look. Just bloody call me, would you!*"

"Oh dear," said Reg. "His knickers really are in a knot, aren't they? You'd better call him, Gerald, before something unfortunate happens to his wedding tackle."

He spared her an exasperated look and made the call. After a few moments Monk's face bloomed in the depths of the crystal ball. "Gerald! It's about bloody time!"

"What's wrong?" he demanded. "It's not my parents, is it?"

"Your parents?" said Monk blankly. "No. It's *you*! You've gone and triggered the international thaumograph, you stupid bastard! I've nearly killed myself avoiding a Code Red investigation! How could you *do* this to me? You've only been there five minutes and I've already had three heart attacks!"

*Damn.* King Lional's bloody cat. He sat on the nearest stool. "Monk, I'm sorry. I totally forgot about the DoT's monitoring station."

"I *know!*"

"Look, I can explain—"

"Explain? You can *explain* an unauthorised Level Twelve transmog? How the hell can you explain that? How the hell did you *do* it? There are currently only *five* certified Ottosland wizards rated for that incant, *three* of them are in my family and *none* of them are in New Ottosland! According to the current status bulletin you are the *only* wizard in New Ottosland right now, Gerald, and *you—*"

He raised his hands placatingly. "I'm *sorry*, Monk. I never meant to cause a panic, it's just the situation got away from me a bit and—"

"*You think so?*" Monk took a deep breath and let it out. "You're damned lucky nobody else has the monitoring capabilities we've got or you'd be up to your eyeballs in an international incident! What did you transmogrify, anyway?"

"A cat into a lion."

Monk gave a gurgling cry and clutched at his chest, glaring. "That was heart attack number four, in case you were wondering! Gerald, for the love of serendipity, *why?*"

He scrubbed a hand across his face. "It's a long story. Look, who else there knows what happened?"

Monk glowered at him out of the crystal ball. "Nobody. I had a funny feeling I should keep an eye on you, so I gave young Harris an early mark and finished off his monitoring shift. If I hadn't shut off the alarms a split second before they sounded, mate, you wouldn't be talking to me, you'd be talking to a Department board of enquiry. And trust me when I say they have *no* sense of humour."

Appalled, Gerald swallowed. "Thanks, Monk. I owe you."

"Damn right you owe me! Look, Gerald, you're not yanking my chain over this, are you? I mean, this isn't just some malfunction in our equipment? You really pulled off a Level Twelve transmog?"

Deep within, a flicker of pride. "Yes. I really did."

"Bloody hell," said Monk, awed. "Gerald, d'you realise what this means? It means you're a genuine card-carrying *genius*!"

Coming from Monk Markham, enfant terrible of the Research and Development community, it was a compliment past price. "Really? A genius?"

"Yes. *And* a raving bloody *menace*! Now you promise me, mate, right here and right now, you won't try anything so crackbrained again!" Monk demanded. "Because I might not be around to save your roasting chestnuts next time, understand? Your paperwork says you're a Third Grade wizard, Gerald, so a Third Grade wizard's what you'll be until the boffins in Aptitude Testing say otherwise. So. How soon can you get back here? A few days? A week?"

Oh, no. He had *no* intention of surrendering himself to the Scunthorpes of the DoT. "I don't know, Monk," he said evasively. "Not that soon. It's complicated. I'm under contract and there's a . . . situation . . . here I've promised to help sort out."

"Let someone else sort it out," Monk retorted.

"There's something bloody funny going on with you, Gerald, and we have to get to the bottom of it before whatever it is blows up in our faces."

Reg rattled her tail feathers. "He's right, sunshine. Since the cat's out of the bag now there's no point hanging about this dismal backwater."

Ignoring her, he shook his head. "Nothing's going to blow up, Monk. I've promised no more funny business and you know I'm a man of my word. I'll just potter along, same as I always do, and when the time is right I'll ask the king to let me portal back for a day."

Monk pulled a hideous face. "I suppose that'll have to do."

"Yes. It will."

"Fine. But in the meantime, mate, you just keep your nose clean."

"I will. My word as a wizard. And—thanks, Monk. For everything."

Monk rolled his eyes. "Level Twelve bloody transmogs. What'll the idiot think of next," he muttered, and severed their connection.

"That's a very good question," said Reg. "What *are* you going to think of next, Gerald?"

"Nothing," he said, and slid off the stool. "Next I'm going to have a bath. *Alone,*" he added, as she opened her beak.

She shut it again with a snap. He patted her on the head and headed for the bathroom.

# CHAPTER NINE

**P**rince Nerim, only surviving brother to the Sultan of Kallarap, woke from his fitful sleep with a cry, momentarily confused as to where he was.

And then he remembered . . . and hung his head.

How *shameful*, to fall asleep during the day beneath the roof of—well, he supposed he couldn't call the King of New Ottosland an *enemy*. Kallarap and New Ottosland were not at war. Not yet, at least. Not until the gods decreed it. If they did decree it. It was hard to see how they could decree anything else, though, given the barbaric behaviour of New Ottosland's king.

Sitting up on his uncomfortably soft bed in the guest quarters provided by the oathbreaking infidel Lional—he could call him *that*, anyway, since that's what he was—Nerim hugged his knees unhappily.

He wanted to go home.

New Ottosland was so *green*. There was grass *everywhere*, and trees, and flowers, and all kinds of hairy *animals*. The air was so full of smells it was heavy, sitting on his skin like a dirty blanket, and no amount of washing in New Ottosland's profligate waters could cleanse him. It was true: New Ottosland was an unclean, godless land. Not like Kallarap, with its burning deserts and sharp, unscented air and the living presence of the gods all around, their tears, shed for love of the Kallarapi people.

Oh, he wanted to go *home*.

But he couldn't, not until Shugat said. Not until they'd had their audience with New Ottosland's king and spoken the words of his brother the sultan, may he live forever. And when that audience would happen was anybody's guess. The appalling king was keeping them waiting and waiting and waiting . . . the insult was calculated. Unforgiveable. His brother should force the infidel Lional to his knees for that alone. Shugat should beseech the gods to smite him and all his kind from the face of the world . . .

Imagining the gods' wrath Nerim shivered, even though there was a fire burning in the room. That was another thing wrong with New Ottosland. It was too cold during the day and too hot at night. How could these New Ottoslanders *live* here? What were the gods *thinking*, to have given them—

Horrified, scrambling, he prostrated his body on the carpeted floor. What was he *doing*? He was questioning the gods! Oh, great Grimthak and Lalchak and Vorsluk forgive him! This New Ottosland was a disease, rotting his brain!

Paralysed with penitence, he began to pray.

A voice above him enquired, dryly, "What are you doing, Nerim?"

For one terrible moment he thought it was the flaming voice of Grimthak himself. "I—I—"

"Oh, get up," said the voice. "You look ridiculous."

It wasn't Grimthak. It was Shugat . . . which was almost as bad and practically the same thing. Shugat was Kallarap's holy man, the most powerful man in all of Kallarap after the sultan, may he live forever. Shugat was learned, he was wise, he was beloved of the gods.

Nerim rolled over and clambered to his feet. "Forgive me, Shugat," he said, and pressed his hands to his heart. "I was praying for strength."

Shugat nodded, looking stern. He always looked stern. And old. It was impossible to imagine Shugat unwrinkled and unbent and subject to the follies of youth. "Strength for what, Nerim?"

He chewed his lip. He hated confessing his weaknesses to Shugat, who had none, nor patience for anyone else's. "I—I—" He winced. "I don't think I can bear this terrible place another day!" he whispered, trying not to wail. "I want to go home!"

Shugat nodded again. "As do I."

"When will the king see us, do you know? It has been *days*. Does he truly expect us to deliver the words of our sultan, may he live forever, to a mere woman? And not even a beautiful one!"

"The woman is of high estate among her own people," said Shugat. "Mock not the ways of other men, Nerim. The gods permit all peoples to live their lives in accordance with their rules."

He stared. "But she is *ugly*, Shugat! And forward and immodest and she speaks like a man! She is an *insult*!"

Shugat smiled, revealing his gums. "Of course she is. But the insult comes from her brother, not her. Be at peace, Nerim. The king will see us when he judges we have been suitably humbled."

"*Humbled*!" He felt another surge of rage. "He is an infidel, not worthy to clean my brother's boots!"

"Even an infidel may have a purpose," said Shugat, shrugging. "We are here because the gods sent us. We will leave when we have done what they desire us to do, in the fashion they design for it to be done." He paused, his expression darkening. "Do not presume to question the gods, Nerim. That way lies madness and pain."

The look on Shugat's face was the one he wore just before administering a sharp clout to an offender's ear. Nerim bowed, hurriedly. "As always you are right, Shugat. Forgive me."

"I forgive you," said Shugat, and with a weary sigh lowered himself into the bedroom's chair.

"Are you . . . well, Shugat?" he asked hesitantly. Asking him personal questions was always a risky undertaking; Shugat resisted all attempts to engage in normal conversation. Only with the sultan, may he live forever, was he seen to laugh and even then not often. But the strain of this mission was beginning to show: there were dark circles beneath the holy man's eyes, and the healthy colour in his cheeks had faded.

Shugat waved a dismissive hand. "I am well," he said curtly. Then he sighed. "But also . . . troubled."

Eagerly he sat on the bed. "By what, Shugat? Tell me. I am the brother of the sultan, may he live forever, sent with you to speak the words of the gods' chosen ruler of Kallarap. Gladly will I lend you my wisdom. Speak to me as you would my brother, your friend, and I will listen with his ears."

Shugat's eyes widened. He was silent for a moment, lips twitching. Then he nodded. "Very well, Nerim. There is a man of great power in this kingdom. His presence here . . . concerns me."

"Concerns *you*? How can that be?"

"Many things concern me, Nerim," Shugat said sharply. "The heat of the sun, the pallor of the moon, the fall of a sparrow from the sky. But this man . . . he is a wildness. An unpredictability. He is chaos given form. I sense that our fates flow together like the mingling of two springs becoming one beneath the sand . . . but how or why this should be, I cannot tell. And so I am concerned."

He frowned. "But . . . you are Shugat, the wise and holy. Surely no man of flesh and blood can concern *you*. As well to say the gods themselves fear him!"

Shugat stood, his eyes flashing. "Bite your tongue, Nerim, you witless boy! I said nothing of fear, nor of the gods! And only a fool pays no heed to a man of power! Are *you* a fool? Did your brother the sultan, may he live forever, send a fool with me to talk of broken oaths and forsaken honour with the King of New Ottosland?" His left hand lifted and his gods' eye, the crystal embedded in his forehead, pulsed with the fire of a thousand suns.

Horrified, Nerim fell to his knees, arms rising to

shield his face. "No, no, Shugat! I spoke in ignorance but I am no fool! Do not punish me. Please,
please, *do not punish me!*"

An age passed before Shugat spoke again. "Of
course I will not punish you, Nerim," he said at
last, sounding weary beyond bearing.

"Thank you, thank you!" he cried. Then he gasped
as Shugat raised him to his feet and lightly shook
him. Despite his fear he opened his eyes. The fierce
crystal was dormant again, and Shugat's expression
was a blend of impatient kindness and urgency.

"But you must not wake my ire in such a fashion!"
the holy man warned him. "The gods sleep very
close to the surface of my dreams in this place, boy.
And the power I feel here scrapes my nerves as a
sandstorm at noon scours the sky."

Trembling, Nerim let his legs fold him back to
the bed. "Why did you not speak of this man and
his power when first we arrived?"

"When first we arrived he was not here," said
Shugat. He too resumed his seat, and his thin brown
fingers wrapped themselves about the arm of the
chair. "But he is here now. His power is newly
woken . . . and it is mighty . . . and what his presence means to us I do not know. But it does mean
something, Nerim. Of that I have no doubt."

He didn't understand, but he nodded anyway. It
seemed safest. "What do the gods say of this man?
What do they say we must do?"

Shugat frowned, and shook his head. "They say
nothing, Nerim. Which means they are not yet ready
to speak. We must be patient. When it is time for

the gods' purpose to be revealed it will be revealed, and not a moment before."

"Yes, Shugat," he said obediently. "Shugat—"

But he was interrupted by a forceful knock upon their guest quarters' outer doors. Shugat went to answer it. He heard the holy man say, in the horrible New Ottosland tongue, "Ah, Your Highness. How may I assist you?"

He pulled a face. What did the ugly immodest woman want *now*? Not more sightseeing, surely. He was sick to death of monstrous New Ottosland architecture. He joined Shugat in the foyer, wishing he could avert his eyes from the king's lowly sister who dared appear before them with her face uncovered and in clothing that outlined her—her *legs*.

And they weren't even *attractive* legs.

The king's lowly sister nodded at him. "Thank you for seeing me, Prince Nerim. I just stopped by to let you know His Majesty would be pleased to grant you an audience tomorrow afternoon at three, if that should prove convenient to yourself and Holy Shugat."

He nodded. "Certainly, Your Highness." The honorific nearly stuck to his tongue but Zazoor had impressed upon him the need to observe all niceties of good behaviour. And Shugat had promised him a clout on the ear if he forgot. "It is a meeting which we have long looked for."

"Yes," said the woman. "Well—"

"His Majesty is a busy man with the weight of a kingdom on his shoulders," said Shugat smoothly. "He must be miserly with his favours."

The king's lowly sister nodded. Nerim winced;

truly, he'd seen prettier camels . . . "Your graciousness is appreciated, Holy Shugat," she said. "I'm sure now that an amicable outcome will be achieved."

Shugat shrugged. "The gods determine all outcomes."

"Ah. Yes," she said. "Of course. Well, that's all I wanted. Unless you particularly desired another carriage ride into the city?"

"No," said Shugat. "No more carriages."

The king's lowly sister nodded again, and left.

Nerim resisted the urge to pull a face at the closed door. "An audience at last!" he said, returning gratefully to their own civilised tongue. "What do you think this means, Shugat?"

Shugat's leathery features creased in a frown. "The gods know. I shall withdraw and meditate, that they might tell me what they require."

"And me, Shugat?" he said eagerly. He was the sultan's brother, after all, may Zazoor live forever. He was instrumental in this very important mission. "What should I do?"

Shugat sighed. "Go back to sleep, Nerim."

Instead of returning to her office and tackling more prime ministerial problems, Melissande decided she needed a moment's respite from care. She headed for Rupert's butterfly house. A few precious moments discussing nothing more important than insects was exactly what she needed right now.

The *gods* decide all outcomes? Well *phooey* on the gods! If that was the case then it was about time the gods pulled out their collective finger and got this ridiculous tariff situation sorted *immediately*.

"Because I've had enough, all right?" she demanded as she trounced down the staircase leading to the palace's south saloon vestibule. "Are you listening? Did you hear me? I-have-had-*enough*!"

A startled footman tripped over his mop and bucket. "Your Highness?"

She helped him to his feet. "Sorry, Norbert. I wasn't talking to you."

Mystified, Norbert dabbed soap suds off his elbow. "Very well, Your Highness."

"Carry on, then," she said grandly, and pointed to a grimy patch beside the nearest wilting pot plant. "You missed a bit."

Rupert was in the meticulously tended garden attached to his butterfly house, snipping the heads off dead flowers. When he saw her his face lit up. "Melly!"

She joined him, kissed his grubby cheek then surveyed the flowerbeds. "Hey, Rupes. What are you doing?"

"Oh, you know, chores. A butterfly keeper's work is never done," he said, his smile fading a little. "It's so sad. All the *Floribunda Magnificos* have died off, you see? So I have to prune them. My poor butterflies won't know what to do with themselves. The *Magnificos* are their favourite supper—almost thirty percent sugar in the nectar, with chambers nearly twice as big as any other flower."

She considered the headless bushes. "And that's good, is it?"

"Oh, Melly, that's *marvellous*," he said earnestly,

waving his pruning shears for emphasis. She took a prudent step back. "Bigger chambers mean their little proboscises don't have to work so hard!"

She had no idea what he was talking about. "How wonderful. I'm so pleased for them."

"Yes," he sighed. "They do love their *Magnificos*. Oh well. They'll just have to make do with the sweet sillies and cuttings from the honeypot tree."

"You really love your butterflies, Rupert, don't you?" she said, and brushed her fingers over his arm.

He blushed. "I know, I know. A grown man in transports over insects; it seems ridiculous. But they're as important to me as Boris is to you and Tavistock is to Lional."

*Tavistock.* She had a blinding flash of memory: Lional's cat, changing. The look on her brother's face. The look on Gerald Dunwoody's face, too. Terrified and exhilarated and shocked beyond the telling. And what *that* might mean she was too afraid to wonder . . .

"What?" said Rupert, anxiously. "Melly, what's happened? Tavistock's all right, isn't he? Don't tell me he's got himself run over by a carriage! Lional will skin the driver alive, he *dotes* on that cat!"

"No. No, Tavistock's not dead." She pulled a face. "But he's not a cat any more, either."

"Not a cat?" said Rupert, bewildered. "Melly, what are you talking about?"

There was a charmingly hand-carved wooden bench a few feet to the left. She sat on it and shoved the hairpins back in her bun. "The new wizard's here."

Rupert looked disappointed. "Oh, no! And I'd promised myself I'd be there to meet him! What's he like? Is he nice? Nicer than Grumbaugh? Although that's not much of a challenge, eh?"

"He seems very nice," she said, cautiously. "Lional likes him, at any rate."

"Yes, well, Lional's liked all of them to start with, hasn't he?" Rupert pointed out. "And then he's either fired them or frightened them away. Why should this new one be any different?"

"Well, for a start, he turned Tavistock into a lion."

Rupert dropped his pruning shears. "He did *what*?"

She slumped against the back of the bench. "And far from being angry, Lional was *pleased*. I'll tell you, Rupert, it's making me very nervous."

He sank onto the bench beside her. "I'm not surprised! I mean, I am, but not about you feeling nervous. If I was standing that close to a lion I'd be *terrified*, even if it was only Tavistock in disguise. And Lional isn't angry?"

She shook her head. "No. He's even meeting with the Kallarapi tomorrow."

"Well, that's good, isn't it?" Rupert said encouragingly. "That's what you've been after him to do ever since they got here! Shouldn't you be happy?"

"You're right," she said, and patted his knee. "I should."

"But you're not."

"I'm not *unhappy*," she said, frowning. "I'm just . . . I don't know." She stood. "I've got a fluttery feeling in the pit of my stomach, Rupes."

"I know that feeling," he said, and grinned. "Butterflies!"

"Oh, *you*," she said, and mussed his hair. "Is that all you can think about?"

"Yes," he said. "Sorry."

"That's all right. To be honest, Rupes, I find it rather restful."

"Oh, so do I," he said cheerfully. "Which is lucky, because we both know I'm not clever enough to be prime minister, or a king. Why, I shudder to think where we'd be if I'd been born first instead of Lional."

He was right. It didn't bear thinking about. But it hurt her, sometimes, to know that Rupert knew exactly how short-changed he'd been when it came to intellect.

She turned back towards the palace. "I'd better be off. I'm only out here to avoid the mountain of paperwork waiting for me in my office."

"Ouch," said Rupert, standing.

"Oh, no, I didn't mean it like that!" she said, and impulsively hugged him. "I just meant—"

"I know what you meant, Mel," he said, hugging her back. "Go on. You're keeping me from my very important chores. And don't worry about the new wizard. If Lional stays true to form he'll have the poor man packing his bags within the month. And then perhaps he'll *finally* give up this nonsense of having a royal court wizard."

"Perhaps," she said. "But I wouldn't bet on it if I were you!"

She left Rupert to his pruning and trudged back

to her office, where Boris was draped helpfully across her desk. He yowled as she entered the room.

"I know," she said, depositing him on the chair. "I agree completely. Tavistock as a lion is taking one-upmanship *far* too far. But I'm afraid there's nothing we can do about it, at least for now. So just you go back to sleep and let me get on with my paperwork!"

Gerald didn't really need a bath. It was just the only place he could think in peace.

Think, and experiment.

He'd snuck his back-up staff into the bathroom with him, bundled into a change of clothes. Soaking in warm, bubble-frothed water, he began to explore the new limits of his power. Simple incants at first, that a good Third Grader could master if he were on top of his game, like turning the towels from white to green and back again; chequer-boarding the white wall tiles orange and puce, then a less eye-searing black and gold.

He rather liked the effect, so he left them that way.

After that he had another look at the advanced incants Reg had pummelled into him, that he'd never been able to perform. The incants he'd reached for back in Ottosland, holed up in his shoebox of a bedsit, and been unable to access.

*I must still have been recovering from what happened at Stuttley's. I needed more time for my body to adjust. Or finish changing. Or whatever the hell it is that's going on with me . . .*

Even though the water was warm, he shivered.

*Talk about butterflies... have I turned into a chrysallised grub? When this is over am I going to hatch into someone—something—completely different?*

He didn't want to think about that. The idea was far too disconcerting.

*Perhaps being a genius is over-rated.*

Heart banging hard he put aside the spare cherry-wood staff and reached for his newmade power. Incanting without a staff was supposed to make the etheretic energies ten times harder to control but he barely noticed the difference. Holding his breath, he constructed bogwights out of thin, steamy air. Unravelled his dull and serviceable brown suit into the shorn marsh fleece it was made from, then re-constituted it into finest grade superior mountain fleece and redyed it, creating for himself a rich purple suit his father would be proud to own. For good measure he changed his plain white cotton shirt to pearlescent silk. Finally he coalesced all the random etheretic energies in the atmosphere into a single glowing ball of raw thaumic energy and let it hover like a burning blue sun beneath the bathroom's high ceiling.

"*Oy!*" shouted Reg on the other side of the bathroom door. "Even *I* felt that! Gerald, what the devil are you doing in there?"

Entranced, he floated in the cooling bathwater and smiled at his bright blue miracle.

*On the other hand I think I could get used to being a genius.*

"Nothing," he called back. "You're imagining things."

Reg retreated in a cloud of muffled curses.

With a snap of his fingers he released the coalesced energy back into the atmosphere, then climbed out of the enormous tub to dry and dress. Reg was waiting for him in the bedroom.

"Nice threads," she said from the bedhead, staring at his remade suit. "And good timing." She nodded at a slightly torn piece of parchment with a broken wax seal, discarded on the bedspread. "That just got shoved under the front doors. His Nibs has invited you to dinner."

He snatched up the parchment. "Reg! How many times do I have to say it? *Don't* go reading my mail!"

As usual the complaint was water off a duck's back. "You're to report to his private dining room at seven o'clock sharp," she said. "Not me. Just you." She sniffed. "I think my feelings are hurt. Gerald—"

He gave her a look. "No. We'll talk when I'm ready to talk and not a minute sooner."

"That might not be soon enough," she retorted. "Gerald, you're not treating this with the seriousness it deserves. What's happened to you, well, it's just not *normal*. And it's *certainly* not something you should be playing with like a shiny new toy. I want you to tell me again what happened at Stuttley's. Now that you're sober you might remember something that—"

He tossed the parchment back on the bed. "No. Reg, I'm fine. I have never felt better. And this is one gift horse I *won't* be looking in the mouth. I'm going to be the best royal court wizard King Lional has ever seen, and when a decent interval has passed I'm going home to get retested and officially regraded. And after that—" He released a long slow sigh of satisfaction. "After *that*, Reg: the world will be my oyster."

She glowered. "Haven't you heard? Oysters give you food poisoning!"

He threw a pillow at her.

"Butterflies are actually very loving, you know, Professor Dunwoody," said His Royal Highness Prince Rupert, confidingly. "Loving and gentle." There were smears of butterfly dust all over his patched mustard yellow velvet dinner jacket, and in his eyes the gleam of the fanatic. His long thin nose was disfigured by a neat strip of plaster.

"Really?" said Gerald, trying not to stare at it. "I didn't know that."

It was twenty past seven, he was seated with the prince and the princess in the king's private dining room, and they were waiting for King Lional to arrive.

Noticing him trying not to notice his nose, the prince blushed and laughed. He sounded like a lamb separated from its mother. "Just a little misunderstanding with one of the *Vampirella Majesticas*, Professor," he explained, giving the bandaged wound a self-conscious tap. "I blame myself, naturally. I mean, the poor little *Vampirellas* can't help themselves. Their instinct is to bite and they follow their instincts, so if one is silly enough to put one's nose in their way, well, one can hardly blame *them*, now can one? Creatures—and people—act according to their natures and there's no point expecting otherwise. Don't you agree?"

Gerald shot a beseeching look across the table at the princess but she wasn't paying attention. She'd brought a folder of work along with her and was busily totting up figures. In honour of the occasion she'd changed her clothes, but despite the fact that silk and satin and a certain amount of lace figured in the ensemble she still managed to look rumpled and tweedy.

He turned his attention back to the prince. "Agree? Certainly, Your Highness."

The prince beamed. "I say, I do *like* you, Professor." He leaned a little closer. "So what do you think of Lional's private dining room? Isn't it the swankiest you've ever seen?"

It was. The ceiling was some thirty feet overhead, and ripe with chandeliers. The walls were panelled with gilded mirrors. The mahogany dining table was laden with gleaming cutlery in four different varieties. There were three different kinds of glasses, an assortment of gold plates and bowls and two napkins for each diner.

Resisting the impulse to tuck one under his chin as a subtle hint that yes, on the whole he *was* ready for his dinner, thanks ever so much, he scowled at the overabundance of ironmongery and cursed himself for cutting short Reg's "Etiquette For All Occasions" lecture.

As a finishing touch, whoever was responsible for setting the table had managed to squash in arrangements of wan-looking flowers. Any minute now they were going to start him sneezing. Behind each gilded dining chair, ramrod stiff and conspicuously not listening to both the conversations of his betters and any rumbling digestive systems, stood a magnificently liveried manservant complete with white gloves and a little napkin laid over the left arm, which was held away from the body at a precise ninety-degree angle. It looked like a desperately uncomfortable way to spend an evening.

Prince Rupert leaned even closer. "Don't tell anyone I told you so," he whispered, "but for what it cost to have the place refurbished three months ago we could've paid the Kallarapi twice what we owe them and still have change left over." One bony finger tapped the side of his bandaged nose. "But there you are, Lional does love his little comforts."

Without looking up, the princess said, "Rupert. No telling tales out of Treasury."

The prince blushed. "Sorry, Mel." He tittered, embarrassed, then nodded. "I say, Professor, I do like your robe. Reminds me of the pattern you find on a Greater Winged Triple-Tipped Thribbet."

"Thank you, Your Highness. It's actually Fandawandi silk. Quite rare."

"*Beautiful*. Where did you get it?"

Back home, wizard robes were largely seen as pretentious affectations from a bygone era. But he suspected they were the kind of thing that would appeal to the king . . . and besides, this particular robe had sentimental value. "It was a graduation gift from my father, Your Highness. He's a tailor."

"*Really*?" Prince Rupert marvelled. "I say, that's fantastic. I'm useless with my hands, I'm afraid. All thumbs. I'd never dare pick up a needle and thread, you know, in case I stabbed myself in the eye. How desperately clever of him, I'm sure."

Gerald considered the prince. Was he being sarcastic? No. No, there wasn't a sarcastic bone in Prince Rupert's daft body. The compliments were genuine. "Thank you."

"And your *hat*!" Prince Rupert added. "*Amazing*!"

Yes. Well. *Amazing* was one word for it. *Embarrassing* was another. Tall, black and ridiculously drooping, and like the robe over a century out-of-date, fashion-wise, the hat had been another gift. This time from his mother. He was wearing it just this once, here where no-one like Errol Haythwaite would see him, so he could put his hand on his heart and say *Yes, Ma, it fits perfectly*, and forever after consign it to the bottom of whatever wardrobe he happened to be using at the time.

At least now he could say, with perfect honesty, it had been admired by royalty. That would cheer her up no end.

Princess Melissande was looking at him, as though she could read his mind. Or perhaps her pained expression came from the fact he was wearing the damned thing indoors. Clearing his throat, he snatched the hat off his head and shoved it under the table, between his feet.

"My mother gave it to me, actually," he explained to the prince. "She'll be thrilled to hear you like it, Your Highness."

Another bleating laugh. "Goodness, Professor, there's no need to stand on ceremony. Plain old Rupert, that's me. A prince in name only, I'm afraid. No credit to the crown." The foolish mouth drooped for a moment. "Sad to say, I'm a trial and a tribulation to the king. No, no, don't try to deny it, Melly. It's true. They think Nanny Prendergast dropped me on my head when I was a baby and never admitted it. I dare say that's true, too. It's the only reason I can think of, at any rate."

"Well, well, well," drawled an impeccable voice from the doorway. How . . . *delightful* . . . to see you all enjoying yourselves so much. Without *me*."

# CHAPTER TEN

King Lional. At his side Tavistock the cat-turned-lion, its expression now unbearably smug: seemingly the animal liked its new look. The king's ring-smothered hand rested negligently on the beast's vast, maned head. He was dressed neck to knee in richest black velvet, the lush fabric carelessly strewn with seed pearls and diamonds. Poised in the doorway, glittering beneath the chandeliers, he looked as though someone had draped him in a section of cloudless midnight sky.

The herald at the doors blew a belated, vaguely musical trill through his horn and announced, "Be upstanding for His Majesty King Lional the Forty-third!"

But Gerald was already on his feet, along with Rupert and the princess. Languid as molten gold, the king made his way to the head of the table; Tavistock padded with him, rawboned tail waving in a parody of greeting.

"So sorry to have kept you waiting," Lional said, smiling as he eased into his throne-like chair.

He didn't sound sorry at all.

"That's quite all right, old chap," Rupert said cheerfully as they sat down again. "We hardly noticed you weren't here, actually. Been having a lovely chat with the new wizard. I must say I think you've made an excellent choice this time, Lional. This one's much chirpier than those other old fossils. Grand, isn't it?"

Princess Melissande shoved aside her paperwork and covered her eyes with one hand. Sprawled indolently by the king's chair, Tavistock complained with a throaty rumble like distant calamitous thunder.

The king's smile widened. "I'm relieved you approve, Rupert. Professor—" he added, as the manservants began pouring wine and serving soup, "allow me to compliment you on your attire. You quite put me to shame."

"His father made it, Lional," said Rupert. "Wasn't that grand of him?"

The king stared, his cerulean eyes wide. "Your *father*? Really?"

Pillock, pillock, pillock and prat. Gerald smiled. "Yes. Your Majesty. He's a tailor. Or at least he was, until he retired."

"Was he indeed?" Lional spread out his napkin with a snap. "Fancy that. Mine was a king, you know."

He felt his fingernails bite into his palms. *Bastard.* "Indeed, Your Majesty. But then I think that to his son, every father is a king."

Silence, broken only by Tavistock's resumed rumbling. Then Lional threw back his golden head and laughed. He sounded genuinely amused. Princess Melissande, the colour flooding back to her face, loosened her grip on her spoon.

"Professor, I believe you're right!" Lional declared. "Let us raise our glasses to fathers, shall we?" He laughed again. "Especially *absent* ones."

The toast was drunk. Abruptly bereft of appetite, Gerald toyed with his bread roll. One of the manservants had given Tavistock an enormous bloody haunch of something to gnaw on. He'd never realised how big a lion's teeth were. Or how sharp. What had he been *thinking*?

Unlike his brother, who slurped, Lional consumed his lobster bisque daintily, fastidiously. Pausing between spoonfuls he dabbed his lips with his napkin and said, "Melissande, I hope you've informed the Kallarapi I'm granting them the honour of an audience tomorrow."

She nodded. "Yes, Lional."

"Excellent. I look forward to showing them the error of their ways. Don't you. Professor? Naturally, you will be in attendance. Lending the appropriate air of gravity and menace."

*Menace?* He cleared his throat, very carefully not looking at the princess. "Of course. Your Majesty. Although you know, my skills haven't been what you'd call honed in the international arena. I wonder if there's not someone else more suited who could take my place? Or at least join us. Her Highness Princess Melissande, perhaps. She is your prime minister, after all." And if she attended the meeting he wouldn't have to worry about the king thinking he was her spy.

Lional's expression chilled. Sublimely oblivious, Rupert pulled a dog-eared book out of his pocket, propped it up against a vase and began to read as he continued to slurp his soup. The book's cover was graced with a watercolour of an improbably smiling butterfly.

"My dear Professor," said Lional. He didn't sound at all friendly. "That won't be necessary. Your experience as a wizard will be quite sufficient for my purposes."

Across the table, Princess Melissande was attempting to semaphore a message via her unplucked eyebrows. Gerald tried to ignore her. "I'm sorry, Your Majesty. Would you mind explaining what you mean by that?"

The king considered him. "Oh, dear. Please don't tell me you're going to be *obtuse*, Professor. I find obtuse people very . . . *wearing*."

*Not as wearing as they find you, I'll bet.* "Obtuse, Your Majesty? No. At least, that's not my intention. I just don't want any misunderstandings when we meet with the Kallarapi. Misunderstandings could give rise to an unfortunate international incident."

The king dropped his spoon into his emptied soup bowl. The manservant behind his chair winced. "I am not concerned about international incidents. No great nation can afford to concern itself with the hurt feelings of its inferiors. I hope you are not suggesting, Professor, that I place the selfish desires of these Kallarapi above the welfare of my own people?"

Oh, thank *God* Reg wasn't here. "Of course not, Your Majesty," he said carefully. "But—"

"There is no *but*, Professor," said the king. "It has

been said that diplomacy is the waging of war by other means. If that is indeed the case then where the Kallarapi are involved *you* may consider yourself my secret weapon."

Secret *weapon*? What the hell was *that* supposed to mean? He snuck a glance at the princess. She was very pink about the face and her fingers were white-knuckled on the stem of her almost emptied wine glass.

"Lional," she said with commendable calm, "is that a good idea?"

Lional ignored her. "Do you know, Professor, what the very best thing about being king is?"

He couldn't help himself. "The hours, Your Majesty?"

Beside him, Rupert surfaced from his butterfly daydreams long enough to bleat his amusement. "The hours! I say, that's a good one! The hours! That *is* a good one, isn't it, Lional? The hours?"

"The very best thing about being king, Professor," said Lional, as though his brother didn't exist, "is that all my ideas are good ideas. In fact since I came to the throne I haven't had a single bad one. Have I, Melissande?"

Rupert said, "Ooh, I don't know about that, Lional, I mean there was that business with the horses, the monkeys and the—"

"*Rupert*," said his brother. "*Get out*."

Rupert flinched. "Sorry, Lional," he whispered, picked up his book and retired.

"All I *meant*," the princess began, and was silenced with a glare that sizzled the air between them.

"It seems to *me*," said the king, his voice lightly

coated in ice, "the time has come for us to remind the world that New Ottosland is a sovereign nation, a kingdom of tradition, antiquity and significant heritage. We must no longer allow ourselves to be dismissed and trifled with because we appear insignificant. The fire ants of Sanarabia appear insignificant yet they can reduce the mighty elephant to bloody bone and sinew. So it may be with New Ottosland, should the unwise choose to render us one whit less than our proper due. For too long nations like Kallarap have treated us with contempt. Well, to that I say; *no longer*. We must assert ourselves as New Ottoslanders, the equals of any nation in the world."

"And I'm not saying we shouldn't," the princess persisted. "But to be taken seriously on the world stage we have to look like a world power. Which means we need things like privy councils, to give us gravitas. *And* supply valuable diplomatic experience."

"My privy council was short-sighted, lily-livered and stuck in the past like hogs in mud," snapped Lional. "Aged relics . . . and their sons are relics-in-waiting. Which is why I banished them to their estates where they can dwindle their dying days in contemplation of the nation they and theirs *might* have birthed had they the least wit, imagination or courage."

Princess Melissande released an exasperated breath. "I *know* they're ancient and irritating, Lional, but as it turns out they actually got quite a lot done around here and I have to say, in all honesty, that expecting me to pick up the slack is a bit unfair. I mean, I'm doing my best, and so are my staff, we really are, but we just can't keep up and—"

"Then I suggest you find new ways of motivating your employees," said Lional, smoothly. "And yourself. Unless you'd like me to do it for you?"

She bit her lip and looked down. "No. Thank you. That won't be necessary."

"I suspected as much," said Lional. Still rankled, he shifted in his chair. "And what about you, Professor? Is there anything *you'd* like to add while we're all feeling so *delightfully* conversational?"

If he said what he *really* wanted to say he'd find himself getting intimately acquainted with a headsman's axe. "Well . . . as a matter of fact there is, Your Majesty. Another question, if you don't mind."

"No," said the king. "I don't mind. Provided it's not *obtuse*."

"Well, sir, in short: what exactly do you mean, *secret weapon*?"


"The man's barking mad," said Reg late the next morning, through the remains of her breakfast mouse. "How does he think *you're* going to make those Kallarapi buggers change their minds about the tariffs?"

Gerald stirred his porridge with his solid gold spoon and frowned. "He didn't say. He just laughed and waved in the next course."

"I mean," she continued, "as far as I can tell, the only thing that's going to stop this tariff tiff before it gets well out of hand is Lional sitting down to a great big slice of humble pie." She sniffed. "And how likely is that, I ask you?"

"Not very," he said, still frowning.

Reg cackled. "Not at *all*, sunshine. Trust me. There's nothing you can tell me about Lional that I don't already know. I was giving his type the cold shoulder when I still had a shoulder to give 'em, and that's more centuries ago than I care to think about. I tell you, he's lost his marbles down the privy."

He winced and looked around the fountain-tinkled foyer. "Careful, Reg. For all we know the walls have ears. Pillock or not, Lional's the king. You can't flap about the place saying he's mad."

With a burp Reg hopped off the back of her gilded chair and started marching to and fro across the table. "Listen, sunshine, the fact he's a king only makes it *more* likely he's off his rocker. Royalty's always inbred. Comes of them being snobs and refusing to marry a good bit of commoner every third generation or so. I mean, look at that Prince Rupert. From what you've told me it's clear he's a grade A nutter. Madness probably runs in the family. You want to keep an eye on that Melissande or next thing we know she'll be after you in the middle of the night with a jewelled dagger and a fixed smile, you mark my words."

He groaned. "*Honestly*, Reg. You do go on."

She waved an emphatic wing under his nose. "Gerald, I'm serious. You need to respect my experience in these matters. Sending a bunch of worn-out dukes and barons and their gormless offspring on a one-way trip to their country estates is one thing. Nothing wrong with that. Did it myself on a regular basis, generally speaking they're nothing but a bunch of parasites anyway. But seriously entertaining the idea that he could use an oath-protected wizard as *any* kind of weapon, secret or otherwise, is clear proof that Lional's two oars short of a rowboat."

On second thoughts he wasn't in the mood for porridge after all. Reaching to the fruit bowl for an orange he said, "His Majesty's not mad, Reg, he's just . . . determined to have his own way. I swear, if he thought I could make the Kallarapi back down by turning up at this meeting naked I'd be well advised to get used to inconvenient breezes."

"Deary deary me, I don't know," Reg fretted, kicking the solid gold toast-rack in passing. "The more I hear, the unhappier I am about staying in this place."

Moodily, he peeled his orange. "It's a crazy set-up, all right."

Reg stopped. "Hallelujah, he's seen the light! You start packing and I'll nip down to madam's office to give her the good—"

"Not so fast!" he said, waving orange peel in her face. "You're forgetting my contract."

She made a sound like an exploding firecracker and turned a complete somersault. "For the love of Saint Snodgrass, Gerald, there isn't a contract signed that can't be broken and lord knows you've got grounds with this one. I ask you, where is the benefit in dancing to the whirligig tune of some addle-brained power-drunk third-rate backwater king?"

There was orange juice running down his fingers. Reaching for a napkin he said, teeth clenched tight, "That's not the point. The *point*, Reg, is—"

"Oh, I know what your point is, Gerald. It's that

bloody princess! You've gone and fallen arse over tea-kettle for Madam Fashion Disaster, haven't you? Oh *Gerald*! How *could* you!"

He could have banged his head on the table. "Reg, for pity's *sake*. I have *not* fallen arse over tea-kettle for the princess."

Reg squinted at him suspiciously. "Are you sure? Because I'm not blind, Gerald, I saw the way you were around her yesterday, dumbstruck with admiration, and—"

"Are you cracked? I wasn't dumbstruck with admiration, I was just dumbstruck!" he cried. "She's even bossier than you are and I didn't think that was possible! I'm telling you, Reg, I am *not* in love with—"

"Good morning," said a bemused voice from the doorway. "I knocked, but nobody answered."

Princess Melissande, even more rumpled and harassed than she'd been yesterday. This morning she was wearing dark blue trousers and a pale green shirt that may or may not have been recently introduced to a hot iron. Her hair was scraped back into a lumpy plait and the freckles on her face remained uncamouflaged by makeup. Behind the glasses, her eyes looked tired.

Gerald dropped the orange and stood. "Your Highness. Good morning. Please, come in."

As he hurried to close the foyer doors behind her she slumped into his vacated chair and reached into the fruit bowl for a candied kumquat. "I interrupted you, Professor. You were saying something about not being in love with . . . what?"

"What?" He glared at Reg, who crossed her eyes

at him. "Ah—oh, yes! The idea of being His Majesty's secret weapon against the Kallarapi. I think, as a plan, it could do with a rethink. Reg agrees."

The kumquat stopped halfway to the princess's mouth. "*Reg* agrees? You were discussing affairs of state with a *bird*?"

"Oh, yes. She's very knowledgeable. Well. About some things, anyway. You'd be surprised."

Princess Melissande continued to stare. "You were discussing affairs of state with a bird."

Reg snorted. "Says the woman with a brother who probably starts the day by asking his butterflies what underpants he should wear!"

"Rupert?" The princess smiled. "Oh, you mustn't mind Rupert. He's quite harmless and very sweet once you get to know him."

Gerald perched on the edge of the tinkling fountain, mindful of splashes. "So . . . what do you think, Your Highness?"

"About what?" she asked around a mouthful of kumquat.

"About Gerald the secret weapon," said Reg. "Oy—you don't suppose that pretty brother of yours has got some bright idea about using him as leverage, do you?"

"You mean is he thinking *literally* a secret weapon? Spells of destruction at thirty paces followed by some hasty handiwork with a mop and bucket?" The princess swallowed and reached for another kumquat. "No. Look, Lional talks big, he always has, but it never comes to anything."

"Are you sure?" said Reg. "I mean, he does know, doesn't he, he can't just point Gerald like a musket and *shoot* this Zazoor when he holds out his hand for the dosh? I mean, he does *know* that?"

"Of course he does," snapped the princess. "Look, Professor, I'm sure there's nothing to worry about. Lional knows perfectly well he doesn't have any choice but to pay Zazoor what's owed. I expect all he wants to do is show you off to the Kallarapi. Make the pill he's got to swallow a little less bitter. *You* may have a holy man but *I've* got a wizard, so *nyah*. Nothing *dangerous*. Just diplomacy."

He pulled a face. "That doesn't sound terribly diplomatic to me. What if things get out of hand?"

"You won't let them." She sighed. "Professor, I'm not a complete ignoramus. I do know that wizards are forbidden to use their magic to cause harm."

Reg rattled her tail feathers. "You might, ducky, but what about that brother of yours?"

"He knows too!" she insisted, exasperated. "You're not the first wizard we've had around here, remember?"

Now there was a point. And an idea. He narrowed his eyes. "Exactly how many were in the job before me, Your Highness?"

The second kumquat eaten, she pretended to be interested in a banana. "A few," she muttered.

"Forgive me, but that's not very specific."

"You want specific? Fine. Five. All right? There were five court wizards before you."

"*Five*?" He slid off the fountain. "The king's had *five* other wizards? I'm his *sixth* wizard?"

"Oh, don't you stand there looking surprised! You've met him!"

"I'm not *surprised*, Your Highness, I'm *deceived*!"

"I did *not* deceive you!" said the princess, shoving out of the chair. "If you'd asked me in the interview how many wizards had been in the job already I'd've told you! You didn't ask!"

Perched on the edge of his abandoned porridge bowl, Reg snickered. "She's got you there, sunshine."

Disgusted, Gerald considered Lional's angry sister. Then he sighed. "Yes. She does. I apologise, Your Highness. That was uncalled for."

"It certainly was."

"But not unexpected," added Reg. "You knew perfectly well he'd never have taken the job if all your dirty linen had been hanging on the line in plain sight, madam."

Princess Melissande sat again, slumping. "What can I say? I was desperate."

Gerald dropped once more to the edge of the fountain. "I know the feeling." He and the princess exchanged tentative, rueful smiles. "So who were they, then? These predecessors of mine?"

"Why does it matter?"

He shrugged. "It doesn't. I thought I might know one or two, that's all."

"I doubt it. They were all years older than you."

"Still . . ."

She rolled her eyes. "Oh, for the love of Saint Snodgrass. As if I didn't have anything better to do than go staggering down memory lane . . ." Then she sighed. "All right. Give me a moment."

As she chewed her lip, he triggered a recording incant under cover of scratching his nose then dabbled his fingers in the fountain's water, waiting.

"Well," she said at last, "*not* in chronological order, there was Humphret Bottomley, the prat."

In the air above and behind her the name *Humphret Bottomley* appeared in glowing silver letters. It hung there unmoving, like liquid smoke. "That's an old-fashioned Ottosland name," he murmured. "Who else?"

She screwed up her face. "Pomodoro Uffitzi. Aloysius Beargarden. Er—er—oh, yes! Grumbaugh. Lord, how could I forget him? Barked in monosyllables and spent most of his time locked up in what's now your workroom, making smelly smoke. And Bondaningo Greenfeather." Her face softened into a smile. "Terribly sinister-looking with all those tattoos and facial piercings but actually very nice. And that's all of them. Satisfied now? Say yes."

With another deceptive nose scratch Gerald closed down the recording incant with its five silver smoke names and stored it in a nearby pot plant. He'd retrieve it later and run the names past Monk at the first opportunity. Get him to find their whereabouts and how they could be contacted. Seeing as how he was going to be stuck here in New Ottosland for a while it seemed only prudent to do some belated homework on his charming pillock of an employer.

"Yes. Thank you, Your Highness," he said. "Your patience is most appreciated. Doubtless you didn't come here to—" He sat up. "Good lord. I'm so sorry. Why *did* you come here?"

# CHAPTER ELEVEN

"To get you all primed to spy on her brother, I'll bet," said Reg.

Princess Melissande gave her a haughty look. "Must you reduce everything to the crudest possible motive?"

Reg smirked. "Told you, sunshine."

"Then perhaps you'd like to tell *me* what else I'm supposed to do?" the princess demanded. "Since you're such a font of wisdom. I have to know what happens in that meeting, this kingdom's future could depend on it, and since Lional refuses to let me be there—"

"All right, all right," said Reg. "I never said you were wrong, did I? No need to get your bloomers in a twist, ducky."

"What she means, Your Highness," Gerald said quickly, "is that you're in a very difficult position and—"

"And I don't wish to talk about it here," said the princess, still glaring at Reg. "You're looking claustro-phobic, Professor. I think you're overdue for some fresh air. Meet me downstairs in the east wing forecourt in twenty minutes."

"Why? Where are we going?"

"Where do you think?" she said, sounding resigned. "Sightseeing, of course. Didn't you know? On top of everything else, I'm New Ottosland's Minister of Grand Tours!"

Half an hour later they were seated in a scarlet and gold touring carriage pulled by a pair of flashy dapple grey horses, bowling along a wide, tree-lined avenue. The sky was cloudless and deeply blue, the air flower-scented and fresh. Delightful. The carriage, unfortunately, was rococo in the extreme, all gilded carved fruit and simpering cherubs with hideously love-struck expressions. Gerald squashed himself into one corner, trying to be as inconspicuous as possible. *Thank God Monk can't see me now. Thank God no-one I know can see me now.* It was bad enough that the pavement strollers and passengers in passing carriages and street-corner vendors and impressively uniformed policemen on foot patrol could see him.

Sitting opposite, the princess noticed his discomfit and snorted. "Welcome to my world, Professor."

"Thank you," he said. "I think."

She smiled wickedly and pointed her predictably no-nonsense green parasol over the side of the carriage. "Now, to your left you'll see the Royal Music Hall. Isn't it pretty?"

He considered the Music Hall's impressive marble steps and its honour guard of pigeon-splattered dead composer statues lining the entrance.

"I was going to say familiar. In fact, *everything* looks familiar."

"You noticed? It's quite simple. We never got over being a colony. There isn't a street or a building here whose original you won't find back in the Old Country." The princess grimaced. "It's ghastly, like living inside an echo. What I wouldn't give to just *once* see somebody else's idea of architecture!"

"What's stopping you?"

She looked at him. "Nothing much. Just a small matter of running the kingdom."

"But you've got staff. And what about His Majesty?"

"Yes?" she sighed. "What about him?"

Gerald opened his mouth to answer but was stopped by Reg whacking him over the head with her wing. She was sitting behind him on one of the cherub's plump bottoms and humming a risqué ditty under her breath in time to the *clip-clop* of the carriage horses' hooves.

"Ow!" he exclaimed, and turned. "*Now* what?"

She pointed at the driver sitting high above them on his box. "Discretion, Gerald! Muggins up there is probably taking notes."

"No, he's not," said the princess. "He's deaf."

"'Deaf as a post' deaf, or 'I'm a loyal servant and it'll cost a lot more than that to loosen my lips, squire' deaf?" Reg demanded.

"Deaf as a post deaf, of course. Why do you think I chose him to drive the carriage? Oh, look," the princess added, and waved the parasol. "There's the Royal Zoo! Do you know, Professor, I'm sure they have a spare birdcage in there somewhere. Would you like me to ask?"

He patted spluttering Reg on the head. "She'd only teach the other parrots rude words."

Princess Melissande sat back amongst the carriage's overstuffed cushions and considered Reg thoughtfully. "I'm sorry but I have to ask. *Where* did you find such a singular creature? If there's another one in existence anywhere in the world I swear I'll eat my parasol. With mustard."

"Good idea," said Reg. "You've the look of a woman who doesn't get enough roughage."

Gerald winced. "*Reg!*"

"Well what do you expect? She called me a singular creature!"

"It was a compliment. Wasn't it, Your Highness?"

The princess looked down her nose. "Not intentionally."

"*Right!*" squawked Reg. "I've had this. You and me, madam, parasols at twenty paces, and—"

He grabbed her and pushed her beak-first among the cushions. "We seem to have strayed from the topic. I believe Your Highness was wondering how Reg and I met . . ."

"Well, yes, I *was*," agreed the princess. "But now I'm wondering what the wretched bird's lung capacity is."

He rescued Reg and dangled her in front of his face. "Have you *quite* finished?"

She spat out a beakful of cushion fluff, gasping. "Gerald Dunwoody!"

"I'm sorry, Reg, but Her Highness—"

"Oh, call me Melissande," said the princess.

"Thank you, Your—Melissande," he said, surprised. "And you can call me Gerald."

Her lips quirked in a wry smile. "Yes, I know."

She was the most *irritating* woman . . .

Wriggling free of his grasp, Reg hopped onto the nearest cherub's dimpled buttocks and scowled. "If you *must* know, madam, and not that it's *any* of your business, Gerald and I met when he helped me out of a sticky situation."

Remembering, he laughed. "Literally. I was in the local woods, looking for fresh wizard's beard for one of my First Year assignments, and practically fell over her. She'd managed to get herself gummed up in some bird lime and was swearing so hard she didn't hear me coming. So I ungummed her and we've been stuck with each other ever since."

"Gracious," said Melissande, dryly. "It sounds positively romantic."

"Romantic?" screeched Reg. "If you don't mind, I'm old enough to be his—"

"Yes?"

"Aunty," said Reg, eyes gleaming. "Gerald's problem is he can't resist a damsel in distress."

"Well then," said Melissande, "lucky for him I'm not in distress."

"Or a damsel."

"*Anyway* . . ." he said quickly, "about the Kallarapi delegation . . ."

Melissande drummed her fingers on her knee. "Yes. About them. Prince Nerim is Sultan Zazoor's younger brother; his official title is Blood of the Sultan. I get the feeling if there'd been another brother to send he'd have been spared a long camel ride.

Shugat is the sultan's holy man. He's the most important religious figure in Kallarap. Nerim's a lightweight. *Shugat's* the one to look out for."

"And what do you think they're hoping to get out of this meeting?"

She pulled a face. "From the number of camels they brought, I think they're expecting to take a lot of our money with them when they go."

"Are there enough funds in Treasury to cover the entire debt?"

Melissande hesitated, her expression troubled. "Barely," she said at last. "But it pretty much wipes us out. Since he took the throne Lional's been a bit . . . extravagant, in places. If we could just get terms for an extended period of payment . . . I'm sure Zazoor would agree, he's not unreasonable."

"And what about His Majesty?"

"I don't know. He—" She stopped, distracted by the delighted cries and excited hand-waving from a long crocodile line of schoolgirls out for an airing. Gritting her teeth she smiled a professional, painted-on smile and waved back. "Sometimes," she muttered, as the schoolgirl's squealed and clutched at each other despite their scandalised mistress, "I think I should just put myself in the zoo and be done with it."

"Good idea," said Reg. "You can have my cage, I won't be using it any time soon."

Melissande glared. "Don't count on it." The carriage rounded a corner into yet another tree-lined avenue of stately buildings, leaving the schoolgirls behind. She heaved a sigh of relief and stopped waving.

"All right," he said. "Let's assume the worst and say the king categorically refuses to pay up. What are the chances of the Kallarapi deciding to, I don't know, take back New Ottosland in lieu of monies owed?"

"I haven't a clue. But let's hope it doesn't come to that," Melissande replied. "If they did decide to invade we'd have no hope of stopping them."

Disconcerted, Gerald considered her grim expression. "Why not?"

"Because quite apart from the fact that the Kallarapi have an ancient and sophisticated warrior tradition and we don't, the only army we've got is Rupert's old tin soldiers in the nursery."

Reg choked. "What do you mean, you've got no army? What self-respecting kingdom doesn't have its own army?"

"We did have one, once," the princess said, defensive. "But nobody ever attacked us. All the soldiers did was sit around eating and playing dice. They were costing the crown a fortune, so one of the Lionals—number twenty-seven, I think—pensioned them off. We never missed them."

*Until now.* Gerald shook his head. *Deary, deary me, as Reg would say. This lot really are in a pickle. What a pity they can't pension off the current King Lional . . .*

"So let me get this straight, Your—Melissande," he said carefully. "In all the centuries since New Ottosland was established the Kallarapi never once tried to invade you or—"

"Never. They're a scrupulously honourable people, Gerald. When they signed the treaty that established New Ottosland they swore an oath to never attack us, and they take their oaths seriously."

"How seriously? I mean, what's the penalty for breaking one?"

"You don't want to know," said Melissande. "Vomiting in public is so uncouth."

This was just getting better and better. "So if His Majesty *doesn't* pay up then as far as the Kallarapi are concerned he's an oath-breaker?"

"Well, nobody's actually come right out and *said* it, but . . ."

"If the crown fits," Reg concluded, and ruffled her feathers. "Glory gumboots. And if the Kallarapi do declare him an oath-breaker then all bets are off. Deary, deary me, you lot really are in the privy, aren't you?"

Melissande sighed. "Yes. To be honest, I'm afraid this audience today might be a case of too little, too late. I've tried to convince myself it's not, but—"

Reg gave a snort of disgust. "But in fact, ducky, the light at the end of the tunnel is most likely the sun glinting on a million righteous Kallarapi swords!"

"I know!" said Melissande, freckles pronounced against her sudden pallor. "Why do you think I'm so worried?"

"*You're* worried?" Reg retorted. "What about my Gerald? Your nincompoop of a brother is obviously under the misguided impression his wizard's a one-man army in disguise!"

In which case King Lional was destined to be bitterly disappointed. "It's out of the question," Gerald said, leaning forward. "I'm not an oath-breaker either, Melissande. I won't be a party to—"

"Violence, I *know*!" she shouted. "But Gerald, you have to do *something*! You said it yourself! It's your duty!"

"*His* duty?" shrieked Reg, before he could protest

on his own behalf. "And what about *yours*? What kind of prime minister lets matters get sucked this far down the gurgler, eh? Well, don't just sit there like a soggy pudding, madam. Answer me!"

Melissande's face now burned a dull red. "You don't understand. It's not as—"

"Oh, I understand, all right!" snapped Reg. "You and your idiot brother have made a complete mess of things and now you expect Gerald to pull your bacon out of the fire before it's burned to a crisp! Well let me tell you something, ducky, I won't have it! I won't have you—"

"Oh, *shut* up, you *stupid* bird!" cried Melissande, and threw the nearest pillow.

"*Hey!*" said Gerald, catching the pillow and tossing it out of the carriage. "Don't you tell her to shut up! She's got a point! I'm a wizard, not a miracle-worker, and I've only been here a day. Now you expect me to solve an international crisis with one snap of my fingers? What are you, *crazy*?"

"Of course she is," said Reg, nodding vigorously. "Didn't I tell you it runs in the family? Perhaps next time you'll listen when I—"

"If you don't *shut up*," hissed Melissande, "I *swear* I'll feed you to Boris! For your information I am *not* crazy, I'm *desperate*! In fact I am *so* desperate I'm prepared to entrust the fate of my kingdom and all its subjects to a Third Class wizard who takes advice from some freakish mutated *parrot* with terminal verbal diarrhoea!" She laughed, somewhat wildly. "Which means I *must* be crazy!" Abruptly, the laughter exploded into a loud sob. "Oh *damn*!" she cried, threw herself face down into the remaining cushions, and burst into tears.

Horrified, Gerald stared at Melissande's heaving shoulders. *Oh, God, what do I do now? She's royalty and we're in public, I can't cuddle her . . .*

Reg jumped over to the seat beside the weeping princess and poked her in the behind with her beak. There was an eruption of cushions as Melissande wrenched herself upright. "How *dare* you? You are the most *repulsive* creature I've ever met!"

"In that case you need to get out more," Reg retorted. "Now just you get a grip on yourself, Madam Watering-Pot. Yours aren't the kind of looks that are improved by blubbering. Besides, this isn't the behaviour I expect from a princess. Or a prime minister. You've got to walk the walk, ducky, not just talk the talk."

As Melissande gaped, speechless, Gerald fished out a handkerchief from his pocket and handed it to her. "She means well, you know. And she's right."

"Really?" said Melissande, snatching the handkerchief and pressing it to her wet face. "What about? The fact I'm a frump or that I'm a failure?"

*Hello, my name is Gerald and I'm between a rock and a hard place . . .* "You're not a failure," he said after a difficult pause.

"Yes I am," she retorted, glowering. "I never should've let Lional start this stupid game of brinksmanship with Zazoor, I *knew* it'd end up pear-shaped." She looked at the soggy handkerchief. "Do you want this back?"

"Not particularly. Besides, I've got another one somewhere."

She shoved it up her sleeve and heaved a shuddering

sigh. "I'm sorry, Gerald. I never should have dragged you into this."

Yes, she was bossy. But she wasn't so bad, really. He shrugged. "It's all right. I let myself be dragged."

"Well, for what it's worth . . ." She managed a watery smile. "I'm glad."

"Oh *please*!" cried Reg, and dove headfirst into the cushions.

Melissande stared at her kicking toes. "She's muttering about arses and tea-kettles. Should we take her to a vet?"

"*Doctor*, if you don't mind!" snapped Reg, sitting up. "And no. *I'm* not the one who needs his head examined!"

A rancorous silence fell. "Look," said Gerald at last, "there's no point getting all worked up over what *might* happen, Melissande. I'll do whatever it takes to keep His Majesty from doing something . . . regrettable . . . in the meeting. I promise."

"Whatever it takes. I hope those aren't famous last words." She sniffed. "All right. Thank you. Now, we'd best get back to the palace. I've got appointments scheduled all afternoon and that's *before* Lional gives me his daily list of Things I Can't Be Bothered Doing Myself So Just Take Care Of Them For Me, Would You?"

"As you wish, Your Highness."

Extracting her parasol from beneath the cushions, Melissande turned and poked the driver between his shoulder blades. When he looked round, expression enquiring, she bawled, "Home, William!" William touched his fingers to the curly brim of his coachman's hat and took a left-hand turn along yet another tree-lined street.

"You know," Gerald mused, "when you think about it, the underlying cause of all this kerfuffle is the fact you're totally reliant on Kallarap for getting things in and out of the country. Why not just arrange for some industrial-grade portals and bypass the Kallarapi altogether?"

Melissande slumped against the carriage cushions. "We can't afford them. The only reason we've got any kind of portal at all is because Pomodoro Uffitzi constructed one for us."

What? What? He'd travelled halfway across the world in an amateur unsanctioned portal? "But—but that's *illegal*!" he protested. "There's international law governing portal installations. They're supposed to be constructed by a specially certified thaumaturgical company and inspected regularly. If something went wrong someone could—"

She appeared surprised. "Nothing's gone wrong."

"No, not yet! But if your portal's a do-it-yourself job by some smart-alec nobody wizard then it's only a matter of time!"

"Oh, but—Pomodoro Uffitzi—he wasn't a nobody, he had *pages* of commendations and awards and references, he wouldn't—"

He could easily have shaken her silly. "Melissande! Portal installation is a specialist's job." He stared at her, aghast, but she didn't seem to realise the gravity of the situation. "Look, I do know what I'm talking about, I used to be a thaumaturgical compliance officer!"

"Well you're not one now," she snapped, flushed.

"Now you're an honorary New Ottosland citizen. And you can't report us, it'd be treason."

*I take it back. She's as bad as the king.* "I was an oath-sworn wizard before I was a New Ottoslander, honorary or otherwise, and—"

"So you keep saying," she said impatiently. "Fine. I'll hang a great big *Out of Order sign on the portal door. Happy now?*"

"Oh yes," he said. "I can just see your brother paying attention to *that.*"

Reg broke the crackling silence with a pointed rattling of her tail feathers. "Yes, well. I suggest we worry about this little hiccup *after* we've dealt with the Kallarapi. What d'you say?"

"Fine," muttered Gerald.

"Excellent," snarled Melissande.

"Oh, *please,*" groaned Reg.

After that there was nothing more to be said. During the forty-five minute journey back to the palace they clip-clopped over the picturesque Canal Bridge, past the fountain-studded Art Gallery, the Mint, the recently vacated House of Ministers, an Academy for Young Gentlemen, a Seminary for Young Ladies, the Royal Playhouse, the Royal Opera House and down the full length of fashionable King Lional High Street where all the important people bought their necessities, apparently.

Eventually they arrived at the palace's rear entrance. Various servants bustled in and out with messages and packages and a constant stream of tradesmen's wagons trundled further along to the loading bay, where another servant was ticking off their deliveries and arguing about payment. They alighted from the carriage and stood looking at each other.

"Well," said Melissande. "That's that, then. You'll come and see me, after the meeting?"

Gerald made sure Reg was secure on his shoulder, and bowed. "Certainly, Your Highness."

"Good. Excellent."

She turned on her heel and marched away. He watched her go, frowning. "I can't believe she let me travel through an unregulated portal. I could've been *killed*."

"*We* could've been killed," Reg pointed out. "But we weren't, so let's worry about it later. Right now there are far more interesting things to worry about."

Yes. Like spying for the princess. He swallowed a groan. "Fancy a walk? I need to air my brain, and those look like gardens over there . . ."

They were indeed gardens. Beautiful ones, spreading out from the palace in a lake of colour and perfume. If they were Lional the Forty-Second's legacy, well, royalty had surely done worse.

*Like now, for instance.*

Reg whistled approvingly as they wandered among the flowerbeds. "Very nice. If more kings stuck to harmless pursuits like weeding and fertilising, the world would be a better place."

"I say!" cried an excited voice. "I say, *Professor*!"

Gerald turned—and there was Prince Rupert, bouncing up and down in the middle of a neighbouring pansy patch. Both hands were filled with plucked blooms.

He smiled and waved. "Good morning, Your Highness."

"Rupert," said the prince. "Remember? I'm just collecting a few treats for my butterflies. Since you're out and about would you like to come and see them?"

*No. I've got better things to do with my time, like panic about this stupid meeting where I'm single-handedly supposed to avert a full-scale international invasion, complete with camels.*

Reg leaned close to his ear. "Say yes," she muttered. "He may be a prat but he's a royal prat. Never get on the wrong side of royalty, sunshine. It always ends badly."

Swallowing a groan, he made himself smile. "That sounds lovely, Rupert," he said. "I'd be honoured."

Rupert beamed. "*Splendid*! Come along, then! Follow me!"

Rupert's butterfly house was situated on the far side of the gardens. Flooded with light, it was filled with beautifully maintained cages, a variety of aromatic mini-habitats and an immaculately arranged workroom containing butterfly food, magnifying glasses, three crammed bookcases, two microscopes and a wide array of nets and other butterfly-catching paraphernalia.

Gerald was surprised. Given Rupert's scatterbrained demeanour he'd not expected such clutterless order and pristine attention to detail. As for the butterflies . . . there were hundreds, in every colour, shape and size imaginable. They were riotously beautiful . . . and he hadn't been expecting that, either. Whoever noticed butterflies?

Rupert was still beaming. "Don't tell Lional, but

I call this butterfly house 'my little kingdom'," he confessed.

"And a well-run little kingdom it is too."

"Well, you know, the butterflies rely on me, don't they?" said Rupert, as they wandered past cage after cage of jewel-bright insects. "If I didn't look after them properly they might get sick, or die, and that would be unforgiveable."

He nodded. "You're right. It would be." He stopped in front of a cage neatly labelled: *Vampirella Majesticas. Danger: Do Not Touch.* The savagely scarlet and black insects clustered on their hunks of fresh raw meat and waved ominous antennae at him. Safely anchored to his shoulder, Reg burbled like a kettle with a sock shoved down its spout. He stroked her wing with a reassuring finger. "So . . . they really are dangerous, then?"

"Everyone's dangerous, Gerald," Rupert said gently. "Or they can be, if you're not careful. I mean, you seem like a terribly nice chap and all that, especially for a wizard, but I expect you could do a mischief or two if you put your mind to it."

"Well, yes, I *could*," he admitted reluctantly. "Only I wouldn't."

"No, *you* wouldn't," said Rupert. "You're a thoroughly decent chap, I can tell. But some wizards aren't so scrupulous, Gerald. I've heard stories . . ."

The sight of the *Majesticas* sucking blood from the raw meat was . . . unsettling. He turned away. "Old stories from our distant past, Rupert. It's true that once upon a time there were wizards who abused their powers, wizards who ran amok doing unspeakable things. But not any more. My colleagues and I are closely monitored. There are terrible penalties for the irresponsible uses of magic these days. Modern wizarding is about humanitarian advances and scientific discovery, not subjugation and warfare and dark deeds in the dead of night."

Rupert beamed. "Well, that's a relief!"

"Honestly," he insisted as they continued to wander past more butterfly enclosures. "Wizardry's perfectly safe and reliable these days. Those other kinds of wizard are history."

"I'm very pleased to hear you say so," said Rupert earnestly. "Because when you get right down to it there's something not very *nice* about a person who likes other people to be afraid of him. A person like that bears very close watching, don't you agree?"

"Er . . . yes. Probably," he said, after a moment. Was it his imagination or was Rupert trying to *tell* him something . . .

Rupert, his watery blue eyes wide, smiled his foolish, tremulous smile. "You're staring, Gerald. Was it something I said?"

"What? Oh! No! Sorry. I just—I was off with the butterflies."

Rupert chortled. "I say, that's a good one! 'Off with the butterflies'! I must remember that! Now, I expect you'll want to be on your way. Busy, busy, busy. I'll see you again soon, though, yes?"

"Yes. Yes," said Gerald. "And thanks for showing me around."

Outside in the gentle sunshine, Reg cackled. "Hard to believe he's related to the other two, isn't it?"

"Practically impossible," he agreed as they headed

back to the palace. "He's such a fluffy, harmless man I feel guilty for getting impatient with him."

Reg snorted. "He's such a fluffy, harmless man that after five minutes in his company I want to rush to the nearest park and find some pigeons to poison!"

"Oh, come on, Reg! You don't! I mean, isn't that practically mur—"

"Why hello, there, Professor," said King Lional, stepping out from behind one of the large, flowering trees that lined the path. "Fancy meeting you here."

Gerald stopped, heart pounding, and managed a ragged bow. "Your Majesty! Ah—you startled me."

Lional smiled. "I'm sure I did."

"Is there something I can do for Your Majesty?"

"Indeed there is," said the king. There was something . . . unsettling in that smile. "You can introduce me to your loquacious little friend!"

# CHAPTER TWELVE

"Bugger," said Reg.

Lional wasn't alone. At his side appeared the muscular watchfulness of Tavistock, whose tawny mane had been shimmered with gold dust. The former cat stared up at Reg with slitted topaz eyes, tail swishing to and fro.

Leaning a negligent silk-clad shoulder against the trunk of the tree that had hidden him, Lional drawled, "Well? What's its name, Professor?"

"Reg," said Gerald. Damn, damn, *damn*. Why the hell had he let Rupert waste his time with butterflies? He could've been up in his suite by now, sending that list of ex-court wizards to Monk. Instead . . . "Her name is Reg. Your Majesty."

"How quaint," said Lional, and straightened. In the bright summer sunshine everything about him glittered: his diamond rings, his ruby and emerald brooch, his bared teeth.

He cleared his throat. "I can explain, Your Majesty. The thing is—"

"Thank you, Gerald, I'm perfectly capable of speaking for myself," said Reg, with a rattle of tail feathers. "Let's start with you not call me 'it', Your Majesty. I'm a sensitive soul and my feelings are easily bruised."

Lional's flawless face was vivid with delight. "Extraordinary," he murmured. "Tell me, Professor, was it a very difficult ensorcelment to perform? Of course, I realise you're a brilliant wizard but even so . . . birds are singularly stupid creatures. To give one such a convincing appearance of intelligence. I can scarcely—"

"Oy!" said Reg. "What d'you mean *appearance* of intelligence! What d'you think I am, some kind of metaphysically enhanced ventriloquist's doll? I'll have you know—"

"I'm so sorry, Your Majesty," said Gerald, Reg's beak caught firmly between thumb and forefinger. "She gets flustered in the presence of royalty. Doesn't know what she's saying."

To his surprise the king didn't appear in the least offended. "Incredible. You *must* tell me how you did it!"

"But I didn't. Your Majesty. Reg was—articulate— when we met."

Lional frowned. "You're telling me this *isn't* your handiwork? How disappointing. But you can duplicate the enchantment, can't you? Recreate the same extraordinary linguistic achievements elsewhere?" One elegant hand strayed to the top of Tavistock's head; the lion rumbled deep in its throat at the touch.

The implication was unmistakable. *Oh God . . .* "Tavistock? Your Majesty wants me to—"

Wrenching her beak free of his fingers, Reg cackled scornfully. "Why? What kind of conversation are you going to get from an overgrown cat? Milk now, scratch my tummy, and somebody empty the damned litter tray. Hardly what you'd call *scintillating*, is it?"

"Scintillating or not . . ." said Lional.

"I'm so sorry, Your Majesty," Gerald said quickly. "I'm afraid it's impossible."

Lional's smile chilled. "Does that mean you can't . . . or you won't?"

*Saint Snodgrass, are you listening? Get me out of this!* "It means I don't know how," he said, with care. "And it would be far too dangerous for me to . . . experiment. I might end up hurting Tavistock and that would violate my oaths. I'm sorry."

For one terrible moment he thought the king was going to argue, or start making threats. A flush of temper mantled Lional's cheekbones and his lips pinched tight. Then he heaved a sigh. "I'm sorry too, Professor. It would've been so entertaining! I shall just have to amuse myself with your bird here, shan't I?"

He wanted to ask "*Amuse how?*" but didn't dare. Instead he bowed. "Your Majesty."

"Very good. Go, now. I shall see you in the Large Audience Chamber at three."

Another bow. "Yes, Your Majesty."

"And Gerald?"

Swallowing a curse, he stopped walking, re-arranged his expression into bland helpfulness and swung about. "Your Majesty?"

Lional was suavely smiling again. "Make sure to wear that splendid robe you had on at dinner. The

Kallarapi are a primitive people, easily impressed by bright display, and we do want to put our best sartorial feet forward, don't we? No need to mention it's hand-made, of course. Oh, and bring your bird, too. I dare say they'll find it . . . charming."

Safely within their apartments once more, Reg gave vent to her feelings in a long, loud raspberry. "Appearance of intelligence, my arse!" Then she whacked Gerald on the head with her wing. "And what d'you mean I get flustered in the presence of royalty! Cheeky bugger! I'd have a bloody hard time of it looking in the mirror every morning if that was the case, wouldn't I?"

Slumping into the nearest chair, Gerald watched her fly outraged laps of the foyer. Each time she passed the caged parrots she paused to engage in rude exchanges. Ordinarily he'd have laughed but he didn't have the energy. He was exhausted and he had another headache; the royal family of New Ottosland was a lot harder going than he'd bargained for.

Temporarily puffed, Reg fluttered to join him on the arm of the chair. "That wretched Lional's a menace," she announced. "He's let inheriting a crown go right to his head. No wonder all his other wizards sloped off or got themselves fired. You mark my words, Gerald, there'll be tears before bedtime if someone doesn't haul him into line quick smart."

"Mine, probably," he said, pulling a face. "Reg, why do you think he's so keen on having you at this meeting?"

She shrugged. "I expect he wants to lord it over

the Sultan's delegates. See, I've got a wizard *and* a talking birdie. So *double* nyah."

"Well, that's just childish."

"I know," she sighed. "But you need to understand, Gerald, you're not dealing with *normal* people now. You're amongst *royalty*. Think Errol Haythwaite and multiply by a hundred. Which means our pretty friend Lional bears close watching."

True, true, damnably true. *And when I've done watching him, what then? I've no authority here, or jurisdiction. I'm not even a probationary compliance officer any more. If I had any sense at all I'd listen to Reg. Get out while the going's good. But even if I didn't have a contract, I promised Melissande I'd help.* He pressed his fingertips into his eyes. *Me and my big mouth.*

He pushed himself to his feet. "I need to get Monk onto finding those former court wizards for me. I know it's a long shot, but if just *one* of them has an idea of how to keep Lional in check . . ."

But Monk wasn't answering his crystal ball. Disgruntled, he retrieved the recording incant, transmitted his predecessors' names with an urgent request for their contact details, then pulled the nearest bell-rope and ordered lunch from the breathless servant who turned up some fifteen minutes later.

Once he'd finished his soup and sandwiches, and Reg had gobbled her chopped chicken liver, it was perilously close to three o'clock.

With a show of devil-may-care he was a long way from feeling, he bathed, changed, then inspected himself in the mirror . . . *Gerald Dunwoody, Wizard Spy* . . . God help him . . .

After that it was time to go. He called for a servant to guide him through the labyrinthine palace corridors and made his way to the Large Audience Chamber with Reg uncharacteristically silent on his shoulder.

As for his spare cherrywood staff, he left it behind. Something told him he didn't need it any more.

Lional was already in the audience chamber, ensconced on yet another extravagant throne. From head to foot he was swathed in gold and studded with rubies. Tavistock, freshly groomed and sleekly oiled, gleamed at his feet. As the herald's announcement of his arrival echoed beneath the lavishly frescoed ceiling Gerald made his way from the doors to the dais. The walk took forever: the room was absolutely enormous. "Right on time, Professor," Lional greeted him, glittering in the chandelier light. "How gratifying. Do come and stand beside me. We must present a united front, musn't we?"

He climbed the dais stairs. "Certainly, Your Majesty." Taking up a position discreetly to the rear of the throne, he looked around the empty chamber. "Ah—I thought there'd be more people here. Attendants. Minor aristocracy."

Lional laughed. "I have no need of them, Professor. On occasions similar to this one my late father, when he could be prised from his wheelbarrow, surrounded himself with ministers and secretaries, courtiers and chamberlains, experts all . . . and yet still we find ourselves in our present invidious position. He was a timorous fellow, my father. Too afraid to seize life by the throat. Too willing to let others do the thinking for him. In that respect, Professor, as in so many others, I am *not* my father's son."

Which was a great shame. At least his father hadn't brought the kingdom to the brink of a war it had no hope of winning . . .

The herald positioned at the chamber's open doors cleared his throat. "Your Majesty?" he called. "The Kallarapi delegation is approach—*ow!*"

"They can wait a minute!" declared Melissande, having shoved the hapless herald aside. "Lional, hold your horses! I want a word with you!"

"Blimey bloody Charlie," Reg muttered as the shaken herald hurriedly closed the chamber doors. "She wants a word with a fashion consultant is what *she* wants."

The princess, marching towards the dais, had made a valiant effort to match her brother's habitual magnificence . . . and failed. Gerald felt his jaw clench, and his guts turn over in horrified sympathy.

*Melissande, Melissande . . . what were you thinking?*

Her rust-red hair was tortured into an odd looking construction on top of her head and stabbed to death with crystal-topped pins that looked like an outbreak of colourful warts. Her face—minus its glasses—was coated in makeup: bristly mascara-laden eyelashes, startled blue-rimmed eyes, embarrassed cheeks and lips the colour of over-ripe plums turned her ordinary features into a poster for bad abstract art. Her dress was a bilious green satin sack trimmed with blue-dyed feathers and finished about the hem with voluminous mulberry-coloured netting. To complete the ensemble she'd chosen thick dark tights, laddered at the ankle, and brick-like shoes in a moth-eaten black.

The only part of the outfit that worked was the matching pearl necklace and earrings.

"Melissande?" Lional enquired, his voice suggesting that hidden within its velvet sheath was a *very* sharp knife that could see the light of day at any moment. "Would you care to explain?"

She halted before the throne. "Look," she said forcefully, "sorry to interrupt. Lional, but who's the damned princess around here anyway? I'm just as much Blood of the King as Prince Nerim is Blood of the Sultan and on top of *that* I'm the prime minister. I *deserve* to be in this meeting!"

Lional frowned. "Melissande, you'd be well advised not to take that tone with me. *I* wear the crown in this family, not you."

She waved a pointed finger under his nose. "Exactly! So why are you letting the Kallarapi tell you who can and can't be present at a meeting in *your* audience chamber?"

Lional leaned back on his throne and considered her from head to toe. Eventually he said musingly, "I don't suppose you know exactly *who* is responsible for that fetching gown you're wearing, do you?"

"I might," said Melissande, suddenly wary. "But only if you want to write them a card saying how nice it is."

"That wasn't my first thought, no."

"In that case," she replied, chin up, "I found it in the bottom of my closet and I don't have the faintest idea how it got there."

Lional sighed and passed a weary hand across his eyes. "If only I didn't find that so easy to believe."

Through gritted teeth his sister said, "If I've told you once, Lional, I've told you a million times, I'm not a clothes horse. If you want a decorative female around here you'll have to marry one. Now can I stay or can't I?"

There was a long silence, punctuated by Tavistock's heavy breathing, during which Lional stared into the distance with half-lidded eyes and his lips pursed. Then he nodded. "Very well. On one condition."

Beneath the layers of makeup Melissande blushed with pleasure. "Name it."

Lional turned. "Dear Professor. Be a good chap and fix her, would you?"

Taken off guard, Gerald answered without thinking. "Fix her? I didn't know she was broken."

Lional waved an impatient hand. "Her *presentation*, man. Do something about that *abominable* frock . . . and the rest of her."

He didn't dare look at Melissande. *She'd kill me, she'd kill me, I'd wake up dead.* "Ah—forgive me for saying so, Your Majesty, but do you really think it's *appropriate* for me to—"

"No, it isn't!" snapped Melissande. "There's nothing wrong with how I look! *Honestly*, Lional! I'm in a dress, what more do you want? I'm not going to have *him*—"

"*Melissande!*"

Her eyes were very bright. With tears or temper, Gerald wasn't sure. "Sorry."

Lional's fingers drummed on the arm of his chair.

"It's your choice, prime minister. Change your unfortunate appearance or leave."

Melissande let out a shaking breath. "Some choice," she muttered. Then she turned, glaring. "Well, Professor? What are you waiting for? Get on with it."

Gerald swallowed. "Certainly, Your Highness. If I might just have a moment to confer with my—my—fashion consultant?"

She made a rude sound and glared at the ceiling. Lional sighed. "A very brief moment. I'm sure I have nothing better to do with my time than kick my heels while you and your feathery friend natter about last year's hemlines."

He bowed then put some distance between himself and the royal siblings. "Help, Reg!" he demanded in an urgent whisper. "If I put her in the wrong frock I'll offend her, Lional *and* the Kallarapi!!"

"The Kallarapi are going to be offended no matter what frock she's wearing, sunshine," Reg pointed out. "And I wouldn't worry too much about offending her, either. Not if that sack she's wearing is her idea of fashion that flatters." She snuck a look under her right wing. "Give me strength! If only she wasn't such a *box* of a girl!"

"*Reg!*"

"All right, all right!" She heaved a long-suffering sigh and stuck her head under her wing for another look. "Cripes. Just don't expect a miracle."

He closed his eyes and concentrated as Reg whispered into his ear. When she'd finished designing Melissande's new ensemble, she shook her head. "And that's the best I can do on short notice."

"Thanks." Turning to Melissande he said, "I'm ready, Your Highness. Are you?"

"Yes." The word came out cold and clipped, and in her eyes a promise of hot words later.

He swallowed annoyance. *Because this is all my fault, of course . . .* The words of the incant hovered on the tip of his tongue, waiting to be spoken.

Opening his mouth he let them fly free.

Power licked his bones with a lascivious warmth. Revelling in it, he uttered a silent command that summoned to his inner eye an image of the princess as she was at this moment: vertically challenged— horizontally overcompensated—crowned with that unfortunate hair—slathered with all the wrong makeup and swathed in that dreadful dress.

But not for much longer.

Preserving modesty, the bilious green satin darkened and transmuted to a rich, glowing blue-green shot-silk taffeta which melted over the feathers and the tragic squashed-mulberry netting, swallowing them entirely. For a moment it slipped and slid around her as though making up its mind. Then the fabric settled sinuously into place . . . and Melissande was wearing an elegantly simple frock with a demure v-neck, long sleeves and tapered skirt that finished a decorous two inches below her knees.

"So far, so good," Reg whispered. "Now for the shoes."

He snapped his fingers and recited the next incant. The little Melissande before his mind's eye squeaked as the black bricks disappeared from her feet and she immediately became four inches shorter. Then she squeaked again as new shoes appeared.

Slim, elegant midnight blue shoes, with just enough heel to enhance her posture and lengthen her legs, and a gently tapered toe to lend an air of sophistication. The finishing touch: sheer silk stockings. Black. Unladdered.

"Very nice," approved Reg. "Hair next."

Still watching his inner Melissande, Gerald uttered a new incant. Obediently the princess's rusty red hair untangled and became a smooth, shining fall of rich auburn that rearranged itself into a gleaming helmet and rolled into a smooth twist at the back. The warty crystal pins disappeared, replaced by pearl-headed pins that inserted themselves diplomatically and discreetly, keeping the twist in place without the least sign of frenzied skewering. They matched the jewellery perfectly, which he left alone.

Reg clacked her beak. "Well done. Now gild the lily."

He frowned. Gild the—oh. Melissande's makeup. Yes. Of course. But *makeup*? He took a deep breath and thought of his mother's quiet, understated elegance.

With a raised fingertip he erased the virulent blue eye shadow, the clumping mascara, the clown-red rouge and the flaming lipstick. Replaced them with a discreet feathering of lavender, a tinting of eyelash, a hint of blush on the cheek, a suggestion of rose on the lips.

Tentatively he opened his eyes to check the result in the flesh, and only just stopped his jaw dropping in shock. "*Wow*! Your Highness, you look . . . wonderful."

"I'll be the judge of that," she said, nervously truculent. "So don't just stand there. Fetch me a mirror!"

With a careless snap of his fingers he produced the full-length cheval-glass from his own dressing room. Melissande looked at her reflection. "Oh," she said at last. Her expression was unreadable.

Eyes glittering, Lional stared intently at his sister. Slowly, as though in a trance, he slid off his throne, stepped down from the dais to the chamber floor and prowled around her in rapt silence. Then he turned.

"Professor, you are . . . magnificent."

"Oh, no, Your Majesty," he said, his eyes not leaving Melissande's face. "Not me. But I think Her Highness might be."

She was still vertically challenged. Still horizontally overcompensated. Her hair was still, at heart, a rusty red. But any suggestion of frumpiness had vanished. She was sleek now, and polished, and she looked like Lional's sister.

"Cor!" said Reg. "It *is* a bloody miracle!"

Diffidently, he stepped forward. "Your Highness? Is it—you know—all right? I can change it if you're not satisfied. Just say the word."

Slowly, as though waking from a dream, Melissande tore her gaze away from her elegant, polished reflection. She appeared dazed. "No," she said faintly. "That won't be necessary. Thank you very much."

She didn't sound terribly grateful, though. If anything, she sounded . . . despairing.

"Yes indeed," said Lional, and poured himself back into his throne, gold on gold. Beside him, Tavistock purred. "That's another debt of gratitude you've incurred, Professor. At this rate you'll see me beggared!"

He bowed. "Not at all, Your Majesty."

Still dazed, Melissande said, "Lional, we'd better not keep the Kallarapi waiting any longer."

"Indeed not! Professor, get rid of the mirror. Melissande, invite our guests to join us."

Gerald returned the mirror to his suite and watched Melissande cross the vast expanse of carpet to the audience chamber's doors. Wearing high heels she even *walked* differently. Almost . . . alluringly.

"Remarkable," Lional murmured.

She opened the doors and said something to someone in the anteroom beyond. There was a pause, and then the sound of a male voice raised in protest. Melissande's shoulders stiffened. She tried to speak again and was over-ridden. She stepped back, closed the doors and marched back to the dais.

So much for allure. The way she was walking now, those high heels were deadly weapons.

"They won't come in," she announced, flushed with anger.

"Won't come in?" said Lional, eyebrows lifting. "Whatever do you mean?"

"Exactly what I said, Lional. The Kallarapi won't come in while I'm here. Prince Nerim refuses point blank to discuss *anything* with a woman present."

Lional sat up. "Well, that's unacceptable! You're not a woman, you're my prime minister! How dare he insult me in this fashion? He'll meet with both of us or go back to Kallarap with his tail between his legs and an empty purse to boot!"

Melissande sighed. "No. New Ottosland's future

is a million times more important than my pride. Or yours, for that matter. It's all right, Lional. I'll go."

For a moment it looked as though Lional was going to argue, then he nodded. "Very well. Your sacrifice is appreciated, Melly. And don't you worry: I'll make sure the Kallarapi pay for this insult."

"Thank you. I think." She turned, her expression strenuously neutral. "Professor? Good fortune attend your first encounter with the Kallarapi. I look forward to hearing all about it."

So. It was back to spying again. *Damn*. Gerald bowed. "Thank you, Your Highness."

As she disappeared through a small, discreet door in the wall behind the dais, the chamber's main doors flung open.

"Your Majesty!" the herald shouted. "I present to you Prince Nerim of Kallarap, Blood of the Sultan, and Shugat, Holy Man of the Kallarapi."

In walked the Kallarapi delegation to the strains of a blistering fanfare. Gerald let out a hard breath. *Here we go, then. Saint Snodgrass defend me.*

From the look of him, Prince Nerim hovered somewhere around eighteen years of age. His height was average, his build slender. Olive skin was moulded over high cheekbones and a broad brow. His deep-set eyes, fringed with extravagant lashes, were a clear light brown. A short black beard jutted from his chin, barbered and pomaded into a ruthless point which was tucked into a gold ferrule. His shirt and trousers were of pristine white linen. A belt of solid gold studded with emeralds clasped his waist. On his feet were curly-toed golden half-boots decorated with diamonds and on his head a cloth-of-gold turban. Fixed front and centre was a yellow diamond bigger than a hen's egg, with four curly white feathers dipped in gold sprouting above it. Shiny black ringlets curled from beneath the turban's edges, shyly brushing his shirt collar.

"Talk about sending a boy to do a man's job," breathed Reg, swallowing a snort of disgust. "That popinjay's window dressing, Gerald. It's the *other* one we need to worry about . . ."

*The other one.* Kallarap's holy man.

Shugat was so old his spine had curved him over like a sapling under heavy snow. A scraggly grey beard adorned his brown leather face and his bald, polished head was bare. He wore a plain brown robe, rough-spun and ill fitting, which was belted around his concave middle with a ratty old bit of rope. His callused feet were encased in scuffed leather sandals and his gnarled, ringless right hand grasped a knobbly wooden staff taller than he was.

Set into his forehead, above the bridge of his fiercely hooked nose, some kind of rough-hewn crystal the colour of dirty milk and no bigger than a bantam's egg.

Shugat looked up, revealing deep-sunk eyes as bright and burning as newborn stars . . .

. . . and Gerald felt a shocking shudder run right through him as he fell headlong into that molten gaze.

Waves of power were suddenly radiating off the Kallarapi holy man, distorting the surrounding air. Holy man? Try *wizard*. Even from thirty feet away Gerald could feel his skin crisp and his hair curl from the raw thaumaturgical energy Shugat emitted. On his shoulder, Reg was gasping.

All that power . . . and he'd never sensed so much

as a spark of it even though they were living in the same palace. He'd never met anyone who could hide himself so completely. Shugat was to First Grade wizardry what elephants were to ants.

*Bloody hell! Lional thinks he can tell this man what to do? He thinks I can tell him? He really is mad. Shugat could squash us flat with the blink of one eye.*

This meeting was a waste of time. Doomed to failure before it had even begun. The Kallarapi didn't *need* an army. They had Shugat . . . and all New Ottosland had was him.

*Damn. I really should have listened to Reg.*

# CHAPTER THIRTEEN

Just as Gerald thought he'd have to look away from Shugat or burst into flames, the holy man's measured strides faltered and his sulphurous gaze shifted abruptly to Reg and then to Tavistock. The lion stared back, lazily insolent. Reg gurgled in her throat.

Shugat halted, thrusting his head forward like a hunting dog in search of prey. Prince Nerim glanced back and stopped, surprised. Opened his mouth to query or protest and was silenced by Shugat's upraised hand.

Gerald felt his heart rate treble. Blimey, *now* what? He risked a glance at Lional. The king was perfectly relaxed, faintly smiling, as insolent as Tavistock as he sprawled on this throne.

Shugat's nostrils flared and his wild eyebrows shot up, then slammed down over his eyes in a ferocious scowl. He took three slow steps forward then halted again, lifted his staff and struck it onto the crimson carpet with all his might. The ensuing thunderclap shivered the chandeliers and rattled the lead-lined window panes. Tavistock leapt to his feet, roaring.

"*Blasphemy*!" the holy man roared back. The crystal in his forehead burst into burning life, pulsing like the sun. Prince Nerim was cowering.

"This is bad, Gerald, this is *bad*," Reg muttered.

"I know, I know, shut *up*!" he muttered back, then sidled closer to the throne. "Your Majesty?"

Lional was smiling, one hand stroking Tavistock's head, the other dangling idly over the side of the throne. "Now, now, Professor. Blasphemy is in the eye of the beholder. The trick is to appear profoundly unimpressed. I encourage you to follow my example."

*Mad, mad, and with a crazy death wish*. With an effort he smoothed his face to match Lional's bored, sleepy expression. "Yes, Your Majesty."

Now the Kallarapi delegation was huddled in conference. There was more staff-thumping, some fist waving and hissed ranting from Shugat and a lot of anguished whispering from Nerim.

"Perhaps, gentlemen," said Lional, poisonously polite, "you'd like to step outside until you're quite ready to meet with us? I'm sure we have nothing better to do than twiddle our thumbs while you rehearse your presentation."

Nerim and Shugat broke apart. They exchanged looks: Nerim's pleading, Shugat's grim. After a fraught pause Nerim wilted and the tatty old holy man advanced towards the throne. His eyes still blazed but the burning crystal in his forehead was quiescent again.

"You king of New Ottosland!" Shugat's voice was gravelly, his Kallarapi accent pronounced; he made no attempt to shorten vowels or soften consonants. "You mock us with your blasphemy!"

"*Mock* you, sir?" said Lional, vastly innocent. "I think not. Incidentally, do feel free to make your obeisances at your earliest convenience."

Gerald stopped breathing. What was Lional doing? Putting on a good face was one thing, playing with fire another. Surely even *he* could feel the power pouring out of the Kallarapi holy man? Did he think a trinket crown would save him? If so he was sadly mistaken.

Before Shugat could incinerate everyone within a mile of the audience chamber, Prince Nerim leapt forward and clutched at his arm. There were more exchanged looks: this time Nerim's mute appeal was so desperate his eyes almost popped out of his head. Another fraught pause, then Shugat nodded grudgingly and stepped back.

Gerald started breathing again.

Nerim cleared his throat and bowed. Not deeply, but sufficiently enough that Lional's faint smile remained undiminished. "O King," he said, his voice quavering slightly, "mine brother, His Glorious Magnificence Sultan Zazoor, may he live forever, of the Holy, Great and Immortal Empire of Kallarap, bids me greet you in his name." Unlike Shugat, his accent was barely discernable. Boarding school polish, Gerald decided. Like his brother.

Lional inspected his manicured fingernails. "That's nice."

The prince's eyes flashed. "Mine brother the sultan, may he live forever, also commends to you his holy man Shugat."

With obvious and severe reluctance Shugat offered Lional a parsimonious bow. Lional inclined his head in return, teeth glittering in a smile. "Welcome to my court, gentlemen. And allow me to present to you Professor Gerald Dunwoody. My royal wizard."

Shugat thudded his staff again: the chandeliers overhead tinkled to the faint echo of thunder, rolling on some distant horizon.

"*Not* wizard! Blasphemer!" he retorted. "As are you, little king! It is not for outsiders to know the faces of our gods: the Dragon, the Lion, the Bird!"

Gerald felt his heart stutter. *That's* who the Kallarapi worshipped? Animal spirits? Spirits like Reg and Tavistock, who were here now because of him? Oh no.

*Is this a coincidence or does the king know something?*

On his shoulder, Reg was moaning.

Lional held up his hand and admired one opulent diamond ring. "I know more than their faces, Shugat. I know their names."

Nerim gasped. For long moments there was silence as Shugat's seamed features reflected some bitter inner battle. "No outsider knows names of our secret, sacred gods."

Lional sighed. "Grimthak, Vorsluk and Lalchak," he said, counting on his fingers. "Sound familiar?"

*Not a coincidence. This is more than knowing, this is a plan. And I'm a part of it . . .*

Oh no. He *really* should have listened to Reg.

Shugat staggered as though he'd received a mortal wound. "Not possible! Not *possible*!" he hissed.

"And even more than their names, Shugat," continued Lional, inexorable, "I know *them*. And I welcome them. With open arms and a loving heart do I welcome the gods of Kallarap to New Ottosland."

With a slash of his staff Shugat indicated Tavistock and Reg. "*These?* You say these mimicking beasts are *our gods?*" Letting out a harsh cry like the lamenting of crows he plucked free the crystal from his forehead, leaving a bloodless crater in his flesh, and held it aloft. Incandescent light flooded into every cranny and corner. "*Woe to the blasphemer, for he shall burn in the fires of the Dragon. The Bird shall tear out his wicked tongue and the Lion devour his heart. So says Shugat, Holy Man of Kallarap!*"

With a shriek Prince Nerim fell to his knees, arms cradling his head. He began sobbing.

Lional laughed. Ignoring the stricken prince, ignoring Shugat and the light from his terrible crystal, he leaned over the side of his throne and said conversationally, "Did you know, Professor, there are so many holy men in Kallarap I'm sure you can't cross a single sand dune without falling over one."

Gerald unglued his tongue from the roof of his mouth. Melissande was going to *explode* when she heard about this. "Really, Your Majesty?" he croaked.

"Really. But the *sultan's* holy man is accounted something special. According to Kallarapi folklore, the *sultan's* holy man speaks to their gods on a daily basis. Imagine!"

And when the gods spoke back after today's little debacle three guesses what they were going to say . . . "That sounds very . . . religious, Your Majesty."

"It certainly does," agreed Lional. "Of course now that I come to think of it, as far as I'm aware nobody has actually *witnessed* this miraculous event. As far as I'm aware, the sultan's holy man just totters out of his little temple or cave or whatever *claiming* to have received a list of instructions from the gods and, for some reason I don't altogether understand, my old school chum Zazoor *believes* him." He shrugged. "Mind you, Zazoor always was the gullible sort."

The incandescent light faded, leaving Shugat's crystal dull and unreflecting. Still holding it the holy man rammed his staff into the carpet yet again. "*More* blasphemy!" he shouted over the echoing thunder.

Lional frowned. "Shugat, old chap, I feel compelled to point out you're getting tedious."

With a nervous glance at Shugat, Prince Nerim swallowed his sobs and clambered to his feet. "Hasty words, O gracious king. Holy Shugat was merely . . . taken aback."

Shugat glared and thumped his staff; the chandelier overhead danced and tinkled as the rolling thunder died away. "Do not speak for me, Blood of the Sultan! These beasts are blasphemy and so is doubting my speech with the gods! Now you tell me, King, how our sacred secret ways are open to you."

"Ah," said Lional. "You suspect some foul magic, perhaps? Sorry, but no. As it happens a little sultan told me."

Shugat's head snapped back. "*Zazoor?*"

"While we were at school. We were both a little drunk, you see, and had a bet regarding . . . well. Never mind. The point is, I won. Oh dear," he added, eyes alight with malicious amusement at the identical looks on Shugat and Nerim's faces. "Was he not supposed to say anything? Perhaps you should ask the gods to smite him, you know, just a little bit, the next time you're chatting."

Nerim said hoarsely, "Your Majesty, surely these matters are for the holy men of our nations to discuss at another time and place. The sultan, may he live forever, did not send us here to talk of gods, but of—of—" He swallowed convulsively. "—debts unpaid."

"Ah . . . yes . . ." said Lional. "Well, I think you'll find the two matters are more closely connected than you thought."

Nerim threw Shugat a desperate look. Leathery face creased with displeasure, Shugat nodded. "We will hear your words on this, King. And then—" He smiled ominously. "You will hear ours."

"By all means," said Lional. "If there's time. Now. As I was saying, Gerald," he continued, shifting a little on his throne so that one shoulder was presented to the Kallarapi delegation, "the sultan's holy man claims to be the sole recipient of his gods' wisdom. And certainly I can see why he would. Any man with the exclusive ear of the gods is in a remarkable position of power, as I'm sure you'd agree."

Gerald couldn't trust himself to speak. If he spoke he'd unleash a torrent of abuse that would get him thrown into a dungeon or worse. If he spoke he'd likely do even more damage to New Ottosland-Kallarap relations than the king was managing all by himself.

*I have to see this through, I have to wait till we're alone. Then I'll tell Lional what I think of him. Then I'll let him know that I quit. And if Melissande has the brains of an ant she'll quit too and come back to Ottosland with me.*

"Mmm," he said, and somehow managed to hide his rage.

"Yes, indeed," Lional continued, as though the inarticulate comment was a ringing endorsement. "A man with exclusive access to the gods is a man in a unique position. But what if the gods have been telling him something he doesn't want to hear? What if they want to change a few things and this holy man prefers things to stay the same? Prefers it so strongly that he ignores the gods' wishes? Might the gods then not choose *another* way of communicating their desires?"

Prince Nerim goggled. "I am confused . . ."

Lional sighed and rolled his eyes. "Of course you are. You know, I must introduce you to mine brother Rupert. The two of you would get along splendidly."

With a withering look Shugat shouldered Nerim aside. "You say *you* now speak for Kallarap's gods?"

The king spread his elegant hands wide. "I'm not saying anything, old chap. I just draw your attention to this lion and this bird, the very embodiments of Lalchak and Vorsluk, newly come to my court as *you* arrive to press your dubious claims upon me."

"And what of Grimthak the Dragon?" Shugat rasped. "First among the gods. Where is he?"

"I'm sure I've no idea," said Lional. "*I* don't presume to tell a god where and when he should present himself for inspection. Perhaps you do. If so I must say you're a braver man than I."

Shugat rammed his staff into the floor so hard that smoke puffed out of the carpet. When the ringing echoes of the latest thunder clap had finally died he shouted, "The Holy Ones do not dwell in New Ottosland! They are the gods of Kallarap!"

Lional picked some lint from his knee. "I see. So what you're *saying*, and do correct me if I'm wrong, is that *you* are in a position to dictate to three *gods* where and upon whom they bestow their favour? Is that what you're saying, Shugat old chap?"

Shugat's mouth worked soundlessly for a moment, spittle flecking his lips. Then he raised his staff overhead and shouted, "The gods strike you dead, King! The gods smoke your bones and boil your eyeballs in their sockets!"

Silence. After a moment, Lional raised his eyebrows. "Oh dear. It appears the gods aren't listening, Shugat. At least not to you."

Reg leaned close. "*Now* do you agree we should've got while the going was good, sunshine?"

Gerald nodded, feeling sick. *For once I don't care if she does say "I told you so". I deserve it. Oh lord, what a mess.*

Prince Nerim was staring at his brother's holy man, the first cracks of doubt showing in his armour of belief. Shugat brandished his staff some more. A short sharp wind swirled around the audience chamber, rattling the chandeliers. "Blood of the Sultan, you *will not* heed him. He is a trickster!" he shouted at Nerim. "A defaulter of debts! *Oath-breaker*! *I* am the holy man! *I* speak to the gods!"

"Well, Nerim, as *I* understand it," said Lional into the fraught silence, "what Shugat *actually* does is converse with a lump of carved wood that's supposed to *represent* the gods, more or less, in a rough, pre-modern impressionistic kind of way." His hand drifted to Tavistock's head and rested there, suggestively. "I have to say *I* prefer a more—*direct*—method of communication."

Shugat's face suffused with blood. "These beasts are not our gods!"

"I never said they were!" Lional protested, wounded innocence incarnate. "What they *are*, I believe, are the gods' emissaries. Sent here by the gods themselves to make their wishes known."

Gerald bit his tongue so hard he tasted blood. His shoulder stung where Reg's claws had pierced his robe, clutching him in shock. She was burbling hysterically under her breath. "*He's mad, he's mad, he's totally bonkers . . .*"

Shugat scowled, squinting at Reg. "This bird looks not like Vorsluk. It looks not like any bird I have ever seen."

"I'm sure I wouldn't know," said Lional. "Not being an expert on birds. But I must say it seems very comfortable, doesn't it, sitting on my wizard's shoulder? You'd think they were old friends."

Shugat surged forward and pointed his staff. "You there. Wizard. You claim friendship of Kallarap's gods?"

*Oh shit.* He stared at Lional. Lional stared back. He was smiling with his lips but his eyes were terrible. "Now, now, Professor. There's no need to be shy," he said, so eminently reasonable, so deceptively sane. "Answer the holy man, there's a good fellow. Truthfully, of course. Gods are very particular about truth, I believe. And certainly *I* don't want you to lie. *So*. Are you and the bird friends?"

He had no choice. No *choice* unless he wanted to start a war right here, right now. Damn damn *damn* . . .

"Yes," he croaked. "We're friends."

Lional jumped to his feet, arms wide. "And there you have it! Now, Nerim, Shugat, I expect you're wondering what this means. Well, what it means is *this*. The gods desire New Ottosland and Kallarap to forgive all debts and grievances and henceforth live together as loving brothers!"

Stony faced, Shugat looked from Lional to Tavistock to Gerald to Reg. "This is what *you* say the gods mean. *I* say they mean for you to pay us all the money you owe and cease your unholy oath-breaking on pain of death!"

"Oh," said Lional, disappointed. "Well. In that case it would seem we've reached what's known as an impasse." He clapped his hands. "*I* know. How about this?" He gazed at the frescoed ceiling. "Gods of Kallarap hear my plea! If I have wronged you and sinned in your sight, show me your displeasure! Strike *dead* this bird and this lion in a demonstration of your holy wrath!"

Nothing happened.

Very slowly Nerim turned to the silent holy man. "Shugat? He has spoken to our gods and our gods have answered him. Yet they did not answer *you*. How can this be?"

"It is a trick," said Shugat. His voice trembled. "This man is an unbeliever, O Prince. He is not of the Blood or the faith. He cannot have the favour of the Three."

"I do not understand," Nerim whispered. Shatteringly close to tears he retreated, leaving Shugat stranded on the crimson carpet with only his staff for support. Then he looked up at Lional. "Mine brother the sultan, may he live forever, will want—I must explain—" He turned again to Shugat. "Give me your wisdom, holy man! Tell me what to do!"

Still and silent as stone, Shugat leaned upon his staff like one entranced, blindly staring at the floor.

With a light-hearted leap, Lional bounded from the dais to rest a hand on Nerim's sagging shoulder. "I have an idea. Why don't you ask the *gods* what you should do? I mean, no offence to Shugat, old chap, but everybody knows what happens when you rely on middlemen and start passing messages along. Bits get misheard, or left out or . . . reinterpreted . . . and before you know it, what started as 'Let's all be friends' becomes 'Cut off the infidels' heads' and I don't know about *you*, Nerim, but *I* think that's taking paraphrasing just a *little* too far."

Frightened, Nerim stared at him. "But the gods *never* speak to us directly. Only through Shugat, our most revered holy man."

"Things change, Nerim," said Lional, shrugging. "And we can change with them or we can be left in the dust. I'll bet there are simply *dozens* of things you've always wanted to ask the great Vorsluk. Now here's your chance. Ask away!"

As Nerim dithered, Reg again pressed her beak to Gerald's ear. "Do something. Stop him before this gets right out of hand!"

*How?* he wanted to shout. How do you stop a runaway tram? He'd halt time if he could, turn it backwards, undo the damage he'd unwittingly caused, but magic didn't work like that. Or if it did, he didn't know how.

*Where's Monk Markham when I need him?*

Unmasking Lional was out of the question. Shugat would likely slaughter the king on the spot . . . a scandal that would make Stuttley's look like a rained-out garden party.

But he had to do *something*. Put on the brakes . . . ?

"Ah . . . Your Majesty?" he said. "Are you quite sure we're worthy of speaking directly to the gods? Perhaps we should all spend a night in prayer and fasting first. The last thing we want to do is offend them with—with—uncleanliness."

The look Lional gave him was lethal. "I hope you're not suggesting the Blood of the Sultan is *un*worthy, Professor. Or *unclean*. That might be construed as a grave insult. Prince Nerim might feel compelled to return to Zazoor with a poor report of our meeting. He might even go so far as to beseech the gods to strike us down in retribution!" He turned to Nerim. "Pay no attention, old chap. My wizard is merely concerned—*needlessly*, I might add—for your safety. Please. Vorsluk's emissary is waiting."

*"Silence, oath-breaker!"*

Nerim took one look at Shugat and his upraised staff and shrieked, then flung himself face-down on the carpet, hands clapped to his ears. A split second later the audience chamber shuddered as crack after crack of thunder exploded beneath the frescoed ceiling. Two window panes shattered and one of the chandeliers plummeted to the carpet in an explosion of blue diamond splinters. From the crystal in

Shugat's upraised hand writhed a white-hot whiplash of light.

As Tavistock heaved to his feet, roaring, and Lional, shouting, grabbed at his mane, Gerald threw himself behind the throne. Reg tumbled to the floor beside him.

"*God*, Reg! *Say* something! Quick, before he kills Lional!"

"*Let* him kill Lional!" she yelled. "It'll serve the mad bastard right!"

"No! If Shugat kills Lional there really *will* be a war, even if Rupert has to draft his vampire butterflies! Go *on*! Whatever happens after that *can't* be worse than this!"

"That's what you think!"

Heart pounding, he inched his way out from behind the throne to see what was happening. Shugat advanced towards Lional, the whip of light lashing back and forth, seeking contact. Lional let go of Tavistock and faced the holy man, lips curving in a strange smile. His hands came up, as if to ward off death . . .

"Speak, Reg! You have to! *Now!*"

With a furious curse and a cackling cry she launched herself into the air. "*Vorsluk! Vorsluk! Vorsluk speaks!*"

"Look, Shugat!" shouted Nerim and pointed, still prone on the carpet. "The gods are with us!"

Shugat's mouth fell open. The whiplash of light abruptly died, the rolling thunder stopped and the audience chamber ceased its shaking. Turban askew, Nerim staggered to his feet and stared at Reg as though he'd never seen a bird flying in his life. Lional, still smiling, lowered his hands.

At the far end of the chamber the doors flew open and a cohort of palace guards tumbled in, ceremonial pikes flailing.

"Your Majesty!" cried the chief guard. "Are we under attack?"

"No!" said Lional. "Get out, you fools, and close the doors!" As the guards retreated in confusion he turned his attention to Reg. "Oh, mighty Vorsluk, great god of Kallarap, *speak* to us! Reveal your sacred will!"

Still flying, Reg let out another wild cackle. "Hear ye, hear ye, hear ye! Mighty are the deeds of Vorsluk and also Lalchak and Grimthak! Great is their power and just their retribution! The Three watch over all, understand all, judge all. Patience will be rewarded. Events shall unfold as the Three desire. Attend your duties and be obedient."

"*Aiieeee!*" cried Nerim. "The god speaks!"

Shugat stayed standing, clearly shaken but stubborn to the last. "That—that—is not how Vorsluk speaks to me."

As Reg, panting, landed on the back of Lional's throne, Nerim managed a shaky bow. "King Lional, the gods of Kallarap have favoured you mightily. I shall return to mine brother the sultan, may he live forever, and—"

"*Silence*, Nerim!" Shugat shouted. "You are dazzled by trickery, like a child in the bazaar! The gods do not—"

"I am no child!" Nerim retorted. "I am the sultan's brother! His Blood, and his emissary in this land.

Did you not tell Zazoor the gods *wished* you to come here? This is why! So their will might be revealed!"

The crystal's fire woke briefly as Shugat shuddered. "Now *you* explain to me the will of our gods?"

"No, no, Holy Shugat!" Nerim gasped, his momentary defiance wilting. "But do you not teach the Three are omnipotent? All that is come to pass here *must* be their doing . . . mustn't it?"

Shugat stilled. Gerald, stranded on the dais, hauled himself back onto his feet and held his breath, not daring to look at Reg. Three feet distant Tavistock shook his maned head and grumbled.

Lional said brightly, "Of *course* it must. Dear Shugat, can you think that *I* am not amazed? I never *dreamed* your gods would come to us. They never have before. But here they are and we must obey."

Saying nothing, Shugat pressed the crystal back into his forehead. Nerim, nodding, said, "Yes, O King. That is our sacred duty."

"Exactly," said Lional, and perched on the edge of the dais. Still grumbling, Tavistock joined him. The grumbling became a pleased rumble as Lional petted his face. Gerald watched Nerim's awestruck expression and felt sick all over again.

*I'll never undo this damage now. Not ever. What a bloody disaster . . .*

Eagerly Nerim said, "You say the gods wish us to be friends? Then we are friends!"

Lional frowned. "Well, I thought we already *were*, Nerim. I've always felt nothing but affection for the Kallarapi nation. How could I not after six happy years getting to know its sultan in the rough and tumble fashion of schoolboys everywhere?"

Nerim blinked, and glanced at Shugat for some kind of guidance. But Shugat was once more a man in a trance, silent and uncommunicative. Eyes dull and hooded, supporting himself upon his staff, he appeared weary to the bone, all the fire in him burned to ash.

"I am sure mine brother the sultan, may he live forever," said Nerim, with a last worried glance at Shugat, "will be pleased to hear you say so, O King. And with the gods' help I know we can put our misunderstandings behind us."

"Of course we can," said Lional. "Tell me, Nerim, Zazoor hasn't gone and found himself a wife lately, has he?"

"A wife?" Nerim shook his head. "Alas, O King. The gods have not yet seen fit to choose a woman worthy of such an honour." He flickered another glance at Shugat and lowered his voice. "It has been a matter of some concern. Perhaps, O King, since you have the gods' favour, you could speak to them on our behalf?"

Lional smiled, his ringed fingers threading through and through Tavistock's gold-dusted mane. "What a lucky coincidence, Nerim. As it happens the gods have already made their wishes known to me."

"They have?" said Nerim, incredulous. "Truly, O King, the gods of Kallarap are great! Who is the woman?"

"Someone you've already met," said Lional, one arm draped possessively across Tavistock's shoulders. "Someone very close to my heart."

Gerald pressed a hand to his roiling guts. Oh *God.* Not *Melissande*...

Reg flapped from the throne to his shoulder. "*Criminy*," she muttered. "He can't be *serious,* madam'll go *spare*..."

Nerim looked confused. "Yes? And this someone is...?"

"My sister!" said Lional, impatient. "The princess!"

"The princess?" Nerim echoed, and turned again to the holy man. "Shugat, did you hear? The gods wish for the sultan, may he live forever, to take Princess Melissande as wife!"

Shugat said nothing.

"I knew you'd be pleased," said Lional, beaming. "I know *I'm* pleased."

Nerim swallowed. "Er—I fear the honour is too great, O King..."

"Nonsense," said Lional briskly. "It's what the gods want, Nerim. And we've already agreed that what the gods want the gods get." He laughed. "Nerim, Nerim, don't you realise what this *means*?"

"No, O King," Nerim whispered. "What does it mean?"

*Hell's bells and buckets of blood!* cried Gerald inside his aching head. *That's what it means!*

"It means we'll be *brothers,* Nerim!" Lional crowed. "You and I and Zazoor. Oh. And Rupert of course, unfortunately. On second thoughts, let's forget Rupert, shall we? It'll be you and I and Zazoor! One big happy family, with Melissande playing mother. Isn't that just wonderful? Aren't the gods *divine*?"

# CHAPTER FOURTEEN

There was a loaded silence in the audience chamber once the stunned Kallarapi delegation had departed.

Lounging on his throne Lional looked at Gerald, eyebrows elevated. "'Prayers and *fasting*', Professor? Do feel free to explain *that* little unsolicited piece of inspiration." Sprawled at his feet, Tavistock snarled.

Through teeth gritted so hard they were nearly breaking, Gerald said, "My apologies, Your Majesty. I thought you might appreciate a chance to think about what you were doing."

Lional's fingers drummed on the arm of his throne. "Well, I didn't."

"No, Your Majesty," he replied, reckless with rage. "It's clear to me now you had no intention whatsoever of *thinking*."

As Reg, still on his shoulder, made alarmed noises in his ear, Lional considered him. "Do you know, Professor, I liked you much better when you were diffident and ingratiating. Recall, if you can, that I am your *king*."

"You're not *my* king! I'm Ottoslandian, we don't have kings! And after what just happened I can see why!"

Lional sat up. "I'm warning you, Professor. You're on very thin ice."

"*I'm* on thin ice? *I* am?" Choking, he took a stamping half-turn around the dais. "And what do you call that little stunt *you* just pulled, Your Majesty? *I* call it tap-dancing on a melting ice floe! Have you forgotten that Sultan Zazoor has an *army*? And don't you understand that when he figures out he's been had he's going to introduce us to it? Intimately?"

"I suggest, Professor," said Lional, coldly, "that you moderate your tone."

"To hell with my tone!" he retorted. "You've spent the last hour playing fast and loose with a foreign power's religious icons! You forced Reg into impersonating one of them and manipulated *me* into upholding the lie! I don't have enough fingers and toes to count all the rules I've just broken! And you tell me to *moderate* my *tone*?"

Lional sighed. "I must say, Professor, you disappoint me. What I have done, sir, is solve the punitive Kallarapi tariff crisis, thus rescuing New Ottosland from certain bankruptcy and thousands of my subjects from suffering, *and* I've taken the first steps in consolidating a lasting alliance with our Kallarapi neighbours while incidentally saving Melissande from the tragedy of spinsterhood. All in all, it's been an excellent afternoon's work. I deserve congratulating, not scolding."

The man was serious. He really thought what he'd done was *praiseworthy*. Oh, dear *God* . . .

"And what about Mel— I mean, Her Highness?" he said, suddenly exhausted. "What if she doesn't want to marry the Sultan of Kallarap?"

Lional looked baffled. "What she wants is irrelevant. The Melissandes of New Ottosland have always married to further the interests of the kingdom."

Which may be true . . . but he wondered if anyone had thought to remind the current Melissande of that. "All right. What if the sultan doesn't wish to marry the princess?"

"Oh, I don't think that's very likely," said Lional, carelessly. "Not want to marry a young woman in the prime of her child-bearing years, capable of giving him a fistful of sons to carry on his quaint camel-breeding empire?" He shrugged. "I admit Melissande's not exactly *beautiful*. But you know what they say, Professor. All cats are grey in the dark. Really, you mustn't fret so. You'll give yourself indigestion." A lazy smile. "Besides. Zazoor will do whatever his gods tell him to do. In that respect he's as gullible as his gormless little brother."

If there'd been something handy he would have thrown it at Lional and the consequences be damned. "But, Your Majesty, *think*. What if Shugat wasn't as convinced by our little charade as he led us to believe? What if he takes a moment on the way home to stop for a chat with his gods and the gods say 'Wedding? What wedding?' What do you think is going to happen then?"

"My dear Gerald . . ." said Lional tartly. "Calm yourself. Shugat is nothing but a moth-eaten old man with delusions of grandeur. And as for the gods of Kallarap . . . surely you've worked it out by now?"

"Worked *what* out, Your Majesty?"

"The gods of Kallarap don't exist!"

Gerald stared. "You don't know that!"

Lional let out an exasperated groan. "I'll tell you what I know, Professor. I know that when Shugat asked his gods to kill me, they didn't. And when I stood here and invited them to strike me down in my stockings, nothing happened *again!*"

"Actually, you invited them to strike down Reg and Tavistock."

"Mere detail," said Lional. "What *matters* is there was no striking of any kind. Which leads me to one of two conclusions. Either the gods don't exist *or* they approve of what I'm doing! Either way, I win." He smiled. "And Zazoor loses."

On his shoulder, Reg heaved a sigh and scratched the back of her head. "You know," she mused, "I hate to admit it but he's got a point."

"*There*. You see?" said Lional. "Even your little feathered friend agrees there's nothing to be concerned about."

Reg sniffed. "Well, I didn't say *that*."

Lional sat back. "I think, Professor, you need a little quiet time to reflect upon this momentous occasion. Given your excellent assistance I shall overlook the tone and content of your recent remarks. *This* time. Don't feel obliged to join me for dinner. I shall look for you in the morning. We'll go hunting."

"*Hunting?*"

"Yes indeed," said Lional, nodding. "I'll see you in my private stables at seven, Professor. Just you, I think. No need to rob Vorsluk's emissary of her beauty sleep."

"Sarky bastard," muttered Reg. "I'll give him beauty sleep . . ."

"Hunting," said Gerald. Oh, lord. He'd thought Melissande had been joking about that. And just when he thought things couldn't get any worse . . .

"Don't be late," added Lional. "I can't abide unpunctuality. It puts me in *such* a bad mood."

It was a dismissal. Gerald bowed, jerkily, and made his escape before he forgot every last oath he'd ever taken as a wizard and turned King Lional the Forty-third into a toad.

Nerim sat in an overstuffed armchair in the palace guest quarters' salon and shivered. He couldn't remember the last time he'd felt so afraid.

It was hard to say which scared him the most: the fact that for the first time in his life he'd been in the living, speaking presence of the gods . . . or that in the half hour since he and Shugat had returned to their suite the holy man had refused to utter a single word. Instead he remained motionless and cross-legged on the floor under the window, eyes closed, hands in his lap.

From birth every Kallarapi knew his people were the gods' chosen. Never once had Nerim doubted it. Some of his earliest memories were of sitting on Zazoor's knee in the private temple of their father the sultan, may he dwell with the gods in perpetual peace, listening to Shugat pronounce the desires of the gods.

Shugat, whom the gods now refused to answer.

When he and Shugat had left Kallarap it had been in the safe and sure knowledge the gods were sending them to give New Ottosland's king one last chance to honour his sacred oath and pay to them the tariffs required by treaty. Shugat had said so. Shugat had said the gods were enraged by King Lional's refusal to follow the path laid down by his honoured ancestor King Lional the First. He'd said this was a sacred mission to restore the honourable bonds of mutual obligation between Kallarap and New Ottosland. He'd said the gods would *reward* them for doing their holy duty.

Shugat had said *nothing* about weddings and new alliances and the gods revealing their presence to the New Ottosland king. Surely he would have mentioned it if the gods had told him about any of that? So . . . what was going on?

Had Shugat somehow offended them? Had his refusal to acknowledge their presence in New Ottosland turned them against him? And if that were true what did it mean for the rest of Kallarap? If Shugat had sinned did it mean the punishment must fall upon all Kallarapi? Upon *Zazoor*?

Nerim barely stifled his cry of grief and terror. Flinging himself from the armchair to his knees before the ominously silent Shugat, he held out his hands in desperate entreaty. "O Holy Shugat, I beseech thee . . . speak to me! Are we forsaken? Are we abandoned? After a thousand years of protection do the Three now belong to *New Ottosland*?"

Shugat's eyes snapped open. They were black as night and blazing with the heat of countless suns. Startled, Nerim fell backwards. So ferocious was the fire in Shugat's eyes that he scuttled behind the safety of the armchair and cowered there as the holy man stared and stared at nothing he could see.

At long last the leaping black flames died and Shugat's eyes were his own again. The old man stirred. Flexed his fingers in his lap and nodded his bald head in answer to a question only he could hear. Using his staff to help him, he got to his feet.

"Come, Nerim," he said. "It is time to go home."

Because he was too angry to wait for a native palace guide and subsequently made every wrong turn it was possible to make, sometimes more than once, it took Gerald forever to get back to his suite from the king's audience chamber. Slamming open the doors, he stormed inside.

"Dammit!" he shouted, stamping about the sun-dappled foyer. "Dammit, dammit, *dammit*! That bloody man! That insane, megalomaniacal, off-his-rocker, *bastard*!"

Reg jumped off his shoulder and perched instead on a handy chair back. "Careful now, or you'll do yourself a mischief. And close those doors before somebody hears you and repeats what you're saying to our little blond friend!"

Whirling, he gestured wildly at the open doors; they slammed shut so hard the hinges nearly buckled.

"What am I going to do, Reg? What the *hell* am I going to do?"

Reg sighed and stretched one wing above her head. "Well, for starters you're going to calm down."

"*Calm down*? How can I calm down? You were there! You saw what happened! If word of this gets out I am *finished*! I am sanctioned into the middle of next *century*! And most likely I'm in *gaol*!"

She sighed, and stretched the other wing. "Stop panicking, Gerald. Word isn't going to get out."

"You don't know that!" he shouted. "Good God, with *my* luck five minutes after the Kallarapi delegation unsaddles its last camel there'll be a report on its way to the Department!"

"Oh, *Gerald*! Enough with the hysteria! Shugat could just as easily go home and tell his sultan 'Slight change of plans, sunshine. Put on your prettiest turban, you're going to a wedding!' So how's this for an idea? Why don't we wait to see what happens before you start picking out a fetching prison ensemble?"

He groaned, still pacing. "*Wedding. Oh lord.* Melissande's going to *kill* me."

Reg tipped her head to one side consideringly. "Not necessarily. The wretched girl might be secretly in love with Zazoor. This could be the best news she's had since she heard about sensible shoes."

He stopped pacing. "You think?"

Reg sniffed. "Well . . . no. But at the rate you're going you'll be throwing yourself into that fountain to drown and I can't see me pulling you out in time. Not with my arthritis. And anyway she won't blame you. How can she? None of this is *your* fault. Lional's not *your* barmy brother."

"Trust me, that won't make any difference!" he retorted. "I was there and I didn't stop it! Of *course* it's all my fault!"

"Well, you heard what His Raving Majesty said. It's

a question of duty. She might not like the idea of marrying Zazoor but she is a Melissande and—"

"Oh Reg, come on!" he said, and started pacing again. "Can you see her meekly trotting off to live the rest of her life in a *tent*? Leaving Lional here with no-one but *Rupert* to keep him in check?"

Reg deflated. "Damn. Now you've got a point." Then she brightened. "I know," she said, cackling. "Maybe we'll get lucky and old Shugat'll stir Zazoor up for an invasion and when the sand settles there won't be any Lional left to explain away or cause any more grief!"

"*Reg*! That's a *terrible* thing to say!"

She snorted. "Maybe, but are you going to tell me the idea doesn't give you a happy tingling feeling?"

Possibly it did but that wasn't the issue. "This isn't about getting him *killed*. I'm a wizard, not an assassin."

"I know, I know," she said, placating.

"*God*." He pressed the heels of his hands against his aching temples. "What the *hell* am I going to do?"

"Call that Markham boy."

Abruptly tired of pacing, Gerald slumped into the nearest chair. "Why? The last person I can tell any of this to is Monk."

"Of course you can't! You can't talk about today to anybody outside this foyer!" said Reg. "But you do need to find out if he's tracked down any of those other wizards yet. They might be your only hope for keeping Lional under control!"

Of course. He'd forgotten all about his predecessors, and asking Monk to track them down. This damned place was getting to him . . .

"I got your message," said Monk from the uncertain depths of his crystal ball. "And I've started tracking those wizards' whereabouts. Bottomley's one of ours, I should hear something about him soon but—" Then he scowled. "All right. I know that look. What's gone wrong now?"

Draped across his workshop bench, Gerald swallowed. "Nothing."

"Don't you try that 'nothing' mouthwash with me, Dunnywood! I can read you like a book and the page I'm looking at has 'Trouble' written all over it. What's going on?"

"I *told* you, Monk. *Nothing*," he insisted. Then added, as his friend's expression scrunched warningly, "Much. Nothing I can go into right now." He dragged his fingers through his hair. "Let's just say it's not easy being court wizard to His Sovereign Majesty King Lional the Forty-third of New Ottosland and leave it at that, eh?"

"Uh huh," said Monk, unimpressed. "Fine. Just so long as you haven't gone and transmogrified anything else!"

With an effort, he made his voice cheerful. "No. No, I haven't done that."

"Good!" Then Monk's ferocious scowl cleared. "Look, Gerald, if the job's such a stinker chuck it in. Come home. I'll hide you in the cupboard till everyone's stopped talking about Stuttley's. Honestly, there's bound to be a fresh scandal any day now."

He sighed. "I wish I could, Monk. But it's out of the question. Things around here have got a bit . . . complicated."

"*Complicated*?" Monk slapped his forehead, aghast. "I *knew* it! Didn't I say I can read you like a book? Ha! I can read you like bloody *hieroglyphics*, mate!" He groaned. "Complicated means politics, doesn't it? Go on, doesn't it? God, I *hate* politics."

*Not as much as I do, trust me.* "I told you, I can't discuss it. And even if I could, I wouldn't."

Monk's eyes squinted suspiciously. "Why not?"

"Plausible deniability."

"Bloody hell, Gerald, what *is* it with you?" his friend demanded. "This was supposed to be a cushy little job in the middle of nowhere, a doddle, a giggle, a walk in the park, and now you're talking complications and plausible deniability and all of a sudden—"

"Hang on," he interrupted, distracted by the sound of loud erratic banging in the foyer. "I have to go, Monk, there's someone at the door. Get back to me about those other wizards as soon as you can, okay? Leave a message if I'm not in. Thanks. Bye!"

"He's right, you know," said Reg, perched on her ram skull. "We should skedaddle while the skedaddling's good."

He snatched at the fraying ends of his temper. "*Reg*—"

"I know, I know!" she said. "You've got a contract, you made a promise, blah blah blah. But I'm right, sunshine. If we stay you'll be sorry."

He was already sorry. "*Look*—"

The loud erratic banging started up again. Reg tutted disapprovingly. "Would you listen to that? Go on, see who it is before they knock the doors flat to the floor."

He went.

"Cheery pip pip, Professor!" a fatuously smiling Melissande greeted him. Precariously propped against the doorframe she waggled her magically manicured fingers at him while Boris, draped around her neck like an evil moulting fur stole, leered and flicked his tail. Melissande patted him, cooing, then burped.

Gerald recoiled in automatic self-defence as a pungent wave of alcohol fumes wafted over him. *Oh hell. This is all I need.* "Your Highness. How . . . unexpected."

Beaming, she held up a bottle half-full of something that looked suspiciously like whiskey. "Care for a little drinky-poo, old bean, eh what? We have news to celebrate! Lional informs me I'm about to be *married*!"

His heart sank. "Oh lord."

"Who is it?" Reg called.

He raised his voice. "One of our chickens coming home to roost."

"Eh?" said Melissande, peering blearily through her glasses. "Who are you calling a chicken?"

"Nobody," he said helplessly, and stood back from the door. "Would you like to come in?"

Another burp. "Why I don't mind if I do!" she trilled, and tottered all the way into the foyer on the midnight blue patent leather high heeled shoes that he'd so kindly and *stupidly* conjured for her. Boris turned his head to look back over her shoulder. He was still leering.

Gerald closed the foyer doors, took a deep breath and shouted, "*Reg*! I think you'd better get out here! *Now!*"

Twenty minutes later, they still had company.

"Oh God," he said, one hand pressed firmly over his eyes.

"Which one?" asked Reg.

"I'm not fussy," he replied, and groaned. "I can't look, Reg. What's she doing now?"

"Well, she's just climbed into the ornamental fountain," said Reg. "And she's standing on the goldfish."

"Oh, *God*! What's that dreadful noise? Did she slip? Is she drowning? Tell me she's not drowning!"

"No, she's not drowning," said Reg, after a pause. "And neither's Boris, more's the pity. He's scarpered under the nearest table. She's—and I use the word in its *loosest* possible context—singing."

It was no good. He had to look.

And promptly wished he hadn't. *Oh blimey. And to think I thought Stuttley's was the worst trouble I could get into.* "I don't believe this, Reg," he muttered. "We have to get her *out* of here. If somebody comes in and finds her it'll be whoops-a-daisy and chains for two in the dungeons!"

Melissande, soaked to the skin and blissfully warbling, threw her head back and hit what she fondly imagined was a High C.

"At least the dungeons would be quiet!" Reg shrieked, and launched herself across the foyer to the fountain. "Oy! You! Princess Diva! *Put a sock in it!*"

Arrested in mid-arpeggio, Melissande blinked. "Oh. It's you. The funny-looking feather duster with verbal diarrhoea." She leaned forward confidingly. "My cat Boris doesn't like you."

"I'm shattered," said Reg grimly, perching on the

edge of the fountain's top tier level with Melissande's bloodshot eyes. "And you're drunk."

"Yes," said Melissande, and fished at her feet for the bottle of whiskey. Raising it with a flourish she swallowed another big mouthful, burped loudly, and beamed upon the world at large. "I rather think I am."

Reg rolled her eyes. "And that's going to help matters, is it?"

"Well it can't bloody hurt them!"

"Tell me that again tomorrow."

"You know," said Melissande, frowning, "you really shouldn't take that tone with me. I *am* a princess. *And* the prime minister." Suddenly noticing the haphazard modesty of her sodden clothing she squeaked, and with fumbling fingers started to rectify the situation.

"And you're doing a fine job of both, I must say," scolded Reg. "Drunk and disorderly in the private residence of an unmarried gentleman, madam? What kind of an example is *that* to set for this year's crop of debutantes? You're a danger to the fabric of society, not to mention my eardrums if you start singing again! Why don't you take yourself back to your own apartments, put your head in a nice big bucket of iced water and we'll agree to forget this unfortunate interlude ever—"

Modesty more or less restored, Melissande took another generous swig of whiskey then waved the bottle under Reg's beak. "Don't look at me in that tone of voice, you disreputable cleaning implement. Didn't you hear me? I'm a *princess*. And I'm getting *married*, to a *sultan*, which means I'll be a *sultana*—"

She stopped and thought for a moment. "That can't be right. Sultanas are wrinkly grapes. I am *not* a wrinkly grape."

Reg sniffed. "Stay in that water for much longer and you'll be doing a pretty good impersonation."

But Melissande wasn't listening. "In fact, if you put it all together. I'll be a princess sultana. Or a sultana princess."

"Yes, yes," said Reg impatiently. "The International Sultana Growers' Alliance will probably make you their mascot and then won't some poor fool in a grape suit be relieved. The point *is*, you stupid girl—"

"You can't talk to me like that!" Melissande spluttered, swaying dangerously. "I'm a princess, a prime minister and very nearly a wrinkled grape! And you haven't congratulated me! *No-one's* congratulated me."

"Probably no-one's been game to," said Reg. "Now why don't you be a sensible little sultana-in-waiting and put down the bottle, eh? I mean, don't you think you've had enough?"

"No," said Melissande, and took another huge swig of whiskey. "I haven't had *nearly* enough."

Reg opened her beak to argue, reconsidered, and said, "You know what? You're right. Most marriages are best conducted when at least one of the victims is pickled. In which case can I fetch you another bottle? Or would you prefer a keg?"

"Reg, are you out of your mind?" Gerald demanded, and pushed away from the bit of foyer wall he'd been leaning against. "Just—go away! You're not helping! Your Highness—" As Reg retreated to the nearest chair, hugely offended, he inched towards the fountain, ready to break Melissande's fall and be crushed to a pulp if she did a sudden nose-dive over the side. "You're right. I'm sorry. Please accept our condolences—I mean *congratulations*—on your impending nuptials. This is wonderful news."

Melissande staggered a pace sideways, the better to thrust an outstretched finger into his face. "*Wonderful?*" The flattering hairstyle he'd conjured for her was proving no match against water, headtossing and the effects of a determined splurge of drinking; trailing vines of rust red hair waved about her flushed face and plastered themselves to her damp cheeks. "What makes you think it's wonderful? It's *terrible*, you stupid wizard! And it's *all your fault!*"

*I knew it. I knew it. Of course she's blaming me.* He stepped back, stinging with guilt. "Look here, Your Highness, that's bloody unfair. I'm not the one who pass-the-parcelled you over to Sultan Zazoor. That was your brother's idea, not mine."

She stamped her foot splashily. "Don't worry, there's plenty of blame to go around!"

"What's *that* supposed to mean?"

"It means marrying me off to Zazoor might have been Lional's idea but he *never* would've thought of it if *you* hadn't tarted me up like a prize cow for the market!"

"Prize cow?" he echoed. "Well, thank you very much! For your information I did *not* make you look like a *cow*, I made you look beautiful! And then what happened? Instead of sticking around and doing your duty as princess and prime minister you caved in to the antiquated notions of those stupid bloody

Kallarapi and left me in there all alone with your insane brother and everything went arse over tea kettle and I *still* don't know how I'm going to fix it! I don't even know if I *can*! I mean, I could've done with you in there for some moral support, Melissande, I *needed* you there for moral support. The only reason I was in there in the first place is because you manipulated me into fighting your fight for you. The *least* you could've done was be there in case of slight catastrophes! But no! *You* were too busy piking out! And anyway, do you honestly believe I *wanted* this to happen? Do you think I had any idea that it *could*? Well I *didn't*! Brothers don't give their sisters away to virtual strangers where *I* come from. That's just a quaint New Ottosland custom! And—and—"

He stopped shouting and waving his arms, suddenly and acutely aware that Melissande, Reg and even Boris were all staring at him in mute astonishment. He shoved his hands into his trouser pockets and cleared his throat.

"Yes? And?" said Melissande, with ominous sweetness. "Don't stop now, it's just getting interesting."

"And I never intended for things to get so out of hand," he finished lamely. "I'm sorry."

She brandished the whiskey bottle at him. "*Sorry*? What good does *sorry* do me, Mister Professor Gerald Dunweedin', or Dunnywood, or whatever your name is? I mean if you're so *sorry* why don't *you* rattle off to Kallarap on the back of a camel to be their sultana and *I'll* stay here being the princess prime minister!"

He stared. "I don't want to be their sultana."

"*Well neither do I!*" she cried, stamping her foot so

hard she sent a wave of water over the side of the fountain. "*I* never asked you to make me look beautiful, did I? *I* never asked you to stick me in this dress and these shoes and fix my makeup or my hair! What do you think I am, *blind*? Of *course* I know how appalling I look! Didn't it ever occur to you that I dress like a frump on *purpose*? Don't you think I'd figured out by the time I was *three* that slender pretty New Ottosland princesses get bartered away like—like—primary produce? I've spent *years* cultivating my Chubby Fashion Disaster Persona! And then *you* and your *bird* come along and ruin it in five minutes flat! How could you *do* that to me, Gerald? I thought you *liked* me!" She was weeping now, overflowing with rage and whiskey.

On *purpose*? She'd done it all on *purpose*? Why the hell hadn't she *said* so? "I—I do like you," he stammered, appalled. "I just had no idea. You mean the trousers and the sensible shoes and the awful hair are *camouflage*?"

"Of *course* they're camouflage, you dolt!" she shouted. "And so is the chubbiness! All designed to make sure nobody would look at me as marriage market material so I could stay here in New Ottosland where I'm needed, and where I can keep both eyes on Lional! So congratulations, Professor! You've just scuttled the careful work of a lifetime!"

"Bloody hell," he said faintly. "You should've told me! This morning, in the carriage, I thought—it just seemed to me that you didn't like—"

"Being a frump? I *hate* it, but that's not the point, is it? I was doing it for New Ottosland and *now*—" Overcome with alcohol and emotion she sat down in the fountain, the whiskey bottle cradled in her arms. "What I don't understand is *why*," she said, fishing a sodden handkerchief out of her cleavage and mopping her tear-streaked face. "*Why* has Lional suddenly decided he wants to deepen our close ties with Kallarap? What close ties? We don't even have adjacent *strings*! And he *despises* Zazoor, so how could he possibly want him as a brother-in-law? It doesn't make any *sense*!"

# CHAPTER FIFTEEN

Gerald looked at Reg, who shrugged. "She's got to find out sooner or later, sunshine. At least right now she's anaesthetised."

He put his aching head in his hands. Forget about being born beneath an unlucky star. Clearly he'd popped out beneath a misfortunate bloody *galaxy*.

The princess was staring at him suspiciously as she wrung out the sopping handkerchief. "Find out what, Gerald? What exactly happened after I left the audience chamber?"

*Oh lord.* "Well, Melissande," he said, "it's got something to do with New Ottosland's foreign policy."

"Foreign policy?" she echoed. "Don't make me laugh. The closest thing we've got to foreign policy is 'oh look, here comes a stranger, let's throw a rock at him but make sure you get his money first!' Trust me. Lional doesn't care about foreign policy."

"Where does he stand on religion?" said Reg, scratching the side of her head.

"As far away from the church as he can get while

still being in New Ottosland." She sat up a little straighter. "Why? What's religion got to do with this?"

Gerald looked at Reg, who shrugged again, short-hand for *Get on with it, sunshine.* Oh hell.

"Everything," he said, bracing himself. "The king told the Kallarapi delegation that their gods want New Ottosland and Kallarap to join together as one big happy family."

Melissande's jaw dropped. "He told them *what?*"

"Don't worry, it gets worse," added Reg. "What he actually *said* was the Kallarapi gods told him in person that they've chosen you to be Zazoor's bride."

"And the Kallarapi *believed* him?"

He nodded. "Apparently. They're going back home to give Zazoor the glad tidings."

Dazed, Melissande slumped against the fountain's centre pedestal. "In person? How? That's not even remotely possible. It's completely *im*possible."

"I think you'll find 'impossible' is a relative term, Your Highness."

She fixed him with a terrible stare. "Tell me exactly what happened, Gerald. All of it."

*So much for her being anaesthetised.*

By the time he'd finished re-enacting the meeting with Kallarap's delegation, all the hectic colour had drained out of her face, leaving her chalk-white with horror. "No! Lional *wouldn't.*" And then she laughed. "What am I saying? Of course he would! Oh, Melissande, you fool, you idiot. Stupid, stupid, *stupid* . . ." Beside herself with anger and regret she started pounding her fist into her leg.

Gerald caught her wrist in his hand. "Steady on. You'll hurt yourself."

"*Hurt* myself?" she said, wrenching free. "I should behead myself. He used Tavistock and your stupid bird to make the Kallarapi think their gods, which we aren't even supposed to *know* about, are on his side! And when they realise it was all a put-up job we're going to be up to our eyeballs in a religious war!" She buried her face in her hands. "Oh, Gerald. How could you let him do it?"

And look! It was *his* fault again! "Let him? Are you saying I could've *stopped* him?"

"You could've tried!" she retorted, raising her face to him once more. Her eyes were brimful of tears again. "You're the court wizard, Gerald. You've got a responsibility to this kingdom and its people to protect them from harm!"

Now hang on, that was just downright unreasonable. "From *harm*, yes!" he shouted. "But nobody ever said I had to protect them from the *king*! You left that little detail out of the job description, didn't you, Your Highness?" Stung into movement, he stamped backwards and forwards in front of the fountain. "In case you hadn't noticed, Melissande, your brother Lional is as mad as a meat axe!"

"He is *not*! she shouted back. "He's temperamental, I grant you. Impatient. Occasionally insensitive. And yes, all right, sometimes he acts without considering the consequences and then expects other people to clean up the mess! But he's not *mad*!"

As he turned, exploding with baffled outrage, Reg flapped into his face. Hovering with difficulty she said, eyes flashing, "Don't say it don't say it don't *say* it!"

"Say what?" he hissed, sticking out his arm for

her to perch on before she had a heart attack. "I wasn't going to say anything!" He snuck a quick look at Melissande, who was gurgling down the last of the whiskey and surreptitiously wiping away tears. "But you know I'm right. You said it yourself. Lional's stark staring bonkers!"

Reg clacked her beak impatiently. "Look, Gerald, you know that, I know that, probably the apprentice scullery maid knows that . . . but there's no point saying it to *her*. He's family and that'll always come first. At least to someone like Melissande."

He stared. "You just called her Melissande. Are you feeling all right?"

Before Reg could stab his eye wtih her beak, the princess cleared her throat. "Excuse me, I don't mean to interrupt or anything but we happen to have a *crisis* on our hands, in case you hadn't noticed!"

*I swear, the bloody woman is as bad as her brother.* "A crisis? Really?" He parked Reg back on the chair and marched to the fountain. "Are you sure? I thought it was just an interesting variation on the giddy social whirl that is life in the royal court of New Ottosland!"

She glared at him from behind her foggy glasses. "That's not funny!"

"No? Well, neither was being in that meeting!"

"And for all the good you did, Mr Royal Court Wizard, it's a great pity you *were* in it!"

"Ha. Royal court wizard," he said bitterly. "And what a crock *that's* turned out to be. I don't mind telling you, Melissande, accepting this stupid job was the *biggest* mistake of my *life*!"

"And the biggest mistake of *my* life, *Gerald*," she

retorted, precariously thrusting her face into his, "was *offering* it to you!"

They glared at each other, nose to nose. After a fraught moment Reg cleared her throat. "Entertaining as this is, I don't think it's going to get us very far past a double homicide. I suggest we all take a deep breath and discuss the situation rationally."

"You know," said Melissande, splashily slumping again, "I was just starting to like you, Gerald. I really thought that together you and I could work to make New Ottosland a better place. But now . . ."

Still fuming, he watched as her green eyes overflowed with yet more tears. This time he had the nasty suspicion they came from her heart and not a bottle of whiskey. He crossed his arms and stared at the ceiling.

"Oh, no. You're not getting me with that trick. The tears of a woman are to me as rain on a statue. I am impervious. Unmoved. See?" He looked at her. She was still crying. "Oh *bugger*," he said, pulled off his Fandawandi silk robe and climbed into the fountain beside her.

Melissande shifted over to make room. "And this is supposed to make me feel better, is it?" she enquired, sniffing. "Well, it won't. The only thing that's going to make me feel better is waking up in my bed to discover this has been nothing but a very bad dream."

*Which makes two of us.* "Look, Melissande. I would've stopped the king if I could but everything happened so fast and, to be honest, I was afraid of making things worse."

She patted his knee. "It's all right," she sighed. "I

know what Lional's like when he gets the bit between his teeth. I'm the only one who's ever been able to stop him, and even then, not often. I should've been there. This is my fault, not yours."

"No, it's Lional's fault," said Gerald, and covered her hand with his.

Reg glided from the back of her chair to the top of the fountain and looked down at them, her head on one side. "Go on then, kiss and make up. You know you want to."

Only the crystal ball's off-key chiming from the workshop saved her.

"What's that racket?" said Melissande.

Still glaring at Reg, Gerald said, "My crystal ball. Someone's trying to contact me."

Reg was grinning. "Better answer it then, sunshine. With any luck it'll be that Markham boy."

Melissande's eyebrows lifted. "What Markham boy?"

"A friend," he said. "Who may have some information that can help get us out of this mess."

She shoved the wet hair away from her face. "Gerald Dunwoody. You haven't gone blabbing about this to a complete *stranger*, have you?"

"Monk's not a stranger. He's my very good friend."

"Well he's not *my* very good friend! I don't have any friends, unless you count Boris. And Rupert. And *don't* bother telling me how pathetic that is," she added to Reg. "I know perfectly well how pathetic that is."

"It's all right," Gerald assured her hastily. "You can trust Monk. And no, he doesn't know anything."

"Then how can he possibly help?"

"Blimey," said Reg, rolling her eyes. "Make up your mind, ducky."

As Melissande threw a handful of water at her he summoned the chiming crystal ball with a hurried "*Ventifastioso.*"

A moment later it floated into the foyer and came to a gentle halt midair in front of him, pulsing an urgent bright blue. As he waved his hand in front of it the pulsing stopped, the blue faded, and Monk appeared in the depths of the crystal, cutting off a chime in mid-ring.

"Ooo-kay," he said, a grin spreading slowly over his face. "I'm not even going to ask."

"Good," said Gerald, acutely aware of Melissande squashed damply beside him. "What have you found out?"

Monk waved a reproving finger. "Hang on, hang on, not so fast. Aren't you going to introduce me?"

"Do I have to?"

"Only if you want my help."

He sighed. "Monk, Her Royal Highness Princess Melissande. Your Highness, Monk Markham. There. You're introduced. Now I'm kind of in the middle of something here, so—"

Monk grinned. "No kidding."

"*Markham!*"

Monk relented. "All right! Keep your hat on, Dunnywood." Another grin. "And everything else while you're at it."

*You can't kill him, you need him.* "Monk. Have you managed to track down any of those wizards yet?"

"One. Sort of," said Monk. "Bottomley. The others are all foreign nationals, that takes more time."

"What do you mean, sort of?"

Monk shrugged. "I mean I've got him entering New Ottosland, but not leaving."

Melissande shoved herself into the ball's field of vision. "Do you mean *Humphret* Bottomley?"

"Yes, Your Highness."

"And why are you investigating the whereabouts of Humphret Bottomley?"

"Because Gerald asked me to."

*Thanks, Monk.* "Look, Melissande," said Gerald. "I'll explain later."

She glowered. "You certainly will." She turned back to the crystal ball. "I don't know where you learned this, Mr Markham, but I suggest you recheck your source of information. Humphret Bottomley certainly *did* leave New Ottosland. Months ago, and good riddance."

"Call me Monk," said Monk, cheerfully. "Your Highness, I don't know what to tell you. Two weeks after he started work at your brother's court his family got a letter saying he'd been offered an even better position somewhere else and he'd contact them when he got there. But they've not heard a peep from him since. There's an official investigation been launched but I don't know what it's found out, and if I start poking around asking questions—"

Alarmed, Gerald straightened. "Hell, no, don't do that! The last thing I need is the DoT noticing me." He chewed at his thumb. "How soon will you be able to track down the others?"

"How should I know? I'm a wizard, Gerald, not a miracle-worker," Monk said severely. "Trust me, I'll call you when I've got any news."

He couldn't ask for more than that. "Thanks. Monk, I really appreciate it. Talk to you soon, bye!" And he severed the connection before any awkward questions could be asked.

Melissande poked him. "Are you going to tell me what's going on or do I have to—"

"Yes. But first—" He sent the crystal ball back to the workshop then, with a certain amount of grunting and scraped shins, clambered out of the fountain and held out his hand. "Your Highness?"

She let him assist her back to dry land. "Thank you." There was a pause as she extracted a distressed goldfish from her décolletage and dropped it back into the water. Then, cheeks pink, she cleared her throat. "Ah . . . look, Gerald . . ."

With a wave of his hand and a hex muttered under his breath, he dried them both off. "It's all right, Melissande. The idea of marrying Sultan Zazoor would drive anyone to drink."

Her lips twitched. "Marrying Zazoor and the rest of it. Gerald, what are we going to *do*?"

"Find a way out of this that doesn't involve gods, swords and blood leaking all over the place," he replied. "The reason I asked Monk to find my predecessors is so I can ask them for any tips on how to keep Lional in line. *Now* I'm thinking I need to know if they managed to dig up any dirt on him."

Her eyebrows shot up. "*Dirt?*"

He cleared his throat. "Yes. Sorry. But if he's as bent on gaining acceptance on the world stage as you say, the chance of being cold-shouldered by all the other nations might be the only thing to make him think twice!" He pulled a face. "Which I suppose is treason."

Melissande managed a swift, wry smile. "You *suppose*?" Then she sighed. "Oh well. We'll be skipping hand-in-hand to the headsman then, because I have no intention of marrying Zazoor even if he wants me, which he won't. The next time I see Lional I'm going to tell him where he can stick his wedding plans."

Uh-oh. Brave but foolhardy, surely. "Is that a good idea?"

"Probably not," she said, her expression grim. "But at least it'll take his mind off the Kallarapi for a while. And that might buy your friend Monk enough time to find Bondaningo and the others. Unless . . ." She looked suddenly hopeful. "Surely today's fiasco would put any number of important nations off-side? If you threatened to tell—"

"I can't do that!"

"Why not?"

"Because chances are the king would call my bluff and I'm as culpable as he is! I aided and abetted in duping the Kallarapi. Not only will I get clobbered for that, they'll find out about Tavistock—"

"And me," added Reg, flapping from the chair to his shoulder.

He rubbed her wing with the side of his finger. "Yes. And Reg. I can't risk—"

Melissande frowned. "You're not telling me Reg is some kind of bewitched criminal, are you? Because that would certainly explain a lot."

He shook his head. "No. She's not a criminal. And she really does grow on you, I promise."

"So does fungus," Melissande observed. "Are they related?"

"*Oy!*" said Reg.

"The thing is," he said quickly, "Reg is—unusual—and the fewer people who know about her the better."

"Especially *official* people?"

"Exactly."

"And Tavistock?" Melissande said delicately.

"Tavistock was . . . unsanctioned." He scrubbed a hand across his face. "Look. Lional's invited me to go hunting with him in the morning, and since I don't suppose there's any hope I can get out of it . . ."

"None whatsoever," she agreed. "Short of death. And even then I wouldn't put it past him not to tie you to the saddle as an example to any other slackers who might be watching."

She was right. Lional would. "Okay. So perhaps while we're cavorting about the countryside I could persuade him to forget this whole wedding idea."

She snorted. "Good luck."

"What? You don't think I should try?"

"Well, you can certainly *try*," she said. "But don't hold your breath waiting for Lional to agree. Not unless blue is your colour."

"Then what would you suggest?"

She sighed. "Honestly? I don't know. I need to sleep on it. In the meantime, I have work to do. Enjoy your outing with Lional tomorrow. And please don't get yourself killed. With my luck I'd inherit the bird."

She turned and headed for the door. He took a step after her. "Melissande—wait—"

She stopped. Looked back. "I apologise for barging in here the way I did," she said stiffly. "And for the things I said. Most unprofessional. I don't know what got into me."

"I do," said Reg. "The best part of a very large bottle of Orpington's Superior Single Malt."

The foyer doors banged shut with a bad-tempered thud.

"*Honestly*, Reg . . ." said Gerald, and collapsed into a convenient armchair.

"Well, she called me a fungus!" Reg complained, and flapped from his shoulder back to her chair. "Cheeky young besom. I'll give her fungus . . ." She rattled her tail feathers. "So. What now?"

*Now I go looking for my own large bottle of Orpington's*. "I find out what Lional's *really* after. Because I'll never believe he's been pining for Zazoor as a brother-in-law. There's a hell of a lot more to this than meets the eye, Reg." He thumped the chair with his fist. "Losing my temper with him was a mistake. I'll have to work twice as hard now, to make him believe I'm on his side."

"On his side?" said Reg. "What are you talking about? You're not on his side!"

"No, but I have to make him think I am."

"You mean *really* spy on him?" she shrieked. "Gerald Dunwoody, are you out of your *mind*?"

He snorted. "Probably."

"Then get back into it! That Lional's as flash as a rat with a gold tooth! You'll never bamboozle him into thinking you're after a life of crime. What do you think you are, a government secret agent?"

"Of course not," he said impatiently. "But I'm partly responsible for what's happened. If I don't do everything in my power to put things right I don't deserve to be a wizard. Now you can either help me or get out of my way."

After a brief internal battle she heaved a sigh, wings drooping, and said, "All right, Gerald. But when you're up to your armpits in alligators, don't say I didn't warn you."

He blew her a kiss. "I won't."

"I think I should come with you in the morning," she added. "Just to be on the safe side."

"You can't. Lional said to leave you behind, and flouting a royal command won't help me discover his secrets." Brooding, he picked at a loose thread in his trousers. "I wonder if a truth incant would work on him? I don't see why it shouldn't. I mean, they work on everyone else . . ."

Reg fluffed up her feathers. "You don't know any truth incants."

"No," he agreed. "But I'll bet you do."

"That's not the point," she said, looking harassed. "Truth incants are restricted to law enforcement, *and* for very good reason. They're extremely temperamental and can even cause brain damage if something goes wrong. I won't be responsible for turning you into a vegetable, Gerald."

And there she went, treating him like a wayward little brother again. He sat up. "Look, Reg, I appreciate the concern but I'm prepared to risk it."

"Well I'm not," she said. "Just you stick to your original plan, sunshine. At least for now."

"And if I can't convince Lional to let me in on whatever he's scheming? What then?"

She shrugged. "Then we'll just have to wait for the other shoe to drop, won't we?"

"When the other shoe drops," he said sourly, "it's going to hit me on the head and give me concussion. And when that happens, Reg, I'm going to blame *you!*"

After a restless night filled with disquieting dreams, Gerald walked into Lional's private stable yard at two minutes to seven. It was a pretty cobblestoned place with neat flowerbeds and some twenty stables with horses in most of them. Another ridiculous extravagance; what did one man need with twenty horses? Lional was little more than a gluttonous child, snatching at everything he saw just because he could.

*And everyone else in the kingdom goes without to keep him in ponies.*

Whoever thought royalty was a good idea?

It was a dank, cool morning; mist draped the treetops and curled in tendrils across the damp ground. Moisture beaded his hair and stippled his shiny black boots, his breeches and the jacket hastily conjured up from his existing wardrobe. Maybe when this was all over, provided he was still in one piece, he could set up shop as a *magical* tailor? He was certainly getting enough practice with clothes . . .

Lional, of course, had arrived before him. The king stood in the middle of the yard surrounded by a milling horde of black and tan hounds, all barking and snapping and slavering, competing for his attention. Lional laughed at them, his face alight with pleasure. He was sheathed in silk and supple leather, dark as midnight. A long-bladed hunting knife rode his right hip.

"Good *morning*, Professor!"

"Good morning, Your Majesty," Gerald replied, giving the hounds a wide berth and trying not to look at the prancing black monstrosity of a horse making a spirited attempt to flatten its handler as it was led from its stable. If Lional thought he was going to ride *that* thing he really *was* mad.

"Looking forward to our little expedition?" said Lional, taking the black monstrosity's reins and feeding it a sugar lump. "I know I am!"

"Ah . . ." Even though his belly was empty, he still wanted to be sick. "Certainly, Your Majesty. Wouldn't miss it for the world."

"*Excellent.* Now, let's mount up, shall we?" He clapped his hands. "Stable boy! The professor's horse, if you please!"

Oh hell, oh shit . . . He turned, braced for the sight of a second fire-breathing monster.

"This is Dorcas," said Lional as he vaulted—*vaulted*, the bloody show-off—into the black horse's saddle. "I'm sure the two of you will get along like peas in a pod."

Dorcas was a pony. A short, fat, mud-brown pony with a resigned expression and sleepy eyes. She stared at Gerald with a minimum of interest and he stared back with a maximum of surprise. Then he realized. Of course he was riding a Dorcas: how likely was it that Lional would risk being upstaged by his wizard?

"Get a leg over, Gerald!" said Lional, as his wild black horse fought the restraint of the bit and plunged amongst the excited hounds like something possessed. "The morning gallops away, sir, and so must we. Come, Demon!" Clapping his spurred heels to the black horse's flanks he charged out of the stable yard, scattering gravel and grooms. The hounds bolted in his wake, yelping.

The stable boy rolled his eyes as he manhandled Gerald into the saddle. "Have fun, sir."

He managed a faint, sickly smile. "Oh, yes. Fun. I knew I was doing this for a reason . . ." And then he bounced up and down until Dorcas reluctantly took the hint and shuffled off in the black horse's vanishing wake.

# CHAPTER SIXTEEN

It didn't take long for the hounds to flush their first quarry. Lional and Demon pounded after them across the open fields that stretched towards the woodland on the west side of the palace. Gerald and Dorcas laboured doggedly in their wake. Despite his rapidly increasing physical discomfort and his distaste for the purpose of the outing, he had to admit it was good to be outside breathing clean, fresh air. He felt . . . released.

More swiftly than he could believe, the palace and its problems had become his whole world, swallowing him alive. He felt like a sailor whose ship had been shrunk and forced into a bottle, its confines so close he could reach out and touch them with his fingertips.

And with the wide world beyond the bottle unattainable, the narrow world within it became . . . everything.

Far ahead, Lional drew rein and beckoned impatiently. His voice floated back on the damp morning breeze. "Hurry *up*, Professor!"

"Aye, aye, Captain," he muttered. Gritting his teeth, he clapped his heels to Dorcas's unenthusiastic sides and hurried.

Seven rabbits and two foxes later, he swore he'd never go hunting again.

Lional had let the hounds devour the rabbits and the foxes but their latest prize, a deer, he forbade them. By this time they were plunged deep into the Crown Forest, according to Lional an exclusive royal hunting preserve. The mist had cleared and the sky was a patchwork of blue and green, with golden columns of sunlight shafting cathedral-like between the lacework branches overhead. The only sounds as they rode further and further in were the muffled thudding of the horses' hooves, the panting and padding of the hounds, the jingling of harness, the occasional startled cries of invisible birds . . . and the last desperate gasps of the doomed creatures who could run no more.

Lional looked up from wiping his hunting knife on the flank of the slain doe. "Ah, Professor! There is nothing to match the taste of freshly roasted venison. Particularly when the kill is your own. We shall dine like kings tonight!"

The deer had been brought down in a small clearing littered with leaf mould and pocked with poisonous-looking mushrooms. Gerald, who couldn't bear to watch Reg humanely despatch a fieldmouse, swallowed nausea. He'd be dreaming of dagger teeth snarling and brown eyes glazed crimson with terror for the rest of his life. He slid down from happily dozing Dorcas and tied her reins to the nearest tree branch. Demon, trained to a hairsbreadth, stood like a statue with his reins still trailing.

"Well, Your Majesty, one of us will, anyway."

Lional laughed. "You're a witty man, Professor. I like witty men."

He nodded. *I wonder if he also likes men who vomit at the sight of blood?* He snuck a glance at his watch. Four hours they'd been out here, charging across the countryside, and all he had to show for it was blisters on his backside. In four hours the only thing he'd gotten Lional to discuss was how much he enjoyed killing things.

Good thing he *wasn't* a government secret agent. After a dismal performance like this one he'd be fired from that job, too.

Lional slid his knife back into its sheath and rose to his feet with smooth, athletic grace. "Yes," he mused, leaning his shoulder against the mossy trunk of a convenient tree. "I do like you, Gerald. Far more than the other tedious fellows I hired."

*And is that supposed to reassure me?* Gerald bowed. "A compliment indeed, Your Majesty. Thank you."

Lional smiled. "You're welcome."

"Speaking of those other wizards . . ." He throttled any sign of eagerness, kept his tone casual, uncaring. "Do you mind if I ask, sir, why none of them suited?"

"Not at all," said Lional. "I'll even answer you, Professor. In short they were dullards."

Well, that was a big help. "Dullards, Your Majesty?"

"Yes. Each time I had such hopes . . . and each time, alas, my hopes were dashed," said Lional, regretful. "You see, Gerald, I was searching for a man like myself, a man of *vision*. A man who understands the world and how it works. Who appreciates that timidity is the refuge of cowards. I sought for that rare man amongst the world's premier ranks of wizardry and had come to think I'd never find him. And then, just as I was about to surrender to despair . . . *you* came along." He laughed. "What a pity Melissande didn't ignore my hiring instructions long ago. Then I needn't have wasted so much time." His amusement faded and he frowned. "She's being difficult about the wedding, you know. Tiresome wench. As if she's ever going to get a better offer. As if she's going to get *any* offer apart from this one."

Condescending, patronising bastard. "It's just shock, Your Majesty," he said carefully. "Once it passes I'm sure she'll be eager to marry Sultan Zazoor. As you know, women don't possess the most powerful of intellects. They find it almost impossible to see the big picture."

Lional's eyebrows lifted. "And what big picture would that be, Professor?"

The surrounding forest had fallen deeply silent. Even the bright shafts of sunlight had faded, dimmed by incoming rain clouds high overhead. The hounds' panting as they lay sprawled around the carcass of the deer sounded even louder, impatient and foreboding. Gerald glanced at them uneasily and they stared back, eyes shining.

Here was his chance. It was now or never.

"The one you are painting, sir, with breathtaking brushstrokes. Your Majesty, I owe you a humble apology. I spoke hastily and without thought yesterday after the Kallarapi departed."

"You certainly did, Gerald," said the king, his

guarded gaze sharp and watchful. "Indeed, I was brought to the brink of doubting you."

"Your Majesty, it shames me to hear you say so," he said, and lowered his head in what he hoped looked like heartfelt contrition. "In my defence, allow me to say that your actions took me by surprise."

"I'll allow it," said Lional, after a moment.

*So far, so good.* He risked lifting his head. "It also shames me, Your Majesty, to recall my childish response to your bold attack upon the Kallarapi's rapacious demands. It is clear to me these are a rudely primitive people, desperately in need of New Ottosland's civilising influence."

"They certainly are."

"To be frank, Your Majesty, after my ill-judged actions yesterday I wouldn't blame you if you chose to dispense with my services and sent me packing."

Even though Lional appeared relaxed as he leaned against the tree trunk, there was about him the air of a nocked arrow, quivering and ready for flight. He smiled. "Oh, no, Professor. That would be quite the over-reaction. You are young, and allowances must be made for youth."

Gerald pressed his hand to his heart. "Your Majesty is graciousness personified."

"Yes, I am, aren't I?" said Lional.

"Then . . . I am forgiven?"

"Of course you are."

*But only because you want something from me. What is it, you smarmy sanctimonius maniac? What else do you want me to do for you?* "Thank you, Your Majesty. How can I repay such generosity?"

"Oh . . ." Lional waved a careless hand. "I'm sure

I'll think of something." Pushing away from the tree, he began a casual circumnavigation of the clearing. The hounds watched him, ears pricked, tongues lolling. "See here, Gerald, this dead deer," he said, and kicked it casually in passing. "It's dead because I killed it. Because tonight I will be hungry and require sustenance. There was no malice in my action. Certainly I committed no *crime*. I merely obeyed an immutable law of nature: the strong devour the weak in order to survive and prosper."

As Lional circled, Gerald found himself turning too so the king never managed to get behind him. Suddenly it was very important Lional not get behind him. His mouth was dry. "As you intend to devour Kallarap, Your Majesty?"

"Is that what you think?"

He nodded. "Of course. Marrying Melissande to Zazoor is but the first . . . mouthful of the meal, is it not?"

Lional laughed, a soft whisper of amusement. "You disapprove?"

*Yes, yes, yes!* "Not at all, Your Majesty. The strong must always overpower the weak. As you say, it's the law of nature."

"But you are curious, Gerald. I see the question in your eyes. Why bother with conquering Kallarap? That barren wasteland of sand and sun. What use can it be to lush delicious New Ottosland?"

"I assume for access to the trade routes, Your Majesty," he replied. "They represent significant financial value to New Ottosland, after all."

"Yes," agreed Lional. "But they are merely the beginning."

Deep in his eyes burned a fervid, greedy flame. Seeing it, Gerald felt his chest tighten. *Here it comes . . . here it comes . . .* "Princess Melissande has told me Kallarap possesses a formidable army, Your Majesty, while New Ottosland stands defenceless. If they should resist . . ."

"New Ottosland defenceless?" Again Lional laughed. "Not at all, Professor. New Ottosland has you."

*Me? What the hell?* The tightness in his chest increased almost to suffocation point. "Forgive me, Your Majesty. I'm afraid I don't follow you. I am but one man. I can't defeat an army."

Lional stopped walking and skewered him with a stare. "But you're *not* a man, Gerald. You're a *wizard*."

Oh . . . bugger. *Of course. Of course.* "Actually, Your Majesty, I'm both."

A heartbeat's pause, then Lional started circling again. "I'm only interested in the wizard. Take my advice, Gerald: put the man in a box, lock it and throw away the key. He'll only get in our way."

He took a deep, painful breath and let it out slowly. "*Our* way, sir?"

"Yes, Gerald. I'm asking you to join me."

"Join you? In . . . conquering Kallarap?"

"In creating a kingdom the likes of which this world has never seen," said Lional. "In driving New Ottosland to the very pinnacle of international power and prestige where she has always deserved to be! Every king of New Ottosland before me was a weakling, a coward, a slave to tiny dreams! Not I! *This* Lional is a visionary. *This* Lional has greatness. *This* Lional is man to be *reckoned* with!"

As his voice rose higher and louder, the panting black and tan hounds surged to their feet and howled, refusing to lie down again until he kicked them into cowering submission.

"Well, Gerald?" he demanded, once the hounds were subdued around him. "Will you join me? I know you possess the ambition, I can see it in your eyes! You think you hide it but you're mistaken, my friend! We're cut from the same cloth, we hunger for the same things. You're no more for a small life than I am, Professor! You have dreams too, of glory, of greatness! Don't dare to deny it for I'll know you're lying!"

Gerald felt his face heat. Ambition wasn't a crime . . . so why did it sound shameful when Lional talked of it?

*Because his ambition demands the subjugation—the destruction—of anyone or anything standing in his way.*

He looked at the forest floor, afraid Lional would read the thought in his eyes, where he'd already read too much for comfort or safety.

"Well, Gerald?" Lional said softly. "What do you say?"

*I say you're mad, you're crazy, you're stark staring bonkers.* He kept his gaze lowered, hoping Lional would take it for humility. "Your Majesty, speech is almost beyond me. The honour—the trust—where do I begin?"

"By saying yes, Gerald. Say yes and I'll make you the most powerful man in New Ottosland after myself. No pitiful rules. No pathetic regulations. Your word will be law. And the Scunthorpes of this world will be as dust beneath your feet."

His head snapped up. "*Scunthorpes?*"

Now Lional's smile was wicked with mischief. "Foolish fellow. Did you think I'd grant you access to my court without knowing *exactly* who you are? An hour after our first meeting I knew everything about you, Gerald. Where you were born. Went to school. Qualified as a wizard. Your first job. Your second job. Your disaster at Stuttley's. None of it matters. You made me a *lion*."

And see where that pride, that *folly*, had led him. When he could trust his voice he said, "Your Majesty is too kind."

More laughter. "Kind? Kings can't afford to be kind. Now answer my question."

*Will you join me?* How could he possibly join Lional? Help him force Melissande into an unwanted marriage—conspire with him to destroy the Kallarapi—and after that, who knew?

*But I started this, God help me, and then I kept it going. So if the only way to beat Lional is to join him . . .*

He bowed, so deeply his nose nearly touched his knees. "I would be honoured to join you, Your Majesty."

"How honoured?" said Lional, regarding him playfully.

*Now* what? "Your Majesty?"

"Honoured enough to make me a dragon?"

"A dragon," he said blankly, after a long pause. "Your Majesty, dragons don't exist."

"Ah, but Gerald, they *do*!" replied Lional, exultant. "They exist in our imaginations. And what can be imagined can be created. After all, you turned my cat into a lion. Now you can turn a lizard into a dragon. I have the perfect specimen, as it happens, all ready and waiting."

"Your Majesty—"

"Now, now, don't go getting *coy* on me, Gerald! And don't try telling me you can't do it, either, for I shan't believe you."

A *dragon*? Why the *hell* would Lional want a—

*Oh hell. Oh no.* The third and final deity of Kallarap, mightier than the other two put together. Grimthak, whose earthly form manifested as a dragon.

*What have I done?*

This was his fault, all of it. If he hadn't been so desperate to stay in New Ottosland, to prove he was brilliant, if he hadn't turned Tavistock into a lion then Lional would never have hatched this plan. Or even if he did, without Tavistock-the-lion, without Reg at his fingertips, he could never put it into action.

*If one person dies over this I'll be a murderer.*

No matter what happened he must never give Lional what he wanted. He must never turn *anything* into a dragon.

"I'm sorry, Your Majesty," he said, pouring as much regret into his voice as he could muster. "I'm afraid I'm not good enough for that kind of magic."

Lional slid a hand into his breeches pocket. "On the contrary, Gerald. I'm afraid you're far *too* good."

He frowned. There was a note in Lional's voice that he'd never heard before. Gone was the petulance. The peevishness. The volatile good humour. The handsome face was suddenly older. Grimmer. Suddenly Lional's face was . . . frightening.

He felt himself take an unintended step backwards.

His heart was beating so hard he felt sick. "You knew all along I had no intention of joining you."

Lional laughed. At his feet his hunting hounds whimpered. "Of course. It's true you have ambition—just not enough. Or the right kind. But it was amusing watching you try to pretend. A piece of advice, Gerald: don't go on the stage. I'm afraid as an actor you make a very fine wizard."

His heart pounded brutally against his ribs. "*Are* you mad, then? Or are you evil?"

Lional shrugged. "I'm both. Or neither. It's not significant. They're just words, Gerald. Hot air. Blah blah blah."

"You must know I'm oath-bound to stop you."

Another shrug. "You're oath-bound to *try*." Lional's lip curled, sneering. "You orthodox wizards, you're all the same. Cowards. Hidebound by rules and regulations. Rigidly unadventurous. Suffering from a catastrophic failure of imagination. Incapable of seeing past your oaths and your artificially imposed boundaries to what is possible. Just *once* I wish I could meet a wizard who—"

Without warning and with blinding speed he pulled his hand from his pocket and threw something, very hard and very fast.

Gerald flinched. Pure, unthinking reflex raised his hand, outstretched his fingers, curled them around the flying missile . . .

*Oh my God!*

. . . and he was caught, trapped in a web with strands of metaphysical steel. He could breathe, move his eyes, but that was all. He couldn't run. He felt his fingers convulse around the thrown lump of rock . . . and then he cried out, assaulted by a tornado of dreadful images and excruciating pain. Faces screaming. Flame-licked bodies writhing. Greasy smoke spiralling into the air. And Lional, his golden face a glowing mask of power . . .

"I must say, Gerald, it's rather a pity you have to die," said Lional, plucking the rock from his nerveless grasp. "There are a number of incantations requiring the involvement of two wizards that I'd really like to try and you're the first wizard I've met who could manage them. Ah well. Life is full of small disappointments. I'll just have to console myself with the taking of your formidable powers." A gentle hand reached out and patted him on the cheek. "I expect you're wishing you'd made me that dragon now, aren't you?"

Speech was beyond him, his mind and will held as fast as his body. But inside the confines of his skull he was screaming.

*I'll kill you . . . I'll kill you . . . you bastard, I'll kill you . . .*

"Useful little gadget, this, don't you think?" Lional said brightly, tossing the rock from hand to elegant hand. "It's called a Wizard Trap. An appropriate title, don't you agree? I made it courtesy of an interesting little book I—well, let's just say *I* inherited it."

There was sweat beading on his forehead, rolling down his face and into his eyes. *Lional's a wizard? That isn't possible. This can't be happening . . .*

Lional's smile widened. "Ah, Gerald . . . but it *is*."

And then the forest clearing was filled with power, a black seething maelstrom that boiled inside Lional's deceptively commonplace aura as though searching for a way to burst free. The hunting hounds howled and fled into the shadows. Dorcas broke her bridle and bolted. Demon, sweating, stayed where he was.

Ignoring them, Lional stepped forward and raised his hands, eyes narrowed, face contorted into something no longer human. From between his lips hissed a stream of filthy words that burned the air to a stinking foulness . . . and a searing ball of power exploded from his outstretched fingertips.

It struck Gerald over his heart. Lifted him high into the air. Flung him against a tree.

The world ended.

The first thing he heard as consciousness begrudgingly returned was a voice saying, "He's not dead, is he? Please tell me he's not dead. You've no idea of the paperwork that's involved if he's dead."

A second voice said snippily, "Your stupid brother almost gets him killed and all you can think of is *paperwork*?"

The first voice replied, seeing the snippy and raising it a snide, "If anybody here is stupid it's your precious wizard, falling off *Dorcas* for the love of Saint Snodgrass! The wretched pony's one hundred and one in the shade and can barely get out of a trot!"

A third voice said silkily, "Melissande? What are you doing here? Have you changed your mind about marrying Zazoor?"

Gerald unglued his eyes. Slowly, grindingly, the world swam into fuzzy focus. He was in bed. Somebody was sitting on his aching chest. They were wearing feathers and an outraged expression. *Reg.* And to his left, camouflagingly trouser clad, on her feet and staring at his bedroom doorway with a mixture of hostility and apprehension, was Melissande.

"Oh," she said, chin lifted. "Lional. I can explain. I was just—"

"Returning to your apartments. Where you shall remain until you agree to do your duty. I shall be along presently to chastise you."

"*Chastise* me!" she echoed, furious. "You're not my father and I'm not five years old! How *dare* you—"

"*Melissande.*"

She went red, then white. "Fine. Banish me to my rooms. Put a guard at the doors while you're at it, why don't you, and see to it I'm fed on nothing but bread and water from now until doomsday! I don't care. You're making a mistake with the Kallarapi, Lional, and the only duty I have is to see that you realise that!"

She marched from the room without a backwards glance. Lional stepped aside to let her pass then approached the bed, his expression grave. Despite his pounding head Gerald tried to sit up. "Your Majesty . . ."

"Gerald!" screeched Reg. "You're awake!"

"More or less. What happened?"

"What happened?" Lional echoed. "Don't you remember?"

"No," he said, after a moment's frantic thinking. "The last thing I recall is riding out of the stable yard. I take it I fell off?"

"Comprehensively," said Lional, smiling. "I'm afraid Dorcas put her foot in a rabbit hole and threw you headfirst into a tree. It's a miracle you didn't break your neck. You are concussed, though, according to my doctor."

"Ouch," he said, and with tentative fingers explored the top of his head. "*Ouch!*" He looked at Lional. "What about Dorcas? Is she all right?"

"Who cares?" said Reg. "Are *you?*"

He took a quick inventory. "I think so. Apart from my head . . . and my chest."

"Your chest? Ah. Yes," said Lional. "Possibly you were bruised by my saddle. I carried you home on Demon, you see." He laughed. "Draped before me just like a kill."

Oh. How *embarrassing.* "Your Majesty, I'm sorry, I—"

"I say!" said an excited voice from the bedroom doorway. "He's awake? That's *marvellous!*"

Rupert. Underneath a voluminous green apron he wore canary yellow plus-fours and a bright violet shirt. His socks were striped red and pink.

"Blimey," breathed Reg. "That's no sight for a sick man to bear!"

Lional speared his brother with a look. "Yes, Rupert. Now isn't there a butterfly somewhere you can chloroform?"

Rupert blinked. "No. I *never* chloroform my butterflies, not unless they're suffering."

"Trust me, Rupert, that can be arranged! Now go away. The professor doesn't need to be disturbed by your mindless drivel, he needs to rest."

"Oh," said Rupert. "All right. If you say so, Lional. I'm so happy you're not hurt, Gerald. If you're feeling up to it later perhaps you'd like to come visit me?

The Grandiose Feather-Headed Lobbet babies hatched an hour ago and they're ever so sweet."

"That would be very nice, Your Highness," he said weakly, not daring to look at Lional. "Once my head stops aching."

"Wonderful!" said Rupert, beaming. "Only Grandiose Feather-Headed Lobbet babies don't stay sweet for very long, so—"

"*Rupert.*"

Rupert departed. "*Dreadful* man," said Lional, shuddering. "I sometimes wonder if he isn't a changeling." Then he smiled. "Now, Gerald, you must rest. There are urgent matters of state about which I must ask your advice, as soon as you feel up to it."

Wonderful. Just what he needed. *I really feel rotten. I'll never ride again.* "Of course, Your Majesty," he said weakly. "Thank you, Your Majesty."

"Oh, no, Gerald," said Lional, and pressed a friendly hand to his shoulder. "Thank *you.*"

"Well!" he said as the door closed quietly behind the king. "Do you suppose he's concussed too?"

"Don't know, don't care," said Reg. "How bad are you feeling really? Can you get up?"

He raised his head from the pillow and nearly vomited. "I don't think so. I feel hideous. And why would I want to get up, anyway?"

"Because we're leaving."

"*What?*"

Reg lowered her voice. "Look, sunshine. I don't know exactly what happened out there because I zigged when I should've zagged and lost you for a bit in all that dratted greenery, but I do know this. *Whatever* happened didn't have anything to do with that horse sticking its clumsy hoof down a rabbit hole!"

His jaw dropped. "You were *following* me?"

She had the grace to look guilty. "I had a feeling, all right? And my feelings are never wrong." She leaned closer. "I think Lional tried to *murder* you."

Oh, for the love of Saint Snodgrass. This was taking the little brother routine *way* too far. "*Murder* me? Why would Lional want to *murder* me?"

Her expression became mulish. "There could be any number of reasons. Lord knows *I've* been tempted once or twice. But when I finally found you in that wretched forest, Gerald, you were laid out like a corpse at the base of a tree and Lional was staring down at you as though you'd just swallowed the keys to his Treasury. Proper put out, he was, swearing and muttering and carrying on." She sniffed. "Very un-royal behaviour."

He rubbed his aching head. "Really? Knowing you I thought it was par for the course."

"Gerald, stop trying to be clever and *listen*! Not only was that sluggard Dorcas nowhere to be seen, because it had bolted for home, when I looked it over in its stable I couldn't find hide nor hair to prove it'd fallen flat on its face."

"So?"

"So a fall like Lional says it had, should've broken its knobbly knees! That nag shouldn't have been able to hobble ten yards, let alone gallop all the way home to bed!" Reg snapped. "And I'll tell you something else. There wasn't a rabbit hole within a hundred yards of that tree you were supposed to have been thrown against. Show me your chest."

"What? No, I'm not going to show you my chest!"

With an impatient cackle she tugged open his night-shirt. "Lional says his saddle bruised you. Well, I'm not looking at any bruises, sunshine, I'm looking at three chest hairs and some underdeveloped pectoral muscles. And what does that tell you?"

"That you've got no respect for a man's privacy," he muttered, covering himself again.

"No, you idiot! Lional's *lying*! If you got yourself knocked silly by falling off that pony then I'm Shugat's maiden aunty. And trust me, I'm not."

"Reg, this is ridiculous. If Lional wanted to murder me he could've done it while I was unconscious on the ground! Why bring me all the way back to the palace? You've got this all wrong."

"Oh, *Gerald*!" said Reg, stamping one foot for emphasis. "Forget about my outside and remember what I am on the *inside*. What I *was*. I *know* about these things, you fool, they were my meat and drink and they put me in a feathered dress for the rest of my unnaturally long life and I don't want you to end up the same way, or worse! Just because I don't know *why* Lional wants you dead doesn't mean he *doesn't*! Or that he won't try again! That's why you've got to get out of here. You might not be so lucky next time."

He frowned. He'd never seen Reg this upset before. She was really frightened. He felt an answering stab of fear. If *Reg* was really frightened . . . He brushed a fingertip across the top of her head. "Sorry," he said gently. "It's just a little hard to believe, that's all. As a rule, tailor's sons from Nether Wallop don't have kings trying to kill them."

She rattled her tail feathers. "Not unless they've done a *very* poor job with their pin tucks, no."

It was ridiculous. But Reg was so convinced . . . "Oh lord," he groaned. "What's Melissande going to say when I tell her you think her brother tried to kill me?"

"Nothing useful," Reg said briskly. "She probably won't believe you. Lional's got her well and truly hoodwinked, the cad."

"Well, I have to tell somebody in authority here." He screwed his eyes shut against the pounding pain inside his skull. "I suppose I could tell Rupert."

Reg laid a wing across his forehead. "Don't look now, Gerald, but fever is making you delirious."

He managed, just, to push the wing away. "He's next in line for the crown, Reg. It's my duty to tell him."

"And *if* you tell him, Gerald, what is he going to do? Send his trained attack butterflies to carry Lional off the throne and put him under lock and key?"

He hardly heard her exasperated question. Suddenly there was a fuzzy kind of ringing in his ears and the world was going smeary round the edges. "No. No, of course not," he said vaguely. "But something . . ."

"Gerald?" said Reg, sounding alarmed and querulous. "What's wrong? Gerald! Talk to me!"

He tried, but his tongue felt like a fat roll of flannel, his eyes wouldn't focus and none of his limbs would obey him. Reg was saying something else but he couldn't hear her, she sounded as though she were speaking from the opposite end of a very long tunnel.

And then all the lights went out, and he tumbled headfirst into welcome oblivion.

# CHAPTER SEVENTEEN

When Gerald opened his eyes again, morning sunlight was streaming through the bedroom window, bathing his face in golden warmth and painting the cream bedspread butter yellow. His headache was gone, and the dull pain in his chest with it.

"Hmmph," said Reg's slightly muffled voice from above him. "You're awake." He looked up: she was sitting on the bed's padded headboard, consuming a mouse. "It's about time. The clock's just struck seven."

"Reg! How many times do I have to say it? *No* eating in bed!"

"Now, now, keep your underpants on," she replied, unmoved. "I'm not a young woman any more and a sight like that might do me a mischief."

"So help me, Reg, if you leave the tail in the bed-clothes again . . ."

Hopping onto a convenient pillow she slurped down the last inch of mouse and gave a genteel burp.

"Happy now? Right. The way I see it, if we get a move on we should be back through the portal to Ottosland before that murderous lunatic Lional has even opened his eyes. Do you want to start packing or shall I?"

He sat up. "Neither. I'm having a bath."

Closing the ensuite door on her outraged shrieks, he inspected himself in the mirror as the tub filled with steaming water. The lump on his skull had almost disappeared and the sore spot on his chest barely protested when he poked at it. That was the good news. The bad news was his memory still hadn't returned. And, after yesterday's hours in the saddle, the rest of his body felt like it had been racked.

Inching himself into the bath, moaning as the seeping heat began to unknot his tortured muscles, he closed his eyes and tried to make sense of the chaos that was currently his life. In the sober light of morning, and without that vicious pounding headache, the idea of Lional as a homicidal maniac seemed increasingly unlikely. Not only was the king completely without motive, wizards just weren't that easy to murder. They had in-built alarms. Extra sensitivities. Wizards got murdered by other wizards, not civilians, even if said civilians were royal.

So. That disposed of one problem. Unfortunately it still left him with several others, the most pressing of which was the Kallarapi situation.

Even if Lional *had* tried to murder him, which he *hadn't*, he couldn't possibly leave New Ottosland before making sure he'd prevented a full-scale religious conflict with the kingdom's neighbour . . . or found a way to stop Melissande's unwilling marriage to Zazoor.

If Lional was so keen on asking for his advice, he'd make sure to give him some. Forget the marriage. Pay your debts. Pull your head in. And *no* religious hanky-panky.

Once all that was accomplished *then* he'd go home to Ottosland.

Much cheered, he finished bathing.

Reg had made herself comfortable on his pillow and was in the middle of a half-hearted primping session. She took one look at his face as he emerged pink, damp and towel-wrapped from the bathroom and groaned. "You're not leaving, are you?"

"I'm sorry," he said, hunting through his chest of drawers for fresh clothing. "I know you're worried but I can't leave until I've stopped Lional from provoking a war when he doesn't have an army to protect his kingdom with."

"He doesn't have one *now*," said Reg. "But that doesn't mean he can't get one."

He looked up from buttoning his shirt. "How? There's no such thing as a mail-order defence force."

"There doesn't need to be. You forget that somewhere in this drafty old pile of a palace there's a nursery with a whole battalion of tin soldiers in it."

"So?"

"So you've got a nifty knack of turning one thing into another, haven't you?"

He gaped at her. "*What*? You think I'd turn tin soldiers into *real* ones? That could *hurt* people?"

"Not willingly, no," said Reg. "But I think if Lional put his mind to it he could be very . . . persuasive."

"I would *never* use my magic to make something that could hurt people, no matter *what* Lional said!"

Reg considered her wing tips. "It's not his pretty speeches that worry me, sunshine."

"So now you're saying he'd try to—to *torture* me? How? I'm a wizard, Reg! A damned powerful one as it turns out. He wouldn't get close enough to torture me, I'd have him flat on his back and across the other side of the room before he took one step towards me."

Reg shrugged. "He managed to lay you out cold and get you to forget how it happened, Gerald. Right now I wouldn't put anything past him."

"Oh, don't start that again! For Lional to do what you're suggesting he'd have to be a wizard himself, and he's not. I can smell a wizard a mile away."

She considered him steadily. "Really? You didn't smell that tatty old Shugat, did you, till he was right under your nose."

*Damn.* He didn't think she'd noticed that. "Shugat's not a wizard. Not in the accepted sense of the word. He's a holy man. All bets are off when it comes to religion. And Lional is *not* a wizard. The only thing he smells of is expensive aftershave. Anyway, if he was a wizard he wouldn't need me, would he? Now can we *please* not talk about this any more?"

She flapped from the pillow to the chest of drawers. "What about Humphret Bottomley?"

He retreated to the bedroom armchair and threw himself into it. "What about him?"

"He's missing."

"No, he's not!"

"That Markham boy says no-one's heard from him in months," she retorted. "In my book that's called missing." She sniffed. "But in yours, apparently, it's called wilfully disregarding the facts."

"What facts? There are no facts! There's just you having some kind of mid-life crisis!"

She fixed him with a gimlet glare. "Trust me, sunshine, when I'm having a crisis you'll be the first to know. Now wake up your crystal ball and call that Markham boy. Tell him what's happened around here in the last day and see if he doesn't agree with me. And while you're at it, see if he knows how many more of Lional's ex-court wizards have disappeared."

He drummed his heels into the carpet. "Reg . . ." But it was depressingly clear from the look on her face that she'd give him no rest until he indulged her, so he stamped to the workshop, activated the crystal ball . . . and completely failed to get a call through to Monk.

"Did you get the address right?" said Reg, flapping from the bench to Gerald's shoulder. "Try the wretched thing again."

"Yes of course I got the address right," he said, teeth gritted. "And I was just about to try again."

He did. Still nothing.

"Maybe it's the ball," said Reg. There was just the faintest hint of panic in her voice. "It's an old ball, Gerald, it was fourth or fifth hand when you got it and it's taken a bashing in the last few years. Try it again. Third time lucky."

"Or unlucky, as the case may be," he said a moment later, staring at the inert lump of crystal in front of him. "Now what?"

Reg clattered her beak. "Now we sneak into Madam Fashion Plate's office and use *her* crystal ball."

"Why sneak? Why don't I just go and ask Melissande—"

"Because she's being guarded under lock and key, remember? We don't have time to fart about with all that. Being underhand is faster."

"What about my breakfast?"

"Bugger your breakfast, Gerald!" snapped Reg, launching herself into the air. "We have to get cracking. I've got a very bad feeling about this!"

Groaning, he followed her out of the workshop. "Wait, Reg, I really need my breakfast!"

But she was already on her way to the foyer, so he shoved his sockless feet into his shoes and hurried to join her.

"You'll have to pick the lock," said Reg, as he rattled Melissande's office door-handle. "Quick, before a lackey comes along."

Gerald rolled his eyes. "A lackey would be useful, Reg. I could ask them to let us in."

"At this hour of the morning?" she snapped. "Go on, you know how to diddle it. Stop dithering and get us inside!"

He turned his head to stare at her nose to beak. "*What* has gotten *into* you?"

"I told you. I've got a very bad feeling."

"So have I," he muttered, and sprung the lock with a word and snap of his fingers. "Doctors call it dangerously low blood sugar." They slipped into the office. "So where's the crystal ball?" he whispered, staring at Melissande's desk. "It was right there, she was using it as a paperweight."

"Search me," said Reg. "She must've had an unexpected fit of tidiness and put it away somewhere. Start looking."

*If Melissande finds out about this she's going to kill me.* He hunted in the cupboards, behind the books in the bookcases and in the filing cabinets. Opened all the desk drawers, including the ones that were locked, and nearly bit his tongue at what he found in the last.

"Reg!"

"You've found it? Excellent!"

"No," he said, and held up a book bound in dimpled red leather. "But I found this!"

"Gerald," said Reg severely. "We don't have *time* for reading!"

"It's a textbook," he said, flipping open the cover. "Monk's sister Emmerabiblia's got the same one. Melissande's been studying witchcraft!"

"So she's got a hobby! At least it's not butterflies! Now is that crystal ball in here or not?"

"Not," he said, tucking the textbook under his arm.

"Maybe she took it with her when Lional locked her in her apartments," said Reg. "We'd better go and ask her."

"How can we ask her? Guard, lock and key, remember?"

"So we get rid of the guard, unlock the doors and *then* we ask her."

"I don't know which part of the palace she lives in."

Reg groaned. "That bang on the head really rattled your marbles, didn't it? You've got her textbook, haven't you? Use it!"

Oh. Right. Feeling like an idiot he spread his fingers flat against the book's cover and closed his eyes. "*Locatio Melissande anuxi.*" An answering tingle of energy ran through his hand. The book quivered and tugged. "All set," he said, and headed for the door. "Let's go."

Melissande's suite of rooms was four staircases and three corridors away from her office. The good news was that only one guard stood sentinel. The bad news was that he was young and athletic. But if the expression on his face was anything to go by he was also bored to sobs and therefore not inclined to be a martyr to his job. Back to good again.

Reg nipped Gerald's ear. "Come on, then. Get rid of him."

Ducking back around the corner before the guard noticed them, Gerald shoved the book under one arm and wrestled with his conscience. He wasn't going to hurt the man, not really. Creating an illusion of discomfort wasn't the same as actually hurting someone. *And* it was in a good cause. An *excellent* cause. If the guard knew how he was helping his kingdom he'd probably volunteer.

Reg bounced on his shoulder. "*Gerald!* What are you *waiting* for?"

He took a deep breath and peered around the corner. The guard was still there, scratching his armpit. Softly, Gerald let out his held breath and with it the hex a very tipsy Monk had once invented as a practical joke.

"What's happening, what's happening?" Reg demanded.

"Shh," he hissed. "Any second now . . ."

The guard, who had short black hair, pimples and an impressive pair of biceps, stopped looking bored and started looking puzzled. After a moment puzzlement grew to unease. He began to shift himself from one foot to the other and back again as his brows knitted tighter and his hands bunched into fists.

Half a minute later he was trying to cross his legs without falling over. Half a minute after that he uttered an anguished moan and fled.

"Right!" With Reg clinging to his shoulder Gerald rushed to the double doors of Melissande's apartments, opened them, eased through the gap and locked them again. Then he turned to see exactly where they were.

Reg groaned. "Oh my deary gracious me. What is this, a boudoir or a second-hand bookshop?"

"Well technically, Reg, it's a foyer . . . but I know what you mean. Blimey!"

Floor to ceiling, from one side of the room to the other, the walls were lined with bookshelves, and the bookshelves were crammed with books. Thick books, thin books, yellow and red and brown and blue books, old books and new. They were piled on the floor as well, little towers of books listing alarmingly to port and starboard. Somewhere beneath all the clutter were a few scattered rugs, faded and threadbare.

Reg sneezed. "That girl is beyond redemption!"

The girl in question walked through an open

doorway on the far side of the foyer, head down and nose in a book as she came.

Reg sneezed again. "You really weren't joking when you said you didn't want to get married! Well I don't think you've got too much to worry about, ducky. This lot's better than a chastity belt!"

Melissande's head snapped up and she froze mid-stride. "*You*! How did you two get in? You didn't do something awful to Ronnie, did you?"

Gerald hid the textbook behind his back. If she'd just turn around for a moment he could stick it on a pile with some others and she'd never know he'd had it . . . "Ronnie? You mean the guard?"

"No, the pot plant in the corner. Of *course* the guard. What have you done with him?"

"You're on first-name terms with your guard?"

"Please. He's two months younger than I am and we've known each other all our lives. Now stop trying to weasel out of answering the question! Did you do something awful to him?"

He managed a weak smile. "That would depend on your definition of awful."

"Tentacles and exploding boils leap to mind."

"Nothing of the kind!" he said, offended. "What kind of a wizard do you think I am? I just made him think he needed to answer a call of nature."

As Reg cackled her amusement, Melissande snorted. "Very creative of you. Juvenile, but creative. The nearest loo is two floors away. What do you want?"

"Your crystal ball," said Reg. "Ours is on the blink and we need to reach Markham."

"Who?" said Melissande, then held up a hand.

"No. I remember." She shuddered. "Unfortunately. All right. It's in the study. Just because I'm locked up doesn't mean I don't have work to do." She stepped aside and with a sweep of her arm indicated the doorway she'd just walked through. "After you."

*Damn.* So much for surreptitiously ditching the textbook. He waited for Reg to fly through the open doorway then finagled his way past the princess, who followed him in and headed straight for a paperwork-cluttered table in the middle of the study. This room, like the foyer, was stuffed to the gills with books.

"Nice to see you've kept the motif going," observed Reg as she landed on the back of a ratty old armchair piled high with leather-bound tomes. "Very thematic."

Melissande looked up from tidying the mess, frowning. "Are you here to use my crystal ball or give me interior decorating advice?"

"I can do both," said Reg, scratching her head. "It's no skin off my beak, ducky." She peered around the room suspiciously. "Where's that Boris?"

"Out. Just because I'm a prisoner there's no need for him to be one as well."

Reg sniffed. "Typical. Bloody cats. Wouldn't know the meaning of loyalty if it bit them on the bum."

"So. Gerald," said Melissande, pointedly ignoring Reg as she sorted through the clutter. "Why do you want to get hold of Markham so urgently?"

Taking advantage of her distraction he shoved the textbook into the general disorder and took a step back. "Oh. Ah. I need a second opinion."

"If it's to do with your bird I'll give you—ha!"

With a pleased smile Melissande unearthed the crystal ball from beneath a tumbled pile of ledgers.

"No. It's nothing to do with Reg."

"What, then?" she said, polishing the crystal ball with her sleeve. "Has something *else* happened I should know about?"

*What she doesn't know can't hurt her.* "Ah—no."

She looked at him, eyes narrowing behind those unflattering glasses. "Gerald?"

"Why don't you ask him how he's feeling?" said Reg, all spurious sweetness. "Mere hours ago he was writhing on a bed of pain . . . or had you forgotten?"

Melissande's cheeks coloured. "Sorry. Of course. How are you feeling, Gerald?"

"I'm fine. Starving to death, but fine."

"Now ask him what *really* happened yesterday," Reg added.

Exasperated, Melissande planted her hands on her hips. "What *are* you talking about?"

"In a nutshell? Your pretty brother lied, ducky."

Melissande laughed, and started to make more space for the crystal ball. "Don't be ridiculous! Lional's the king. He doesn't need to lie. If you don't mind I've got a lot of work to do, so call Markham and—"

"Oh," said Gerald. "Ah—I can explain that."

She'd noticed the pilfered textbook. "I left this in my office," she said, picking it up. "At the bottom of a locked drawer."

*Damn, damn, damn.* "Your Highness—"

"Have you been *spying* on me, Professor?" she demanded, her fingers bloodless as they gripped the book. "Did *Lional* put you up to this?"

He turned on Reg before she could speak. "Don't. All right? Just *don't*. Let *me* handle this, all right?"

Reg closed her beak, fluffed up all her feathers, and retreated into sulky silence.

Hesitantly he took a step closer to the furious princess. "Melissande, listen. Please. It's not what you think."

Her chin came up. "It isn't? So you *didn't* break into my office and go through my desk? My book just magically appeared out of thin air and dropped into your lap?"

"No, of course it didn't," he said. "You're right. I broke into your office and I went through your desk. But trust me, not for Lional!"

"*Trust* you?" She tossed the book back onto the table then wrestled her temper under control. "All right. Why, then? And I give you fair warning, if I don't like the answer you *will* be sorry."

*I'm already sorry.* "It's like Reg said," he told her, carefully. "I need to get through to Monk and my crystal ball's not working."

"So you thought you'd steal mine?"

"Borrow."

"It's only borrowing when you ask first!"

He risked a smile. "Believe me, I wish I had. I didn't want to disturb you. Sorry."

She just looked at him, stony-faced. Clearly the smile wasn't working. "Well, there's the ball. Use it and go."

He nodded at the discarded textbook. "I didn't realise there was a Witches' Academy here in New Ottosland."

"There's not," she said stiffly, arms folded. "If you

*must* know I'm doing a correspondence course with Madam Ravatinka's Exclusive School of Witchery. It was advertised in a back-issue of *The Ottosland Express*. And don't you *dare* sneer. You're a correspondence-course graduate yourself!"

"I wasn't going to sneer," he protested. "Are you any good?"

She unfolded her arms. "I'm not *had*. I've passed all my First Year tests. But so far it's just been theory. We don't start the practical stuff till next year." Calmer now, she flicked him a sharp look. "Gerald, did Lional really lie about your accident?"

The nearest chair was piled high with books. He shifted them to the floor, buying some time, and sat down.

"Go on," said Reg. "Tell her."

He sighed. "Well . . ."

"For the love of Saint Snodgrass *stop* trying to *protect* me!" cried Melissande. "I'm not a little girl, I'm—"

"A princess and a prime minister. I know," he said. "Melissande, I'm not trying to protect you."

Her eyes were scornful. "No?"

"All right. Perhaps I am. A bit. But I'm protecting me, too."

"From what?"

"The consequences of unfounded accusations. Reg has a bee in her bonnet but I don't hear it buzzing. At least not very loudly. There's suspicion but no proof to back it up and until there *is* proof . . ." Troubled, he considered her. "But leaving yesterday aside, it's likely things are going to heat up around here anyway. With the Kallarapi. I don't suppose you'd consider leaving? I could get you to the portal undetected. You could go and stay with Monk till the dust settles."

Melissande stared. "Leave? Run away, you mean."

Reg clattered her beak. "Run away, make a strategic withdrawal, charge in a backwards direction, make tracks, bugger off—does it matter what you call it? Just answer the question, ducky. If he gave you the chance would you scarper?"

"And if I did?" said Melissande, still staring. "Who'd take over as prime minister? Rupert? He wouldn't last five seconds against Lional."

True, true, lamentably true. "You could take him with you."

"Well that'd be nice and inconspicuous, wouldn't it?" said Melissande, rolling her eyes. "Me, Rupert and five thousand butterflies all sneaking out of the country together. Because you'd never get him to leave them behind, you know. And I wouldn't leave him. If I was going. Which I'm not. Shocking as this may sound, Gerald, you aren't the only one around here who's sworn an oath and takes it seriously. Or do you think only wizards have a sense of honour?"

Stung, he stood up. "Of course not."

"So I guess that answers your question, doesn't it?"

"Yes. I guess it does."

Reg cackled. "I'll give you this, ducky. You may have the deportment of a demented mongoose but you've got guts to go with it."

Melissande looked at her. "Thank you. I think."

"More guts than sense is what you've got," Gerald

retorted. "If you'd give me some privacy I'll rustle up Monk, then Reg and I'll be on our way."

She shook her head. "Whatever you have to say you can say in front of me. Unless it has nothing to do with New Ottosland." Her eyebrows lifted; for a moment she looked like just Lional. "Has it?"

For a heartbeat he considered lying. For her own good, naturally. Then he discarded the idea. Not only would she probably not believe him, if she did then found out later he'd deceived her, well . . . "Fine. On one condition: whatever gets said in this room *stays* in this room."

She sighed. "Naturally. Shocking as it sounds I do have a passing familiarity with discretion, Gerald."

Also with sarcasm. He nodded. "Right."

But when he tried to put the call through, nothing happened.

"Don't look at me," said Melissande. "It was working last night when I spoke to the Babishkian Minister for Trade about their last shipment of *grooslok*. Try it again."

Stomach churning, he tried it again. Still nothing.

"Maybe it's you," said Melissande. "You're concussed, that could—"

"No," said Reg, frowning. "It's not Gerald. The etheretic transductors have gone hinky."

"The what?" said Melissande blankly.

Reg looked down her beak. "The etheretic transductors, ducky. The squillions of teeny tiny thaumaletic particles bumping around in the atmosphere acting as crystal ball carrier waves." She sniffed. "I hope you didn't pay a lot for this Madam Rinky Tinky's correspondence course. Because if she doesn't know enough to teach you about etheretic transductors, madam, I'd say you've done your dosh."

"It's none of your business how much I paid," said Melissande, colouring. "And anyway, all that technical stuff isn't covered until next year."

"Well, if this Madam Rinky Tinky doesn't know enough to teach her First Year students about etheretic transductors, the dangers associated with, I'd be very surprised to learn she had any Second Year students on her books at all!" retorted Reg. "In fact it's a wonder to me you haven't blown yourself to smithereens already!"

"I'll have you know," Melissande said hotly, hands on hips, "that Madam *Ravatinka* is a highly qualified expert and—"

She was interrupted by the sound of her apartment doors opening and an autocratic voice crying, "Melissande? Where are you? Come out here immediately, I wish to talk to you!"

"*Lional*!" whispered Melissande. "*Damn*. If he finds you two here we're cooked. I'll get rid of him. Whatever you do don't make a sound or tonight the three of us will be sleeping in chains!"

# CHAPTER EIGHTEEN

Heart thumping, Melissande plastered a welcoming expression onto her face, pulled the study door not quite closed behind her and shoved her hands into her pockets. "Good morning, Lional."

Lional tossed the book he was perusing onto the floor. She tried not to wince as the cover loosened, spilling pages. "What took you so long?"

"Sorry. I was working." She cleared her throat. "Actually, I'm glad you're here. I need to make an urgent call on my crystal ball and it won't connect."

"Why tell me?" said her difficult brother. "I'm a king, not a crystal ball repairman. And I don't recall giving you permission to have a crystal ball in here while you're under house arrest."

*Oh, Saint Snodgrass. Give me strength . . .* "I may be under house arrest, Lional, but I'm still the prime minister. Who's going to shuffle the paperwork if I don't? Unless you'd like to fire me and appoint Rupert to the position instead?"

He frowned. "Don't be ridiculous. Rupert is an idiot."

"I rest my case."

"Why won't the wretched thing work?" he demanded, eyeing her with cold, impatient displeasure. "Did you drop it?"

Her fingers clenched inside her pockets but she managed, just, to keep her temper. Losing it now would be fatal; Lional was clearly in a precarious mood.

"No, Lional, I didn't drop it," she said, flawlessly reasonable. "The etheretic transductors are on the blink. Tell Gerald—Professor Dunwoody—to fix them, would you? It's about time he started earning his keep."

"Thank you, Melissande! I will be the judge of who's earning their keep in my kingdom and who isn't! And speaking of which—"

"Of what?" she said, after a moment. "Lional?"

Lional stared into thin air, his expression suspended. Then he stirred. "Did you just say . . . *etheretic transductors*?"

Taken aback, she blinked at him. "Yes. Why—don't tell me you've heard of them?"

"As a matter of fact, I have. And they're on the blink, you say?"

"They are. Yes."

"Ah. Then it would appear we've been struck by polarised lightning," said Lional. "In which case there's nothing our good Gerald can do. Wizards can't reverse the effects of a polarised lightning strike. Nobody can. All one can do is wait for the etheretic conditions to return to normal. So, Melissande. About this wedding . . ."

"Forget about the bloody wedding, Lional!" she snapped before she could stop herself. At the look on his face she whipped her hands from her pockets and held them out placatingly. "At least for the moment, and tell me what you're talking about. I've never heard of polarised lightning. How do you know what it is, or what it does to etheretic conductivity?"

He let out a short sharp sigh. "Polarised lightning is an extremely rare, practically unheard of thaumaturgical phenomenon, a bizarre concatenation of colliding atoms, random particles and misfiring tetrothaumical emissions."

Well, Madame Rink—*Ravatinka* had definitely *never* mentioned *that*. "It is?"

Lional glared. "Didn't I just say so?"

"Er—according to who?"

"Former Court Wizard Grumbaugh, actually. The city was struck by it during his brief and unlamented tenure. Grumbaugh was most put out. He couldn't use his crystal ball for nearly three days. Yes, and it knocked out the portal too. Most inconvenient."

Lional could be the most plausible liar when he felt like it. But why would he lie about something like this? *Sorry Gerald, it looks like you're clean out of luck*. "And why is this the first I'm hearing of it?" she asked, feeling slighted.

"You were away at the time, officiating at some dreary little village ceremony somewhere unimportant," said Lional, waving away her annoyance. "By the time you got back the disruption was over. It must've slipped my mind."

"But I was working practically all last night and I didn't see any lightning."

"You wouldn't," he said promptly. "It's black, apparently. More or less invisible even during the day. But etheretic disruptions are a classic indicator of polarised lightning activity. Grumbaugh left behind some kind of monitoring apparatus, he said we were uniquely prone to the problem because of the desert and other technical claptrap I didn't listen to." Lional's expression subtly shifted and his eyes took on a militant glitter. "If you don't believe me I can fetch it and—"

"No, no," she said swiftly. "Of course I believe you, Lional. It's just a nuisance. I've got so much *work* to do."

"Leave it to your staff," he said coldly. "That's what they're for. You, Melissande, have a wedding to plan."

Bloody hell, the wedding *again*? When would her impossible brother *listen*? "Lional, *please* reconsider! How can you do this? Hand me over to a man you despise as though I were a—a—*lamp* you didn't care for? Don't *my* feelings come into this? Doesn't it *matter* to you that I don't want to marry Zazoor?"

"Putting it bluntly, no," he said. "All that matters is my kingdom. And I'll use any coin I have to secure its future, Melissande; even my own flesh and blood."

She couldn't swallow a choked protest fast enough. "How can you be so cruel? I thought you loved me!"

"I do!" he cried. "Do you think this is *easy* for me? That I relish the thought of Zazoor's hands upon *my sister*? I don't. The idea revolts me. But it's a sacrifice I'm willing to make for the good of this nation."

"How very . . . *noble* . . . of you," she said unsteadily, when she could trust herself not to scream. "But Lional, can't you see that marrying me to Zazoor will do far more harm than good? His people will never accept me. I'm an outsider, probably an infidel. And as for this ridiculous charade involving the Kallarapi gods—oh, Lional, change your mind! New Ottosland *needs* me, surely you can see that!" *You need me, you fool, if you're not to destroy yourself and the kingdom with this madness!* But she didn't dare say that aloud. Instead she just stared at him, willing him to hear her for once. This once.

He shook his head. "You're needed in Kallarap more."

"Well, I'm sorry, Lional, I don't agree." On a deep breath, she folded her arms. "And I can't—I *won't*—do it. I won't marry Sultan Zazoor."

In silence he looked at her. Not raging. Merely . . . unreachable. "Then I'm sorry too, Melly," he said at last. "Because until you change your mind the most you'll be seeing of New Ottosland is the view from your windows. And while you contemplate that view I suggest you contemplate this as well. There are cages much less gilded than this one, far beneath our feet. Don't be fool enough to think I won't use them, and far more swiftly than you'd like. In the meantime . . . consider yourself my *ex*-Prime Minister."

The foyer doors slammed hard behind him. She stared at them, feeling her insides tremble. Fighting to hold back the tears. *What's happened to you, Lional? You never used to be like this . . .*

Behind her Gerald's voice said, "Don't lose hope, Melissande. This isn't over, not by a long shot."

She nodded, unwilling to turn or trust her voice.

"You listen to Gerald, ducky," the bird said bracingly. "You'll be a card-carrying member of the Spinsters' Club a good while yet—especially if you don't engage a decent interior decorator."

When she was sure she could speak like a princess she said, "You heard what he said? About the—the polarised lightning?"

"Yes," said Gerald.

Now she turned. "And?"

He and the bird exchanged swift looks. "And I suppose we'll just have to wait for the etheretic disturbance to subside. Sorry to have bothered you, I know you're busy."

His quite plain face was impossible to read. "So . . . you have heard of it, then. This polarised lightning."

"I think I recall a passing reference in a couple of trade journals. It's . . . rare."

"Ah." She nodded. "I see. Well, you two should go now, in case Lional sends for you."

Another shared look with the bird. "Yes. But what about you? Will you be all right? We heard what he said about cages, too."

If he started getting all solicitous she was going to cry, and she'd done enough crying lately to last the rest of her life. "Don't worry about me," she said briskly. "I'll be fine. Just . . . fix this, Gerald. Please. Fix it."

Gerald didn't reply, but touched her arm in passing. With Reg hunched on his shoulder he pressed his ear to the foyer door, nodded to himself, whispered something under his breath and waited. A couple of moments later he eased the doors open and slipped outside.

Once more, she was alone.

"All right," said Gerald, having gotten them safely outside the palace and into a section of the gardens full of flowers but not gardeners. "Have *you* ever heard of polarised lightning, Reg? Because *I* haven't!"

Reg snickered. "I knew you were fibbing."

"Yes, well, Melissande's got enough on her plate. So. Have you ever heard of it?"

She clacked her beak thoughtfully. "I can't say I have, and you know how long I've been around," she said eventually. "But the world's a large strange place, Gerald, full of fantastical things. You've only got to look at madam's hairdos to realise that. For all I know, polarised lightning could be a phenomenon peculiar to New Ottosland. It is the only country in the world surrounded by weeks of desert, after all, and who knows what strange things lurk in the sands of Kallarap? It's not like anyone's ever explored them." She sniffed. "Not unless you count camels. What do your wizarding senses tell you?"

He stopped and closed his eyes. Breathed deeply for a moment, trying to ignore the hollow pit in his stomach where his breakfast should be, then let his instincts quest outwards.

*Silence. Stillness. An odd kind of muffling . . .*

"Bloody hell!" he said, and opened his eyes. "The whole place is *dampened*!"

"Dampened?" said Reg.

"Like—like—fogged in. There's enough ambient

energy to ignite the smaller incants but that's all, I think." He stared at her. "You really can't feel it?"

She sighed. "Of course not. I'm a witch in name only these days, Gerald, you *know* that."

As always, behind the tartness he heard the aching regret. "Sorry," he said, and reached up to stroke her wing. "I'm a bit distracted."

She flapped from his shoulder to the back of a nearby garden bench. "You must be if you didn't notice this before."

Thoroughly disconcerted, he slumped onto the bench beside her. All of a sudden food didn't seem so important. "Do you think it's a side-effect of this polarised lightning?"

She shrugged. "I suppose it could be. *If* such a thing does exist."

"If it doesn't," he said slowly, "then Lional was lying. Why would he do that?"

"Deary me," said Reg, rolling her eyes. "Have I taught you nothing? He's *royalty*, Gerald. As far as royalty's concerned truth is what happens to other people. Unless of course telling the truth will gain us an advantage, in which case we're as honest as the day is long."

"That still doesn't explain why he'd lie about this." He drummed his fingers on his knee. "I suppose the timing could just be a coincidence . . . me not being able to contact Monk right when I need to talk with him, urgently, the morning after I have a mysterious accident in the woods. If it *was* a mysterious accident."

"*Trust* me," said Reg robustly. "It was mysterious. But what of it? If Lional's *not* a wizard and he *isn't* trying to kill you, which is what *you're* saying, how can this sudden communications blackout be anything *but* a coincidence?"

He looked at her. "You know, it makes me nervous when you agree with me."

She snorted. "But I *don't* agree with you, Gerald. And I *certainly* don't believe in coincidence. This entire situation stinks to high heaven. I might not understand the details yet but I do know this much: that Lional's a weed and he needs to be pulled!"

"I know, Reg," he sighed, and rubbed his aching head. "The trouble is I'm not a gardener. I'm a failed probationary compliance officer who can turn cats into lions to impress mad kings and in my spare time ruin an innocent woman's life while pushing two entire nations to the brink of armed conflict." He groaned. "How long have we got, do you think?"

She stared down her beak at him. "To do what, sunshine? Avert a war, depose a madman and rescue a princess?"

"Is that the plan?" He sighed again. "Yes, I suppose it is. The war part, anyway. If I don't stop that the rest of it won't matter."

"Not a lot, no," said Reg.

"We're going to have to move fast," he said. "The Kallarapi will be back, and in strength, you can bet on it. That show we put on may have fooled Nerim but it didn't fool Shugat, no matter what Lional thinks. And when Shugat pays us a second visit he won't just bring the sultan's gullible brother. He'll come with hordes of Kallarap's fiercest warriors."

"Which means we'll need reinforcements," said Reg, and began to march back and forth along the garden seat's back. "You're a wonderful young man with unplumbed talents, Gerald, but you aren't an army. That Markham boy *has* to be told what's been happening. He may work in Research and Development but he and his family know everyone who's anyone in wizarding, domestic and foreign. *And* they've got the clout to cut through the red tape."

She always was one for stating the bleeding obvious. "I *know* that, Reg, but *how*?"

She stopped, tipping her head to one side to stare at him intently. "You say there's still some etheretic juice in the air?"

"Yes."

"Enough for an *accelerando maxima*?"

He nearly fell off the bench. "A *Speed-Em-Up* hex? Reg, are you out of your *mind*? No. It's out of the question. We've got some time up our sleeves yet, camels can't run that fast. I'll contact Markham once the ether clears, then—"

"And what if it doesn't?" said Reg, severely. "What if this dampening effect lasts five days, not three? Or a week? Or forever! With a good strong hex to help me along I'll be back in Ottosland in just over two days. I can—"

"Explode into so many pieces there won't be anything left to bury!" he retorted. "The Speed-Em-Up was *never* designed to be used on living things! Don't you remember the bookmaker and the racehorse? It was *disgusting*! And *that* was using the hex at quarter strength!"

Reg snorted. "The wizard that bookmaker hired was a third-rate hack who couldn't tie his shoelaces without a diagram and a scantily clad assistant. I have total faith in your ability to do the thing correctly, Gerald. You're a metaphysical prodigy, remember? There's absolutely no reason to assume I'll explode, provided you take the proper precautions. Besides, what other choice is there? We have to reach that Markham boy somehow."

She was right, dammit, but *hell*. The *risk*. "What about Lional?" he demanded, desperate. "What if he wants you? What do I tell him?"

"Tell him I'm sick."

"And if he doesn't believe me?"

"Then tell him I'm dead! Boo-hoo your eyes out, put on a show. Now stop arguing, Gerald! We both know I have to do this."

Overwhelmed, stomach churning, Gerald pushed to his feet, stamped to and fro for a minute then collapsed to the grass against a handy chestnut tree and closed his eyes tight. He could hear the drone of bees amongst the flowers, the twittering of birds in the branches overhead, the laughter of children playing two gardens along and the measured *snick-snick* of secateurs somewhere off to the right. The morning sun was warm on his face, the heady perfume of roses and luvvyduvvies tickled his nose. He felt Reg's claws prick gently through the fabric of his trousers as she jumped onto his knee.

"Come on, my boy," she coaxed. "I'll be fine, you'll see. I'm a smart old bird and I have no intention of blowing myself to kingdom come on behalf of that oink Lional."

Unconvinced, he banged his head against the tree trunk and welcomed the pain. He was familiar with the *accelerando maxima* hex. For a while, until

Scunthorpe played spoilsport and put an end to the hijinks, he and a bunch of other probationary compliance officers had spent their lunchtimes souping up some model cars and zooming them round the Department car park, to the amusement and bruised ankles of all. The employment market for top-notch speed wizards was excellent, and lucrative; the international car-racing circuit paid a fortune for wizards with the knack of making race cars go really, really fast. Briefly he'd dreamed of the big-time himself, but mostly his model cars had crashed. Of course that was before Stuttley's. The hex would work now. He knew it would.

*I am, after all, a metaphysical prodigy.*

Suddenly he was angry. If only he could be the old Gerald Dunwoody again, the Gerald Dunwoody who'd forgotten New Ottosland even existed, who'd honestly believed he'd found his level and was—if not happy—then resigned to staying there, doing what good he could for the welfare of wizardry and civilians alike. Where was *that* Gerald Dunwoody when he needed him?

*Gone.*

And in his place breathed a wizard of untried, untested limits who held the fate of two nations and who knew how many thousands of souls in his ill-prepared and sweating hands.

With his heart like frozen lead in his chest he opened his eyes to meet Reg's expectant gaze. "Do you even know how to find Markham from here?" he asked tiredly.

"More or less. Trust me, Gerald, that's the least of my worries." She rattled her tail. "So. Does this mean you'll do it?"

"Do I have a choice?"

"Sorry," she said. "You really don't."

No. He really didn't. *If I get out of this mess in one piece I'm retiring. The world will be a safer place without a wizard like me let loose in it.* He looked at Reg. "Well. Are you ready?"

She ruffled all her feathers. "And waiting, sunshine."

"All right then," he sighed. His chest hurt. "But if this doesn't work and your wings fall off or your brain explodes or you fly in one side of a mountain and out the other don't you *dare* come back to haunt me because I'm telling you right now, for the record, I think this is a *very bad idea.*"

Reg rolled her eyes. "Yes, Gerald. I hear you, Gerald. Now can we please get *on* with it, Gerald, because I'm not getting any younger!"

She hopped down from his knee and crouched on the grass before him, eyes gleaming with determination, wings outspread and ready. He leaned forward and rested a finger lightly on the top of her head. Closed his eyes. Sought for the power hidden within and felt it shudder, waiting. "*Accelerando maxima,*" he whispered. "*Accelerando maxima qui. Accelerando maxima deco dea.*"

Nothing happened.

"Gerald, if you're waiting for me to change my mind you're much sillier than I ever gave you credit for!" said Reg, flapping her wings. "I'm going and that's all there is tooooo—ooooh—ooooh—Geeeraaaaaald!"

And she was gone.

        \*       \*       \*

For a long time he sat in the shade of the chestnut tree, listening to a nearby gardener's tuneless humming and staring at the point of sky into which Reg had launched herself like an arrow of flame. He lost track of time. Felt bodiless, as though he were nothing but a vast and pulsing pain contained within a tissue-thin sack of skin. As though at any moment he would tear to shreds and the pain would come pouring out in a torrent of tears to soak into the grass and put an end to him entirely.

He thought that might be a good thing. Because if anything happened to Reg . . .

Then a voice cried: "Oh *there* you are. Professor! I've *found* you!" and he was dragged back into passing time and aching flesh and solid sorrow.

*Oh no. Not Rupert. Not now. Someone make him go away.*

He closed his eyes, but when he opened them again Melissande's batty brother stood directly in front of him, beaming like a little boy who'd found his lost teddy. He was dressed in a puce velvet suit with lace trimmings, and wore a butterfly like a hair ornament.

"Rupert," he said, struggling for rudimentary good manners. "Hello. Ah . . . on your head—there's a—"

Rupert's smile widened. "Oh, yes, that's Esmerelda. Isn't she beautiful?" Collapsing his knees and ankles he dropped to the grass to sit cross-legged in the shade. The green and white butterfly clinging to his tangled hair fluttered its wings but didn't fly away. "I named her after my mother. Her name was Esmerelda, before she became a Melissande. She was beautiful too. Lional looks just like her. Unfortunately

Melly and I seem to have taken more after Father's side of the family." He reached up a gentle fingertip; the butterfly stepped onto it, dainty as a ballerina. "Esmerelda's a Dumb Cluck," he added, grinning soppily at the docile insect.

*I can't stand this, not right now . . .*

"A *what*?" Gerald said, ungritting his teeth.

"It's a specialty breed," Rupert explained. "Designed as a house pet. They can't fly so they almost never escape. If you're not careful though you tread on them, with unfortunate consequences. But they do make excellent companions, provided you remember to look where you're stepping." He winced. "Or sitting."

Gerald tried to imagine the kind of person who'd go to all the trouble of purpose-breeding a butterfly that made a good pet but couldn't fly.

Probably they looked a lot like Rupert.

"The Dumb Clucks used to be very popular," said Rupert, carefully returning the insect to his head. "But *then* Andrea Wallington-Finch successfully crossed a Dumb Cluck with an Exciteable Clampet." He sighed. "And after that hardly anybody wanted a plain old Cluck in the family. I suppose I have a certain amount of fellow feeling for the poor things."

There was no way to answer that politely, so he nodded. "Hmm."

"Now tell me, Gerald, how are you feeling this morning? All recovered from that nasty fall?"

"Yes. Quite recovered. Thanks for asking."

Rupert peered at him. "Are you sure? Because when I saw you just now I thought: Oh dear, Gerald's having a relapse."

*Reg.* With a supreme effort he banished the haunting fear. "No. No relapse."

"You'd tell me if you were, though, wouldn't you?" Rupert said anxiously. "I mean, if there was anything upsetting you, you'd tell me? I know I'm a bit of a ninny but I'm a very good listener. You'd be surprised, I think, the things people tell me. Especially the staff. They all come to me with their little problems because they know I'll listen. Sometimes I even solve them, only please don't go repeating that because Lional doesn't like me getting familiar with the staff."

Tell Rupert his little problems. There was an idea. *Your brother probably tried to murder me, I accidentally arranged for your sister to be sold into a loveless marriage, I've almost certainly plunged your kingdom into a religious war and there's a good chance I've just killed my best friend.* He dredged up a smile. "That's incredibly kind of you Rupert, truly. But I'm fine."

The prince beamed. "I'm *so* glad you're calling me Rupert. It makes me feel like we're proper friends. You don't mind, do you?"

He stared at Melissande's dotty brother, ambushed by compassion. What a *sad* man Rupert was. Hardly even a man, really. More a case of tragically arrested development. A figure of idiocy, with his tremulous mouth and his watery eyes, his shrinking posture and his grating laugh. Dressed in that dreadful suit . . . crowned with a butterfly . . . and everywhere he turned—Lional. Tall and handsome and mercurially gifted. Poor Rupert, doomed to be a perennial scholarship boy in the university of life.

"No," he said gently. "I don't mind at all."

"Wonderful. That means I can tell you what's bothering me!"

His heart sank. "Bothering you?"

Rupert nodded eagerly. "Yes! You see I'm rather worried about Melissande. She and Lional are very alike you know, Gerald. Both dreadfully stubborn."

"You don't say?"

"Oh yes. They both take after Father in that respect. Once Father's mind was made up you couldn't have changed it with a block and tackle. And I really do think that the more Lional says 'you *will* marry the sultan', the more Melly will dig her heels in and say 'I *won't*'." Rupert chewed his lip. "And to be honest, Gerald, although it hurts me to say so because he *is* my brother, if Lional doesn't get his own way he can be a trifle . . . snarky."

He kept a straight face, just. "Really? That's hard to believe."

"Well I promise it's true," said Rupert earnestly. "*I* don't think she should marry Zazoor either, no matter *what* the Kallarapi gods say. Quite frankly, what business *they've* got making wedding plans for *my* little sister I'm sure I don't know. And as for Lional agreeing with them . . . I don't understand it. But he won't explain why. He just shouts and stamps and makes Tavistock look at me with all his teeth." He shuddered. "*You'll* have to speak to him about it. Gerald. He won't make Tavistock look at *you* with all his teeth."

Oh lord. He rubbed his aching head. "Rupert . . ."

"He won't," Rupert insisted. "He likes you. He's always liked wizards, ever since he was a boy he's been fascinated by magic and all those terribly secret and peculiar things you chaps get up to. Actually,

I think he'd have liked being a wizard himself but he's got next-to-no aptitude. Very put out about that, he was. He made the men from the Department test him *six* times."

"That must have been disappointing," he murmured.

Rupert bleated. "Oh, Gerald, you don't know the half of it! Anyway, the first thing Lional did when he took the throne was hire himself a court wizard. Although," he added, frowning thoughtfully, "as it turns out Professor Uffitzi wasn't quite what he was after. None of them were. But he thinks the world of *you*, Gerald. In Lional's eyes you can do no wrong. He already likes you more than he'll ever like me. In fact . . ." His face lit up. "Why don't *you* marry Melly? That way you'll be Lional's brother-in-law, which will *more* than make up for me."

Gerald staggered to his feet. "Marry Melissande? *Me*? Rupert, are you *cracked*?"

Rupert got up, one hand over his head to safeguard Esmerelda. "I expect so," he said cheerfully. "But that doesn't make me wrong. I mean I know she's not exactly beautiful, at least not on the outside, and she can be a bit bossy, but really that's just her being organised and goodness if she wasn't organised I don't know what would happen to the rest of us, and then of course there's Boris . . ." He thought for a moment then sighed. "No. I can't think of a single nice thing to say about Boris. Still. Nobody's perfect, are they?"

Oh, *hell* . . . "Look," he said helplessly. "I'm sorry, Rupert, but I can't marry your sister. I will talk to His Majesty, though, and see if I can't convince him to reconsider her marriage to Zazoor. How about that?"

"Well," said Rupert, patently disappointed. "All

right. If you think it's worth a try. In fact . . ." A growing expression of unease spread over his gormless face. "Why don't you go talk to him right now?"

The unease was contagious. "Why right now?" he said, suspicious.

This time Rupert's smile was sickly. "Because I've just remembered why I came looking for you. Lional wants to see you. In his private dining room. Something about lunch and state business."

"Bloody hell, Rupert! Why didn't you *say*?"

"I meant to," Rupert said meekly. "I got sidetracked. Sorry. Do you remember how to find the dining room?"

*Idiot, idiot, idiot!* "Yes," he said, walking rapidly.

Behind him, Rupert cleared his throat. "And Gerald?"

"*What*?" he demanded, over his shoulder.

Idiot Rupert was pale and agitated. "I think I'd *run*, if I were you."

# CHAPTER NINETEEN

"*Half an hour!*" shouted Lional, sitting bolt upright and radiating fury. "You've kept me waiting for *half an hour*, Professor! It simply isn't *good* enough!"

As a relieved servant closed the private dining room's door behind him, Gerald glanced warily at Tavistock, disapproving beside Lional's ornate chair, and bowed. "So sorry, Your Ma—"

"My instructions were perfectly clear, not even a moron like *Rupert* could've misunderstood me!" Lional seethed. "Which means you've kept me waiting on *purpose!*"

The dining table was set for two and laden with tureens and platters and sauceboats of food. Poached fish. Roast duck. Delicately spiced gravies. Green beans and artichokes swimming in garlic butter. Their combined aromas teased and tantalised. On the sideboard a towering confection of cake, as yet untouched, with cream and chocolate and the seductive scent of coffee liqueur.

Almost deafened by his abruptly rumbling belly, Gerald swallowed the saliva pooling in his mouth. "Please forgive me, Your Majesty. I intended no deliberate slight or disrespect. I think His Highness had some difficulty finding me."

Eyes narrowed, lips pinched, Lional drummed his fingers on the table, vibrating the used cutlery on his emptied plate. Then he reached for his wineglass, tossed its blood-red contents down his throat and thrust it forward. "Well, man, don't just stand there! Pour me another one!"

Hastily he poured Lional more wine from the large crystal carafe on the table. The king half emptied the glass then sat back in his chair, suspicion and anger still not fully allayed. "So what were you up to, Professor, that Rupert couldn't find you?"

*Damn.* Of course Lional had to ask. "Up to? Ah—" Inspiration struck. A chance for two birds with one stone, no pun intended. "I was out looking for Reg, Your Majesty."

Lional's eyes narrowed again. "The bird? Why? Where's it gone?"

Schooling his face to an expression of innocent anxiety he said, "Actually, Your Majesty, I'm not entirely sure."

"Not *sure*?" Lional sat up. "You mean you've *lost* it?"

Reg, hexed to the eyeballs and hurtling home. *Oh lord, I hope not.* "No, no, Your Majesty. Not lost. Just—"

"Good," said Lional. "That bird is an integral part of my plans for this kingdom. I would be excessively . . . *disappointed* . . . if you'd been so careless as to misplace it, Gerald."

*I bet you would, Lional.* "Yes, Your Majesty."

Lional didn't look entirely convinced. "I should warn you, Gerald, that I don't much care for being disappointed."

*Too bad. Because you're long overdue and if I have my way* . . . "I'm sure you don't. Your Majesty."

Without warning, Lional smiled. One hand drifted down to scratch Tavistock between the ears. "Well, you're here now so I mustn't complain. Do have a seat, Professor. You look positively peaky. Help yourself to some food and while you're eating you can explain what has happened to your little feathered friend."

"Thank you," said Gerald, and sat at the table's other place setting. He was so hungry he felt lightheaded and ill. He was so hungry he didn't care he'd be eating with Lional and Tavistock for an audience.

Plate hastily filled, he tried not to fall on the food like a starving wolf or choke when Lional poured wine for him into his glass.

"Drink up, Professor," the king urged, positively genial. "Your blood could do with some fortifying, I think."

*It certainly can. Reg, Reg . . . please be all right.* "Thank you," he said, and swallowed a mouthful of the wine. It was exquisite, rich and robust and full of fruit. Just what he needed. He swallowed some more. Ate the fish and roast duck. Savoured the buttery garlicked artichoke. The rumbling ache in his belly eased, mouthful by mouthful. He drank the rest of the wine. It was fabulous.

"Another half-glass?" suggested Lional, crystal carafe raised invitingly.

He shook his head, which was swimming gently like the goldfish in his foyer fountain. "My thanks. Your Majesty, but—"

Lional ignored him. "And now that your appetite is assuaged," he said, expertly pouring, "do feel free to tell me *all* about Reg. Where *has* the charming little wretch got to?"

His blood felt replaced, not fortified; rich red wine pumping in time with his heart. He almost emptied his refilled glass in a single swallow. It was so *good*! He'd been worried about something. What was it? "Reg?" he echoed. "Oh! Yes! Reg! Well, Your Majesty, she went out early this morning to stretch her wings. She said she'd only be gone an hour but she still hasn't returned."

"I see," said Lional, gently frowning. "And you're anxious? You feel there could be some cause for alarm?"

"Well, I was. I did. I mean I am! I do! Although . . ." He leaned towards Lional confidingly. "Just between you and me, she does enjoy her little jaunts. Has been known to get a bit carried away in the sight-seeing department. Your Majesty." He hiccuped. " 'Scuse me."

Lional's smile was camaraderie personified. "Not at all, Professor."

"The thing is, Your Majesty, I think I was over-reacting," he admitted. "She's no spring chicken, is our Reg. Been about a bit in her time. You'd be surprised. She'll be fine. Be back before we know it. My word on it, believe me."

Lional patted his arm. "You're the wizard, Gerald. If you say that's the case, of course I believe you. And doubtless the gods of Kallarap will protect her." He smiled again. "Have some more wine, my friend. It wants drinking up." He poured for the third time.

Gerald didn't need encouragement. All his knotted muscles were unravelling, leaving him loose and delightfully mellow. He raised his glass. "To your good health, sir!"

"Thank you, Gerald," said Lional, sitting back. "I'm touched. Tell me, how are you feeling? No unfortunate repercussions from yesterday's tumble?"

Tumble? Tumble? *Oh yes! I fell off a horse, aren't I clumsy?* He stifled a giggle. "None at all, Your Majesty."

"Ah, you wizards. Tough as old boots." Elbows propped on his chair's gilded arms, Lional laced his fingers. "And your memory of our little outing? Any sign of its return?"

"My memory?" he said vaguely. "No, Your Majesty. I'm afraid it's as blank as ever." He did giggle this time, a ridiculous sound. "So if you happened to ravish a milk-maid or three while we were romping about the countryside, I promise your secret's safe with me!"

He held out his empty glass with a hopeful smile. Watched Lional fill it yet again. Drained it dry. Reached for the carafe himself this time, without asking, and sloshed more red gold into his glass.

Good old Lional. Excellent fellow. *If only Errol Haythwaite and his cronies could see me now, chatting over lunch with my friend King Lional.* They'd be greensick with envy. And Scunthorpe, too, that miserable old paper pusher. *Bet he'll be sorry when he finds out the calibre of wizard he let slip through his fingers. Too stupid to see the genius right under his nose, Scunthorpe. They all are. Idiots! They'll rue the day they disrespected Gerald Dunnywood!*

Replacing the carafe on the table with exaggerated care, he realised Lional was watching him intently. "Cheers, Y'Majesty!" he said, and raised his glass in salute. "Bloody nice drop this, innit?"

"Bloody nice indeed," said Lional. He reached into his green silk coat's inside pocket and withdrew a red velvet covered box. Placing it on the tablecloth between them he added, "And I hope you'll find this equally nice."

He leaned forward, peering muzzily. "Wazzat?"

"A gift, Gerald. A trinket. The merest token of my appreciation for all your efforts."

"For me?" He felt his jaw drop. "Y'Majessy . . . y'shouldn't have!"

"Of course I should! You've no idea how much I owe you, Gerald. Or how much more I'll owe you very soon. Open it."

Fumbling, his fingers stubbornly uncooperative, he wrestled with the velvet box's lid. Inside, nestled in white satin, was a heavy golden ring set with a single cabochon-cut sapphire; the blue gem winked and flashed in the chandelier light.

Lional smiled. "It's a signet ring. A gift from my father."

"Y'father?" The box slipped from his clumsy fingers into a puddle of congealed gravy on his plate. "Oh—no—can't take it—too precious—"

"Nonsense," Lional said robustly. "I never wear the wretched thing. Come. Put it on."

"Oh, no, I—"

"Gerald! Please! You must, it's a gift! Do you want to hurt my feelings?"

Hurt Lional's feelings? Good old Lional, his mate, his chum? "No, course not!"

"Then put it on, Gerald. Let me see how it suits you."

It took him two attempts to fish the box clear of his plate. Growing dizzier by the second he gave it a half-hearted swipe with his napkin. "Sorry, Y'Majessy," he mumbled. "Must've drunk a bit more than I realised."

Lional laughed. "Not to worry, old chap. We all get a bit tipsy from time to time. Quickly, now. Slip on the ring. Or I'll think you've not been truthful and you don't care for my gift."

"No, Y'Majessy! Lovely gift! Never expected it!" With difficulty he extricated the ring from its box. It was cool, heavy, and slid on as though made for him. Weighted his hand and—

– *closed around his left forefinger like a vice. He was caught, trapped, held fast in a web with strands of metaphysical steel. He could breathe, move his eyes, but that was all . . .*

In a searing burst of pain and light his foggy mind cleared and he remembered everything. The hunting expedition. The Wizard Trap. The captured images of all those other wizards screaming, burning, their powers ripped from them by magics fouler than the deepest pits of hell. Lional, laughing . . .

*Make me a dragon.*

Drenched in sweat and horror, he stared. *Oh, God. Oh, God.* "I remember."

Lional appeared mildly interested. "Really? I wondered if you might."

Gerald's gaze shifted to the almost empty crystal carafe. Rising fast, understanding laced with bitter shame and self-derision. *When Reg hears about this she'll go spare . . .* "The wine?"

"Your glass," said Lional. He was smiling, a thin nasty curve of unkind lips. "Coated with a neat little concoction I cooked up in my spare time. Very handy for rendering impotent any wizard who might fight back."

He tried to wrench the ring from his finger but he couldn't even lift his hand. His body was like a sack of wet sand. Inert. Immoveable.

*You fool. You fool. You let your guard down . . .*

Lional laughed. "There's no escape, Gerald. Not even you are strong enough to break this binding. Trust me, after what happened in the woods I made quite certain of that."

*I'll bet you did, you murdering bastard.* He'd never felt anything like this before. As though he were a puppet and his strings had been cut. "You're wasting your time," he said, forcing the words out. "I won't make you a dragon."

"No?" Lional shrugged. "Well, we'll see. Now look into the sapphire, Gerald."

Head pounding, he fought the command. The effort hurt him all the way to his bones. Lional's binding incant held a compulsion element too. "No."

"*Look into the sapphire.*"

Lional's voice lashed him like a whip, breaking his

fragile resistance. Against his will his gaze began drifting downwards. He tried to close his eyes, turn his face away, but the impulse to obey was overwhelming. *No. No. Fight him, you have to!*

It was hopeless. On a despairing cry he stared into the sapphire's heart. The gemstone flared from blue to crimson, pulsing like a captive sun. He was falling . . . falling . . . fallen.

The crystal held him fast, like a fly in blood-soaked amber.

"Dear me, Gerald," Lional said lightly as he stood and crossed to the dining room door. "Didn't anyone ever tell you? Never accept gifts from strange wizards."

Voiceless and paralysed, he watched as Melissande's murderous brother opened the dining room door and snapped his fingers. Almost immediately a nervous servant entered the chamber and bowed. "Your Majesty?" With a friendly smile Lional rested a hand on his shoulder. "Davenport, isn't it?"

The man paled. "Yes, Your Majesty."

Lional nodded and brought up his other hand in front of Davenport's face. His fingers crooked into a strange, vaguely threatening, almost obscene gesture. Davenport stiffened, his brown eyes bulging.

"Listen carefully," said Lional, silkily persuasive. "The professor and I are retiring to my private chambers, where we are not to be disturbed. Shortly after that he will return to his apartments for extensive meditation upon matters of grave magical importance. Nobody is to be concerned if they neither see nor hear from him for some time and under no circumstances is he to be called for or have his contemplations interrupted."

Davenport's eyes were glazed in his blank face. "Yes, Your Majesty," he whispered.

"You will share this information with every palace servant assigned to the professor's suite, Davenport, and any others you happen to encounter."

"Yes, Your Majesty."

"This conversation did not happen."

"No, Your Majesty."

Transfixed, Gerald watched Lional pass his crooked fingers before Davenport's face left to right, right to left, down and up, and finally up and down. Then he pressed the ball of his thumb to the man's forehead. Davenport gasped as though the collision of flesh and flesh was an agony. A white hot brand burned like a furnace between his eyes.

Lional stepped back. "Go now. Take Tavistock with you and make sure he gets a nice rump of something for his supper."

By the time Davenport reached the door, a complaining Tavistock at his heels, the brand had faded. With a flick of his fingers Lional swung the door open then shut it behind them. He was grinning.

"I'll bet you weren't expecting *that*, Professor! Clever, aren't I?"

Diabolically. Gerald's stunned and captured mind reeled.

*Reg, Reg, come back. I'm in trouble.*

"Oh dear. Has the king got your tongue?" Chuckling, Lional sauntered to the wall opposite the door. Ran his hands over the patterned wallpaper, pressed the centre of one floral bouquet and watched, humming cheerfully, as a part of the wall swung soundlessly inwards to reveal a small wooden platform and a spiral staircase, leading down. "Come, Gerald. Time to go."

Numb, enslaved, he felt his body jerk. He stood, then plodded gracelessly forward. When he reached the opening in the wall Lional held up his hand and he stopped, teetering on the brink of darkness. Lional snapped his fingers and torches set into the wall above the wooden platform sprang into life.

"After you, Professor, and do mind your step," said Lional, jaunty as a bus conductor.

And although he didn't want to, although he struggled against the force of Lional's voice until it felt like his heart would burst, he stepped through the hole in the wall, onto the platform and down the spiralling staircase. Lional came close behind, swinging the door closed in their wake, a steadying hand on his shoulder. He felt his skin crawl at the touch.

They travelled in a capsule of light, torches dying behind them, kindling ahead. Down and down they climbed, stair after stair after stair. The air was clean but faintly stale. Exhausted, he stopped fighting the merciless grip of the incant wrapped round his mind and threaded through his bones. Instead, he let it move him as it willed and surrendered himself to waiting.

After a lifetime of stairs they reached ground level and continued along a low-ceilinged, narrow-walled corridor of stone. On and on it unwound, sinuous as a snake. The temperature fell. Here and there the torchlight flickered on threads of moisture trickling down the dark, dank walls.

He lost track of time and distance. Thought suspended, he just put one foot in front of the other, following Lional without question or hope of defiance. Eventually there was no more corridor so they stopped. Set into the rock wall before them was an ancient rough-hewn door. Ugly glyphs, crudely carved into the weathered timber, marred its splintered surface. The shape of them woke fresh dread, reminding him of the obscenity of Lional's fingers as he worked his will upon the servant Davenport.

Humming again, Lional pulled a ring of keys from one of his pockets and began to sort through them. After a moment he turned, his shadow-flickered face grotesque with self-mockery. "Aren't I a silly? You'd think I'd remember which one it is by now. Ah! Here we are . . . You know," he added confidingly, a big brass key in his hand, "I could just as easily lock this with a spell but there's something so *satisfying* about a key." He fitted it into the door's lock and turned it. There was a click. Lional pushed and the door swung open. "After you, Gerald."

The space beyond the open doorway was pitch black and cold. He felt loose dirt underfoot. Lional locked the door again and pocketed the keyring. There was a snap of fingers and a whispered word and the absolute darkness disappeared in a coruscation of light. Unable to shield his eyes Gerald squeezed them tight shut instead and saw the world as a blood-red shadow.

"Come along now, Professor, don't be a spoilsport," Lional's hateful voice reproved him. "Don't you want to see your new home?"

What he wanted was to wake up from this

nightmare to find himself safe in his shoebox room at the Wizards' Club. He wanted to be nothing more exalted than a probationary compliance officer, answerable to Scunthorpe, despised by Errol Haythwaite and benignly bullied by Reg.

*Reg.*

Oh, lord. How long before she reached Ottosland and Monk? How long before she could raise the alarm?

"*Gerald!*" said Lional and slapped him, hard. "Pay attention!"

Cheek burning, he opened his eyes.

He stood in a cave as large as a ballroom. It was lit like a ballroom, too, bobbing round lights clustered high beneath the rocky ceiling. Unlike most caves, this one had no mouth. The only way in or out was through the carved wooden door behind him.

"Excellent!" said Lional. "You know, Gerald, you'll find we'll get along very much better if you just do *what* you're told *when* you're told and *how* you're told to do it."

He tried to speak but the words wouldn't come. He heard himself grunt, an animal sound.

Lional frowned. "Oh dear. I think we'd best put you back the way you were, Professor, before you embarrass yourself." Pulling a green stone out of one black silk trouser pocket he breathed on it, whispering, then held it up before his captive's eyes. "Look deep now, Gerald."

Helpless, he looked.

A rush of burning, as though the incant sunk through his flesh and bones had suddenly caught fire. A spinning dizziness, the feeling of being drawn swiftly upwards by an invisible thread. The ring on his finger flared, searing. He cried out in pain, another animal sound.

And then he was free. He staggered backwards until his shoulder-blades met the unforgiving cave wall, ripped the signet ring from his finger and threw it into the dirt.

"Reg was right. You tried to *kill* me."

Lional considered him thoughtfully. "Not . . . precisely. And really, is that *any* way to treat a present?"

"Fine. You tried to steal my power *then* kill me."

"Close enough," Lional conceded. "The goal was indeed to appropriate your *magicali potentia*, as I appropriated the *potentias* of the five wizards who came before you. Your death, like theirs, would've been a convenient side effect."

Gerald laughed, unwisely triumphant. "But I'm not like those other wizards, am I? You *failed* . . . Your Majesty."

A muscle leapt along Lional's jaw. "Don't get your hopes up, Gerald. I haven't failed yet." His eyes lit with an inner fire and his aura ignited, crackling fiercely, silently, in a nimbus of purple and black. "I am a wizard, after all."

Despite himself, he flinched. The malevolence radiating from Lional's display was choking. He felt befouled, nauseated. "You're no wizard. You're just a thief."

Lional's fist quenched the flare of power. The fire in his eyes dwindled to a pinprick of crimson light, flickering deep. "Wrong, Gerald. I am *unique*."

"What you are is stark staring bonkers. Raving lunacy on legs."

All of Lional's masculine beauty vanished. Twisted

with hate and a brooding malice he took a step forward, fist raised. "Don't push me, Gerald! I can be quite . . . vengeful . . . when I'm pushed."

"You've already been pushed, mate, right over the edge!"

"*Insolence!*" hissed Lional. "Hold your tongue, peasant! It's time for you to make me a dragon."

Gerald swallowed. *Keep him talking.* That was all he could do, keep the mad king talking and pray that Reg got back in time with Monk and the Department's cavalry. "Are you deaf as well as insane?" he sneered. "How many times do you need me to say it? *I will never make you a dragon.* And anyway, even if I did it, wouldn't do you any good. The Kallarapi aren't stupid. You just wish they were. Shugat won't buy your fake dragon any more than he bought Reg and Tavistock. He'll let loose his holy man powers on you and once you're dead the world will be a better place!"

"*Shugat?*" Lional laughed, the sound raggedly bouncing from wall to wall. "Shugat will burn! *Zazoor* will burn! Every last Kallarapi shall burn to ash and bone and their desert will be *mine!*"

And that really was crazy. "Yours? Why the hell do you want their desert?"

An indrawn breath, then Lional stopped. The fury and rapacity wiped clean from his face, as though his features were made of fine pale sand and a smoothing hand had passed across them. He smiled politely, urbanity incarnate. "All in good time, Gerald."

He pushed away from the wall. "I don't have good time. I'm leaving."

"I don't think so," said Lional and clapped his hands. "*Impedimentia implacato*."

Gerald's feet froze to the cave floor in mid-stride; he paddled the air frantically, trying not to fall over. Balance regained, he snapped his fingers. "*Nux nullimia!*"

Nothing happened.

"You're wasting your time," said Lional, eyes glinting with petty amusement. "Ingeniously hidden in this cave is a lodestone, calibrated to suppress all thaumaturgical signatures except my own. A rather clever modification I designed, feel free to be impressed. Until I say otherwise, your formidable powers are completely inaccessible to you, Gerald. So you see? You have no choice but to help me."

A lodestone. Things just kept on getting better and better . . . "I'll help you all right. All the way to a full tribunal hearing at the United Magical Nations and from there into a not too comfortable cell where you can spend the rest of your miserable, manipulative, *criminal* life!"

"No, I can't say that's what I had in mind," Lional mused. "I was thinking more along the lines of us crushing the Kallarapi and ushering in New Ottosland's bigger, brighter future."

"*Us?*" Gerald laughed. Even to himself he sounded unsteady, on the edge. "There's no *us* here. There's just me and a well-dressed murderer."

Lional pulled a face. "Oh come now, Gerald, there's no need to be *parochial*. You're a *wizard*, man. You have to think beyond the mundane. Yes, some people have died. But it was in a good cause. *New Ottosland's* cause. Their sacrifices will be remembered, I promise. I'll put a plaque on a wall somewhere with all their names on it, how does that sound?"

"Insane," he said grimly. "Just like you."

Lional lifted a warning finger. "Careful, Gerald."

He gasped as a bolt of pain shot through him. Blood trickled down the back of his throat. He swallowed, gagging at the metallic taste.

*Don't antagonise him, you fool. Keep him talking. He wants to boast. Show off. Encourage him, don't make him angry. Every minute he keeps talking is a minute that gets you closer to rescue.*

"You put the kybosh on the crystal ball."

"I did," said Lional, smiling complacently. "I wasn't entirely convinced your memory was gone. Didn't want to risk you making any inconvenient calls. *Polarised lightning.*" He laughed. "I do wish I could've seen your face as I fed Melissande that rigmarole. I expect it was priceless!"

Gerald felt his fingers clench into fists. "You knew I was there."

The complacent smile returned. "Of course. The *potentias* of five wizards, remember? Why do you think I made up all that drivel in the first place? For *Melissande*? Hardly."

"Well I'll give you this much, Lional. You may be crazy but you're not an idiot."

"No, Rupert's the idiot in my family," said Lional, then raised a sharp finger. "And I'd appreciate it. Gerald, if you addressed me with just a *little* more respect."

Another flaring bolt of pain. Another rush of blood down the back of his throat. Anchored to the floor by Lional's incant he dropped to his knees, nearly breaking both ankles. "All right, all *right*! I'm sorry, *Your Majesty*!"

Lional looked down at him. "That's better."

"Fine. Now would you please release the *impedimentia implacato*? You said it yourself, I can't hurt you in here and I think the blood's stopped flowing to my feet."

After a moment Lional nodded. "Very well. Since you asked so nicely." He waved one hand and whispered under his breath.

Gerald felt a tingle run through his legs. Moving carefully, he levered himself back onto his feet. Stamped them to get the feeling back. "Thank you." Lional's eyebrows lifted. "Your Majesty." *Keep him talking, keep him talking.* "I wonder . . . can I ask you something else?"

"If you must," sighed Lional.

"Rupert—His Highness—said you had no magical aptitude. If that's true how is any of this possible?"

"*Rupert* said?" Lional frowned. "Well, well. What a little rattle-tongue young Rupert is proving to be. I shall have to speak to him. Severely."

*Damn.* "Don't! Rupert's as harmless as one of his butterflies, you know he is. Leave him alone." With an effort, he moderated his tone. "Please, Your Majesty."

Lional considered him. "Well . . . perhaps you're right." He shrugged. "And so is Rupert. I have no real natural metaphysical aptitude of my own."

"Then *how* did you steal—"

"You'd like me to explain?"

"Yes. I would." Because he really did want to know. Not just for himself but so—in the unlikely event he got out of this mess—he could tell the authorities. One Lional in the annals of thaumaturgy was one too many.

Lional consulted his pocket watch. "I suppose we've a few minutes before we must get down to business. Pull up a patch of dirt then, Professor, and I'll tell you my fascinating story."

He sat on the floor with his back against the rough cave wall and watched as Lional closed his eyes and raised one finger. A moment later an armchair appeared beside him; with a pleased smile, he sat in it.

Gerald swallowed dismay. *Oh, hell. A thought. He can translocate objects with a thought. And we must be miles from the palace, we walked for ages. He can translocate objects over miles with just a thought.*

His only consolation was that Lional was unable to steal his *potentia*. Why that was he didn't know or much care. So long as Lional couldn't rip it out of him, as he'd done to Bottomley and the others, there was still a chance of thwarting the mad king's plans.

*I don't know how, but there must be a chance. Because if I don't stop him people are going to die.*

Lional cleared his throat. "Are you listening, Gerald?" he demanded, a distinct and razored edge to his voice.

He wrapped his arms around his knees. *Keep him talking, keep him talking. Whatever you do, don't make him angry.* "Yes, Your Majesty."

"Then in the tradition of all good fairy tales we shall begin with 'Once Upon A Time'," said Lional, legs crossed, hands elegantly at ease, the epitome of genteel sophistication. "So. *Once* upon a time, the kings of New Ottosland were magically talented in their own right. As far as I can tell they never actually *did* anything with it, but nevertheless the talent was there. Unfortunately, over the ensuing generations and most likely due to indiscriminate breeding, our abilities became more and more diluted. In fact until recently we were good for little more than parlour tricks. I mean, Melissande's a dab hand with a crystal ball, Rupert can make butterflies land on his head and with a lot of effort and some nose bleeding *I* could levitate a pencil half an inch into the air." He chuckled. "I can do a trifle more than that now, of course."

*Bastard.* "Only because you—"

"*Manners!*" Lional said sharply.

Gerald winced as a frisson of fire whispered through him. Hating Lional so fiercely he could taste it he said, "Sorry, Your Majesty."

Lional nodded. "Very well. But don't make me remind you again. Now, to continue. I've always known that to create the New Ottosland of my dreams I'd need power. Wizard power. My stupid father, may he rot in hell, wouldn't give me a wizard of my own, growing up. I had to wait till he died, which wasn't nearly soon enough. But die he did, at long, *long* last, and I lured Pomodoro Uffitzi into my employ. I wanted him to help me develop my meagre skills. I didn't believe those fools from your Department. I thought all I needed to become a powerful wizard was the proper training."

"All the training in the world won't help you if you lack raw talent."

"Careful, Gerald." Eyes narrowed, Lional shifted in the chair. "Pomodoro considered himself the world's foremost thaumaturgical scholar. He had an extraordinary library of magical texts—but he refused to let me see it, can you imagine? Claimed there were books no eyes but his own were fit to look upon. But, like you, Uffitzi underestimated my . . . dedication."

He hated giving Lional the satisfaction but he had to know. "What books, Your Majesty? What didn't he want you to see?"

Lional gazed thoughtfully at the cave's ceiling. "Well . . . there was *Pygram's Pestilences*—that one's fun. Lots of interesting plagues and things to play with in that one. Then there was *The Ebony Staff*. Some fabulous curses in there, Gerald, you'd be amazed. Hands turning into hooves. Noses falling off, not to mention other bits. Oh yes. Perfectly ingenious. Now, what else? Ah . . . of course. The most important book of all. The one that changed my life." He released a slow, ecstatic sigh. "*Grummen's Lexicon*."

Gerald bit his tongue so hard he drew blood. "That's impossible. There are only two copies of that book in existence, neither of them intact. They've been split into seventeen sections and dispersed between six different countries, held in separate secret locations, bound by curse and key. You can't have one."

Lional smiled. "I'm afraid whoever told you that was a trifle misinformed, Gerald. There are *three* copies of *Grummen's Lexicon* in existence. And I keep mine on the bedside table."

# CHAPTER TWENTY

Shaken to sickness, Gerald tried to hide his horror. *Saint Snodgrass save us all. Grummen's Lexicon?* His belly churned with acid, with undigested food it wanted to reject. "Yours? You mean Pomodoro Uffitzi's."

Another amused smile. "Technically. I suppose. But you know what they say, Gerald. Finder's keepers."

With an effort he swallowed the scalding bile. *Keep him talking.* "And it was the Lexicon that showed you how to strip another wizard's power from him and take it into yourself?"

"Amongst other things," Lional agreed. "I'm not saying it was easy, mind you. It wasn't. I had to *perform* other tasks first, things to prod and provoke my own pathetic *potentia* into life." He sighed theatrically. "I suffered, Gerald. No-one can imagine how I suffered. But I didn't care. I was doing it for New Ottosland."

*For New Ottosland?* he wanted to shout. *For your-*

*self, you murdering madman!* The more he heard, the more he realised just how dangerous Lional truly was. Powerful, ruthless . . . and armed with magics so foul, so evil, no sane wizard had ever risked the using of them.

*Except Lional's not sane, is he? And he's been studying* Grummen's Lexicon. *How the hell am I supposed to beat him?*

He took a deep steadying breath. "So you killed Uffitzi and the others," he said, careful not to sound accusing. "Took their *potentias.* Then why try and take mine? You can't need it, you're already more powerful than any wizard in history."

Lional shrugged. "You'd think so, wouldn't you? Alas. All I can do is what *they* could do, Gerald. Better, admittedly. With more force, to be sure. But not *one* of them had the ability to turn Tavistock into a lion. Don't you *know* how rare that is? How *special*?"

*I do now. And I curse the day I ever thought of becoming a wizard.* "I never thought about it . . . Your Majesty."

Leaning forward, face alight, Lional said, "It's incredible. I tried to take your *potentia* three times. The third attempt nearly finished me. *Why*? What makes you impervious?"

Gerald shook his head. "I've no idea." *And even if I did I wouldn't tell you.*

Lional sat back, eyes glittering. "I heard that, Gerald. I'll bet you would, you know. Eventually."

It took everything he had but he didn't drop his gaze from Lional's face. "You still haven't told me what's so important about Kallarap's desert."

"No. I haven't. And why do you care? Unless . . ." Lional thought for a moment then gasped. "No! *Surely* you don't think you're going to escape and raise the alarm? Save the day? Be a *hero*? Oh, *Gerald*!"

He let Lional's mocking laughter wash over him. It didn't matter. Nothing mattered but buying more time.

"You're right, Your Majesty," he said, striving to sound hollow and beaten. "You've won. I can't escape . . . and I'm no-one's idea of a hero."

"But you'd like to know what it's all about? Of course," said Lional, mockingly sympathetic. "And I'll tell you. I'm not an unreasonable man. If one is to die, one at least should know what one is dying for. That's only fair."

*If one is to die* . . . "If I'm dead I can't make you a dragon, Your Majesty."

Lional's smile was lethal. "I meant afterwards, naturally."

Naturally. "In which case what incentive do I have to obey you?"

Again, the lethal smile. "Trust me, Gerald. I can provide all the incentive you require. But we can discuss that later. You wanted to know about Kallarap's desert?"

If he let himself think too closely about what Lional was implying he'd lose the last of his dwindling courage. "Yes, Your Majesty."

Lional resettled himself comfortably in the incongruous armchair. "The Kallarapi Desert, Gerald, far from being a barren, desolate wasteland, is chock-full of gemstones that will fetch untold millions on the international market. Millions that will pave the way to New Ottosland's glorious future."

He stared. "*Gemstones*?"

"Yes. Gemstones." Lional rolled his eyes. "Cast your scattered wits back to our little meeting with the Kallarapi delegation. Do you recall that undistinguished lump of dull grey rock embedded in Shugat's forehead?"

How could he forget? "Yes."

"Once properly cut and polished those rocks become rare and priceless gemstones. The sands of Kallarap are littered with them. The Kallarapi call them 'The Tears of the Gods'," said Lional, his voice curdled with contempt. "They regard them as sacrosanct. Only their holy men may touch them, and only then for arcane religious purposes. For the most part the Kallarapi just leave them lying around in the desert. They're too stupid to know the rocks' true worth."

"Well . . . isn't that their choice? These rocks belong to them, after all."

"Not for much longer," said Lional.

"So you think if I make you a dragon," said Gerald, after a disbelieving moment, "and you tell the Kallarapi it's their greatest god Grimthak, they'll hand over these rocks to you without so much as an 'excuse me, but'?"

Lional laughed, a soft, shivery sound. "It's a pleasure doing business with you, Gerald. For a moment there I thought you were going to be obtuse. Yes of course the Kallarapi will hand them over. They are a gullible and superstitious people and they'll do whatever Grimthak tells them to."

No, no, no. Lional couldn't be serious. "Your Majesty, I'm sorry, but your plan is flawed. I wasn't lying when I said I couldn't make an animal speak. Even if I did make you a dragon it wouldn't be able to tell the Kallarapi *anything!*"

Lional shrugged. "A minor technicality. I'll do the speaking for it. Or Reg can."

"*Reg?*" Gerald nearly laughed out loud. "Forget it. You'll never get Reg to play along with this!"

"I think I will, you know," Lional contradicted gently. "It appears she's rather fond of you, Gerald. I wonder how many of your detached fingers it will take to persuade her that cooperation is in your best interests?"

Gerald pushed himself to his feet. "Saying something like that only proves you don't know Reg. You could cut off my *head* and she'd never do it! You're wasting your time!"

"Let me be the judge of that," said Lional. His eyes were narrowed, his fingers steepled. "And now, Gerald, it seems to me our avenues for conversation are exhausted. The time has come for you to make me my dragon."

Okay. This charade had gone on long enough. *I can't afford to wait for Reg and the cavalry. For all I know they're not even coming. I'll have to fight him myself, here and now, for as long as I can. I'll probably die. It probably serves me right.* "Get a grip, Lional! You can't seriously think I'm going to transmogrify a dragon so you can terrorise the people of Kallarap into believing that their gods want you to steal their sacred stones and *sell* them? For *money?* To make you *rich?*"

Lional stood, his expression cold and severe. "Guard your tongue, sir, lest it talk you into trouble."

"I'm already in trouble," Gerald retorted, feeling reckless. Feeling desperate. "But so are you. You're crazy if you think Shugat and Zazoor are going to fall for a stunt like that. The sultan was at school with you, he knows *exactly* what you are. You may be powerful, Lional, but you're only one man. You won't stand against the sultan's army, or even against Shugat. That holy man will blast you into a million pieces!"

"*Silence, idiot! You will not defy me!*"

"Are you kidding? To my last *breath* I'll defy you, Lional! I won't be a party to your—"

And then he was flying through the air, boneless as a rag doll. He cried aloud as he crashed into the wall on the cave's far side. Cried out again as Lional's sweeping arm hurtled him into the ceiling, and yet again as he was thrown mercilessly into the dirt at Lional's feet.

"*Now* do you see who you're dealing with, Gerald? *Now* do you see that I *will* have my way?"

Dazed, bruised, his body harsh with pain, he stared up into Lional's demented face. "And what about Melissande? Where does she come into this?"

Lional laughed. "She's my tool, Gerald, just like you and your little friend Reg! By the will of the gods that I've created, Melissande shall marry Zazoor and bear him a son. Once that's accomplished Zazoor and his ridiculous brother will die and *I* shall rule Kallarap in her name. Kallarap will cease to exist, desert and oasis both shall be New Ottosland and New Ottosland shall be the most powerful nation in history, ruled by the greatest wizard king this world has ever known!"

Breathing hard, Gerald sat up. There was blood

running down the back of his throat and trickling down his face from a cut on his cheek. He touched it with unsteady fingertips, wincing as he found the split flesh. "Oh Lional," he whispered. "You really are insane."

"All the great visionaries throughout history have been called so," said Lional. "We do not heed the gabbling of our inferiors."

"Well, you'd better heed this, *Your Majesty*," he said, his jaw clenched tight. "You might as well go ahead and kill me now because I will *never* make you a dragon."

"Really?" said Lional. "Are you quite sure?"

Gerald watched, uncertain, as Lional reached into a pocket, withdrew a fine silk handkerchief then dropped to one knee beside him. Flinched, as Lional dabbed the still-wet blood from his cheek.

"Dear, dear Gerald," he said caressingly, and leaned close. His pupils were enormous, empty black pits. "So eager for death. You have no idea . . ." His hands came up, confining, restraining.

"No!" Gerald protested as Lional pressed warm lips to his open mouth and exhaled. Revolted, he shoved the madman away and rolled over, smearing a dirty sleeve across his mouth. "What was that? What the hell did you just do?"

Smiling, Lional stood and tucked the bloodstained handkerchief back in his pocket. "Patience, Gerald. You'll see."

Gagging, guts roiling, he sat up. There was a foul taste in his mouth. A buzzing in his head like a rampaging swarm of wasps. Wasps with stings. And they were *stinging* . . .

"Now, Gerald," said Lional as he fell sideways against the rough cave wall, retching. "Tell me again how you won't make a dragon?"

The torment continued for hours. For days.

Lost in a sea of suffering he was dimly aware that Lional came and went at will. Countless minutes passed, each one lasting an eternity. From time to time he fainted in an attempt to escape the misery but the blessed darkness never hid him for long. Lional's clever curses always found him and dragged him, screaming, back to the light.

Every time Lional returned to the brightly lit cave he asked the same question: "*Gerald, will you make me a dragon?*" and every time he returned the same answer. "*No.*"

Then Lional would sigh with counterfeit sorrow and breathe another pestilence into his mouth. Boils, or carbuncles. Lesions. Rashes. A bloody flux or stones in his kidneys. Racked with pain and a kind of fascinated horror, he watched his flesh swell and fissure, watched the pus well and drip into the dirt of the cave floor where eventually he lay naked, because the torment of fabric against the open sores on his skin was impossible to bear. His body seared and sweated and convulsed in protest against the afflictions Lional visited upon it. His hair fell out in scab-encrusted clumps. His fingernails rotted softly in their beds, consumed with fungal infections. His teeth shivered in their shrinking sockets. Ulcers colonised his mouth and tongue and cataracts blurred his bloody sight.

And still he said: "*No.*"

Eventually Lional's patience began to wear thin. "I think you're labouring under a misapprehension, Gerald," he hissed, his lips pressed close. "Do you think this is a competition you can *win*? It's not. And you can't die, either. Not unless I say you can. But I won't. How will I have my dragon if you're a discarded sack of bones and bile? No, Gerald. You will live. Like this. Abandoned to a life of solitude and suffering."

Gerald dragged open his pus-filled eyes. His gums were bleeding. "*You wouldn't . . .*"

Lional gently touched what was left of his filth-matted hair. "Of course I would. I will. Or, Gerald, you can make me a dragon."

"No," he whispered. "Never."

Lional clicked his tongue disapprovingly. "Never is a very long time. Would you like to know how long? I'll show you . . ." And he whispered foul words into the air, and laughed, and left.

Then came pain so complete, so obliterating, that everything he had suffered before was as an overture to a symphony. The cave disappeared into roaring flame and he lost all track of who he was. Where he was. What he loved and believed in, and why. Lost track of everything except the endless sound of his screams.

The next time Lional leaned close and said, "*Gerald, will you make me a dragon?*" he couldn't speak. His throat was swollen shut and his tongue refused to obey him. Nor could he remember what he was doing here or why he suffered so unspeakably. His mind was breaking, the weft and warp of his intellect unravelling, he could feel it as he now felt everything: with a keen and cruel clarity that could not be escaped. The words of his wizard's oath whirled in his giddy brain like autumn leaves, whipped to a frenzy by the wind.

"I, Gerald Dunwoody, wizard, do pledge my powers for good and good alone. Utterly and forever do I renounce the forces of darkness and ne'er will do any soul harm. So say I, unto death and whatever may come thereafter.

But there was no *thereafter*. There was only this.

"A living death, Gerald . . . from now unto the end of time," whispered Lional. "Can you endure it? Can you prevail? Your mind is going. Soon you'll be a moaning, witless beast, drooling in its piss and shit. *Is that what you want?*"

He heard himself moan. Heard a sob force its way past his pulpy lips. He shook his head.

"Of course it isn't," crooned Lional. "Poor Gerald. You've been so brave. But now it's time for the torment to stop. I can make it go away. I *will* make it go away. My word as king, how can you doubt it? All you have to do is make me my dragon. Will you, Gerald? Will you make me my dragon?"

He unbent one bloody, nail-less finger, rested its tip in the cave's dirt floor and with the dregs of his strength, wrote *No*.

And then, so slowly, he wrote again. *Yes*.

Lional kissed him. "Oh, *well done*, Gerald. I *knew* you would."

And then he left.

After that, Gerald slept. When he woke it was to a confusing absence of pain. Curled in a ball he wondered about that, teasing at his foggy memory to supply a reason. Memory obliged.

*Forsworn. Forsworn. I don't believe it. I'm forsworn.*

Tears of shame and misery rolled down his face. He wept until he was exhausted then fell asleep again. When he woke a second time it was to find fresh clothes folded neatly by his head, a jug of sweet water and some ripe peaches. His skin was whole. No fissures. No blisters. No blood, bile, pus or seepage of any kind and his nerves, so recently ablaze, were quiet once more. His hair and fingernails had all grown back.

He found a note from Lional, written in a grandiose hand. *There now, Gerald. Doesn't that feel better? How silly you were to defy me for so long.*

Starving, thirsty, he ate the peaches and drank the jug dry. Pulled on the clean shirt and trousers then sat in the armchair Lional had left behind. He wondered how long he'd been down here, and discovered he had no idea. With no sunrise and sunset to guide him, just the constant illumination from Lional's magical lights, he was adrift in time. The whole world might have ended and he'd never know it.

*Did Reg ever come back? Did she even make it home in one piece? I guess I'll never know now. Reg, I'm sorry. I failed you.*

The thought of her dead was almost unbearable. The thought of her thinking *him* dead just as bad.

*If she did make it back would Lional tell me? He says he needs her. Does that mean she's safe, if she's here? If he's got her, would he hurt her to keep me in line? Would he hurt me again to make her do his will?*

Yes he would. Lional would do anything to get what he wanted. He had no conscience. He had no soul.

*If Reg came back, did she bring Monk with her? Is he a prisoner somewhere too, tortured as I was? Corrupted as I was? Or is he dead? If he's dead . . . if they're both dead . . .*

He had no way of knowing. Not until Lional came back and he asked. Even then, Lional might lie. Would probably lie.

*How did this happen? How did I let it happen? Why didn't I stop it?*

He knew the answers. They made him sick.

*Because I was stubborn. Because I was greedy. Because all I cared about was being the great wizard.*

Yeah. Well. He wasn't so great now, was he?

Desperate for a distraction from his self-loathing thoughts he tried casting a spell, a simple colour change to make his blue shirt green. It didn't work. Clearly Lional's lodestone remained in operation. He looked and looked, but couldn't find it. Nor could he find the door out of the cave. Lional must have masked that too.

Lional, who wielded the power of five First Grade wizards and had read *Grummen's Lexicon* and wanted a dragon.

He returned to the chair, despairing.

*Once upon a time there lived a wizard named Gerald, who'd truly believed the worst thing that could ever happen to him was accidentally destroying a staff factory.*

What an *idiot*. A gullible, naive, ignorant *idiot*.

Well. That Gerald was dead. Burned to ashes in the crucible of Lional's cave. He'd been replaced by someone who might look like him and sound like him but in reality was hollow inside except for the things he knew and the memories that mocked him. Cruel, terrible memories . . .

He tried to go back to sleep but no matter what he did, how hard he pounded his fists against his forehead or ground the heels of his hands into his tightly shut eyes, he couldn't escape.

It was a relief when the door in the cave wall opened and Lional reappeared. "Gerald!" he cried as he sealed the door behind him. "You're awake! How splendid. Did you sleep well?"

"What do you think?"

Lional chose not to notice his surly tone. He smiled. "*Excellent.*"

With a grunt of effort he stood. "What time is it? How long have I been here?"

"It's six o'clock in the morning and you've been here for nearly nine days."

*Nine days.* "Reg? Has she come back? Is she all right?"

Lional sighed. "Regrettably, no. She hasn't come back, which doubtless means that she's dead. Now that's enough small talk. We've an enormous amount of work to do and we've already wasted a lot of time, so I'd like to get started straight away."

Gerald felt his heart thud dully against his ribs. *Dead? No. Not Reg. Not after so long, after everything she's survived. I won't believe it. Not until I see her body with my own eyes.*

*Reg is not dead.*

"Gerald?" said Lional, eyebrows raised. "Is something the matter? You've *such* a look on your face . . ."

For a moment he was so choked with disbelief he couldn't speak. Who was this man? *What* was he, that he could stand there after every hideous thing he'd done, stand there with his perfect grooming and his exquisite clothes and an actual look of concern on his face and ask, quite genuinely, *Is something the matter?*

Dazed, he backed up until he bumped into the cave wall. What was he thinking? Was he *mad*? How could he even *consider* helping Lional? Lional was a monster. A perversion.

*If I help Lional what does that make me?*

Lional frowned. "Oh dear." Step by deliberate step the king closed the distance between them until only scant inches separated their bodies. Rested a hand against the rock on either side of his face and leaned close. His breath smelled of peppermint. "Now Gerald, I do hope you're not thinking of changing your mind. That would make me very disappointed. And if you believe nothing else I say, believe this. Disappointing me would be the biggest mistake of your life."

Gerald closed his eyes. This was it. His last chance to reclaim his dignity, his self-respect, his honour. What was the point of living if your life was paid for with a broken oath? In his hands rested the fate of two nations, of thousands upon thousands of innocent lives. How could he buy his own comfort with such precious coin?

*I can't.*

Stomach churning, he opened his eyes.

"Think before you speak, Gerald," Lional advised. "For you must know by now the true heart beating in my breast. If you defy me I will hurt you in ways no man could tell."

"I don't care," he whispered. "There's nothing you can do that could be worse than knowing I'm forsworn."

Lional sighed. "Ah. Well, Gerald, I'm afraid that's where you're wrong." A heartbeat later he was holding an oval-shaped hand mirror, bright as a full moon. *His* mirror, from the dresser in his palace suite. "Let me show you."

Against his will Gerald looked at his reflection and saw the dreadful changes that had been wrought in his face. Then his hollow-cheeked, haunted-eyed image faded and instead he was looking at a different self. Hanging in midair, spread-eagled and held fast by invisible chains. His head was thrown back, the great tendons of his neck distorted, distended, and his mouth gaped wide in a soundless scream. His shirt hung in rags and the skin and muscle covering the left side of his chest was missing. Through the gleaming cage of his ribs he could see his heart frantically beating, pumping his blood in a scarlet river from the mouths of countless wounds hacked into his prisoned flesh. Some kind of serpent, green and glistening, was wrapped around his right leg. Another clasped his right arm. They were eating him. Tearing great bloody mouthfuls of him from the bone. And as they chewed and swallowed and hissed, his ravaged flesh grew back again, swift as blizzarding snow. The serpents bared their razor teeth, bent their bright-scaled heads, and filled their bellies again. And again. And again.

Against all possibility he felt the pain.

Bones melting with horror he turned away, cheek pressed hard to the rough cave wall.

Lional's remorseless finger beneath his chin turned him back to the nightmare. "There is no mercy in me and I won't be denied. My kingdom has suffered ignominy for seven centuries and if you don't make me a dragon, Gerald, *you* will suffer for even longer." He raised the mirror. "Defy me and this will be your reward, forever and ever unto the end of time. And *nobody* will come to save you. I promise. So, Gerald. Do you defy me? *Do you?*"

He dragged his eyes away from that unspeakable image of suffering and forced himself to meet Lional's pitiless gaze.

*Forever and ever unto the end of time.*

Courage died, brief and blazing as a falling star.

"No," he whispered. "I don't. I'll do it, Lional. I'll make you a dragon. Please . . . don't hurt me again."

"Of course I won't, Gerald," said Lional and banished the mirror. "Provided you continue to be reasonable."

*Reasonable.* The word was nearly his undoing. Fingers compressed into fists held his grief at bay . . . but only just.

*At least my parents will never know.*

With a theatrical flourish Lional summoned a wooden crate from . . . elsewhere . . . and stood there looking at it with a gleaming gloating smile. Then he looked up.

"Oh Gerald, you're not *sulking*, are you? *Don't*, I implore you. It's desperately unattractive. Now come here, quickly. I've something to show you."

Clumsily, as though his muscles had forgotten their purpose, he joined Lional beside the crate.

Two feet long and one foot wide, its base and four sides were solid timber; the top consisted of narrow slats nailed in place to allow ventilation but no escape. From inside the box came the rustle of claws in dry grass and a long sibilant hiss. He glimpsed a vivid scaled hide striped crimson and emerald. Black eyes, malevolently glinting. A crest of spines, each sharp tip oozing a viscous green fluid. The creature opened its mouth to hiss again, revealing row after row of diamond-bright teeth and a long slimy tongue. It took a deep breath and spat something crimson at the bars keeping it caged in the box; the wood smoked and belched green fire but remained intact.

"Isn't she beautiful?" crooned Lional. "She's a Bearded Spitting Fire Lizard from the darkest jungles of Lower Limpopo. You wouldn't believe what I had to go through to get her. I mean, Bondaningo was almost as stubborn as you've been when it came to helping me. But of course he saw reason in the end. Amongst other things. I think she'll make a splendid dragon, don't you?"

Speech still beyond him, Gerald could only shrug.

Lional looked at him sharply. "I said *no sulking*, Professor. If you can't stop by yourself I have a remedy of my own we could try . . ."

He felt his guts spasm. "I'm not sulking, I'm—" *Craven. Beaten. Pathetic.* "Tired. That's all. I'm just tired."

"Not too tired to make me my dragon, I hope?"

"Look. Lional. What if—" He cleared his throat. "What if I can't do it? Transmogrification on this level is almost unheard of. The mass conversion ratio, the inverse thaumaturgical fluctuations . . ." He gestured at the crate. "That's a big lizard but compared to a dragon it's *tiny*. What you're asking for might not be metaphysically possible to achieve no matter who was trying."

"Well, for your sake, Gerald, I hope that's not the case," said Lional coldly.

He flinched. "All right then. Say I can turn this lizard into a dragon. How are you going to control it? It's not like Tavistock. He may have the body of a lion but in his head he's still your cat. This lizard is a wild animal. It's lethal, a killing machine. It'd kill us both now if it could. What hope is there of controlling it once it's dragon-sized?"

Lional's smile was smug. "I was wondering when that would occur to you, Gerald. Don't worry. I really have thought this through very carefully."

With a pointed finger and a sharp command he collapsed the lizard's crate then immobilised the creature before it could recover from its surprise and start spitting. Next he snapped his fingers and produced a small knife with a wicked blade and a carved ivory handle.

Staring, Gerald felt sluggish memory stir. "You can't—you're not actually going to risk—"

"The *Tantigliani sympathetico*?" said Lional, glancing at him. "Well spotted, Gerald. And yes. I am."

"You *can't*! Tantigliani was mad!"

Without hesitation or any sign of pain Lional sliced open his left palm from one side to the other.

"Tantigliani," he said, as thick red blood welled from the wound, "was a misunderstood genius."

"He was an *assassin*! Over a hundred people died because of him!"

Lional shrugged. "Perhaps, but he was a *brilliant* assassin. Only at the very end did anyone so much as suspect that the horses, the dogs and the bulls that killed their owners were anything but deranged creatures run amok."

No. No. This was *beyond* insane. "Lional, you can't do this! What if you lose control? This lizard's not a *horse*, it's not *domesticated*. How can you hope to impose your will upon—"

"I don't hope, Gerald," said Lional, serene. "I know." Crouching beside the unmoving lizard he fisted his wounded hand above it. Blood flowed between his fingers and down his wrist, staining his white silk shirtsleeve. "*Absorhidato.*" Carefully, his expression intent, he dripped the blood over the lizard's hide in a complex pattern of splatters and blotches. Within seconds of it touching the brilliantly hued scales the blood vanished.

"You think all those stolen *potentias* will protect you," said Gerald, chilled with fresh horror. "What if you're wrong?"

"I'm not," said Lional. He stroked a fingertip along the lizard's length from nose to tail. "*Manifesti retarto.*" Then he rose smoothly to his feet. Lifting his wounded hand to eye level he turned it palm outwards to show the gaping crimson slash, whispered a command, and smiled again as the still-dripping blood crawled backwards into the wound and his flesh knitted itself whole again. "As you can see, Gerald, my control is absolute."

# CHAPTER TWENTY-ONE

Numb, Gerald nodded. "Yes, Lional," he said dully. "I can see."

"Good." Lional smiled. "And now, my friend, I believe it's your turn."

*My turn? No, I have to stop him. Think, Dunnywood. Think.*

"I need a First Grade staff."

"*You?*" said Lional. "Surely that's not necessary?"

He felt his lips peel back in a snarling smile. "Better safe than sorry."

"Oh, very well." Lional held out his hand. The air shimmered, then he was holding a staff. Tall. Slender. Bound in gold. "But a word of warning first. Just in case you're thinking of heroics after all and intend sacrificing yourself in order to do me a mischief with this little toy. As we speak, Melissande is metaphysically imprisoned in her royal apartments. Should I not return to release the incant or be so badly injured I can no longer function, she will die a slow excruciating death. So you can see, Gerald, it's in her best interests that you mind your manners."

*Damn.* His heart thudded painfully. "You're lying."

Lional shrugged. "It's possible. But are you willing to bet Melissande's life on it?"

*I should be but . . .* "You won't hurt Melissande. You can't. You need her. She's a part of your crazy plan."

"A small part, yes. But without the dragon it's all meaningless, Gerald. Which makes my sister meaningless too."

"And what if the dragon kills you?"

Another shrug. "Then she dies. But I've already told you, Gerald. That isn't going to happen." He tossed the staff.

Gerald caught it midair. Inspected it closely as a buzz of latent thaumic energy prickled his skin.

"That was Bottomley's staff," said Lional. "Inadequate for my purposes of course, but—" He stared. "I fail to see what's so amusing."

Chased into the gold filigree, an audacious claim: *Stuttley's Staffs, Finest in the World.*

"Nothing," he said, and with an effort throttled the urge to laugh . . . or weep. "Nothing."

"Then I suggest you get to work."

"The lodestone?"

Lional snapped his fingers. "Is now deactivated."

For one dreadful moment Gerald almost attacked. His fingers spasmed on poor Humphret Bottomley's staff and the words of yet another incant Reg shouldn't have taught him caught fire in his racing mind.

*You have to. He's evil. Melissande would understand . . .*

"Incidentally," said Lional, closely watching.

"Melissande's is not the only life you hold in your hands. The entire palace is under my control. That's hundreds of lives, Gerald. Think about that before you do something unfortunate. I promise you will never remove the binding incant yourself."

Damn. Lional *had* to be lying. Making it up as he went along.

*But what if he isn't?*

His fingers unclenched; blood rushed back, painfully. "How big do you want this dragon?"

Lional smiled beatifically. "As big as you can make it, Gerald."

"What about the *sympathetico*?"

"I'll trigger it once you've made the dragon. Now, no more *questions*. Get on with it!"

He nodded. "You'd better stand back. If this works the cave is going to get . . . crowded."

As Lional retreated to the furthest stretch of wall Gerald turned his attention to the still-motionless lizard. Closed his eyes and sought the words he'd used to change Tavistock from cat to lion. And there they were, burning in his blood.

*Damn Reg for ever sharing them. Damn me for making them work.*

A thought struck him. What would happen if he just . . . *changed* them a little? Sowed a seed of destruction within the incant itself? Some kind of time-delayed unravelling spell perhaps, that could—

"*Gerald* . . ."

He opened his eyes, praying his expression was blank. *I can do this, I'm redeemed* . . . "I need to concentrate, Lional."

"Of course you do. Most of all on *this* . . ."

The staff slipping from his grasp Gerald dropped to his knees, felled by a single searing flame that licked along every last nerve in his body. He would have screamed if there'd been room in him for anything but pain. Gasping, he forced himself to meet Lional's blazing eyes.

"Don't take me for a fool, little man. I'm sure the thought is very tempting but I'll know if you try to spoil things."

"I wasn't, I—"

Lional's fingers closed into a fist. Gerald felt himself spasm, felt his spine and all his frozen muscles twist and tangle in one huge convulsion of agony.

"Of course you were," said Lional, impatient. "I *know* you, Gerald. You're an honourable man. Don't insult my intelligence by pretending otherwise! But even honourable men have their limits . . . and we both know that I've found yours. I suggest you end this pitiful self-delusion and do as I ask."

Bowed almost in half, vision smearing and blearing, Gerald managed to nod. To grunt, "Yes. Yes."

"All right then," said Lional, releasing him. "But remember. I'm watching."

When the last whispers of pain had faded into silence he retrieved the staff, used it to regain his feet and shuffled around till he was facing Lional's immobilised lizard.

*If you're listening, gods of Kallarap, this would be an excellent time to strike me dead . . .*

The gods of Kallarap chose not to oblige.

The gold-filigreed staff thrummed in his sweating

hand. Blanking his mind of everything but the terrible words he was about to say, Gerald pointed it at the lizard.

"*Innocuasi cumbadalarum! Amini desporati animali contradicti draco dracorum!*"

For the second time in his life he felt the stirrings of an immeasurably formidable power as the transmogrification spell formed in the invisible ether.

"*Incantata magicata spellorantum infinatum! Enlargiosa dragonara expellecta lizardizo!*"

For three frantic heartbeats, no response. And then the kaleidoscope fracturing of his mind. The rush of energy like a hot dry wind, pleasure and pain and a wild, wild freedom. He closed his eyes, buffeted by a catastrophic glory as the golden staff shuddered and writhed. The chaos of power consumed itself and vanished . . . and he opened his eyes.

There was a dragon in the cave.

It was thirty feet long from nose to tail. Twelve feet tall at the shoulder. Like the lizard it used to be, its hide was banded crimson and emerald. Its massive wings, folded neatly against its breathing sides, were crimson. Its eyes, the size of soccer balls, were a fathomless and glowing black. It opened its mouth and yawned: a spittle of green poison trickled down one long, daggerish tooth and puddled on the cave floor. The dirt melted.

It was beautiful.

It was a monster.

It looked at him, eyes blinking lazily.

Gerald stepped back. *Oh God. What have I done?*
Lional laughed then raised his right hand, fingers

pointing. "*Manifesti asbsolutum! Tantigliani sympathetico obedientium singularum mi! Nux nullimia!*"

The dragon froze. Deep in each dark eye a crimson flame flared to life, burned sun-bright then subsided into a glowing ember like a coal at the heart of a banked fire.

"Did it work?" Gerald croaked. "Can you control it?"

"Let's see," said Lional. Throwing his head back he slowly, slowly extended his arms out to each side. Slowly, slowly, obedient as a reflection in a mirror, the dragon unfolded its wings and stretched them until their tips brushed the sides of the cave. Lional smiled. His eyes drifted shut. He lowered his outstretched arms and the dragon's wings echoed him. "What an extraordinary feeling!" he whispered, his face alight with wonder. "I'm in her mind. Such a hot and hungry place . . . and beautiful. So beautiful. It's like coming home. Ah, my love, my lovely. The things we'll do together, you and I . . ."

Gerald risked a sideways shuffle. When neither Lional nor the dragon objected, he retreated all the way to the nearest bit of wall and collapsed against it, the staff slipping from his fingers to the ground. All its gold filigree had melted, the oak beneath it charred and spoiled. His legs were trembling and his heart hurt with pounding.

*I made a dragon. I made a dragon.*

Lional was crooning to the creature, a song of welcome and delight. His hand pressed against one crimson-scaled cheek. The dragon's tail lashed lazily across the cave's dirt floor and its enormous eyes blinked as it drank Lional's worship like wine.

"And now, my darling . . ." Lional whispered. "Let us explore the limits of our power." His voice was dreamy and in his half-lidded eyes Gerald thought he saw a glimpse of something . . . inhuman. Lional drifted towards the rear of the cave, fingers caressing the dragon's hide as he passed, and came to a halt before the rough-hewn back wall. "*Revellati*."

The rock rippled . . . and disappeared.

Gerald swallowed his shock. Beyond the vanished cave wall was a dawn-kissed valley; in the burgeoning light he saw fields and flowers and trees but no hint of human habitation.

He breathed in the fresh air. *Freedom*. It was just scant steps away.

"Gerald . . ." said Lional. "Please don't. We would hate to hurt you."

He turned away from the dawn. "I thought you were going to kill me now you've got your dragon."

Lional smiled, and the dragon bared its teeth. "I was. But then I thought—what if one dragon isn't enough? She might like a mate. A squadron. An *armada*. Until I've decided, I think you'd better live."

Was that good or bad? He had no idea. *I made a dragon. I'm going to hell.* A sweet breeze was teasing the nape of his neck. He tried to ignore it. "So. Lional. What now?"

"Now?" Lional looked into the rising sun. "Now we spread our wings, Gerald. We survey our kingdom . . . and we taste the new day. Come. You won't want to miss this."

He stared. "Come where?"

"Where do you think?" said Lional, eyebrows lifted. "Into the sky, with us."

For a moment he couldn't grasp what Lional meant. Then he looked at the dragon and choked. "You're going to *fly* on that thing?" He took a step back. "Not with me."

"*Come!*" said Lional. His eyes flickered crimson. "Don't make me chastise you, Gerald."

So he was going to die after all. Smash himself to pieces falling off the dragon he'd so cleverly created.

*Some might call that poetic justice.*

He watched as Lional called the dragon to him; the creature went eagerly, tame as a kitten. Then he stepped out of the cave after it, treading with care. The sunlight was warm against his chilled skin.

"Come closer," said Lional. "She won't bite you. Not until I tell her to."

Reluctantly he approached the dragon.

With a combination of oiled muscle and metaphysical suggestion, Lional tossed him onto the monster's back. He landed with a thud behind the massive juncture of wing and body. The heat radiating from its hide was fierce; he could feel it like a furnace though his trousers.

Then Lional vaulted lightly behind him and all he could think of was that he was sitting on a beast created from myth and magic and there was nothing to hold onto and the enormous wings were lifting . . . lifting . . . and Lional was laughing . . .

. . . and then the ground fell away in a sickening swoop as the impossible beast leapt into the blushing sky, a hissing shriek bursting from its throat even as Lional, still laughing, cried aloud in glee.

Desperately Gerald clutched at the knobbly protrusions at the base of the dragon's wings and concentrated on breathing, just breathing, because fear was a fire in his chest, consuming oxygen. Consuming him. He closed his eyes.

Lional's merciless hand clasped his shoulder. "Don't be afraid, Gerald! We won't let you fall. Look! *Look*!"

Reluctantly, he obeyed. Rising before him was the dragon's crimson and emerald neck, round as a tree trunk and just as solid. The crested spines lay flat to its hide, their poison quiescent. On either side of him the giant wings rose and fell, rose and fell; he could feel the slick slide of bone and muscle between his wide-stretched legs as the dragon's rib cage expanded and contracted, each stroke cleaving the air with a crack like thunder. The cold air streamed into his eyes and all his exposed flesh chilled.

And then he looked down . . . and the fear returned, roaring, to burn his churning insides to ashes.

They'd left the hidden valley far behind. Beneath them unrolled field after field of grain, of grazing cattle and somnolent sheep. Farmers toiled, slaves to the rhythms of the natural world. As the dragon passed overhead, roaring and lashing its tail, they looked up . . . Heart breaking, he saw terror and disbelief contort all their faces, human and animal alike. Plough horses screamed and bolted, cows stampeded, the sheep huddled shoulder to shoulder and bleated their distress.

Then he cried out as the dragon dived lower, neck outstretched, mouth wide and gaping. Behind him, Lional was breathless with laughter. "Not yet, my lovely, hold your hunger at bay! We shall feed soon,

I promise you sweet one! We shall feed till our belly bursts with blood!"

The dragon wheeled away, head swinging from side to side in grumbling resentment. Gerald wanted to turn back, to shout his warnings and his regrets to the tiny fleeing figures on the ground far below. Fresh guilt seared him, churned his guts and spasmed his legs about the dragon's heaving sides.

Now in New Ottosland there'd be widespread panic . . . running and screaming and lives plunged into terrified chaos . . . and it was all his fault.

*I should've made him kill me. I should've found a way.*

Then, as he continued to clutch at the base of the beast's wings, he thought he *felt* something. Or heard it. Two voices whispering on the far edge of reason. One human, one not. Closing his eyes again he strained to hear what the voices were saying.

Behind him Lional was crooning again, a ceaseless, sibilant, disconcerting song. Startled, he recognised it as the human voice he could feel through his contact with the dragon's hot hide.

Which meant the other voice belonged to the dragon. No words, there. Just a burning stream of thought and feeling, like lava flowing down a mountainside.

As the countryside unrolled beneath them like a map unfurling, as fields surrendered to houses and paved roads, he tried to see and hear more clearly . . . and was startled almost into falling to his death.

Lional and the dragon's voices—their *minds*—were twining like two separate cords, crimson and black, weaving and counterweaving through and about each other to form one dissoluble thread. Soon there would be no unravelling one from the other. They would be a single entity, a unified intelligence. A man-dragon. A dragon-man.

Despite the seething fear and the pain as he blistered his fingers on the dragon's wings, Gerald turned around. Lional's face was frozen in an expression of bliss, lips soundlessly framing the words he could still hear as faint echoes in his reeling mind.

"*Stop* it, Lional!" he shouted. "You're losing yourself! The *sympathetico*—it's backfiring! Break free of the dragon while you still—"

And then he cried out in terror, because Lional's hand was anchored to his shirt collar and Lional's inhumanly strong arm was lifting him off the dragon's back—was dragging him over the dragon's side—was dangling him above the roofs of the houses passing beneath them. His shirt collar was strangling him, his bare flailing feet kicked at thin air. Then Lional hauled him back again and settled him safely behind the dragon's wings.

"*Hush*, Gerald," he whispered. "Didn't your mother tell you? It's rude to interrupt."

Speechless, Gerald clung to the dragon and stared at the ground beneath the creature's belly. At the horse-drawn carriages milling in disarray on every street of the capital. At the pointing, shouting people of New Ottosland whose lives were being torn to pieces even as they clutched one another, weeping, or ran away as though running could save them.

The dragon swooped down on them, its terrible jaws open, fire and poison falling like rain. Gerald stared, sick with horror.

*Fire? Fire? How can there be fire? It was only a lizard, it couldn't breathe flames!*

Except that everyone knew dragons breathed fire. In every story ever written about dragons, in every painting ever put on canvas, there was the dragon . . . and there were the flames.

*I did this. I changed the lizard to fit my imagination. I didn't know I could do that. I can't believe I made things worse . . .*

He heard the screaming, smelled the smoke of carriages burning, horses burning, people . . . burning. Saw them burning, silhouettes of flame.

"Lional, *no!* What are you doing? Those are your subjects, you took an oath to protect them!"

Lional said nothing, he was communing with his dragon. The beast swooped lower, almost skimming the ground. Its massive tail lashed side to side, smashing the nearest buildings to rubble, splintering trees like so much kindling, tossing men and women and carriage horses through the air as though they were made of paper.

Perhaps they were. They burned like paper.

Gerald hid from the sight behind one blistered hand, overwhelmed by annihilating grief.

*It's my fault. It's my fault. I was right. I'm a murderer.*

With a last roaring cry the dragon wheeled away from the city and headed back to the hidden valley. As they left the chaotic streets and the broken buildings and the dead and those mourning them far behind Lional fell silent, along with the dragon. Because they had nothing further to say, or because they no longer needed speech, Gerald didn't know.

He didn't want to know.

The dragon landed like thistledown at the mouth of the cave. Lional pushed Gerald to the ground and stared down at him disdainfully from the dragon's high back.

Shivering like a man with fever he staggered to his feet. "Lional, why did you *do* that? Why did you attack your sovereign subjects?"

Lional shrugged. The dragon shrugged with him. "Because we wanted to. Because it amused us. Because we are their king and they are ours to play with."

*We. Us.* He didn't want to think about that . . . "It was wrong. They were innocent. And they're not *yours*, you don't *own* them."

Lional and his dragon sighed. "Ah, Gerald. We hoped you would see. We hoped at last you would understand. But you do not. Your thoughts to us are clear as glass, and empty. No greatness in you for all your powers. You are puny and your purpose is served. Crawl into your cage and wait for us, little man. We will return when you are required."

*I could refuse. I could defy him. The dragon would kill me and this would be over.*

Except he couldn't. That would be taking the coward's way out. As long as he lived there was a chance . . . no matter how remote . . . of somehow finding a way to stop Lional. To undo the damage. To make good, in part at least, his terrible mistakes.

He backed up slowly till he stood once more in his rocky prison. "When will that be? When will I be . . . *required* . . . again?"

"We do not know." As Lional smiled, poison

dripped smoking from the dragon's open mouth. "But we do have news for you. We saved it for this moment."

"What news?"

"The bird has returned."

*Reg.* Disbelieving joy surged through him, momentarily banishing grief. "She came back? She's all right? Can I see her?"

Lional's smile widened; the dragon hissed. "If you like." He snapped his fingers and a moment later was holding something limp. Feathered. Dangling. Lional tossed it. There was a thud as it landed in the dirt at Gerald's feet.

He couldn't look at it.

Lional stroked the dragon's crimson and emerald hide. All its spines stood upright, glistening. "Yes, my friend, the bird came back," he said dreamily. "And it was rude. So Lional killed it."

Gerald staggered sideways, groping for the solidity of the cave wall. He still couldn't bring himself to look at the thing at his feet.

Lional snapped his fingers. "*Vanishati.*"

The air before Gerald's eyes rippled. Solidified. Became rock. Once more he was imprisoned inside the cave, with a few bobbing lights to alleviate the dark. Only this time he wasn't alone. After a long, long moment he lowered his gaze to the floor.

Bent and broken feathers. Brown, with a tracing of black. Creamy flecks on breast and face. A brown band across the glazed unseeing eyes.

*Reg.*

Without warning all the little lights still clustered

against the roof went out and the cave was plunged into utter darkness.

Gerald fell to his knees. Fell further. Lay face down in the dirt, and wept.

# CHAPTER TWENTY-TWO

The Sultan of Kallarap's palace was a modest, single-level, twenty-room affair built of mysteriously acquired blue and grey marble slabs. Located in the middle of a small but fertile oasis, it basked in shade provided by groves of date palms. The desert's dry air tinkled with the music of fountains and songbirds, thrummed with the rushing eagerness of cunningly designed miniature waterfalls. Gentle breezes stirred perfume from lovingly tended flowerbeds. Peace; tranquility; reverent calm: all surrounded the sultan's home, drowsy in the sunshine.

Mid-morning's hush roused briefly as a camel barked from the comfort of its bed in the stable yard beyond the gardens, where the sultan's peerless racing team lived in luxury.

Moments later all the camels were barking as a train of their brethren returned from a long hot journey beneath the burning sun, across daunting miles of sparkling sand and treacherous, shifting dunes.

As camel boys tipped out of their hammocks and raced to succour their weary charges, Shugat slid creakily from his saddle and blessed his beast, for it had carried him well and the gods liked their children to be appreciated. Then he turned to the sultan's regrettable brother and said curtly, "You will wait in the gods' room while I seek their guidance. Once the will of the Three is revealed we will report to the sultan, may he live forever, the outcome of our mission."

Nerim slid off his camel in such a rush that he nearly sprawled on the mud brick ground. "But Shugat, the gods have *already* spoken! Zazoor must—"

He stepped close to the prince and glared. "Be silent!" he hissed, with a quick glance to make sure the camel boys weren't listening. "It is not for you to say what was seen and heard in the court of New Ottosland's oath-breaker king. Remain silent or I shall petition the gods to shrivel your tongue and your manhood both! Now do as I bid you, Blood of the Sultan, may he live forever. I will join you presently."

Chastened, with the whites of his eyes showing his proper fear, Nerim clasped his dirty hands palm to palm before his chest and bowed. "I hear and obey, Holy One."

Shaking his head, Shugat glared after Zazoor's foolish brother as he hobbled away, then collected his staff from his camel's saddle, silenced the protests from his aged muscles and turned his back on the chattering camel boys to seek the solitude and wisdom of his gods.

Surely they would speak to him here in holy Kallarap.

He lived in a dwelling apart from the palace, but still within its grounds. No elegant marble edifice, his, but a squat and simple mud brick box, its roof a thatching of dried palm fronds plastered against the infrequent rain with cured camel dung. It was part of the arrangement the most senior holy men of Kallarap had made with the Three from the dawn of time: an austere life without adornment, accolades or the trappings of position, with simple clothes of undyed linen, plain meals of dates, camel milk and goat flesh, and every day of their allotted span spent in selfless service; in return they were gifted the glory of the gods' words and power enough to pluck a star from the sky should a single candle fail in the dark of night.

At the first touch of his gods' vast and fiery minds, all those years ago, he knew he had by far the better part of the bargain.

He knelt before their shrine now, still stinking and smudged with the grime and sweat of his long ride home. Devoutly carved into the precious wood, rare mahogany from a distant unknown land, inlaid with crafted and polished *andaleya*, the Tears of the Gods, they bent their ruby eyes upon him, the Dragon, the Lion and the Bird, waiting with their infinite patience for him to open his heart to their desires.

So he did. And after the long silence that had frightened him as he had never felt fear in his life . . . the Three heard his prayers and spoke to him.

He wept.

When at last they had imparted their desires, he

levered himself to his feet with his staff and went frowningly about the business of preparing for an audience with the sultan, who had no chance at all of living forever and moreover, unlike some of his forbears, knew so full well and was at peace with the knowledge.

Which was but one among many reasons why he liked Zazoor and had vowed to protect him and his honour to the last drop of blood and breath in his aged and wasting body.

Most especially he intended to protect him, and all of Kallarap, from the soulless predator known as His Sovereign Majesty King Lional, Forty-third ruler of New Ottosland.

The palace's gods' room was a high-ceilinged, incense-scented place of worship and contemplation. Hand-woven carpets of rich blues and greens covered the marble floor so that the sultan and his dependents might properly prostrate themselves before the Three set high upon their plinth in the chamber's centre.

Sunlight shafted through the attenuated windows, piercing the cool shadows and striking splendid sparks of colour from the gods' silver and gold wrought bodies, their ruby eyes, their diamond teeth and claws. Not wood, these icons, not even for the sultan. Only the most-blessed sultan's holy man, touched by the might and majesty of the Three, knelt before wood in a desert land where no wood was to be found.

As instructed, Nerim was waiting for him beneath the swathes of silk draped overhead from wall to wall. Less expected was the sight of Zazoor, an older mirror image of Nerim but, by some strange alchemy, more real, more vital, by the gods' grace distilled to the purest essence of intellect and honour. Kneeling on the carpets beside his young brother, head lowered and eyes half-closed in concentration, he listened to Nerim prattle breathlessly about—

Shugat frowned. Without hearing a single word he knew exactly what Nerim was prattling about. In his tightened grasp his staff quivered, and the single gods' Tear in his forehead flashed white fire.

Zazoor glanced up. One hand lifted, silencing his brother's rattling tongue. After a long, steady look at his holy man he turned his head, lips brushing Nerim's sun-scorched cheek. He whispered something into his brother's crimson-tipped ear. Nerim nodded, smiled, kissed his brother's hand, placed Zazoor's palm atop his head in formal obeisance and withdrew, skipping past like a camel colt caught in mischief.

Zazoor looked after him, a rueful smile thawing, a little, his natural reserve. "We both know there is no wilful disobedience in him, my holy man," he said, voice and dark blue eyes tranquil. "He was but overwhelmed by his experiences in New Ottosland. Did he drive you to complete distraction?"

Shugat scowled. "Not quite complete. My sultan—"

Zazoor raised a placating hand. "I know. I know. His intellect is . . . feeble. But he has a good heart and in some ways he is closer to the people than I, their sultan. It's why I sent him with you, Shugat. As a barometer."

"You think I did not know that?"

"No," said Zazoor. "I can hide nothing from my redoubtable Shugat. What did you learn from him?"

He snorted. "What you already knew, Zazoor. That weak eyes are easily dazzled."

Zazoor grinned, a rare flashing of white teeth, and uncoiled from the carpet to stand lightly on the balls of his feet, poised for any challenge the Three saw fit to provide. "So you did not care overmuch for my dear old school chum Lional?"

He would have spat, were it not that he stood in the gods' room, in their presence. "A veritable sand viper, Zazoor, and I fear I slight the snake to say so." He grimaced. "Even a sand viper may be spit-and-roasted if starvation is the only other choice. Not so this *Lional*. The flesh of New Ottosland's king would dissolve a man's teeth in his gums and burst his belly with acid bile."

"In other words," said Zazoor, "he hasn't changed." He indicated one of the marble benches set into the wall of the gods' room, in deference to the old and the infirm and the very young who found themselves in need of the gods' succour or assistance. "Come. Let us sit and talk, old friend."

Shugat bowed to the Three, shining in the sunlight, then took his place at Zazoor's side. Leaning back into the seating alcove, right knee drawn up to his chest, arms linked loosely about it, Zazoor considered him, one eyebrow raised in silent enquiry.

"This Lional is a bad man, my Sultan," he said, shaking his head. "He wishes us nothing but ill."

Zazoor frowned. "How do you know?"

He bared his stumpy teeth in a grim smile. "He offers you the hand of his only sister in marriage."

"Princess Melissande? Yes. So Nerim said." Zazoor pursed his lips in thought. "I met her. Years ago. A squat child with hair like rusty nails. I don't suppose . . ."

"Alas, no. Outwardly the lowliest maid in your smallest village is more comely to the eye."

"Ah." Zazoor sighed. He was a kind man. "A pity, then, for her sake."

"The palace servants say she is strict but fair, honest and overworked," he added. "Beauty burns away beneath the sun, Zazoor, but an honourable heart withstands even Grimthak's mighty flame, I judge Princess Melissande's heart to be most honourable. She would make a worthy wife and mother of your sons but she is not for you."

Zazoor's eyebrow lifted again. "That is not what Nerim says. Nerim says the gods most earnestly desire me to marry Lional's sister."

"As ever, Nerim snatches at the truth like a child greedy for a sweetmeat, who takes only the wrapping and leaves the real prize behind," he said, disapproving. "It is Lional who says the gods desire you to marry the girl. This is untrue. I say it again, great Sultan of Kallarap: the Princess Melissande is not for you. Her destiny lies along a different path."

"Ah," said Zazoor, then fell silent. At length he stirred, the merest hint of a rueful smile touching his lips. "No word yet, I suppose, on who is for me?"

He rapped his staff lightly against the side of the sultan's head. "When the gods choose your proper wife you will be the second to know."

Zazoor flattened his hands to his heart, the sign of obedient acceptance. "Lional thinks, of course, to void the treaties with this proposed marriage. Perhaps more, and worse. Knowing him as I do, his offer does not surprise me."

"More and worse," Shugat said grimly. "You have the right of it. You must refuse the king's offer in such a way that he cannot vent his rage upon his sister. For that, I judge, is the honour of *his* heart."

Zazoor smiled. "As always, friend Shugat, your eyes see a man's soul as keenly as Vorsluk." Then his smile faded and his face took on a solemn cast. "Nerim says Vorsluk and Lalchak were present in Lional's court. He says they answered Lional's plea but not your own. He says Vorsluk *spoke* on Lional's command." His breath caught in his throat as though he were nearly overcome. "These are wonders I did not think to hear, Shugat, and I confess I find them hard to believe . . . but can I deny them? Nerim is my brother and for all his foolishness he does not lie."

Shugat rested his chin on his chest and sighed deeply. "Nerim's faith is pure. He looks at the world with the eyes of a child, Zazoor, and in his breast beats the heart of a child. Like a child he cannot conceive of wickedness and perfidy. I may at times long to beat him, but still I would have him thus till the end of his days if to have him otherwise gave him the eyes and heart of a man like Lional. Nerim saw and believed what he was intended to see and believe. There was a bird, and it did speak. But it was not the voice of Vorsluk that Nerim and I heard."

"Then what was it?" said Zazoor, after a moment of silent surprise.

He shrugged. "What else but some feathered thing captured and taught to mimic speech? Trained to speak on Lional's command."

"It is possible, I suppose," Zazoor agreed, frowning. "But what of Lalchak? Nerim says the Lion showed Lional great favour and did not smite him with tooth or claw."

"Lions, too, can be tamed and trained."

"Then this was trickery?" said Zazoor. "But how can that be? The Three are hidden from all but the Kallarapi. How could Lional know them if this was a ruse?"

Shugat smoothed his rough robe over his knee. "So there is one thing Nerim did not tell you."

"I do not understand," said Zazoor, staring.

"Perhaps not. But do you recall, my sultan, a time at school when you succumbed to temptation? Drank wine to excess? Gambled with Lional . . . and lost the bet?"

As sleeping memory stirred the blood drained from beneath Zazoor's golden skin, leaving him pale and shaken. "Grimthak burn me . . ." he whispered.

"My sultan, unburden your heart. Purge yourself of this sin that we might take undistracted action against New Ottosland's dishonourable, oath-breaking king."

Zazoor nodded, suddenly looking no older than Nerim. Looking shamefaced and sorrowful. "As you say, Shugat. As a young student I was foolish and intemperate. I made a wager with Lional and I lost. On my knees I begged him not to demand the forfeit. He insisted. Said only a man without honour would *welch* on a bet. So I told him what he wanted to know. I—I gave him what I should not have possessed." Zazoor closed his eyes. "The smallest shard of *andaleya*."

Shugat flinched. He had not been expecting *that*. "You took one of the Gods' Tears to school with you?"

"Yes," whispered Zazoor. "When I returned for my second year. I was so unhappy there, Shugat. Lional made my life a misery. I wanted a piece of home to give me comfort."

*Zazoor, Zazoor.* "That was not well done, my sultan."

"No. It was not." Zazoor stared out of a window, remembering. "I begged Lional never to show the *andaleya* to anyone or repeat what, honour-bound, I had revealed of the Three. He agreed. And to my surprise he kept his word. I had forgotten it ever happened . . . or not permitted myself to remember." Still stricken, Zazoor bowed his head. "Shugat, I am shamed. Unworthy."

He patted Zazoor's arm. "And yet the gods saw fit to make you Sultan."

"You are right," Zazoor said slowly. "They did. They have a task for me to complete." His clenched fist drummed his bent knee. "If I could but fathom Lional's intentions! There is more to this business than treaties and tariffs, Shugat. Some greater treachery stirs the sands. In my dreams I feel a breeze that promises to become a mighty storm, strong enough to drown us all in a river of blood."

"As ever, Zazoor, your heart is open to hear the gods' whispers," he said. "This is a true dream. It is clear to me now that Lional desires you to marry his sister so he might gain access to all the *andaleya* in our desert. To his infidel eyes it is a treasure to be exploited. He does not believe the Three even exist."

Zazoor closed his eyes and lowered his forehead to his knee. "So it is war. After centuries of peace. War, because one child disliked another. Nursed his hurts, fed them and watered them, cosseted them until he grew to manhood and they to hatred. *War*, Shugat, for no other reason than a warped man's greed for wealth and revenge." He sprang to his feet and began pacing the blue-and-green carpets. The heels of his red leather boots thumped softly, like the beating of distant drums. "New Ottosland has no army. With but a tenth of my warriors could I grind their green fields to dust. Is Lional *mad*?"

Shugat nodded. "Yes, my sultan. Mad as a scorpion, or a man boiled too long in the sun. But he does not think it will come to war. You know he sees us as little more than superstitious tent dwellers grubbing in the sand. Nerim's gullibility easily convinced him that we think our gods are on his side."

Zazoor turned, his eyes ablaze. "And what of you, Shugat? What did you do to show Lional his error? To show him that the Three are *our* gods and do not truck with outsiders?"

He hesitated. "Nothing," he said at last.

Zazoor spread his arms wide in entreaty. "*Why*? I sent you to New Ottosland as I would have sent myself. Why did you not *act*?" Then he lowered his arms and took a step back, the fire in his eyes doused with shock. "You *believed* him?"

"I—" Shugat took a firmer hold of his staff. In his forehead he felt the heat as a small pulse of white fire beat deep in the heart of the *andaleya*. "I was unsure," he admitted. "At first. When I called upon the gods to strike Lional down and they did not, I thought—it seemed—" He rapped the staff into the carpets. "When I asked them for guidance they did not reply. I do not question the gods, Zazoor! Silence answers as loudly as a shout!"

Sudden anger spent, Zazoor stepped close, placed a hand on each of his shoulders and rested their foreheads together. "I understand," he whispered. "Forgive me for doubting you."

For the briefest moment Shugat cradled his hand to the back of Zazoor's neck; then he smacked the side of the sultan's head in remonstration. "You're forgiven," he growled. "But do not do it again."

Like a child in the schoolroom Zazoor dropped cross-legged to the carpeted floor and stared up at him, his face once more calm and composed, all shame wiped away. "The gods are *not* with Lional."

His smile was fierce. "No. They are not."

"They have told you this, Shugat?"

"They have." He raised his staff. "My words are the words of the Three, of Grimthak and Lalchak and Vorsluk, Holy of Holies, greatest of all gods," he said, his voice taking on the singsong cadence of holy pronouncement. "Hear their words and obey or perish in Grimthak's flame, by Lalchak's teeth and Vorsluk's talons."

Zazoor pressed his face to the floor. "What is their will, Holy Shugat? I will hear it and obey."

"You will ride to New Ottosland at the head of an army," he intoned. His eyes were rolled in their sockets, now, till only a yellow-white crescent remained, and the stone in his forehead blazed like the sun.

"A large army?"

He felt his crescented eyes flicker. "Fifty men from each village one day's ride from the palace."

"As soon as the sun sets I shall send the proclamation to each village leader on the swiftest camels," Zazoor promised. "And after that, Shugat?"

Slowly Shugat lowered his staff, blinking. His vision returned to normal and the *andaleya's* incandescence faded. Frowning, he stared at a fading shaft of sunlight then at last stirred and looked down at the sultan. "After that you wait, Zazoor."

Zazoor sat up. "For what?"

"For the whisper in your heart. It will tell you what to do."

Zazoor nodded. Then he said, hesitantly, "Forgive me, Shugat, but does it not seem to you, as it seems to me, that the gods' pronouncements have of late been more *cryptic* than once they were?"

Leaning forward, he patted Zazoor's cheek. "When we are children our parents tell us precisely what we must and must not do, for our understanding is circumscribed and our knowledge of the world incomplete. But when we are grown they nod and say, 'We have taught you well. Go now into the world and remember what you learned at our table.'"

"Indeed," said Zazoor, and laughed. "You are wise, Shugat, and patient beyond understanding. In the name of the Three I praise you thrice."

Shugat nodded, acknowledging, but did not reply. His thoughts again were snared in the sunlight, and the memory of a man who yet disturbed him. A touch on his knee; he looked at Zazoor.

"Shugat? What is it? What have you not told me?"

"There was another man in the audience with Lional," he said slowly. Then he pulled a face. "I say man, but youth is more truthful. A fingerful of years older than Nerim, no more."

"Ah! The wizard. Nerim said. What of him? Lional has had many wizards since he came to the throne, each gone more swiftly than the one before. Nerim says it's whispered in the palace that Lional lacks the loving touch. Doubtless this one will disappear as quickly as the rest."

"He is not like the other wizards," said Shugat. "From afar I read them and remained at peace. But this one? Power like a bud yet to blossom curls within his breast, and all around him a roiling of darkness."

Seeing his discomfort, Zazoor rose smoothly from the carpeted floor, his eyes chilled to cold purpose once more. "He is evil?"

"No . . ." he said, after deep thought. "Not evil. And yet evil surrounds him . . ."

Zazoor's frown was suspicious. "It sounds most strange. What must I do with this wizard when I find him? Kill him? You say he is not evil but there is fear and doubt in your eyes, Shugat! I see it, plain as a bird in the sky. What is to be done with Lional's enchanter?"

Shugat sighed. "I am sorry, Zazoor. On this matter the gods stay silent. I have asked them, for this *Gerald Dunwoody* fills me with foreboding, but all they will tell me is: *wait*."

"Then at least tell me this, for I trust in your judgement," said Zazoor. "Do you think him a danger to Kallarap?"

Shugat pursed his lips, considering. "Perhaps. Or perhaps he is more of a danger to Lional. Or perhaps . . . at the end of the day when the sun has set and the camels chew cud in their stables . . . perhaps the biggest danger he poses is to himself."

"As ever you speak in riddles, my friend."

"The day I speak but plainly," Shugat replied, allowing himself a smile, "is the day the gods have done with me!"

"A day long hence, I implore them!" said Zazoor, and kissed his fingers to the Three. "Shugat, will you ride with me back to the court of King Lional?"

His bones were peevish just at the thought, but he nodded. "I will. The gods decree I must return there and see their desires fulfilled. There is a mystery with Lional, his wizard and his blaspheming beasts that I must pierce to the heart lest it poison us all. For good or ill our future lies with them, and in this brewing storm . . . though why that is I cannot say."

"The ride to New Ottosland is long and slow," said Zazoor. "Can we reach it before the storm breaks?"

"Time has no meaning for the Three. I am given power to bend time, that it might serve our purpose and the purpose of the gods."

"Truly, they are great," Zazoor whispered. "Shugat, pray with me."

Together they knelt before the shrine and prostrated themselves in supplication. What Zazoor heard then, Shugat did not know. But in his heart he heard the whispers of the gods and felt himself complete, and at peace.

# CHAPTER
# TWENTY-THREE

"Oh!" shouted Melissande, and kicked her suite's unyielding front doors. "I hate you! Open up right now or I'll—I'll give you woodworm!"

It was an idle threat. Not only did Madame Ravatinka not believe in teaching practical applications of magic until Second Year, she also frowned on offensive thaumaturgy. Because witches were *ladies*, and ladies were *nice*, and nice meant doing nothing *aggressive*.

Thwarted, Melissande hobbled to the nearest chair, shoved its occupying books to the floor and flung herself into it, feeling remarkably foolish. The doors were locked. She knew they were locked. Expecting them to miraculously open with a threat made as much sense as looking for one lost shoe in the same cupboard you've already searched six times.

Staring at the doors she chewed her thumbnail, savagely.

Something was very *wrong* here. Well, *more* wrong than being cooped up in these wretched rooms unable to do a stroke of work because the etheretic transductors still hadn't returned to normal and Lional had forbidden contact from anyone beyond the palace which meant every meeting scheduled for the past five days had been cancelled and what that was going to do to the Treasury's cash flow and the kingdom's trade balances she couldn't *begin* to think about without a cold compress for her forehead and a very large glass of whiskey for the rest of her.

Oh dear lord how she *loathed* her brother.

Returning to the doors she pressed her cheek to the timber and listened. Nothing. She took a deep breath. "Ronnie? Ronnie, are you there yet? Is *anyone* there? Answer me!"

Silence. Ronnie was gone and no other guard had taken his place. Neither had Bedford responded to her summons via the bell-rope, and he'd been faithfully delivering her meals since this ridiculous incarceration had begun.

It didn't make sense.

"Well," she said to the world at large. "Bugger *this* for a barrel-load of monkeys."

Muttering, she retrieved from her sock drawer the special set of keys she kept hidden there and returned to her stubbornly locked suite doors. Lional wouldn't like it one little bit, her just letting herself out with incanted keys she wasn't supposed to own, but that was too bad. He shouldn't have turned into such an unreasonable bully. He only had himself to blame. She'd get him to see sense once he'd calmed down.

That was one of her greatest talents, getting Lional to see sense in the long run.

*Usually.*

Shoving aside *that* unwelcome thought, she sorted through the key collection until she found the big one with all the curlicues and stuck it in the lock. There was a sharp *crack*, an acrid puff of smoke and a flash of unbearable heat. Crying out, she let go of the key ring . . . and watched the incredibly expensive incanted keys melt and dribble down the varnished timber into a sizzling puddle of bronze on the floor.

Her jaw dropped. "*What?*"

Closing her mouth with a snap she fetched a screwdriver and tried to remove the hinges holding the doors to the wall. The screwdriver sagged like a limp piece of liquorice.

No. *No.* There was a *hex* on her *doors?*

*Gerald, how could you?*

Tears welled. Angrily she smeared them away and dropped again into her chair. At least this explained why she hadn't heard from him in over a week. Meditation? Meditation her fat Uncle Albert! Gerald had *caved,* that's what he'd done. He was aiding and abetting impossible Lional. What pressures her brother had brought to bear on him she couldn't imagine . . . and didn't much care about, actually. Gerald was a scummy turncoat, full stop, end of discussion.

*Damn* him. If *she* could stand up to Lional why couldn't *he?*

What a *mess!* The only person left on her side of the argument was Rupert and there was no point considering help from that quarter, even if she could reach him. Rupert couldn't even help himself.

Expecting him to defy Lional and come charging—no, make that fluttering—to the rescue was like expecting Reg to keep her beak shut.

And as if her personal crisis wasn't bad enough there was the imminent national disaster waiting to explode in all their faces once Lional's dealings with the Kallarapi were made public. But instead of being out there in the thick of the action, doing her job, taking charge, organising some kind of intelligent response, she was stuck in here behind a pair of hexed doors without the first idea of how to get around them.

Which meant she was stuck here *indefinitely*, because those doors were the only way out of her apartments. It was an absolute *catastrophe*. And if she wasn't careful she was *really* going to cry.

From the direction of the bedroom came a heavy, clunking-on-glass sound. She stood up, frowning. What the hell?

*I've had about as much nonsense as I can take for one lifetime. If you're a burglar you're going to be sorry.*

Fists clenched she marched to the bedroom, stopped just inside the doorway and glared into the corners. Then she heard it again, a banging against the windowpane behind those curtains *there*!

Heavy drapes in either hand, panting, she found herself staring nose to beak at Reg, who was hovering like an ugly overgrown hummingbird on the other side of the window.

"Well don't just stand there, you stupid bint!" Reg shouted through the thick pane of glass. "Or do you *want* him to fall screaming to a messy death?"

That's when she noticed the fingers ranged along the window ledge. The window ledge of the window that was seven storeys up the side of the palace wall, that she couldn't escape through because not even all her sheets and blankets tied together would reach the ground and, thanks to Madame Ravatinka, her levitation skills hadn't progressed past lifting and lowering very short thin pencils.

The fingers were bloodless, and clutching the window ledge in a manner that did suggest imminent letting go and a subsequent screaming fall to a messy death.

She opened the window and Reg half-flew, half-fell into the room. "What are you waiting for?" the wretched bird gasped, collapsed in a heap on the floor. "Pull him in!"

She lunged forward and over the windowsill, grabbed the wrists belonging to the slipping fingers, dug her heels into the carpet and heaved. Inch by inch the wrists became arms, became shoulders with a head centred neatly between them, became a whole body kicking and cursing and scraping over the sill and into her bedroom.

With a startled grunt she overbalanced and fell on the carpet, rump first. The body landed on its face between her outstretched legs. After a grumbling groaning moment, it looked up.

She stared. "What the hell? *You're* not Gerald!"

The body shook the floppy black hair out of its face, offered her an engaging grin and waved its inkstained fingers at her. "Hi there, Your Highness. Monk Markham. Remember me?"

*Far* too much whiskey. A dip in Gerald's fountain. A wobbly face in his crystal ball. She repressed a shudder. "Vaguely," she said, and scooted herself backwards to a decorous distance. "How did you get here?"

Markham wriggled himself into a sitting position. "Long story. Where's Gerald?"

She scowled. "I neither know nor care. I consider myself gravely deceived in Gerald Dunwoody."

"*Deceived*?" Reg demanded, heaving herself unsteadily upright. "You watch what you're saying about that boy, there's not an ounce of deception in him! And not for want of my trying, either. A good wizard needs a dash of the devious but will he listen? No, he won't."

"Really?" She glared at Reg. "Then why did he hex my doors so I can't get out after he swore blind he'd help me?"

"How should I know?" said Reg. "I haven't been here. But I'll bet you a new hairdo it wasn't Gerald. Or if it was, he had a very good reason. Probably something to do with saving you from yourself. The ether knows you could do with it. Those *trousers*, girl! With that shirt? With *any* shirt?"

Just what she needed in a time of crisis: more acerbic fashion advice. "Of course it was Gerald, who else could it be? And what do you mean you haven't been here? Where have you been? And what are you doing in my *bedroom*? With *Markham*? Answer me!"

"I would if you'd let me get a word in edgewise!" Reg retorted. "We're in *your* bedroom because we couldn't get into *my* bedroom! And we couldn't get into *my* bedroom because Gerald wasn't there to let us in! Now where is he, ducky?"

"Don't ask me! And *don't* call me *ducky*."

Reg glared. "Why shouldn't I ask you? Are you the princess round here or aren't you?"

"Yes. I am. I'm the princess who's been locked in her suite since the day that rotter Gerald fell off Dorcas! You're his keeper, why don't *you* know where he is?"

"Because I've been out of the country since the day after that!"

Grabbing hold of a handy chair, Melissande hauled herself to her feet. "Out of the country? What are you talking about? What the *hell* is going on around here?"

Markham glanced at Reg, who nodded. He got up, lifted her onto the back of the same chair then pulled a lump of rock from the pocket of his slightly threadbare blue jacket. "Can you keep a secret, Melissande?"

She looked at him. "I'm the prime minister of New Ottosland and I have two older brothers, one of whom is Lional, King of Insane and Inappropriate Wedding Plans and the other Rupert, Prince of Butterflies. What do you think? And don't call me Melissande. It's 'Your Royal Highness' to the likes of you."

"It's all right, Monk," Reg said gruffly. "We can trust her. She's got the manners of a warthog and the grace of a drunken rhinoceros but unlike Rupert she's not a complete ninny."

She goggled. "*Excuse* me? Did you just call me a—"

Markham cleared his throat. "Okay, ladies, probably right now we should be concentrating on—"

"Oh, why don't you put a sock in it, *ducky*!" Reg snapped. "If you can't dress like a princess you can at least act like one. Now listen up. We—"

"Listen *up*? To *you*? The biggest mistake I ever made in my life—after hiring Gerald, that is—was listening to *you*! You're a bird, for God's sake! A scruffy, coarse, drab, irritating, uninvited *bird*! What do *you* know about being a princess? What do you know about *anything*?"

"What do *I* know?" said Reg, clutching at the chair back to stop herself from falling; she was swaying with exhaustion. "A damned sight more than you do, ducky, I'll tell you that for nothing! I may well *die* a bird, dearie, but I sure as shooting wasn't *born* one. I was born a princess and became a queen *and* I was a witch to boot. The most powerful witch in all of Lalapinda!"

Melissande opened her mouth then closed it again. Turned to Markham. "Is that true?"

Markham shook his head and sat on the end of her four-poster bed. "Don't ask me. Reg's past is a closed book, Your Highness."

Frowning, she leaned against a bedpost and considered the bird. "So what happened?"

Reg sighed. "It's not important. What's important is finding out what's happened to Gerald."

"*Nothing's* happened to Gerald!" She scowled. "*Yet.*"

"Um . . ." Markham exchanged a worried glance with Reg. "Look. Not that I make a habit of contradicting royalty, but . . . we're pretty sure you're wrong."

"Why?"

"Because a few hours ago the Ottosland Department of Thaumaturgy's thaumatograph's readings hit the roof, kept on going and are currently headed for outer space," said Reg.

"So?"

"So," said Markham, "the source of the readings was New Ottosland. And their cause was the biggest Level Twelve transmog ever recorded. Gerald's the only wizard I know who's capable of successfully pulling one off."

*Oh.* She rallied. "That still doesn't explain what you're doing here."

"He promised me he wouldn't do another one and he's a man of his word," said Markham. He looked worried. "Gerald must've been under duress."

"*Duress?* From who?"

Markham and Reg exchanged cryptic glances. "We're not sure," he said, cautiously. Then he held up the nondescript rock. "But it's why I risked using this."

"And what *is* that, exactly?"

"I call it a Stealth Stone. It's a kind of portable portal. You can use it to go pretty much wherever you like without needing any physical apparatus or a destination module, and nobody at the other end is any the wiser when you get there."

"A portable portal?" she said, peering suspiciously. "I've never heard of such a thing."

He cleared his throat. "That's because I only just invented it. This is a prototype."

"You *invented* it?" Despite herself she was impressed. "How?"

Markham shrugged. "It just sort of happened while I was mucking about with transdimensional keys."

Reg eyed him with proprietal favour. "He's a bit of a genius himself, is our Markham."

He slipped the rock back in his pocket. "Anyway. I haven't told my bosses about it yet. I wasn't even sure it would work. But when the thaumatograph spiked and the Department brass launched into hysterics I thought it was as good a time as any to try it."

"So that explains how you got *into* the country. But I'm still waiting to hear how Reg got *out!*"

Reg sniffed. "I flew."

"To *Ottosland?* In what, a *week?*"

"Four days. It was supposed to be two," said Reg. "Only the *accelerando* wore off prematurely. I had to hitch till my wings worked again."

"And why did you have to go at all?"

"To find Markham, of course," said Reg, rolling her eyes. "And raise the alarm. He'd just finished finding out what happened to all of Lional's *other* wizards when I reached him, but then he had to convince those idiots he works for he wasn't making it up! I was just about to start cracking some heads myself when the thaumatograph went haywire and they *finally* took him seriously. Except *then* they had to form a committee to investigate and we didn't have time to hang about. So here we are."

She was feeling bewildered, which always made her cross. "Reg, this is nonsense. *Nothing* happened to Lional's other wizards. They quit or he fired them. I *told* you that already."

Markham shook his head. "I know that's what your brother said, Your Highness, but . . . he lied."

Shaken, she shoved a couple of hairpins back into her lopsided bun. "Nonsense. I've got three letters of resignation in my office. I'll *show* them to you, assuming I ever get out of this stupid suite."

"Did the wizards hand them to you in person?"

"Not to me. To Lional. He's the king and they were his court wizards."

"Fair enough," said Markham. "But did you see them afterwards? See them leave, wave them goodbye? Any of them? Or did your brother just tell you they'd gone?"

*No. No. No.* "This is ridiculous," she said automatically. "What are you suggesting, that Lional—" The words died in her throat. "No. You're wrong. He *wouldn't*—"

"What?" Reg said brutally. "Make five wizards disappear? *Kill* them? Why not? He tried to kill Gerald."

"*Kill Gerald?* Are you *crazy?*"

"No, but your pretty brother is," Reg retorted. "That riding accident wasn't an accident, ducky. And those other wizards didn't resign or get fired. Lional retired them. Permanently."

"The thing is," Markham added, "after they arrived in New Ottosland nobody who knew them—family, friends, colleagues—ever saw or heard from them again. I'm sorry. It's pretty obvious they met with foul play."

"What you're suggesting is *ludicrous!*" she shouted, and pushed away from the bedpost. "Lional's not some common criminal, he's a *king!*"

Reg snorted. "Often as not it's one and the same thing. If you'd known the kings *I've* known, ducky—"

"*And* he's my *brother.* Do you think I wouldn't *notice* a little detail like being related to a homicidal maniac?"

"Trust me," said Reg. "Family's usually the last to know."

"*No*. This is *ridiculous*. What *possible* reason could he have for killing them?"

Reg flapped her wings tiredly. "I don't know. Yet. But it won't be good, whatever it is. Face it, dearie. Your brother's demented. Markham checked with the Department's chief Etheretic Weather monitor. As I suspected there's no such thing as polarised lightning. Whatever's wrong with the etheretic transductors around here is wizard-made." Reg scowled. "By Lional, I'm guessing, since he's the one who invented that poppycock story."

She stared. "Lional can't do magic. It was probably Gerald. Now that he's on Lional's side."

Reg's beak fell open. "He is *not*!"

"Really? Then who hexed my door? I suppose you're going to tell me *that* was Lional too?"

"Of course it was! Anybody who'd kill five innocent wizards wouldn't hesitate to hex a door!"

"Stop calling Lional a murderer! You don't know he killed *anybody*! Former witch queen or not you don't know *anything*!"

"This isn't getting us anywhere," said Markham, and headed for the door. "There's only one way to tell if it's Gerald's hex."

"Not so fast!" said Melissande, and blocked his path. "You're Gerald's friend which means you're biased. There'll be no reading of anything without an independent witness!"

She led him out of the bedroom, her insides clenched and trembling.

"Excuse me!" Reg bellowed behind them. "I'm still recovering from a flight to Ottosland and I'm feeling a little fatigued, if anybody's interested!"

She stopped. "Wait here," she ordered Markham, marched back into her bedroom, scooped Reg into the crook of one arm and marched back out again to find that Gerald's disreputable friend had paid no attention to her. She found him in the study, staring at her books.

"You have an . . . unusual . . . library for a princess," he commented, one eyebrow raised.

"So now you're the book police?" she said, and resisted the urge to kick him. "Let's just concentrate on my front doors. Because if you don't remove that hex we'll all be stuck in here for the forseeable future."

"Don't just stand there, Markham," said Reg. "Run!"

She shoved Reg at him and stalked into the foyer. Markham followed, parked Reg on a handy pile of books and moved to consider the suite's front doors.

"They melted my incanted keys and ruined my screwdriver," she said, glaring ferociously sideways. "So don't try and tell me they're not hexed, Mr Markham."

"Call me Monk," he said, then laid his right palm against the carved wood and closed his eyes. A moment later he snatched it away again and shook it, hard. "Ouch! No, they're hexed all right. One hex, very powerful."

"See?" she said triumphantly. "I told you."

"It's the strongest barrier hex I've ever come across. But it's not Gerald's."

"It has to be."

Markham sighed. "I'm sorry, Your Highness. I'd know his thaumic signature anywhere."

"Then whose is it?"

"I don't know. But it's a weird one." He pressed both palms to the wooden doors and shivered. "More than weird. It's *horrible*."

Reg clacked her beak. "Horrible how?"

Markham pulled his hands free and wiped them on his trousers, his mouth pruned with distaste. "I've got an idea but . . . it's crazy."

Reg rolled her eyes. "Then it's probably right. *Everything* in this cockeyed kingdom is crazy."

"Thank you," Melissande said coldly.

Reg shrugged. "No point plucking the messenger, ducky. I just call 'em as I see 'em."

Ignoring the bird she turned to Markham. "Explain."

Markham chewed his bottom lip. "Every incant has a unique signature. Like—a thaumaturgical fingerprint of the person who placed it."

"I know that," she snapped. "So?"

"So this hex hasn't got one fingerprint. It's got lots. As though a whole bunch of wizards performed it simultaneously."

"You're right. That's crazy."

"It's worse than crazy," replied Markham. His expression was strained. "It's hex soup. I mean, I'm good. I'm *really* good. And I've neutralised a bunch of hexes in my time. But I don't think I can do this one."

There was a moment of shared and silent panic. Then she slapped her forehead. "I'm an idiot. And so are you. We don't need the doors, we can use your portable portal to escape."

He hesitated. "Not necessarily. I haven't had a chance to fine-tune it for short distances. We may end up in the middle of the desert by mistake. Or worse."

"Oh." She thought for moment then slapped herself again. "Oh! Of *course*! You can levitate us through the bedroom window!"

Another hesitation, then he shook his head. "I don't think we should go anywhere till I've got a better understanding of this hex."

"*Mister* Markham, I have a kingdom to run," she said sharply. "Get me out of here and you can spend as long as you like studying your precious hex. Better yet, ask Gerald to explain it."

Markham slammed the doors with his fist, eyes blazing. "For the last bloody time, lady, it *wasn't* Gerald! Gerald's in trouble somewhere, thanks to you! And if he ends up another one of your brother's victims I promise you: *someone's* going to pay, big time! And I don't have a problem if that someone is *you*!"

There was an appalled silence. Then, panting and grunting, Reg flapped to the marble-topped table by the doors. "Now, now. Let's take a deep breath and remember what's at stake here."

"I know what's at stake!" Melissande turned on Markham. "And don't you threaten me! I've been threatened by experts and I'm not scared! You—"

Reg let out a screech. "Shut up the pair of you! Wasting time spitting like mangy alley cats when Gerald is out there somewhere expecting us to rescue him!"

Silence. Then Markham ran his fingers through his hair. "You're right, Reg. I'm sorry."

She crossed her arms. "Yes. Well."

"All right, Markham," Reg continued. "You're the genius here, so *act* like it. How many fingerprints can you sense in that hex?"

Markham sighed. "I think . . . five. And they're all First Grade."

Reg scratched her head. "So. Five thaumic signatures . . . five missing First Grade wizards. Even Boris could do the maths on this one." She sniffed. "Where is that long black streak of misery, anyway? Last thing we need is for me to end up as his lunch."

"One of the maids is looking after him," said Melissande. "What do you mean, even he could do the—"

But Reg and Markham weren't listening. They were staring at each other, eyes wide with dismay.

"Is it even *possible*, Reg?" said Markham. "I've never heard of—"

"You wouldn't have," said the bird darkly. "Seeing as you're a nice young man who doesn't read that kind of grimoire. But I've known men who do, Monk, and I'd say it's more than possible. It's the only explanation that makes any sense."

*Grimoire*? "What, so now you're saying there's black magic involved?" Melissande demanded. "I don't believe it. This is getting more and more far-fetched by the minute!"

Markham shook his head. "Sorry. I know this is difficult but we have to face facts. The only way a single hex could contain five different thaumaturgical signatures is if someone stole the *potentias* of those five wizards."

Not someone. *Lional.* Blinking rapidly, she stared at Markham. "That is nothing more than wild speculation."

"No," said Gerald's annoying friend. His engaging grin was entirely absent. Now he looked angry and a whole lot older. "It's not speculation. And I can prove it. All I need is something bearing the thaumaturgical signature of one of the missing wizards."

"Well, ducky?" said Reg, not unkindly. "Can you help him or would you rather go on sticking your head in the sand? Because all three of us know who's behind this trouble."

She returned to the bedroom. Snatched up the brown painted tin horse from its special place on her dressing table and took it back to the foyer.

"I had a birthday a while ago," she said, stroking the toy with one finger. "Bondaningo Greenfeather— Lional's wizard before Gerald—gave me this. When you say a special word it—it—canters in little circles, neighing. Or it did. Now it can barely trot, I'm afraid I ran the magic down playing with it. Silly. It's not like I'm a child."

Markham took the horse from her and lightly held it. "Yes. Yes, Greenfeather's fingerprint is still quite clear," he murmured. "It's a clever incantation." He reached out his other hand and pressed it to the door. Moments later his face twisted and his breathing harshened. He pulled his hand away. "Blimey, that's *disgusting*."

"Never mind disgusting!" Reg said sharply. "Did you recognise Greenfeather's signature?"

Reluctantly, Markham nodded. "Yes. It's in there."

"But not Gerald's?"

"No."

"You're quite sure?" Reg persisted.

"I'm sure," said Markham. "Wherever he is Gerald's still got his *potentia*."

Reg fluffed up all her draggled feathers. "Well, praise Saint Snodgrass for that."

Hardly paying them any attention, Melissande took the toy from his unresisting fingers. Whispered "*tally-ho*" into its ear then put it on the foyer floor. All her insides felt hollowed out, scoured bare with sorrow. As they watched, the little tin horse lifted its head, flicked its tail and pranced in a slow jerky circle, neighing.

It wasn't till Reg said, in a strangled voice, "There, there, ducky. Markham, give her a hanky," that she realised she was crying.

*Lional. Lional. What have you done?*

# CHAPTER
# TWENTY-FOUR

W hat I don't understand," said Markham, "is how Lional managed this in the first place. If he's not a wizard . . ."

Reg let out a thoughtful sigh. "Well, magical ability usually runs in families and madam, there, *is* studying witchcraft. Inadequately, but she's studying it. So maybe he had just enough juice to get the ball rolling. And after that . . ." Another sigh. "Well, Melissande? Did he?"

It was the first time Gerald's appalling feathered companion had ever addressed her by her actual name. Slumped in a chair, still clutching Markham's damp hanky, she looked up. "Did he what?"

"Aren't you *listening*? Did your miserable brother have a spark of magic in him? Sufficient, as it were, to get the engine started? Saint Snodgrass preserve me," she added to Markham. "From the look on her face you'd think I was talking Babishkian!"

"Don't be so hard, Reg," said Markham, disapproving. "She's had a bad shock."

"And she's going to get another one if she doesn't buck up! Royalty doesn't sit around *glooming*, it *rallies*, it *rebounds*, it seeks *revenge*! Look at me!"

Trying to sniff discreetly, Melissande watched as Markham ignored the damned bird, crossed to her chair and dropped to a crouch beside it. With flagrant disregard for protocol he took her hand in his; ridiculously, she felt comforted.

"Your Highness—*Melissande*—I'm sorry about this," he said with surprising gentleness. "I really am. I've got a brother. We can't stand each other but even so . . . I think I know how you feel. I mean, if I found out Aylesbury was a mass murderer . . ."

She pulled her hand free. "Stop calling Lional a murderer. You don't know those other wizards are dead."

"Melissande . . ." Markham's thin face was full of compassion. "It's impossible to take a wizard's *magicali potentia* without killing him. Magic is in the blood, literally. It'd be like having your bones ripped out. Not even a First Grade wizard could survive it."

She wasn't Lional's sister for nothing. "I don't believe you. Show me five corpses and *then* I might accept what you're saying, but until you do, I—"

"*Melissande*," said Markham. His hand took hers again. "The wizards are *dead*."

"And if you bleat 'no, no, Lional isn't a murderer' *one* more time when you know damn well he *is*," said Reg, without any compassion, "I swear on my phoney grave, ducky, I'll poke out your eyeballs like olives and feed them to your precious Boris."

She tried not to think of dear Bondaningo, ripped apart from the inside out. "Fine," she said sullenly. Hating Markham. Hating the bird. Most of all, hating Lional. "Have it your way. They're dead."

Markham chewed on a fingernail. "Blimey, Reg. We've got a real problem. How are we supposed to stand up to a man with the *potentias* of five First Grade wizards?" His expression changed, abruptly. "Especially when one of them had access to texts from the *Internationally Proscribed Index*." He let go of her hand and unfolded to his feet, looking stricken. "*Damn*. Pomodoro Uffitzi held a doctorate in Theoretical Applications of Reverse Thaumatics."

"In Ottish please?" said Melissande, feeling waspish.

"Black magic," he said, distracted. "Uffitzi spent eleven years researching his thesis in several countries renowned for their past dabblings in unsavoury practices. Who knows what grimoires he managed to find in that time?"

"And ever so carefully forgot to declare to the authorities?" said Reg. "Saint Snodgrass preserve us!"

"If I'm right, I have to notify the Department."

"Yes, but *after* we've found Gerald," said Reg. She chattered her beak, thinking hard. "He must be around here somewhere."

Very carefully Melissande laid Markham's damp handkerchief over the arm of her chair. "Lional said he was in private retreat, meditating."

Reg snorted. "Meditating my feathered arse. He's being held prisoner."

"Maybe he's run away."

"Stop being deliberately provocative. I'll bet you a nice pair of high-heeled pumps, ducky, Gerald's 'accident' in the forest was Lional *not* being able to steal his *potentia*. That means our mad king needs him to do his dirty work for him—whatever that is. Trust me, he won't be far away."

"But he will be somewhere with a decent amount of space," added Markham. "We know the dirty work involved a Level Twelve transmog that makes the cat-into-lion trick look puny. Melissande, do you have any idea what Lional wanted Gerald to make?"

She glared at him. "Of course not! Who do you think I am, his evil sidekick? I don't have the first idea what—" And then she turned to Reg.

"Hell's bells," Reg whispered, as they stared at each other in sudden, appalled comprehension. "Are you thinking what I'm thinking, madam? The Kallarapi gods. Tavistock as Lalchak...me as Vorsluk..."

Melissande shot out of the chair. "*Grimthak*! Oh my God, Reg! Gerald's made a bloody *dragon*!"

Reg turned, her dark eyes blazing. "*Markham, get us out of here!*"

He flung himself at the foyer doors. Spread his fingers flat to the polished oak surface and pressed his cheek between them. After a moment he began to hum off-key. A moment after that, alarmingly, his unruly dark hair developed a life of its own, weaving and unweaving itself around his head in a series of bizarre patterns.

"Ah—wouldn't the window have been easier?" she asked.

"Don't distract him!" hissed Reg.

As she watched, holding her breath, Markham's face began to twist with pain. The humming became a groan and a bloody sweat broke out on his forehead. Moments later there was an explosion of light and sound and a billow of foul green smoke. Markham, shouting, flew across the foyer, struck the far wall and slid moaning to the floor.

As Reg exclaimed in the background Melissande dropped to her knees beside him. "*Monk!* Are you all right?"

"I think I'm going to be sick," he groaned.

"Not in my foyer you're not!"

He heaved himself upright. "Okay."

"Good!" said Reg, hovering now between the splintered remains of the foyer doors. "Now come on, you two. Let's find Gerald!"

She helped Markham to his feet. "Give him a moment, you nagging old hag! He was practically knocked unconscious!"

"Gerald's running out of moments!" Reg shouted, flapping madly. "How long will your brother keep him around, do you think, now that he's got his precious dragon?"

"Reg is right," said Markham, still looking sick. "We have to go."

"Go *where*? I've no idea where Gerald is. Have you?"

"No. But if we're lucky I can find him with a locator incant. I'll need something to guide me."

"Then what are waiting for?" demanded Reg, still haphazardly hovering. "Let's get to our suite!"

They raced through deserted corridors and up and

down empty staircases to the palace's official wizard's residence. Gasping for air, Reg landed on a foyer chair and pointed a wing.

"The bedroom's that way. Fetch a used sock, Markham. That should have a good strong scent."

As Markham fetched, Melissande frowned. "Something strange is going on. The place is deserted, we didn't see *anybody* between here and my apartments. Where's everyone got to? There are always servants scurrying around here, it's like a damned anthill."

Before Reg could comment Markham returned with a limp red sock. "This should do it. Now I need a map of the kingdom."

"There's one in the *Guide to New Ottosland* I left here for Gerald."

Reg jerked her beak. "It's in the dresser, underneath that painting of the constipated cow on the wall there."

"He shoved it in a drawer?" said Melissande, offended, as Markham found the pink folder. "Did he even *read* it? I'll bet he didn't. I spent *hours* putting that guide together, you know!"

"And now it's come in very useful," said Reg, "which only goes to show there's a first time for everything. Now be quiet and let Markham focus."

Melissande swallowed. "Will the incant still work if the person you're trying to find is—you know—"

Markham glanced up from spreading the guide's map on the foyer table. "Dead?" he said. "No. It won't."

"Anyway, he can't be dead," she added, desperate for a bright side. "You said Lional couldn't kill him."

"Not with magic, apparently. No."

She didn't need him to elaborate. "Oh."

Reg flapped from her chair to the table and glared. "Any *more* clever questions, ducky?"

"Not for the moment."

"*That's* a relief. Now come on, Markham. Let's get cracking."

Markham nodded curtly, his face pale and serious. He wrapped Gerald's sock around his left hand, extended the index finger of his right hand and held it over the map of New Ottosland. "*Seekati. Revelati. Demonstrati.*"

Almost before the words had left his lips the tip of his pointing index finger flared into life as though a light had been switched on under the skin.

He laughed. "We've got him, Reg! He's still alive!"

"Yes, but where?" Reg demanded.

His pointing finger started zigzagging across the map. "Hang on, it's trying to home in on him now." Another zig and two more zags and his finger jabbed itself to a standstill. "There." He peered at the map. "Tolepootle Valley. Melissande?"

"That's *miles* from here. It'll take hours to—"

"No, it won't. The Stealth Stone's fine with miles. What can we expect when we get there?"

Before she could answer they heard a thundering of feet in the corridor outside the suite and a cacophony of alarmed cries.

"*Now* what?" said Reg, and rattled all her feathers. "Quick, madam, see what's making the natives restless!"

Melissande flung open the foyer doors and accosted the first running servant she recognised.

"Hamish! What in the name of Saint Snodgrass is going on?"

Hamish was too panicked to be polite. "Bloody hell, miss! Haven't you heard? There's a bloody great fire-breathing dragon on the loose! It's already killed people down in the city and now it's flying over the palace!"

She stepped back, shut the doors on all the fleeing servants and turned to Reg and Markham. Instead of gibbering incoherently, she felt unnaturally calm. *It's already killed people down in the city.* "Hamish says there's a fire-breathing dragon flying over the palace."

"He's right," said Markham, staring at the foyer's skylight. "There is."

She looked up.

On the other side of the skylight's glass, floating lazily on an updraft like an enormous crimson and emerald striped seagull—with teeth and talons—was Lional's dragon. As they watched, it opened its massive jaws and belched a fearsome plume of fire.

She felt her heart shrivel to ash. *It's already killed people down in the city.*

"Come on," said Reg grimly. "Let's go. We have to stop that damned thing before it really gets started."

Melissande nodded. For once she wasn't inclined to argue.

When Gerald eventually roused from his exhausted, nightmare-ridden stupor there was still no light in the cave. So he sat with his back to the wall and waited.

There wasn't anything else to do.

A few feet away in the dirt and the dark was Reg.

He didn't want to think about her. Reg was a bruised and bloody mark in his heart, an absence he was only just beginning to realise. Another failure he wasn't sure he could live with. She was dead, she was dead . . . and it was all his fault. Everything was his fault. *All those people, burned to a crisp or soaked in poison.* The terror. The destruction. He pulled his knees to his aching chest and held on tight.

*If only I'd been braver. If only I'd defied him. If only I'd never been born.*

There was no food or drink in the cold dark cave. If Lional changed his mind about wanting more dragons or lost what little was left of his sanity and forgot about him, which seemed more likely, then he was doomed to die in this place.

*Oh God. I hope so.*

Time dragged on, sodden with regrets.

Later, in the unrelenting black, he thought he saw a pinpoint of light.

He stirred. Stared, blinking. What new torment was this? Lional, returning at last to dispose of his tool? Or demand more damned dragons . . . or something worse . . .

*I can't. I can't.*

Ten feet away and six feet in the air, the pinpoint of light grew. Intensified. Glowing, it expanded to the size of a firefly. Against his skin, a sudden tingling crackle of power. Heedless of scrapes and bruises he hauled himself to his feet and leaned against the rough rock of the cave wall, his gaze not leaving the ball of light pulsing before him.

With a flash and a ripping sound the air tore open and three briefly silhouetted figures fell through the hole to land shouting on the cave's dirt floor.

"*Ow*! That's my *face*!"

"Sorry, Melissande. Gerald, are you in here? Um, Your Highness, not to complain or anything but your elbow's in a very precarious part of my anato—"

*I'm dreaming. I must be.* "Monk?" he said tentatively. "Is that you?"

"Oh, yes, fine, ask about Markham first why don't you?" demanded an impossible voice. "When I'm the one sitting here faded to a mere shadow of my former glory after flying *and* hitching from here to Ottosland, then convincing Markham and his idiot colleagues that your life was in danger and then risking my life *again* to get back to this ether-forsaken kingdom using Markham's highly illegal and practically untested portable portal! And why is it so *dark* in here? Why doesn't somebody turn on the lights?"

For a moment Gerald thought he'd finally gone mad. Because that was Reg's voice, being Reg, in the Reggiest way it knew how.

And then somebody snapped their fingers and said *illuminato* and he was blinking, half-blinded by the sudden light, and there on the cave floor shaking dirt out of her feathers was –

"*Reg*!" he cried, and fell to his knees. "Oh my God, *Reg*, you're *alive*!"

She glared at him. "Well if I am it's no thanks to your friend the Mad Scientist!" She swung her beak towards Markham and chattered it. "What kind of a portal exit do you call *that*? Flinging us out at speed and miles above terra firma, I think

I've bent a tail feather, you stupid boy! Do you know how long it takes to grow in a tail feather, you—*awwwk!*"

"Reg!" he shouted, clutching her to his chest. "Lional said you were dead, he said he'd killed you! He *did* kill you, *look*, there's your body! Over there!"

Melissande, grubby and harassed and getting to her feet, stared where he pointed at the forlorn draggle of feathers in the dirt. "Eww. What's that?"

"It's Reg," he said, dizzy with relief. "At least, I thought it was Reg. Lional told me it was Reg."

Wriggling free of his embrace, Reg flapped over to the corpse on the cave floor and inspected it. "That's not me," she said. "That's—" She took a closer look. "That's a dead chicken hexed to look like me. And it's not even a very good likeness." She fixed him with a gimlet eye. "Gerald Dunwoody, are you saying you couldn't tell the difference between me and a hexed dead chook? Please don't tell me you couldn't tell the difference between me and hexed dead chook! *Look* at it! The beak's all wrong *and* the eyes are crossed *and* it's missing a claw on the right foot! And it's *fat*. How could you *possibly* think that was *me*?"

He didn't care that she was scolding. "I'm sorry," he said, getting up. "I was a bit . . . distracted . . . at the time." He stared at them, breathless. "I can't believe you *found* me. How—"

"Locator incant and a portable portal," said Monk.

"A *portable* por—?"

"Monk invented it," said Reg.

"Of course Monk did," he said, dazed. "But how could it work, Lional set a lodestone, it—"

"What?" said Reg. "Gerald, what are you talking about?"

*Oh, hell. The lodestone.* "Lional hid a lodestone in here so I couldn't escape via magic," he whispered, nauseous. "He deactivated it so I could make the dragon . . . and then he lost himself inside the damn thing's mind. He never turned the lodestone back on. And I've been so busy feeling sorry for myself I—"

"I don't know what you're bleating about and I don't care!" said Melissande. "What the hell were you *thinking*, Gerald? Making a *dragon*?"

"I'm sorry," he whispered.

"How did you do it?" she demanded, hands fists on her hips. "Transmog a lizard? What kind? The only exotic lizards we have live in the zoo, and none of them look like that flying monstrosity *you've* set loose!"

He could barely look her in the face. "It was a Bearded Spitting Lizard from Lower Limpopo. Lional said Bondaningo Greenfeather got it for him."

"That's a *lie!*" Her eyes were hot with anger and betrayal. Glittering with tears. "Bondaningo was a good man. He would *never* bring something like that into the country!"

"I'm afraid he did. Your brother can be . . . very persuasive."

"I'll bet!" she said, contemptuous. "So what did he promise you in return for his dragon? Gold? Jewels? Land? *What did he promise you?*"

He made himself meet her furious gaze. "You don't want to know what he promised me, Melissande."

With a subdued flutter of feathers Reg flew from the floor to his shoulder. "She may not want to,

Gerald, but she needs to. It's the only way she'll understand what has to be done."

Gently he prised Reg free. "No," he said, thrusting her blindly into Monk's unready hands. "And don't ask me again."

Monk cleared his throat. "Look, mate . . ."

"Are you deaf? *I said no!*" he shouted, and turned away.

"He tortured you, didn't he?" said Monk. He always was a stubborn bastard.

"Tortured him?" said Melissande. "Don't be ridiculous. He looks fine to me, there's not a scratch on him."

Her fresh contempt was like acid. Gerald spun around, shaking, and whatever she saw in his face drove her backwards till she struck the cave wall.

"I'm *sorry*, all right, Melissande? Sorry I wasn't strong enough, sorry I gave in to him, sorry I made his bloody dragon!"

Her chin lifted. In so many ways she was her brother's sister. "Sorry doesn't help the people it's killed. Did you know that, Gerald? Did you know that it's *killed* people?"

"Yes. I know." He saw them whenever he closed his eyes.

"Then how could you *do* it? How could you make such a monstrous creature? *Why* weren't you strong enough? You're a *wizard*, you swore an *oath*! You as good as killed those people *yourself*!"

"You think I don't *know* that?" he demanded, his voice ragged. "You think I don't know I've got their blood on my hands? I tried to resist your damned brother, Melissande! I did resist him, at least for a while. But in the end . . . in the end . . ." Helpless, he stared at her. "In the end I wasn't good enough. I broke. I failed."

"That's not fair," Monk said quickly. "We know what Lional's been up to, Gerald. The stolen *potentias*. We know he had access to illegal grimoires, the kind of filthy magic he's got at his fingertips."

Melissande turned on him. "How *dare* you make excuses for him, Mister Markham? Haven't you been *listening*? People have *died* because Gerald made that dragon. He's an oath-sworn wizard, *he* should have died before—"

"Do you think I didn't *try*?" Gerald said, grabbing her elbow and hauling her around. "He wouldn't let me, all right? Everything he did was designed to keep me alive. Alive and—and—"

"And *what*?" she said. Her tone was scathing.

He opened his mouth and the memories poured out. By the time he was finished she was crying, Monk looked like a ghost and Reg was stamping to and fro across the cave's dirt floor swearing a blue streak.

"There's something else you should know," he said tiredly, as Reg finally ran out of curses. "Lional's controlling the dragon using the *Tantigliani sympathetico*."

Melissande smeared a dirty sleeve across her wet face. "What does that mean?" she said unsteadily.

"It means your brother and the dragon are two bodies with one mind. He sees through its eyes, it breathes with his lungs. It's got all his cunning, his intelligence, his knowledge. And he's got its . . . savagery."

Shaken, Monk said, "Bloody hell. Every wizard

who's ever tried that incant has gone mad. Even Tantigliani in the end." He frowned. "You said he'd lost himself inside the dragon's mind? Does that mean . . ."

Gerald looked at Melissande. Despite everything he could have wept for her. "Yes." In his memory, Lional and the dragon whispering. "I'm pretty sure it's too late for Lional."

Reg rattled her tail feathers. "Then the only way to stop the dragon is by capturing the king."

"How can we capture him, Reg?" said Monk. "He's as good as half a dragon himself now!"

"Fine," she said, shrugging. "Then we don't capture the bastard. We kill him."

"*Kill* him?" Melissande stared. "You can't! *I* can't! He's my brother!"

"He was your brother," Gerald said gently. "What he is now . . . is anybody's guess."

"It's a simple equation," said Reg. "Kill Lional and we kill the dragon."

"And if we kill the dragon instead?" demanded Melissande, folding her arms.

Monk put his hand on her shoulder. "Lional still dies. But the chances of us killing that dragon . . ."

"Are non-existent and none," Reg said briskly. "Sorry, ducky. Lional's got to go."

Melissande dissolved into tears again. As Monk put his arms around her, cradling her against his chest, Gerald picked up Reg. "Can't you even *try* to be tactful?"

"Who cares about tact in a crisis?" she retorted. "And after what she said to you—"

He sighed. "Forget about what she said to me. It doesn't matter. She didn't understand."

Reg's eyes were bright. Birds couldn't cry but he could tell she was weeping on the inside. "I never should've left you, Gerald. If I'd stayed here with you—"

"There'd still be a dragon. And we wouldn't have Monk with his portable portal." He kissed her beak. "Reg, it's all right. It wasn't your fault." He released a hard breath. "Now, what about the Department? Are they—"

She made a rude noise. "We can't trust those idiots Markham works for to get here in time! They're probably still discussing the matter over crumpets and cocoa! No, Gerald, it's up to us. And if we don't act *now*, it could be too late! For New Ottosland, for Kallarap . . . maybe even the world!"

"She's right," said Monk over Melissande's bowed head. "We can't afford to wait for the Department. We have to deal with Lional ourselves. Or try to."

"How? He's not going to let us just walk up to him and kill him. He'll kill us first, or his dragon will."

Melissande pulled out of Monk's embrace. "*I'll* stop him. He's my brother. He'll listen to me."

"No, he *won't*, Melissande. Haven't you been paying attention? He's not plain old Lional any more!"

"I don't *care*! I have to *try*!" She turned to Monk. "Can that portable portal of yours get us to the palace roof?"

Monk took a nondescript rock from his pocket. "I think so. Or pretty close, anyway."

"How close is pretty close? A six foot fall onto dirt is one thing. A fifty foot fall onto brickwork is something else entirely!"

Monk looked insulted. "I said I can do it."

Gerald grabbed his arm. "Wait. Send me and Reg to the palace. We'll do our best to keep Lional occupied. You and Melissande go back to the Department and kick up the biggest stink it has ever seen until those idiots get off their arses and send some help."

"I'm not leaving New Ottosland!" said Melissande. "You three can go if you like, but I'm staying here. I have to be *seen*. The people *need* me. I won't be the second person in my family to let them down on the same damned day!"

"No—Melissande—the only hope your people have is if you stay safe!" he insisted. "Let Rupert fly the family flag, he—"

Her expression changed. "Oh, lord. *Rupert*. I forgot about Rupert! I have to find him, he'll be terrified. And if *Lional* finds him . . ." Then she rallied. "You can take him with you when you go for help."

"Melissande—"

"*No*! I'm the prime minister, my duty is *here*." She folded her arms and lifted her chin. "So shut up. Gerald, because you're wasting your time. Monk? Get that portal thing working and take us out of here! *Now*!"

# CHAPTER TWENTY-FIVE

The portable portal spat them out a mere two feet above the palace roof. The first thing they did when they regained their feet was look up, but the dragon was nowhere in sight. Neither was Lional.

"Oh hell," said Melissande, her voice almost a sob. "I don't believe this . . ."

In every direction they looked distant pillars of black smoke churned into the sky. Closer to the palace, out-buildings not reduced to mounds of rubble smouldered and burned; the greedy crackling of flames reached them in fits and starts on the erratic, smoke-laden breeze.

She pointed. "Over there! I think that's Rupert's butterfly house!" She ran to the nearest balustrade and leaned over it, precariously. "Rupert! *Rupert!*" And then she looked down, and her next cry died in her throat.

"What?" said Gerald. "Melissande? What is it?"

Passing Reg to Monk he joined her at the roof's edge and stared at the ground far below.

There were great burned patches in the gravel and on the grass edging the palace forecourt, as though someone had upended huge barrels of acid onto them. Even at this height he could smell the acrid stench of the dragon's poison. See the remains of what once had been people. Laughing, living New Ottoslanders, reduced to charred and stinking carcasses. Palace staff, perhaps the very same servants who'd cooked him breakfast. Answered his questions. Bowed to him in passing. The servants he'd never bothered to notice, hardly, and whose names he hadn't asked. His empty stomach heaved.

There were tears on Melissande's cheeks. "Is one of them Rupert? One of them could be Rupert, he could be dead down there, or in his butterfly house, I have to—"

Gerald grabbed her before she could do something stupid. "Melissande, *think*. If he is dead, there's nothing you can do for him now. And if he isn't, that means he's hiding safely somewhere. If that's the case we'll find him, I promise. But like you said, you're the Prime Minister. You've got a lot more to worry about than the fate of one man. Even if that man *is* Rupert."

For a moment she resisted him, her muscles rigid under his fingers. Then she slumped. He let her go. "This is ridiculous," she whispered. "Why did Lional let the dragon do this? Why didn't he *stop* it? I don't care what you say, Gerald. Lional's not *evil*. I grew up with him, for God's sake! He used to feed me my bottle, play piggyback with me all around the palace! All of this . . . it isn't *him*."

A creak and flap of wings. Reg. Balanced carefully

on the balustrade beside Melissande's white-knuckled hand she said sternly: "That Lional's dead, ducky. He's been dead for months. What's stalking this kingdom isn't your brother. It's not even a man, it's an abomination. And abominations must be destroyed."

As Melissande flung herself away, and Monk went after her, Gerald closed his eyes. "I should've been a tailor." His voice broke. "I should've died at birth."

"*Gerald.*" Reg's wingtip touched his hand. "Look at me."

Reluctantly he looked.

"I know it's bad," she said. "I'm not going to pretend it isn't. But you don't have the luxury of remorse right now. Lional and his dragon are still out there and they have to be stopped."

Stopped? *Stopped?* "How?" he demanded, almost hating her. "The bastard's five times stronger than I am and filled to the brim with black magic. He's got a copy of *Grummen's Lexicon*, for God's sake. How can I—"

"What?" said Reg, and flapped her wings at him. "Gerald, *what*? What are you thinking?"

Barely breathing, he stared at her. "Beside his bed. Uffitzi's copy of *Grummen's Lexicon*. If I could get to it, if I could *read* it, I could—"

"Put the same evil, poisonous muck into *your* head?" she said, almost snarling. "And then what? You'll kill him?"

"You said it yourself, Reg. He has to be destroyed. If I *don't* kill him, more people will die!"

She nodded. "I know. And probably you'd succeed, if you did what you're suggesting. But even if you managed to kill that Lional, who'd kill *you*?

Because someone would have to, Gerald. The filth in books like *Grummen's Lexicon* stains your soul forever and makes you *bad*. It'd make you *worse* than bad. Let's not forget, sunshine: you're a *prodigy*."

"That's why I have to do this," he retorted. "Don't you understand? There's a good chance I'm the only wizard available with a hope against Lional and his stolen *potentias*. But *only* if I fight him with the same weapons he's got!"

"No. You're the one who doesn't understand," she said, shaking her head. "With Lional dead, Gerald, *you'd* be the danger. And whoever tried to stop you, well, they'd need to read the *Lexicon* too. And it wouldn't end there, I promise you that. Say this hypothetical wizard succeeded and managed to kill you. All it means is there'd be *another* rotten wizard who'd have to die . . . and so the *Lexicon* would be used again . . . and again . . . and again. Is that what you want, sunshine? Every last good wizard in the world dead because of you?"

He turned on her. "What else can I do? The magic I know doesn't have teeth, it doesn't have talons, it can't kill Lional *or* his damned dragon! I *have* to use the *Lexicon*, Reg!"

"*No!*" she shouted, and with a great fluster of wings launched herself into the air to hover furiously above him. "I'd rather see you dead here and now— I'd rather kill you *myself* than see you—" She stopped. Stared straight ahead, down the long straight carriageway leading from the palace forecourt to the distant palace gates. "Oh *blimey*! That's *all* we need!" Dropping back to the balustrade she looked over at

Melissande, sitting with Monk on the edge of a low rectangular flowerpot. She raised her voice. "Oy! You! Madam-Queen-in-Waiting! Front and centre, ducky, New Ottosland's got visitors!"

Melissande and Monk stared. Monk had a protective arm around her shoulders; strangely, she didn't seem to mind. Gerald sighed. *So that's what arse over teakettle looks like, does it?* "Queen-in-Waiting, Reg?"

Reg sniffed. "Well, once we've dealt with Lional this place'll have a monarching vacancy, won't it? And who in his right mind is going to put Butterfly Boy on the throne? If he hasn't been burned to a crisp, that is."

"What visitors?" Melissande demanded as she and Monk joined them.

Reg pointed a wing. "Those ones."

Shading her eyes, Melissande squinted down the length of the carriageway and further into the distance. "I can't see them. They're too far away."

Gerald summoned the hand-held magnifying glass from his suite's workshop then flicked it with his fingers. "*Binoculari expandarium.*"

"Very nifty, mate," said Monk, impressed.

"Oh yes. I'm nifty all right." He couldn't hide the bitterness.

Monk flinched. "Look . . . Gerald . . ."

"No sympathy," he said quickly. "Not unless you want to see a grown man cry." He handed Melissande the enhanced magnifying glass. "Here. Make sure to keep it six inches from your face or you'll hurt your eyes."

Clasping it gingerly she looked again. "Oh, *what*? It's the Kallarapi army! *Hundreds* of them! *Thousands*!"

"Three thousand six hundred and forty seven," Reg said glumly. When they stared at her she added, "I've always been good at maths. And birds have excellent eyesight."

"Huh," said Melissande. "How the hell did they get here so *quickly*? Lord, look at all those swords! And those camels—those are *war* camels, they're trained to rip out a man's throat with one bite and disembowel with a kick!" Her fingers were bloodless on the magnifier's handle. "Gerald, I can't see their faces properly! Beef this thing up for me!"

"Certainly," he said. "If you want your eyes to pop like overripe plums."

"Not really." She lunged over the parapet, trying to get a better look at the approaching army. As one, he and Monk grabbed her by the shirt tails before she overbalanced and plunged headfirst to the ground. "*Damn*. I'm sure their leader looks familiar. Who *is* that?"

"Trouble, that's who," said Reg. "With his best friend Disaster come to keep him company."

Melissande gasped. "Oh, Saint Snodgrass save us! It's Sultan Zazoor!"

Gerald stared at her. "Zazoor? Are you sure?"

"She's sure," said Reg. "He's riding a black camel. Sultan's privilege, that is. And guess who's at his left hand?"

His heart sank. "Shugat. Who else?" He took another look down the carriageway. The Kallarapi army was much closer now. Sunshine gleamed on the unsheathed scimitars at their sides, and the ominous drumbeat of padded camel feet on the gravel was now just audible.

"Who's Shugat?" said Monk.

"Trust me," he said, still staring at the approaching army. "Nobody you want to meet."

"I don't know," said Reg. "Might not be such a bad thing, him turning up. That ratty old holy man's got power to burn. Maybe if you two worked together, Gerald . . ."

Oh yes, that was likely. If Shugat had come all this way to make friends with the wizard responsible for Tavistock and the dragon *he'd* eat Melissande's parasol, with mustard. "You'd best get down there to meet them, Your Highness," he said to Melissande. "Once you've explained the situation there's no chance Shugat and the Sultan will blame you for what's happened. With any luck they'll be able to protect you from Lional."

"We'd all best get down there," said Reg, with an anxious glance at the cloudless sky. "If that dragon comes back it'll pick us off like pigeons up here." She looked at him, eyes narrowed. "And as for what we were discussing—"

Before he could answer, Melissande said, "Reg is right, Gerald. As your de facto employer I forbid you going anywhere near black magic. If Pomodoro Uffitzi's books are what made my brother—" She stiffened her spine. "—what he's become, then you can't risk using what's in them. I know we have to . . . stop . . . Lional. But not like that. It's out of the question."

"You heard her," said Reg. "And rumour has it she's the prime minister."

"It's not worth the risk, mate," Monk said unhappily. "It's obvious you're something extraordinary, but even so. You'd be mad to try it."

One by one Gerald looked at them, all so anxious on his behalf. "You don't understand, any of you. You don't understand what Lional—"

"We understand what might happen if you use that bloody *Lexicon*!" said Monk, and shoved him. "Just—pull your head in, Gerald. You're not throwing your life away if you don't have to!"

*I don't deserve him. I don't deserve any of them.* "And if I have to?" he asked gently.

Monk stepped back. "We can cross that bridge when—*if*—we come it. But we're not there yet, mate, so for now you'll do as you're told. *Right?*"

*Definitely I don't deserve them.* He nodded. "Right."

"Wonderful!" said Reg, shaking her wings. "So now *that's* settled, can we please go and greet the Kallarapi before their ratty old holy man leaves a calling card we'll never forget?"

By the time they'd flapped and run down and along and through the deserted palace staircases and corridors and out onto the forecourt, Zazoor and his slow-marching army were just a stone's throw away. Panting, sweating, they skidded to a halt on the gravel. Down here the smell of death and destruction was thick enough to turn the stomach; up close the charred bodies were sickening. Gerald watched Melissande's expression harden as she stared at them. Watched her make a conscious decision not to react, not to give way. To be royal . . . whatever that meant.

Back on his shoulder, Reg breathed, "Good girl, ducky. That's the way a princess does things."

"I knew them all," she said bleakly. "But Rupert's not one of them." Letting out a hard breath she shoved loose hair pins back in her bun, then blotted her face on her grubby sleeve. "Right. You lot wait here. I'm the prime minister, I'll take care of this."

They watched her march forward to meet the Supreme Ruler of Kallarap, his holy man and his army.

"You know," said Monk, after a moment. "That's a lot of camels."

Reg snorted. "And warriors. And swords. And spears."

"That holy man." Monk shuddered. "I see what you mean, Gerald."

Power roiled off Shugat like heat from the sun. Gerald nodded. "He's something, all right."

"Every last one of them stinks of magic," said Monk. "Explains how they got here so fast. They must have used some kind of *accelerando* incant. I wonder if—"

"Shut up, Monk," he said, as Shugat's power crawled like fire ants over his skin. "I want to hear what they're saying."

Monk started to object, changed his mind, and shut up.

Standing alone and stiff-backed in the wide gravel driveway, Melissande looked small and vulnerable as Zazoor drew his jet-black camel to a complaining halt before her and inclined his head in greeting. From his unadorned turban to his curly-toed boots he was dressed in shimmering white. His face was clean shaven, lean and hard and unreadable. He looked pristine and cool and frighteningly un-approachable. All his attention was focused on the princess.

Gerald felt sweat trickle the length of his spine. *The rest of us might as well be rocks. Or rose bushes.*

Defiant in her ghastly shirt and trousers and sensible shoes, Melissande bobbed a kind of curtseying bow. "Welcome to New Ottosland, Sultan Zazoor."

"Princess Melissande," Zazoor replied politely. "My gods-betrothed wife . . . or so I am given to understand by your esteemed brother the king."

The breeze had stilled. Nothing stirred. Their voices carried clearly through the warm, death-tainted air.

"Yes. And your gods, Magnificence?" countered Melissande. "Do they agree with my brother?"

Zazoor flicked a glance at Shugat, silently menacing to his left on a camel so white it was hard to look at. "No. They say your brother the king is . . . mistaken."

"Alas, Magnificence," said Melissande, her chin lifting. "My brother the king is mad."

Zazoor pressed a flat palm to his heart. "So my holy man Shugat has also told me. You have my sympathies, Highness."

She nodded graciously then looked at Shugat. "I did not look to see you again so soon, Holy Shugat. Such a short time has passed since you left us."

Shugat's look was inscrutable. "The gods give us wings, Princess, when desiring us to fly towards . . . justice."

"Ouch," Monk muttered. "Think that was a threat?"

"I don't know," Gerald muttered back. "Is your brother a pillock?"

"Shhhh!" hissed Reg, and thumped him with her wing.

Zazoor was gazing around the eerily hushed and deserted palace grounds. At the burned bodies. The blackened vegetation. At the plumes of smoke still rising in the distance. "Calamity has come upon your kingdom, it seems, Highness. The city streets we rode through on our way here were sadly damaged and as empty as this grand royal residence. Tell me, if you can: where are all your people?"

"Indoors. Underground. Run away," said Melissande. "They're hiding from the dragon, Magnificence."

"Well there's no point pretending," said Reg as Gerald cursed under his breath. "The wretched thing could land on our heads any moment."

Zazoor's eyebrows lifted. "*Dragon?*"

"It's . . . an internal matter. Nothing for you to worry about, Magnificence." Melissande looked at the army ranged at Zazoor and Shugat's backs. Silent. Disciplined. Waiting for a signal. "Let us instead address your uninvited presence. You've come for the monies owed to you by our kingdom. With an army, to use force if we don't willingly part with them. Sultan Zazoor, if I had those monies to hand I would give them to you gladly. I don't . . . therefore I can't."

Waving a fly away from his face Zazoor said, "It saddens me to hear you say so."

"And I'm not happy to say it," she replied. "But good neighbours are honest with each other."

"Honest?" Zazoor smiled. "A strange word in these strange times. Highness, it is not your debt that brings me here. Kallarap will not starve without your pennies. I am sent to you by my gods, who would have me speak with you of sacrilege. And treachery. And yes, indeed: of *honesty*."

*Damn.* This was where things went from bad to worse really *fast.* Gerald grabbed Reg off his shoulder, shoved her at Markham and threw himself into the fray.

"Sultan Zazoor, your quarrel is with me," he said, ignoring Melissande's furious protest. "Her Royal Highness is—"

Zazoor raised a silencing hand and looked at Shugat. "This is he?"

Shugat nodded. "This is he."

Zazoor's camel curled back its upper lip, lavishly fringed eyes glinting with displeasure, and stepped forward until it could blow its hot stinking breath into Gerald's upturned face.

"You are the foreign wizard who would presume to usurp our gods," Zazoor said pleasantly. "Why shouldn't my holy man strike you dead where you stand?"

As Melissande gasped, Gerald forced himself to meet the sultan's pitiless gaze. "Your holy man can do whatever he likes to me. I won't stop him. I'll even agree I deserve it. Just not before he helps me kill a dragon. Or a man. Whichever comes first . . . or easiest."

Zazoor's cold expression did not alter. "Both you and the princess speak of a dragon. But dragons do not live in the world, wizard. Unless you wish to claim that Grimthak, Holiest of the Holy, greatest god of Kallarap, has clothed himself in form and flame to anoint the kingdom of New Ottosland?"

He shook his head. "No, Magnificence. This is an unholy dragon. A monster of flesh and blood and magic."

"I see," Zazoor said thoughtfully. "And how does it come here?"

His hands fisted, then relaxed. "Magnificence, I made it."

The briefest spark of surprise showed in the sultan's hooded eyes. "For what purpose, wizard?"

*Tell him, Dunnywood. You've got nothing left to lose.* "For the enslavement of your people and the pillaging of your desert's Tears."

Again Zazoor looked to Shugat. His handsome face was grim. "'Evil', you said, my holy man. And so has evil come to pass."

Shugat nodded, equally grim. "The gods do not lie, Magnificence."

"Tell me, wizard," said Zazoor. "By whose order did you bring forth this unholy dragon, that my people might be made to suffer?"

"I made it for Lional, Forty-third King of New Ottosland."

Zazoor's eyes closed as though he were pierced by a terrible pain. "You did this knowing the dragon was an abomination? Knowing how Lional intended to use it?"

*I did. Hell, I did.* "Yes."

Now Zazoor's eyes opened. His face was terrible. "*Why?*"

"Don't answer that, Gerald," Melissande said quickly. "You're not on trial here, this isn't a court of law. He—"

"Magnificence," he said, touching her hand so she fell silent. "I made the dragon because I'm weak."

From behind him came a cackling shriek of fury. Then Reg landed in a flurry of feathers on his shoulder.

"Weak my granny's bunions! Now you listen to me, Zazoor! If you knew what that bastard Lional did to my Gerald to get that dragon, you'd—"

"The bird?" Zazoor said to Shugat.

Shugat nodded. "The bird."

Zazoor considered her. "*Not*, I think, trained."

"Trained?" screeched Reg. "What do you think I am, a bloody circus act?"

The smallest of smiles touched Zazoor's lips. "What you are is a mystery."

"And I can stay a bloody mystery, all right?" retorted Reg. "Let's just stick to the point. In case you'd forgotten there's an overgrown handbag with wings around here somewhere and we've got to take care of it before this little gathering becomes the biggest outdoor barbecue in the history of New Ottosland!"

Gerald sighed. "Reg . . ."

She whacked him on the head. "You shut up. What's the *matter* with you, telling Mr Turban-head here you're *weak*?" She rounded on Zazoor again. "This boy's just come out of a dark, dank cave where he spent nine days being hideously tortured by that maniac Lional! Suffering things that'd make your camel turn white! And if he *hadn't* given in, nine days would've turned into *forever*! Could *you* endure being tortured forever? No. Could you endure being tortured for nine days? Hah! I'll bet you wouldn't last nine *minutes*! So don't you dare sit up there on your mangy sinking ship of the desert and presume to call Gerald evil or weak or anything like it, or you'll have *me* to answer to! Do I make myself clear?"

If Zazoor was offended by the outburst nothing in his expression hinted at it. Instead he glanced at Shugat, who tapped his camel on the knee with his staff, waited for it to fold its legs then climbed down, staff in hand, to stand before him, his deep-sunk eyes half lidded and his thin-lipped mouth pursed.

Gerald waited, barely breathing. *Is this it? Is that wrinkled old face the last thing in this world my living eyes will see?* He flinched, then braced himself as Shugat pressed one palm over his heart hard enough to bruise. He felt an immense wave of power flow through him like a river unleashed. Grunting, he held his ground. Just.

Shugat's eyes closed. A nimbus of light exploded from his forehead. After a moment he stiffened, his face spasming. Then he sighed, a long slow exhalation of pent-up air, stepped back and looked at Zazoor.

"The bird does not lie, my sultan. The wizard has suffered. His blood still stinks of foul enchantments."

Zazoor tapped one elegantly tapered forefinger against his lips. Then his gaze shifted and he lifted a beckoning hand. A moment later, Monk joined them.

"And who are you?" said Zazoor. "Another wizard?"

Monk cleared his throat. "Yes, Magnificence. I'm—"

"A friend," said Gerald, and silenced Monk with a burning look. "Innocent of these doings. He's not to be harmed."

Zazoor raised his eyebrows. "You would stop me?"

"I'd try."

A flickering glance indicated Shugat and the menacing ranks of waiting warriors. "You would fail."

He held the other man's gaze without flinching. "Perhaps. But not before I'd tried."

Zazoor laughed. "Holy Shugat. This wizard asks us to help him destroy the dragon. What is our answer?"

Withered, sundried and bent beneath his weight of years, Shugat lifted his staff and struck it into the gravelled ground. Thunder rumbled from the cloudless sky. "*No.*"

"*No?*" cried Melissande into the ringing echoes. "Why not? What's the *matter* with you people? You heard Gerald! Lional and his dragon are out to destroy you! You *have* to help us stop them!"

"Kallarap is in no danger from your brother or his dragon," Zazoor said mildly. "Kallarap is protected by the Three. Perhaps you should find your own holy men and ask them to speak to your god so he may provide protection for you."

She spread her arms wide. "Look around you, Zazoor! Do you see any of our clergy rushing to my aid? No, I'm pretty sure you don't, because they've all run away just like everybody else!"

Zazoor shook his head. "Then your god is to be pitied, Melissande, that he is worshipped by such straw men."

"Magnificence, the dragon has flame!" she cried.

"And its venom is instant death! Look around you at my fallen people. You'll burn in fire and acid, just like they did! Your charred remains will stink as theirs do!"

"We are Kallarapi. We will not burn."

"So—what? You'll stand by and watch the dragon kill anyone not lucky enough to be riding a camel?" she demanded bitterly. "And when we're all dead, what then? You'll ransack our Treasury sofas for any spare coins you can find between the cushions then go home to Kallarap secure in the knowledge of a job well done? Is *that* your great gods' plan, *Magnificence*? Is *that* their vaunted justice and mercy? Because if it is—" And she spat on the ground at his camel's feet.

Gerald sighed.

"Melissande, don't!" said Monk, alarmed.

"Steady on, ducky," muttered Reg. "Does the word 'outnumbered' mean anything to you?"

Ignoring them, Melissande stared up at Zazoor, all her freckles blotchy in a face gone ivory-pale with temper. Behind Zazoor a growl as his army sat a little straighter and reached for their scimitars.

The sultan raised a finger and they subsided, reluctantly. "Shugat?"

"He who made the dragon must now unmake it," the holy man pronounced. His eyes had rolled back in his head, leaving slivered crescents of white. "So say the Three, whose words are holy and cannot be denied."

Zazoor looked at Gerald. "You have our answer."

He could've screamed. *Hell.* Were Shugat's deities

*deaf*? "I told you, Zazoor, I *can't* defeat the dragon. Not by myself. Reg, back off please."

With a muttered curse, she jumped from his shoulder over to Monk's. "Gerald, what are you doing?"

What had to be done. He stepped forward till he was close enough to touch Zazoor, then dropped to his knees and looked into the Kallarapi sultan's unforgiving face. "Magnificence, I beg you: listen to my words. Lional knows magics far fouler than those he used on me. I have power, it is true, but I am *not* strong enough to defeat him or the dragon. They're no longer two creatures, but one. *Help* me, I implore you. And when it's done—when Lional and his dragon are dead—I'll return with you to Kallarap to face whatever judgement your gods decree I deserve."

"No, Gerald!"

"Idiot boy!"

"Dunnywood, you maniac—"

Not turning, not shifting his gaze from Zazoor, he raised a hand and his friends fell silent. "Magnificence, *please*, don't let more innocent people suffer because of me."

Zazoor considered him in silence. "My gods' wrath is fearsome, wizard," he said at last. "They punish with fire and tooth and talon. They will show you no mercy. You understand this? You understand what will happen to you if I agree?"

Gerald nodded. For what he'd done he wanted forgiveness . . . but he deserved retribution. "Believe me, I understand. Magnificence—"

"Melly! Melly! *There* you are!"

He looked around. Rupert. Staggering towards

them from behind the palace, an unhappy Boris in his arms. Covered in soot and ash, his blue velvet knickerbockers and orange silk shirt charred in a dozen places and his face streaked with sweat or tears or both.

"*Rupert!*" cried Melissande and ran to meet him.

Flooded with relief Gerald stood and watched as brother and sister fell on each other's shoulders. Yowling Boris bolted into the nearest unsinged shrubbery. Melissande barely spared him a glance.

"Rupes, are you all right?" she demanded tearfully.

"I'm fine. Oh, Melly! Thank God you're unhurt, I was so *frightened* for you. I was frightened for *me!*"

"So was I, Rupert!" Her hand pressed against his grimy face. "You're really here? I'm not imagining this?"

"No, no, I'm really here." He captured her hand in his and held on to it, tight. "Melly, can you believe it? A *dragon*? I thought dragons were made up, I thought—"

Melissande sighed. "They are. It's a long story. Listen, Rupert—"

Not paying attention, he looked at the bodies scattered around them. His dirty, foolish face crumpled. "Oh, *Melly* . . . our *people* . . ." His breath caught on a sob and he pointed. "That's Swifty, Mel. I can tell by his socks, I gave him those socks for his last birthday. He used to help me with the butterflies, sometimes, on his day off."

"I know, I know." Her voice was ragged. "Don't look, Rupert."

"And that's Arabella, from the kitchens," he continued, heedless. "She always saved me a brown egg for breakfast. Oh, *Mel*—"

"I'm sorry, Rupert," said Melissande. "I couldn't save them. I couldn't save anyone."

"Neither could I," said Rupert, equally anguished. "When I tried, the dragon burned down my butterfly house."

"I saw." She cupped her palm to his cheek again. "Oh, Rupert, all your little pretties . . ."

He shook his head. There were tears in his eyes. "It's nothing, they weren't people . . ." Then his expression hardened. Abruptly he looked older and nowhere near as foolish. "This was Lional, wasn't it?"

"Yes," she whispered. "Rupert—"

But he wasn't listening. He was staring past her at the mass of Kallarapi warriors. "What's this, Melly? Why are *they* here? What's going on?" Without giving her a chance to answer he marched across the grass and the gravel to confront the invading Kallarapi, ignoring his sister's warning plea.

"Greetings, Your Highness." Zazoor said calmly as Rupert stamped to a halt before him. "It is good to see you again, although the circumstances are—"

Rupert waved away the pleasantries. "Look, Zazoor, if you've come for a wedding I'm afraid I've bad news. It's nothing personal so don't be offended but—"

Gerald cleared his throat. "It's all right, Rupert. The sultan's not marrying Melissande."

All the determination drained from Rupert's face, returning it to foolish uncertainty. "He's not?"

"No."

Rupert frowned. "Then who is he marrying?"

"Trust me, Rupert," said Zazoor, revealing his

teeth in a smile. "When the gods have decided you'll be the third to know."

"Then what are you doing here? With an *army*?"

Before Zazoor could tell him, one of Kallarap's warriors shouted, pointing.

"*Draconi! Draconi!*"

Lional's dragon was coming.

# CHAPTER TWENTY-SIX

It danced in the distance like a butterfly, crimson and emerald scales flashing fire. Flirting with tree-tops, kissing their crowns with flame, it cavorted without care, its enormous wings shivering snaps of sound from the air that floated towards them, thunder on the horizon.

As everyone else stared at the damned thing, stunned into silence, Gerald grabbed Monk's elbow and tugged him aside.

"Listen. It'll reach us in a minute or two so there's not much time. You've got to portal back to Ottosland. Take Melissande, Rupert and Reg with you and—"

Monk stared. "Leave you here alone with *that* thing? And *Lional*? I don't think so!"

"Out of the question, sunshine," Reg added.

"What's going on?" demanded Melissande, joining them. Rupert hovered by her side, his dirty face drawn, his gaze darting between his sister and the dragon.

"Monk's getting you out of here," he said.

She snorted. "No, he's not."

"Who's Monk?" said Rupert.

"I am," said Monk. "Pleased to meet you, Your Highness."

Rupert looked bewildered. "Yes. Certainly. I'm sorry, I don't understand . . ."

Gerald growled. "He'll explain it later. In Ottosland. Monk—"

"I can't go to Ottosland, Gerald." Rupert objected. "There's a murderous dragon loose in my kingdom."

"I know. And I'll take care of it."

"How?" demanded Melissande. "Look at the thing, half a mile away and it's *still* enormous!"

Shaking his head Rupert bleated, "Really. Gerald, I can't leave now, I—"

He raised his hand, fingers widespread. "*Impedimentia assoluta!*"

Melissande and Rupert froze in mid-protest, voices silenced.

"Whoops," said Reg. "They're not going to like *that*, sunshine."

*Too bad.* "So long as they're *alive* to not like it I really don't care!" he retorted. "Monk, listen. You have to go. Get the Department off its backside, *and* the UMN. Raise merry hell till somebody does something. Melissande, Rupert and Reg can help you, foreign royalty always gets attention. Come back with help, lots of it, as fast as you can."

"And in the meantime?" said Monk. He'd gone very pale.

*In the meantime, I die.* "I'll do what I can to keep Lional and his dragon preoccupied. Stop them from hurting anyone else. But you'd better hurry, mate. So go. Now. *Please.*"

Monk pulled the portable portal out of his pocket. His hand was unsteady. "Dunnywood, for the record, I'm telling you this is a bad idea."

He tried to smile and couldn't. "Probably. Monk—"

With a hiccuping sob Reg threw herself into his arms. "No, no, I'm not leaving you. Gerald! You *need* me! I can *help* you!"

Tenderly he lifted her to eyes level. She felt suddenly small and fragile, a frantically beating heart inside a brittle cage of feather and bone. "Darling Reg," he whispered, and kissed her. "I'm sorry but you can't. Not any more. Now if you love me . . . *leave.*"

"Gerald . . ." she protested helplessly as he returned her to Monk's shoulder.

"All set," his friend said. "Ready when you are."

He nodded. "Take care of each other, you two. And our royal friends. Don't let them boss you. And Monk?"

"What?" said Monk, wrapping one arm round Melissande, the other round Rupert and triggering the portal. "Gerald, *what?*"

He undid the immobility incant. Dredged up a smile. "Good luck with the princess. You're going to need it."

The portal opened and they disappeared.

Zazoor said, "Wizard, that was honourably done."

The stern voice released Gerald from his trance. He let out his pent-up breath, the relief so great it was like a pain. *They're safe, they're safe, thank God, they're safe.* Whatever life was left to him now, be it hours or minutes or scant swift seconds, at least he could face it with some kind of peace. His friends wouldn't pay the price for his myriad failures.

He turned and looked at Kallarap's sultan. "You think I'm the kind of man who'd let one more innocent life be lost if he could prevent it?"

Shugat fingered his staff. "The kind of man you are is yet to be revealed," he said before Zazoor could reply.

The dragon was almost on top of them now, flames and smoke billowing in its wake. The clear air trembled.

He sneered. "What's that, Shugat? More of your gods' *wisdom*?"

"Yes."

Damn the holy man and his cryptic utterances. He took a step towards Zazoor. "Magnificence, don't listen to him. That dragon's dangerous, you—"

"Oh *look!*" cried a lilting voice. "It's a party and we weren't invited. Do you know, we think our feelings are *hurt*."

Lional.

Cold with inevitability, Gerald looked to Shugat and the sultan. Unmoved, they watched Lional make his suave, insinuating way through the ruined flowerbeds to the edge of the carriageway where grass met gravel.

He turned to Zazoor, the blood pounding in his head. "This is your last chance. Help me. *Please*."

Unmoved, unmoving, Zazoor sat on his ebony war camel and stared down at his holy man. Shugat inspected the tip of his staff, leathered face creased in thought, then glanced up at Zazoor. After a moment of silent communion they closed their eyes.

*So. I'm alone.*

Something . . . some hope or belief or faith in the ultimate goodness of man . . . broke inside him. Bled swiftly, quietly, flooding all the cracks and chasms of his soul.

Lional laughed. "Gerald, Gerald. Why are you surprised? Didn't we tell you they're a dreadful bunch?"

He snapped his fingers . . . and in a beating of wings, with a hissing song of welcome, the dragon touched lightly to the ground at his side. Sunlight trembled on its scarlet and emerald scales, striking sparks from the diamond-bright sheen of its spines. Poison, green and glowing, oozed from each razor-sharp tip. Dripped harmlessly down the dragon's brilliant striped hide and Lional's green silk arm. Fell to the ground . . . which at its touch dissolved in a cloud of noxious smoke.

Kissing his palm to the dragon's cheek, Lional sighed. Some subtle flow of flesh and bone rippled beneath his skin. Seemed to elongate his skull and dagger his teeth. Gerald thought he saw a shimmer of crimson scale, swift as fish-scales in a river.

"We were hunting," said Lional in a soft and singsong voice, subtly not his own. "The sheep, the boar, the bullock, the stag . . . blood like crimson nectar . . . but before we'd killed our fill we felt the air change. Smelt the rank unwelcome coming of the nasty little man with his stone of power and we thought . . ."

Abruptly, Lional blinked. The dragon blinked. They stirred as though waking from a dream. Then

Lional smiled, a bright flashing of teeth, and the shadows beneath his skin sank from sight.

"Well, well, well," he drawled. He sounded himself again. "Hello, Zazoor. What brings you and your holy lapdog to my kingdom? *And* without an invitation. So *rude!*"

If Zazoor was unnerved by the ravening beast just feet away he gave no sign. He might have been attending a tedious tea party or receiving a tiresome guest in his own home. "What brings us here, Lional? Fate. Destiny. The will of the Three."

Lional's smiled widened. "Can't you make up your mind? Well, it's nice to see some things never change."

Zazoor's answering smile was deadly. "When we were at school, Lional, I knew you for a cowardly boy who bullied and cheated to get his way. Now you are a man grown and you resort to torture when bullying and cheating no longer suffice. Indeed you have the right of it, my old school chum: truly, some things never change."

Lional's smile vanished. His caressing fingers—with nails longer and thicker than they'd been just yesterday—dropped from the dragon's face and his blue eyes darkened, the flickering red flame in their depths leaping high.

"*Burn them*, my darling. Burn them to *ash*."

The dragon roared, lower jaw unhinging to reveal a cauldron of fire. Flames writhing green and scarlet burst from its dagger-toothed mouth. Swift as a striking snake Shugat snatched the stone from his forehead and held out his hand. A bolt of blue-white light collided with the gushing fire. There was a hissing of steam and stinking smoke like hot lava striking an arctic sea. The dragon screamed, rearing on its hind legs, wings thrashing. Lional, fingers clawing desperately at his mouth, screamed with it.

Gerald turned on Shugat. "See? You can hurt them! For God's sake, Shugat, you *have* to help me!"

Shugat glared, his eyes like the heart of a distant sun. He opened his mouth as if to speak . . . then froze. His eyes rolled back in his head, his arms flung wide and his tight-clutched staff began to shiver and twist.

The stone he held exploded into life.

Its surge of power drove Gerald to his knees. As he struggled to breathe he heard Lional, shrieking, and the dragon's echoing roar. He looked up.

Lional's fingernails had gouged deep furrows in his face; blood flowed from his cheeks, his lips, his chin. The dragon was wounded too, its scales cracked and blackened, thick gore bubbled and stinking. But within moments the scales healed, and Lional's wounds. His hands came up, fingers curved into talons, and his eyes were soaked in scarlet.

Shugat moved in a blur of speed. As a stream of foul curses spewed from Lional's lips he swept staff and stone in an arc that encompassed himself, his sultan and the entire Kallarapi army. In its wake sprang a translucent domed shield; motionless within, Shugat and Zazoor and the warriors of Kallarap waited.

Stranded, unprotected, Gerald watched Lional and his dragon throw flame and vitriol and the worst curses in history at the holy man's shimmering shield. Spittle flew from Lional's mouth and green poison poured down the dragon's teeth, turning the ground beneath their feet to acid mud as the attack went on and on.

Still the shield held.

Exhausted, half fainting, Lional fell back, one hand grasping at his dragon's spines to stop himself from falling. Equally spent, the dragon lowered its head and panted, wings limp and splayed upon the ruined grass.

Inside the barrier Shugat's eyes unrolled. He sighed, arms falling to his sides. Looked at Gerald, one wild eyebrow lifting in sarcastic invitation.

*Oh. Right.* Gerald ran.

The flowerbeds at the far edge of the palace gardens had somehow escaped untouched, with unburned blossoms rising rank upon perfumed, bee-buzzed rank. With the last of his strength he dived headfirst into a cloying collection of hollyhocks, daisies and snapdragons.

Ha.

Panting, he snatched up his arms and legs thinking: *hedgehog*. This far from the palace, to his shamed relief, he couldn't smell the stench of the dragon's kill. Thank God. Images of Lional and the dragon rose like flames before him.

Kill *them*? He'd *never* kill them.

*I'm going to die . . . I'm going to die . . . I'm going to die . . .*

Some six inches from his nose a rustling of leaf litter. He sucked in moist, compost-rich air, unmoving. Another rustle. And then a lizard, a skink, skinny and brown with only one good eye, darted out from under a leaf and stopped, nervously scenting the air with its tiny tongue.

Gerald held his breath. Memory replayed recent, desperate words.

*I'm the only wizard with a hope against Lional. But only if I fight with the same weapons he's got!*

When he'd said it he was convinced that meant using *Grummen's Lexicon*. But what if . . . what if . . .

*You know what they say. Fight fire with fire. Or . . . dragon with dragon?*

His stunned mind reeled. No. He was mad. How the hell could it possibly *work*? As lizards went, this one was pathetic. With its left eye shrivelled, practically *crippled*. Its matrix would make a piss-poor dragon; even with the strongest magic this little skink could never hope to match the brute muscularity and mindless viciousness of the bearded spitting lizard from Lower Limpopo. The dragons would never be equal: magic could only do so much.

*But hey, Dunwoody. Remember your mantra: beggars can't be choosers, and it's the only lizard you've got. Even if all you can do is distract Lional . . . tire him out . . . buy enough time for Monk to return with reinforcements . . .*

He didn't have a staff but that didn't matter. He had no need of staffs any more.

"*Impedimentia implacato.*" On the brink of bolting, the little lizard froze and stared at him with its one good eye, cream-coloured sides pumping frantically for air.

He swallowed a sudden stab of conscience. Poor little thing. So timid. So frail. Did he have the right to do this? Change it? Distort it? Pit it against Lional's dreadful dragon, most likely to its death?

*There's no choice. I have to.*

"Sorry little lizard," he whispered. "It's you and me or everyone else. I promise I'll make you as strong as I can. I just hope you survive transmogrification."

And if it did, there remained the matter of *his* survival. Not just physical but mental. The *Tantigliani sympathetico*. If Lional, with the stolen *potentias* of five powerful wizards, couldn't resist its seductive destructive undertow, then prodigy or not, what chance did he have?

*Little to none.*

Fear like a tidal wave smashed him to the dirt. He couldn't move, couldn't breathe, or see anything in his future but a slow and bleeding insane death.

*You took an oath and then you broke it. Here's your chance to mend it, just a little.*

With infinite care he raised his head high enough to see around the garden, straining sight, hearing and wizard senses. No Lional, no dragon. But the respite wouldn't last. Withdrawing into his scented hiding place he scrabbled in the dirt for something sharp. His questing fingers found a rock, chipped on one side.

It would have to do.

Setting his teeth, he unclenched the fingers of his left hand and struck into its palm with the piece of stone, again and again until he breached the sealing skin and freed the blood below.

The pain was a welcome distraction.

Next he summoned from memory the exact sequence of blotches Lional had made on the crimson and emerald lizard's back to set in place the *Tantigliani sympathetico*.

When he was sure of it he opened his eyes, whispered "*Absorbidato complexus*" and painted the skink with his hot, dripping blood. Then he ran his finger along its meagre length. "*Manifesti retarto.*" Finally, after checking it was still safe beyond the flowerbed, he picked up the skink and crawled out into the garden proper . . . where he set the lizard down on the close-clipped grass, took a deep breath and turned it into a dragon.

A roar of power. A rush of heat along every nerve. Vision incandescent, heart bursting, he felt the ether twist and turn in torment, felt the little lizard's dim-witted astonishment as bones lengthened, wings budded and fire filled its belly.

He opened his eyes and saw his second dragon. A muted, muddy brown. Eight foot high and twelve foot long. No spines. No poison. A teaspoon of fire. He snapped his fingers before it could react. "*Manifesti asbsolutum! Tantigliani sympathetico obedientium singularum mi!*" And then, sealing both their fates: "*Nux nullimia!*"

The skinny brown dragon stirred. Turned its head to look at him, blinking. In a single heartbeat the world turned inside out . . . and he was staring at himself through the dragon's single black eye.

He'd looked better.

The dragon raised its head and scented the rising breeze. Gerald, nostrils flaring, smelled smoke and fire, death and decay. A quick flutter of movement to the right caught the dragon's attention. He turned to look. A hummingbird, black and gold and unaware, paused to sup nectar from a nodding bloom in the next flowerbed. The dragon lashed out its tongue and pulled the hummingbird into the embrace of its gleaming white teeth. He felt fragile bones crack and split and hot blood course down his throat. He bent over, gagging.

The dragon swallowed, and waited.

Straightening slowly, smearing bile from his lips with his sleeve. Gerald inhaled a deep calming breath. Inhaled another. And another. Then he took his dragon and went hunting for Lional.

"*Right*," said Melissande. "I've had just about *enough* of this."

Monk sighed. "I did warn you. Look, Melissande, they'll get to us when they get to us so there's no point—"

"There is *every* point! Because at the rate your precious Department's going I'll have qualified for the pension before they come to a decision!" she snapped. "*And* another thing! *You* may be the one who said 'Call me Monk' but *I* never answered, 'Do call me Melissande'. In fact if memory serves I said '*Don't* call me Melissande'."

Squatting between them, Reg refluffed all her feathers and said, "Oh, give it a *rest*, you two, or I'll do *both* of you a mischief."

They were sitting uncomfortably side by side by side in a drab grey waiting room outside some official chamber or other in Ottosland's antiquated Department of Thaumaturgy building. Apart from the back-breaking chairs there wasn't a stick of furniture. Neither were there windows to look through or any tedious old magazines to read. The room was cold and stuffy and not designed to succour its occupants.

Shivering, Melissande glanced through the open

door to the drab grey corridor beyond. "Where the hell has Rupert got to? It doesn't take *this* long to use the lavatory."

"Ha," said Reg. "He's probably been side-tracked by a moth."

"That's not funny! Whatever you may think of him he really *loved* his butterflies! He's *grieving* for them, you horrible bird, he's probably got his head buried in a towel right now, crying his heart out for those stupid, *stupid*, insects!"

"Reg . . ." said Monk. "Please. You're not helping."

With an effort Melissande pulled herself back from the brink of embarrassment . . . and didn't object when Monk took her hand in his. "Nobody's helping," she muttered. "It was stupid to come here, we should have stayed in New Ottosland. Saint Snodgrass only knows what trouble Gerald's got himself into now. He had *no business* forcing me to come here. I should be at home, fighting for the people, I'm prime minister of New Ottosland and practically the queen!"

Not that she wanted to be. She couldn't think of anything worse. *I wonder if I'll have to change my name to Lional . . .*

"Don't you worry about Gerald," said Reg. "He's a wizarding prodigy. He can take care of himself."

Melissande exchanged a mordant glance with Monk over the top of Reg's head. Clearly the bird didn't believe her own pep talk. *I don't believe it either, I'm afraid. It'll take more than a prodigy to beat Lional and his dragon. It'll take a miracle . . . and I'm not sure they exist.*

"Don't give up, Mel—Your Highness," said Monk. "The Deparment will come through for us, I know it. It's just going to take time. This is a hideously complicated situation, you know, involving five different nations, three of whom currently aren't officially talking to each other."

Ah, politics. *I am sick to death of politics. I think I'll ban them when I'm queen.* She pulled a face at Monk. "I'm not giving up. And call me Melissande."

Even though he was as worried as she was, his lips quirked in a brief grin. "Thought you'd never ask. Look, do you want me to go hunting for Rupert while—"

The main chamber's large double doors opened. "Come in, please," said a discreet secretarial type dressed in sober black. "Lord Attaby will see you now."

Abruptly aware of appearing less than her best, Melissande slid off the chair and lifted her chin, defiant. "And not a moment too soon. I was just about to make a Scene."

As Reg hopped onto Monk's waiting shoulder she marched past the discreet secretary and into the chamber. Stalked across the room's dingy carpet, Monk and Reg at her heels, and halted in front of the long polished oak conference table on the far side of the room. There was a click behind her as the secretary closed the double doors.

To her fury she saw the Ottosland officials at the table had been drinking tea and eating biscuits. *Tea and biscuits while my kingdom is dragged to hell in a handbasket. How dare they?* "Right," she said, glaring at the three men ranged before her. "Which one of you is Lord bloody Attaby?"

The man in the middle, reeking of affluence and

self-importance, inclined his head fractionally. His thinning silver hair was slicked to his skull with something smelly and expensive. "I am Lord Attaby, Minister of Thaumaturgy for the Ottosland government."

She looked left then right at his silent bookends. "And these two?"

"My colleagues," said Lord Attaby blandly.

"I see. And do they have names?"

"None that are relevant to these proceedings," said Lord Attaby. "Madam."

She snorted. "I'm not madam, I'm Her Royal Highness Princess Melissande, Prime Minister of New Ottosland and—and—Queen Presumptive."

Lord Attaby laced his fingers before him, frowning. "Or so you claim."

"*Claim?*" she demanded. "What, you think I'm *lying?*"

"I think you are a young foreign woman lacking both identification and requisite travel documentation who has entered this country by dubious and possibly illegal means," said Lord Attaby, looking down his nose at her. "And who, it would appear, has suborned one of its citizens into breaking some very, *very*, serious laws."

Monk stepped forward. "No, she hasn't, Lord Attaby. That's all on me. And she is who she says she is, I can vouch for that. Unless you think I'm lying, too."

Lord Attaby's chilly expression plummeted below freezing. "It would appear, Mr Markham, you have been labouring under the mistaken apprehension that your illustrious family name would afford you unlimited protection in this matter. Allow me to disabuse you of this naive—"

The man on Lord Attaby's right lowered his raised, silencing hand. Melissande looked at him more closely; anyone who could halt an aristocrat mid-tirade was worth examining. He was extremely . . . nondescript. Unlike Lord Attaby, whose shirt was silk, he wore plain cotton. His watchband was leather, not gold, and he altogether lacked a pampered air. His hooded grey eyes were years older than his round, faintly lined face and mousy brown hair suggested. He didn't look like an enemy. He didn't look like a friend. More than anything he looked like a greengrocer or some other kind of inoffensive shopkeeper.

*How very odd*, she thought. *I wonder who he is?*

The man on Lord Attaby's left took advantage of the silence and said, "Your part in this, Monk, will be dealt with in due course. For now let us focus on the reason for Her Highness's unorthodox appearance in the country."

Melissande glanced at Monk. He was subdued now and pink around the edges. "Yes, Unc—Sir Ralph."

"Lord Attaby," said Monk's important relative, properly deferring. "Do continue, sir. I believe time is a commodity in short supply."

"Time, Lord Attaby, has pretty well run out!" Melissande said hotly. "At least for your citizen Professor Gerald Dunwoody! I'm assuming you *do* care about him at least, even if you couldn't give a toss about the five dead wizards or the people of Kallarap or *my* people in New Ottosland, some of whom are already dead because of this string of disasters! You know, none of this would ever have happened if people like you hadn't failed to monitor Pomodor Uffitzi more carefully! If *he* hadn't got his hands on those dreadful grimoires, *I* wouldn't be standing here thaumaturgically related to a dragon!"

Lord Attaby sat back. "Does this mean your . . . government . . . accepts no responsibility for this? Are you now claiming that your brother King Lional bears no culpability whatsoever for the murder of five wizards, one of whom was an Ottoslander, or the deaths of your unfortunate citizens and his intended invasion of your peaceful neighbour?"

She felt herself turn red. "No," she said curtly. "Of course Lional's culpable. He's also crazy. I'm not making excuses, I'm just giving you the facts."

Lord Attaby smiled. It was extrememly unpleasant. "In my experience, *Prime Minister*, facts are remarkably malleable things. They can be massaged to fit any number of scenarios depending upon a variety of preferred outcomes."

"Really?" she said, seething.

He nodded. "Really."

"How very interesting. Because in *my* experience that's known as falsifying evidence. Manipulating the truth. To be blunt, Lord Attaby, it's known as *lying*. Also *covering your arse*."

The nondescript man on Lord Attaby's right looked down, lips twitching. Monk's illustrious relative frowned disapprovingly. Lord Attaby scowled, his pouchy face burnished dull crimson. "Young woman—"

"No, *not* 'young woman'," she said. "You were right the first time. Do at least try to keep the protocol intact." She leaned her fists on the oak conference table and thrust her face into his. "Now let's get something straight, *my lord*. As far as I'm concerned there's plenty of blame to go around for this fiasco. And when it's over, by all means, let's sit down with tea and biscuits and parcel it out like lumps of sugar. But before that, if it's not too much to ask, could you and your hoity-toity Departmental chums here *stop* pointing fingers for five seconds and do something constructive?" She raked them with a furious gaze. "Because in case you've forgotten, gentlemen, people are *dying*! And in light of that, how I got here and so on and so forth is just a steaming pile of bollocks!"

"I'm so sorry," said a hesitant, apologetic voice from the doorway. "You mustn't be offended. My sister has a temper but her heart is in the right place. And as it happens, this time I agree with her. We don't have time for recriminations."

Melissande spun round. "*Rupert?* Rupert, where the hell have you been?"

As the discreet secretary closed the doors again Rupert walked towards her, one hand outstretched. "Darling Melly," he said. He still looked ridiculous in his ruined blue velvet knickerbockers and orange silk shirt but even so . . . something was different. Something had *changed*. Reaching her, he took her hand and kissed her cheek. "I've been sorting a few things out. Lord Attaby?"

Horrible Lord Attaby was on his feet. So were his bookends. "Your Majesty," he murmured. "I take it you and the Prime Minister have reached an agreement?"

"We have," said Rupert. "Everything's arranged."

Dumbfounded, Melissande stared at Monk then Reg then back at Rupert. "I'm sorry," she said, and pulled her hand free. "*What's* arranged? Rupert, what are you—"

He kissed her cheek again. "I'll explain everything later. You have my word. But right now you need to come with me, all of you. We don't have much time if we're going to save Gerald."

# CHAPTER
# TWENTY-SEVEN

Running unsteadily, almost staggering, with a dull-brown, skinny one-eyed dragon flapping in his wake, Gerald returned to the palace forecourt. Sultan Zazoor, his holy man Shugat and the Kallarapi army were still gathered there, safe within their shimmering domed shield. Not a single expression on a single face changed as he haphazardly approached.

After reeling to a halt he bent over for a moment, hands braced on his knees, and sucked in deep gulps of air. It still stank of burned flesh and acid poison. His stomach protested and he spat out bile. Behind him his pathetic dragon landed gracelessly on the ruined grass, hissing as it caught the scent of its counterpart.

When he could trust his guts he straightened, slowly, and stared through the shield at Zazoor and Shugat. "Where's Lional? Where's his dragon? Did you see which way they went? Do you know where they are now? Can you at least help me that much?"

Zazoor and Shugat looked at him, eyes hooded, expressions remote. Just as eerily silent, the mounted warriors sat on their camels as though posing for a portrait.

*You bastards. I think I hate you.* "What is *wrong* with you people?" he shouted. The skinny brown dragon flapped its wings and hissed softly. "*Look at me*! Look at this *dragon*! Aren't you *afraid* yet? Because if you're not, you bloody well should be! Don't you get it? We're all that's standing between you and Lional! Can that magical barrier of yours reach over your entire *nation*? I don't think so. *Nobody* has that much power!"

Shugat stirred. Blinked. "You are wrong, wizard. Our gods have that much power. They have power enough to shield the world." His voice reverberated strangely within the pearlescent shield.

"Your gods . . ." Gerald felt himself breaking inside, as though all his fault lines were fracturing. "Well *bully* for them, Shugat! And *bugger* you! If you're not going to help me then why don't you and your sultan and your ragtag bunch of camel jockeys sod off home! I don't think Melissande's in the market for a bunch of lawn ornaments at the moment!"

Shugat sighed. "Wizard, you are wasting time. Even now Lional and his dragon replenish their strength. Would you break your oath a second time? If not you must face them. You must face them or be lost forever."

*I change my mind. I don't think I hate you. I know I do.* "Fine," he said bitterly. "I'll face them. And we both know I'll probably fail. It's almost certain Lional will kill me. And after I'm dead he'll come for you. Maybe your shield will hold and maybe it won't. But if it doesn't . . . don't you dare blame me. Whatever happens after this, Shugat, the blood's on your hands, mate. It won't be on mine."

Shugat said nothing. Beside him, Zazoor said nothing.

*So. That's that. They're not going to help me. I'm really on my own.*

Hollow, feeling strangely disconnected from the world, Gerald turned his back on them. Gave a hard tug on the mental leash connecting himself and the skinny brown dragon and left the Kallarapi to their own devices to continue the hunt for Lional and his dragon.

He didn't have to hunt far. The horrific sound of horses screaming led him to Lional's private stable yard where Lional was seated on an upturned barrel watching his dragon feed on equine flesh.

The stables had been ripped apart, bricks and tiles and jagged splinters of timber scattered piecemeal, flame-scarred and acid-etched. The yard itself was a shambles, lumps of meat, shards of bone and ribbons of blood-soaked hair splattered over every surface. Gerald felt his stomach heave. From the available evidence the black and tan hounds had been killed too.

*More blood on my hands. More innocents slaughtered. I'll never be able to make this right . . .*

Lional's dragon darted and whirled amongst the few remaining terror-maddened horses, butchering indiscriminately, biting and tearing and swallowing as though it were starved. In his mind Gerald felt the little brown dragon howl a protest as it scented the kills through the link that bound them. It took all his strength to overpower its will and keep it hidden, safe from being revealed too soon.

Lional's frenzied dragon turned on the last surviving horse and bared its blood-slicked teeth, acid pouring from its mouth and spines. The cobblestones smoked, the air filled with the stench of burning blood.

Gerald leapt forward. "*Stop* the damned thing, Lional, before it's too late! Can't you *see*? That's *Demon*! He's your favourite horse, isn't he? Don't let it eat *Demon*!"

*If you let it eat Demon then you truly are gone.*

Lional's face was white as death. "Demon?"

As the stallion called out to its master in fearful entreaty the dragon killed it. Then, with a hissing cry of triumph, fell upon the steaming carcass and tore it open like it was made of paper.

Light-headed with horror, Gerald watched Lional slide off his upturned barrel and dabble his fingers in the steaming blood pouring from his murdered horse. Watched him lift a cupped brimming handful to his lips and drink . . .

Despite the torment he'd endured at Lional's hand, the rage he felt at Lional's unspeakable wickedness . . . he was overwhelmed with sickened pity.

"Oh, Lional. *Lional*. What have you *become*?"

Hunger satisfied at last, the dragon settled amongst the remains of its butchered feast, wings furled against its bulging sides, eyes half lidded and watchful. With a sigh of utter repletion Lional dragged his bloody hands over his face, his hair. Sucked the red smears from his fingers. Then he turned and smiled. His eyes were crimson.

"Why, Gerald . . . isn't it obvious? *I've become myself.*"

He faltered backwards a step. What? *I.* Lional had called himself *I* . . .

"Lional," he said desperately, "listen. Please. If you are still in there *listen* to me. You have to fight this. It won't be easy, you're nearly gone, but I can help you. Lional, you don't want to be this *thing.* You *can't* want it, you weren't born a monster. In your own twisted way you love New Ottosland. You did this for your kingdom. Your people. Well now they need you, Lional. Not the dragon. *You.* So *fight* this, you bastard. Do you hear me? *Fight* it!"

Lional was staring at him, head tipped to one side. Beneath the blood his expression was gently puzzled. "But Gerald . . . there is nothing to fight. I *am* the dragon . . . and the dragon is me. We are us. We are one. I am . . . I."

In the stinking silence Gerald heard his heart beating. *It's true. They are one . . . which means I've failed. I've failed and doomed this kingdom. Good work, Dunnywood. How's that for a legacy?*

And then he shook his head. *No.* If Reg was here she'd kick his arse for thinking like that.

*She wouldn't quit now and neither will I. It's the least I owe her after letting her down.*

He took a tentative step towards Lional. "Your Majesty, think for a minute. What about Melissande? What about Rupert? They're your *family*, they need you, too. The dragon might hurt them, you don't want that. You—"

"Those names are shadows. I am my own family, Gerald," said Lional, smiling. "Shall we show you?"

Before he could escape, Lional's hands captured his face. The grasping fingers were scorching hot, as hard as dragon's claws. Still smiling, Lional drew him close . . . closer . . . their lips met and he tumbled helplessly into the blast furnace of Lional's dragon mind.

*boiling acid—burning ice—a ravenous hunger that could never he gorged—*

Oh, God. It was over. The transformation was complete. The two thin strands of black and crimson, once two separate minds, were now a single thread melting from crimson to black and back again without beginning or end.

Lional was the dragon and the dragon was Lional.

Protesting the invasion, the tangling of their bond, the little brown dragon in its hiding place threw back its head and roared. Gerald cried out as the echoes of its distress reverberated along the link that Lional had forced with his mind. Lional staggered backwards, crimson eyes wide.

"What is this, Gerald? Don't tell me you've *joined* us . . ."

Head swimming, balance momentarily destroyed, he fell against the stable yard's broken brick wall. "Not exactly."

Lional frowned; the dried blood on his face cracked, flaked, drifted away on an errant breeze.

"What, then?"

"What do you think, you poor mad bastard?"

"Oh! I *see!*" cried Lional and laughed with delight. His dragon opened its mouth wide and hissed; more green poison streamed down its teeth to curdle the blood pool it sat in. "Well, they do say imitation is the sincerest form of flattery, don't they? And I *am*, I'm *flattered!* Where is it, Gerald, your brand-new dragon? Don't be shy! Show it to us! I promise I won't bite . . ."

With a grunt, Gerald pushed himself away from the brick wall. "I don't," he said, and ran.

He'd left the little brown dragon in a bower nearby, not trusting its limited athleticism to a confrontation in close quarters. Once cornered by Lional's emerald and crimson monster it would be dead in seconds, and so would he. Open sky was their only chance of survival . . .

If they had any chance at all.

The brown dragon roared rustily as he rejoined it, wings flapping, head swivelling as it tried to focus with its one good eye. He took a deep breath and brought it back under control. Brought himself under control at the same time, because facing monstrous Lional without focus, without total self-mastery, was tantamount to suicide. He felt his heart ease . . . felt the brown dragon's breathing slow . . . felt their blood pound less frantically through their veins.

*My veins* he told himself sharply as the image of Lional drinking blood assaulted him. *And don't you forget it!*

The thought of succumbing to the *sympathetico* was a gibbering fear in the pit of his belly. To lose himself in the mind of a dragon . . . to turn ravening on his friends, on Reg, and Monk. On Melissande and Rupert who were relying on him to undo the damage he'd done to their country . . . *God, don't let it happen. Please, don't let it happen.*

Subduing terror, he made himself think of more practical things. The nearest open space to fight Lional and his dragon was the palace forecourt. He'd have to make his stand there, Kallarapi or no Kallarapi. There was no way he and the little brown dragon could outrun or outfly Lional and his beast. He could hear their casual approach, the scattering of stones, the heavy, roaring breath . . . they were in no hurry, damn them. For Lional the battle was already won. Why rush breathless to a foregone conclusion?

*Yes, well, don't count your victims before they're actually dead, mate. Your royal court wizard's still got a few surprises for you . . .*

With one hand for guidance on the brown dragon's skinny neck, Gerald eased their way out of the bower and around the flowerbeds, the rose-covered trellises and the ornamental shrubs that flanked each side of the palace's grand entrance. The eerie silence over the grounds continued. He couldn't see a soul stirring anywhere. The palace staff, sensibly, remained in hiding or had fled.

*But the cavalry's not here yet, either. Damn, I wish they'd hurry. Come on, Melissande, this is no time to be shy. Throw your weight around, have a princessly tantrum. Don't let them bully you, I need that help!*

Gravel crunched under his feet, swished beneath the dragon's dragging tail. They were back at the forecourt . . . and the Kallarapi were gone.

For a moment he was disconcerted, but the feeling

quickly passed. *Good*. If the selfish bastards didn't intend to help him the *last* thing he needed was them watching him die . . .

He took a deep breath, banished Shugat, Zazoor and his silent army from his mind . . . and waited for Lional and the dragon to come into view.

Only Lional came.

Gerald fought the impulse to stare into the dragon-less sky. What the *hell* was Lional planning . . .

When the king saw the half-blind drab brown dragon at his side he burst out laughing. "Oh, *Gerald!*" he gasped, tears running from his crimson eyes. "*Surely* you can do better than *that*?"

He lifted his chin. In his mind, his dragon burned. "If you surrender now, Lional. you won't be harmed. If you refuse, I'll stop you, both of you, even if I have to kill you to do it."

"*Stop* us?" echoed Lional, incredulous. "With *that*?"

"With everything I have and everything I am."

More laughter, this time derisive. "Well in that case, Gerald, we have nothing to fear," said Lional, dulcet. "For we know what you have *and* what you are. You were revealed to us in the dark, in the cavern. Shall we tell you the truth of yourself?" Now his beautiful smile was cruel. He wore a crown of black flies, feasting on the dried blood in his hair. "You are a weeper. A moaner. A begger of mercy. A pisser and shitter, who gave in to his pain. Oath-bound and forsworn. Or have you forgotten?"

The words were acid on his soul. *I know what I did, Lional. I remember how I sounded and how I stank.*

*I don't need you to remind me of the cavern. I don't need you to do anything but die.*

"If I'm forsworn what does that make you?" he retorted. "For hundreds of years the kings of New Ottosland have been keepers, not conquerors. Stewards of the people. Your sacred duty was to protect them, Lional, not—"

"The people are *subjects*!" Lional screamed, his inhuman eyes aflame. "Ours to kill or kiss as we desire. Now cease your weary prattling, little worm! The time has come for *you* to die! I offered you greatness and you threw it back in my face. I am affronted, Gerald. You have affronted me. I do not take such an insult lightly. I will kill you slowly for that. I'll make you *pay*."

And then the sky was full of beating wings and lashing tail and furious tongues of fire as Lional's crimson and emerald otherself plummeted shrieking out of the sun.

The little brown dragon hissed, startled. Hissing again, it reared on its hind legs and beat its dowdy wings in answer. Gerald, hands fisted by his sides, took a lung-bursting breath of acid-soaked air . . . and kicked down the door protecting his mind from the dragon's.

*Heat. Rage. A burning lust for death. Wings and claws and teeth for tearing.*

Lional's dragon swooped low and Lional vaulted onto its back, as once he'd vaulted onto poor dead Demon. He rode the dragon as though flesh and bone had melded, skin to scales, a man with wings.

The small part of Gerald's mind that remained just Gerald swore. *Oh that's wonderful. I hate flying.*

He scrambled on board his own small brown dragon and with the gossamer thread of himself that survived untouched he told his creation to *fly, fly*. With a rusty roar of challenge and a thrashing of inadequate wings and tail, they leapt into the stinking air towards their crimson and emerald enemy.

Through the first mad moments of fire and torque, as the dragons danced and he held on for his life, he tried to think of a plan. A strategy. Some way of dealing with Lional that would work once and for all. Tried to think of something more useful than "bloody hell, Dunnywood, don't fall off."

*Maybe if I can get Lional out of New Ottosland . . .*

And that *might* work. Get him over the border and into Kallarap . . . if its gods were real . . . if they had true power . . . the last thing they'd want is Lional in their midst. They'd have to destroy him. They'd have to.

*So much for Shugat. I'll cut out the middleman.*

Even as he decided, the brown dragon swerved left. Headed towards the city, towards the border far beyond it, to the desert of Kallarap and the wrath of its gods.

With a bellow of fury, Lional and his dragon launched in pursuit, streaking flame after them in searing streams. Gerald felt the heat wash over him, felt his small dragon's agony as a whip of flame licked its tail.

*I'm sorry little dragon! Fly faster—fly faster—*

He risked a swift look behind them. Lional was gaining.

Now the city was directly below them, they were flying through smoke from its burning buildings. Eyes smearing, tearing, Gerald stared at the rubble . . . the bodies . . . the ruined streets lined with charred skeletal trees. There were people in the open again, milling like sheep without their shepherd, making vague disorganised attempts to do something about the mess.

And then he really did almost fall off his dragon because *Shugat* was down there. Shugat and Zazoor and the entire Kallarapi army, they were down off their camels and helping the people.

A scream of rage behind him. He turned. Lional had seen Shugat. He was close now, so close. His in-human face was contorted with fury. Abandoning the pursuit, he and his dragon flung themselves towards the ground.

*Oh shit.*

Gerald flung himself and his dragon after them.

Lional's subjects were screaming, scattering, running pell-mell into the park which held the Royal Duck Pond. Shugat stood motionless in the cobble-stoned street, holding his ground. Zazoor retreated, the army retreated, assisting Lional's subjects wher-ever they could. Shugat plucked the rough stone from his forehead and held it high in one outstretched hand. No shield of protection this time. Just a pulse of light and a crack of sound.

It was like flying headfirst into a brick wall.

Gerald shouted as he and his dragon bounced off thin air, were struck hard by Lional and his dragon flailing backwards, smacked just as hard by Shugat's invisible hand. Gerald lost his grip and his balance and fell from his dragon's hot back. As he tumbled like a rag doll he caught sight of Lional. He was falling too.

Gerald hit the park's hard ground and felt something break. Pain flooded through him, and in his mind he heard his dragon howl. Somehow he staggered to his feet, the pain didn't matter. He had to stop Lional.

New Ottosland's mad king was unhurt and finding his own feet again several yards from the Duck Pond. Gerald lurched in a circle, looking for Shugat. *You can help me now, you bastard. You're bloody going to help me now!* But the holy man was gone again. So was Zazoor and his army. They'd melted away like mist under the sun. He felt like crying. *Oh damn you. Damn you. Why won't you help . . .*

Above his head the dragons were fighting.

It was a hopelessly unequal contest. Lional's dragon outweighed the enchanted skink by hundreds of pounds. Its wingspan was half as wide again, its tail as strong and lethal as a battering ram. Gerald stared at the battling dragons, barely breathing. One well-placed blow from Lional's monster would snap his dragon's spine like kindling. And he'd thought his little dragon could *hurt* it?

He must have been mad.

Lional's dragon lashed sideways with its tail: Gerald staggered as it hit the brown dragon a glancing blow. Lional's dragon breathed fire: he cried out as the heat licked him along his arm, blistering flesh. The little brown dragon faltered, one wing seared and smoking. Its wings beat once . . . beat twice . . . it wasn't climbing. The brown dragon let out a hoarse cry of despair.

Watching, triumphant, Lional laughed.

This was the moment. Live or die. Kill or be killed. Succeed or fail . . . and in failing doom two nations to death.

As one with his suffering, struggling dragon, Gerald took a shuddering breath. Ignoring their pain, their fear, for the first time he looked deep within to the source of his power. Vivid as mercury, potent as wine, it poured without end from a reservoir he never knew existed . . . drowning him from the inside out.

Somewhere in his mind something tore loose, shattered, exploded. It was Stuttley's all over again but a million times more powerful. His vision disappeared in a dazzling starburst. When it cleared moments later the world was strangely shadowed. Unreal. And cascading through his blood and bones a torrent of *potentia* that took his breath away. Compared to this, everything that had come before was as an echo, or a memory, or the merest hint of maybe. Flesh and bone fell away and now he didn't *feel* power, he *was* power. And he poured that *potentia* into his failing, falling otherself.

Through a silver corona Gerald watched the little brown dragon spiral away. He *was* the little brown dragon, their burned wing whole again, their broken ribs healed. They heard Lional grunt with surprise and then effort as he sent the crimson and emerald dragon in pursuit.

It was still an unequal fight. The little brown dragon was constrained by its original matrix; no power in the world could change that. And for all his newly woken *potentia* he was still a *good* wizard. Unsteeped in the malice and misery of the *Lexicon*.

He and his brave brown dragon would have one chance . . . just one . . .

Seeing through the magicked lizard's single eye, using senses he knew were his, yet not his, he felt Lional and his ravenous familiar closing the gap. Felt the hot wind of their breath on his back. Heard the greedy roar of hunger in their throat. Closer . . . closer . . . closer . . .

The monster would be on them in seconds. In seconds it would all be over with Lional triumphant . . . untrammelled . . .

With a throat-ripping cry of effort Gerald brought his little brown dragon to an impossible midair halt and somersaulted it over the back of Lional's pursuing crimson and emerald monster. Lional and his dragon couldn't stop. He extended his claws—the brown dragon's claws—and sank them deep into Lional's—the other dragon's—hot and scaly hide. Then he reached out his jaws, snapped off one of the poisoned spines . . . and plunged it into the vulnerable throat of the crimson and emerald monster beneath them.

Lional and his dragon screamed.

Dimly Gerald felt the acid poison burn his mouth, dissolve his teeth, run down his gullet and eat out his guts. His little brown dragon was dying and he was dying with it. Dimly, turning, he saw Lional drop to his knees, hands clawing at his throat. A bloody foam frothed at his mouth. His eyes were wild and staring, green venom bubbled from the gaping wound beneath his jaw . . . and where it touched the flesh curled and smoked and split like rotten fruit, releasing a stench like a thousand drowned bloated bodies.

"*Leave the beast, wizard!*" somebody cried. "*Foolish youth, you cannot save it! Abandon its mind before you are consumed!*"

Unstrung with sorrow he pulled his fading mind free of the little brown dragon. His legs gave way and he collapsed to the grass. As he stared into the sweet blue sky so far above him he saw two dragons . . . one brown, one crimson and emerald, locked in a fierce and dying embrace, falling . . . falling . . .

And then the dragons were gone and it was two tiny lizards, falling . . . falling. They tumbled into a clump of burned pink azaleas and disappeared from sight.

To his left Lional let out a choked, gurgling groan . . . and fell silent.

Gerald couldn't move. Could barely breathe. Every muscle, every bone, every hair on his head was hurting exquisitely. All he could do was lie on the grass of the Royal Duck Pond park and stare at the sky. A sky that was suddenly full of camels and sultans and tatty old holy men, all gathered around him, their dark eyes approving.

Then the sky faded, and the camels, and the Kallarapi . . . and his mind folded in on itself, closing the door to consciousness.

Some time later the door opened again, with resentful reluctance, to the sound of jabbering voices and the feel of brisk but gentle hands pushing him, pulling him. With enormous effort he opened his eyes. Anxious faces crowded above him but he could barely make them out through the waves of searing flame rolling relentlessly through his body. The world seemed strangely shallow . . . for some reason sited at the end of a tunnel . . .

There was Markham, his welcome face white and frightened. His lips were moving, shouting something, but the words didn't make any sense. Melissande, too, with her rust-red hair coming down from its bun. Her dreadful shirt had lost three buttons and she was crying messily. Reg sat on her shoulder, claws clutching tightly, wise eyes brilliant with fury and fear.

He couldn't see any Kallarapi.

He was still on the ground. Rolling his head he caught sight of Lional, dead on the grass a few feet away. The King of New Ottosland was a ruined travesty of his extravagantly handsome former self. The *sympathetico* had consumed him so completely his human flesh had succumbed to distant dragon poison, dissolved and reduced him to raw bloody meat. His blue eyes were open, gazing back with blank surprise.

Beneath the searing flame Gerald felt a vast aching sorrow. *You fool, Lional. You poor twisted fool. It didn't have to end like this . . .*

The world blurred, then. Strong arms lifted him, carried him. Placed him inside a covered carriage. The horses' hooves were too loud, they clattered on the cobblestones, on and on, making his head ring. Eventually the carriage stopped. He was lifted from shadow into sunshine. Carried indoors and up stairs, flight after flight. Taken into a familiar place, his suite in the palace. His bedroom. His bed. Swift hands stripped the clothes from his body, cool sheets scorched his shivering flesh. He cried out wildly in fear and pain. He thought Lional had returned to torment him, all blood and rotting flesh, fed to fatness on gross black magics that held the grave at bay.

He felt himself plunge into a pit of fire . . . knew that he was dying . . . and was desperately relieved.

# CHAPTER
# TWENTY-EIGHT

When Gerald opened his eyes again and realised he wasn't dead after all, but mending, he was swamped with a bittersweet joy. The curtains were drawn and lamps were lit. Night-time, then . . . but which night?

*How long have I been here? When can I leave?*

A sound on the pillow turned his head. Reg, settled as a hen on a nest and tossing down minced chicken. Some small spark deep within him flared to a bright brief life.

"Hey," he said, his voice a scratchy whisper. "How many times do I have to say it? No eating in bed."

She considered him thoughtfully. "So. You're alive after all, are you? How do you feel?"

"I'm horizontal and breathing."

She sniffed. "And that's better than horizontal and *not* breathing, believe me."

"I think . . ." he began, then frowned. Something

was wrong. He closed his right eye . . . and stopped breathing.

"I can't *see* . . ." He opened his eye again. "Reg? Reg, what's happened?"

She wouldn't meet his gaze. "Do I look like a doctor to you, sunshine? Is there a stethoscope hanging around my neck?"

"Oh God. I'm *blind*!"

She rubbed her beak against his hair, a rare caress. "*Half* blind," she said gruffly. "And it may be temporary. No need to panic yet."

The little brown skink had been blind in one eye. Was reborn a half-blind dragon.

*. . . the acid poison burns his mouth, dissolves his teeth, runs down his gullet and eats out his guts. The little brown dragon is dying . . . dying . . .*

A pawn. A sacrifice. Killed without mercy on the altar of his necessity.

"I'm sorry," he whispered as the lamplight dimmed and soft oblivion claimed him. "I'm sorry . . ."

The second time he woke Shugat stood beside the bed, supporting his bent old body with his staff. The bedroom curtains were still closed, and candles burned in their holders. The same night? Another night? He didn't know. He didn't care. He closed one eye and Shugat vanished.

So. It wasn't a dream or his imagination. In darkness he heard Shugat say, "You said you would pay the price, wizard."

Darkness was safe; he decided to stay there. "Your gods did this to punish me?"

He heard a gentle sigh. "No, wizard. You did this."

"To punish myself?"

"Forget punishment," said Shugat. He sounded impatient. "Think . . . consequences. Look at me, wizard."

He opened his eye. Shugat's grave expression rearranged itself into a fierce and unexpected smile. The stone in his forehead was quiet. Unremarkable. "You have courage."

Rolling over beneath the blankets, he pressed his maimed eye to the pillow. *I don't have the strength for this.* "I have blood on my hands, Shugat. That's what I have. The dragon I made killed people. Innocents it was my duty to protect." He had to stop. Gather himself. "And then there's Lional." Another difficult moment. "I helped make him what he became. I showed him what was possible."

"And you destroyed him. That debt is paid."

Lional groaning. Lional dead. *Dead by my hand. Like him I'm a killer.* "You think I'm *proud* of that?"

Shugat shook his head. "There is no place for pride in wizardry; you have learned a bitter lesson."

Resentment welled. "And what have you learned, Shugat? Holy Man Shugat and your omnipotent gods. Where were *they* when people were dying? You're very good at reading lectures—are you going to lecture *them*?"

He flinched as the dull stone in Shugat's forehead burst into life. Power licked his bones, threatened an inferno. Something ancient, something living, pressed him to the mattress like a claw—a talon—a padded paw . . .

"In his short life a man is many things," said Kallarap's ancient holy man. "A lover. A liar. A killer. A king." Shugat bent down, his dark gaze incandescent. "A hammer . . . and sometimes the hand which holds the hammer."

Gerald turned his face from that implacable regard. "So you used me. You and your gods."

Shugat shrugged. "Better to be used by the gods than a Lional."

"I don't want to be used by *anyone!*" he said hotly, glaring now. "I just want to be left alone!"

"The choice is not yours, wizard," said Shugat, shaking his head. "The power within you has seen to that. You can choose your master . . . and that is all."

His fingers fisted in the bedclothes. "I can choose to walk away! I can choose to have no master. What am I, a dog, to be whistled for whenever someone needs something fetched?"

"Not a dog," said Shugat. "A lizard. Reborn a dragon. Destroyer . . . or defender. The choice is yours. Choose wisely, wizard. My holy man's healing is a precious gift. It is not to be wasted."

Heart thudding dully, Gerald stared at him. "You saved my life? I really was dying and you saved my life?"

Shugat nodded.

"Why? It didn't seem to matter to you when you refused to help me fight Lional! The bastard nearly killed me before I—before the end."

Another infuriating shrug. "The gods willed it."

He struggled to sit up. "Why? What have your gods got to do with me? I don't worship them, Shugat. These Three of yours, who the hell do they think they are?"

Shugat thumped his staff into the carpet. Behind

the curtains panes of glass shivered. Echoes of thunder, rolling. "Does the hammer demand of the hand that holds it why the chosen nail should be struck?"

"*This* hammer does, *yes*!"

Incredibly, Shugat smiled. "Yes. It does." Then he nodded and headed for the door. Reaching it, he slowed. Turned. "You tread an interesting path, wizard. We will meet on it again."

Oh terrific. Just the news he wanted to hear. "We will? *When*? *Why*? Shugat—"

But Shugat was gone.

"*Damn!*" he said. And was ambushed by exhaustion.

The third time he woke it was in daylight. The curtains were open, letting in warm sunshine. Melissande sat reading in an armchair close by his bed, and for once she actually looked presentable. Well groomed. Green silk blouse with cream pearl buttons. Darker green linen trousers. Not baggy but tailored, and crisply ironed. No disastrous bun; her auburn hair was sleek and smooth and captured demurely in a flattering braid. She was even wearing . . . *makeup*?

She heard his little sound of surprise. Looked up and smiled at him nervously. "At last. You've been asleep ever since Shugat left and that was three days ago."

Muzzily he stared at the ceiling. "Three days?" He closed his good eye and the ceiling disappeared.

Not temporary, then. So much for Doctor Reg's diagnosis. *I am. I'm blind. It is a punishment.*

Melissande cleared her throat. "Look. I'm not very good at this, all right?"

He unclosed his eye. "At what?"

"Apologising!"

"There's no need. None of what happened is your fault, Melissande."

"Of course it is," she said harshly. "I brought you here."

Her pain was palpable. *I'm not strong enough for this. I don't have the stamina.* "I brought myself. I wasn't kidnapped. Melissande, forget it."

Her eyes filled with tears. "How can I forget it? Lional was my brother."

*Lional.* Memory flexed its cruel, sharp claws. "And so is Rupert. What's your point?"

"Yes . . . Rupert . . ." Despite the tears her lips twitched in a curious smile but it didn't last long. "Gerald, let me talk. I've been rehearsing this speech for three days, all right?"

Oh lord. *Can I pass out again, please? Can I sleep till I'm fifty?* Melissande was staring anxiously. He sighed. "Fine. If you must." *For all the damned good it'll do either of us.*

She dropped the book to the floor and tangled her fingers together. "All my life I made excuses for Lional. I said, he's just temperamental. He's highly strung. Burdened with being the heir. I told myself that people were jealous. He was so . . . beautiful. And he could be kind. When it suited." Her breath caught in her throat, and at last the tears spilled. "I should've faced the truth about him, Gerald. I was a coward, a disgrace to every Melissande who came before me. I should've *stopped* him before—"

He reached for her. "Melissande, don't. Please, just don't. This is my fault, not yours. The blame is mine."

She dragged an angry hand across her wet face. "*Yours*? Don't be stupid. *You* didn't make him read those awful grimoires or murder Bondaningo and the other wizards. You didn't—"

"I made him the dragon." *Oh God. The dragon. Emerald and crimson and brimful of death.* "How many people did it kill? Do you know?"

She wouldn't look at him. "Gerald, don't. You can't—"

"*How many?*"

"Ninety-seven," she whispered. "More than twice that number injured."

His heart boomed like a drum. *Nearly one hundred. Nearly one hundred murdered.* "Were any of them children?"

Her fingers laced and unlaced in her lap. "Twelve."

Retreating into his blindness didn't help . . . but he stayed there regardless.

He heard her swallow a sob. Then the creak of the armchair and the swish of her linen trousers as she stood. "I'll leave you alone. The others can come back another—"

"Others?" Reluctantly he admitted light and the altered world. "What others?"

"Nobody dreadful." She pulled a face. "Well, Reg. But Monk and Rupert, too."

The last damned thing he needed was a conversation about butterflies. Monk, though . . .

"Don't send them away."

"You're sure?"

"Yes. Melissande . . . you will feel better. Eventually."

She folded her arms and raised one eyebrow. "You

mean there'll come a day when I'll wake up and there *won't* be this great gaping hole in my chest where my heart used to be? When every breath doesn't hurt me and every corner I turn in this wretched mausoleum of a palace doesn't ambush me with a memory? And that soon, dear *God*, I'll stop talking like some dreadful heroine out of a book I wouldn't be caught dead reading?"

Incredibly that made him smile. "I promise. Now let the others in before I fall asleep again."

But instead of going to the door she frowned. "I'm so sorry about your eye, Gerald. Did you know it's turned silver?"

"*What?*"

She fetched his hand mirror from the chest of drawers. "Gerald?" she said, as he stared at it, remembering . . . 'What's wrong?"

With a convulsive shiver he banished the clawed memory: *his naked body butchered and eaten . . . the glistening snakes . . . his battered heart, bleeding a river . . . and pain . . . such awful pain . . .*

"Nothing."

He took the mirror and made himself look.

It was true: his left eye shimmered an opaque silver beneath a strange creamy film . . . like the scaled underbelly of a full-grown skink. The mark of the dragon. Magic's thumbprint. Payment tendered . . .

*And so much less than I truly deserve.*

He thrust the mirror back at her. "Thanks."

Standing there, fidgeting with the mirror, she said. "Gerald. Can I ask you something?"

He owed her so much, she could ask him anything. "Sure."

"What was it like . . . to make a dragon?"

Anything but that. "Melissande—" he began, and then stopped. No. She could even ask him that. "It was terrible," he whispered. "And it was wonderful."

And how he was going to live with that, he didn't know.

She swallowed, hard. "Oh."

Then she turned away, put the mirror back on the chest of drawers and opened the bedroom door. "He's awake, but you can't stay long," she said to whoever was outside.

Markham entered first, grinning like a shark. Reg sat on his shoulder, doing smug as only she could. And Rupert—

He sat up, gaping. What the hell? That was *Rupert*?

All traces of the butterfly-obsessed buffoon had vanished. His lank fair hair had lost its tarnish, was neatly trimmed and shining. His faded eyes were bright and sharply focused, his lips firm, not foolishly trembling. The loose-jointed shambling was gone, replaced by a taut and muscular discipline. He was dressed in severely cut black velvet, no puce or lace or butterfly dust in sight.

"*Your Highness*?"

Rupert crossed to the bed. "Dear Gerald. What a relief to see you on the mend. You had us worried you know. If it hadn't been for Shugat— well—" He smiled. "Let's give thanks for miracles, shall we?"

He stared into that new-made face. "You look so—" Lord, no. He couldn't say *normal*. "—different."

Rupert exchanged swiftly amused glances with

Melissande. "I know. Sorry to spring it on you like this. You see—"

Melissande sighed. "Honestly, Rupert. Don't be a goose. Gerald, he's the king now. Rupert the First. Despite appearances to the contrary, he never was a gormless twit. Turns out *he* was wearing camouflage as well." A dark look at her brother suggested the matter was far from being closed for discussion.

"*Camouflage?*"

"Yes," she said. "Don't you remember? Just like me, he was hiding from Lional."

"Of course I remember. I'm half-blind not senile." He stared at Rupert. "So . . . you *knew* what he was?"

Rupert nodded. "For a long time now."

A flicker of rage, building swiftly. "And you kept *silent?*"

"It's complicated, Gerald," said Rupert, his hands coming up. "Please. You must—"

"*Complicated?*" he echoed. A terrible pain blossomed in his blind eye. "Tell that to the children who—"

Reg cleared her throat with an ominous gurgle. "Good morning, Reg, how lovely to see you again, thanks so much for everything you did to get those useless bureaucrats at the Department hopping!"

As he struggled to control the rage, Melissande turned. "*You?* You didn't do anything! That was all me and Rupert! And Monk, a bit. *You* had nothing to do with it!"

Reg bridled. "I beg your pardon? I'll have you know that I looked at those anal-retentive civil servants in a very *meaningful* way, madam! And how would you know what I did or didn't do? You were too busy impersonating a headless chook and bleating 'Save Gerald!'"

Melissande gaped. "I never did! I never once *bleated*! And anyway, chickens don't bleat, that's lambs, chicken *cackle*, just like *you*, and—"

"Well if I cackle, ducky, I'm not the only girl in here who does!" Reg retorted. "So I've got you coming *and* going, haven't I? *Ha!* You'll have to pull off your mismatched flannel pyjamas mighty early in the morning to get the better of *me*, young lady!"

Monk grabbed Reg from his shoulder and plopped her onto the bed. "For ether's sake, she's your bird, Gerald! Take her, would you? She's driving me crazy. And anyway . . ." He pulled a face. "I have to go."

"You can't!" he protested. "You haven't told me what *happened* . . ."

Monk shrugged. "Sorry. Duty calls. Reg'll fill you in, she's dying to do it. Anyway, it's your own fault, Gerald, snoring in bed instead of entertaining your guests."

He knew his friend very well; beneath the disrespectful humour lurked trepidation. "What duty? Monk, what's going on?"

Another shrug and a sheepish smile. "Seems I've got an interview with the Department's Thaumaturgical Ethics Committee. I suspect they want to rap my knuckles over the portable portal . . . and a few other things."

Gerald threw his blankets aside. "Then I'm coming with you. Blimey, are they *stupid*? Don't they *realise*—"

Monk and Rupert bundled him back into bed. Humiliatingly, he couldn't stop them. His body was weak, his muscles petulant and protesting. "Back off! Let me up! I'm—"

"Staying put," Rupert said sharply, but with a smile. "Aside from sore knuckles, Mister Markham will be fine."

"*Fine*? Rupert, you're clueless! You don't know what that damned Department's like! They'll skin him alive and charge him for the labour! They'll—"

"Gerald, it's all right," Monk said. "Honest. My Department bosses do have a point." He glanced at Rupert. "His Majesty's put in a good word for me. I'll survive."

He had to lie down again. Falling against his pillows he said, his voice unsteady, "But your career's cactus because you helped me."

"Not *cactus*," said Monk. "Compost, maybe." Another sharkish grin. "You can grow good stuff with compost, I'm told."

He had to smile. Typical Markham: lemonade from lemons, every bloody time. "Even so . . ."

Melissande patted his shoulder. "Don't worry, Gerald. I'm going with him." She flicked a gaze at her brother. "I'm still the prime minister around here, for a few more days anyway, and I'll make sure those Department idiots remember what Rupert said. Or else."

Rupert considered her. "Melissande . . . it's a lovely gesture and I'm sure Markham appreciates it immensely, but as much as I love you I couldn't in all conscience call you diplo—"

"Oh, *please*!" she retorted. "*You're* calling *my* judgement into question? The man who let himself get bitten by vampire butterflies when it said quite clearly on the box *Do Not Open In The Presence Of Light*? Spare me, I beg you!"

As the king and his sister bickered, Gerald looked at Monk. "Are you sure you want her defending you? She can be a bit . . . overwhelming."

Monk pulled a face. "Right now I'll take all the help I can get. Besides. You should've seen her talking to Attaby and my Uncle Ralph. She nearly threw their teacups at them. She was *magnificent*."

*And you're in love with her.* He knew the signs. Maybe this time Monk's lightning-strike passion would last longer than a month . . . and maybe it wouldn't.

But either way it'd be an interesting ride.

For himself he didn't mind. He liked the princess; perhaps even cared for her. But she wasn't for him. Not like that.

"Ha," said Reg, finally joining in. "Teacups. *I* was all set to poke them in the unmentionables, *that* would've made them sit up and squawk!"

Monk shook his head. "I dunno, Gerald. How do you stand it?"

He stroked Reg's wing with one finger. "Well, you know. She kind of grows on you . . ."

"Yes, yes, I remember. Like fungus," said Reg, and sniffed. "I *suppose*," she added, grudgingly, "the girl didn't handle herself *too* shabbily. I *suppose* I could stand it if I saw her again." Then she shuddered. "But only if she swears to burn her wardrobe!"

Melissande, finished with putting Rupert in his place, turned. "I heard that, bird."

Reg smirked. "You were meant to, ducky."

"I *really* have to go," said Monk, forestalling bloodshed. "If you're coming, Melissande, then come. Your Majesty—" He bowed. "Thank you."

Rupert rested his hand on Monk's shoulder. "No, my friend. The debt is mine and New Ottosland's. Visit us whenever you can."

"I certainly will, sir, provided I'm not chained to my desk. Or a damp wall somewhere deep underground." He turned. "Look. Gerald. Don't do it, mate, all right? Not unless you *really* want to."

Gerald stared. "Do what?"

"I'll see you later. Back in Ottosland."

"Markham! Don't do what? What are you talking about?"

But Monk was gone.

Melissande glared, hands on hips. "I'd better go too. Now you rest, do you hear me, Gerald? Or when I come back I'll—I'll be *snippy*."

Reg rolled her eyes. "*That'll* make a change."

"Melissande!" Monk bellowed from beyond the bedroom.

"You've been warned!" said Melissande, and fled. As Gerald stared after her Rupert sat in the armchair by the bed.

"Well," he said, and crossed his legs. It was incredible. He actually looked elegant. "You'd like an explanation, I imagine."

A headache was brewing behind his eyes. In a strange way he felt almost *betrayed*, though he and Rupert weren't actual real friends. "I think I'm owed one. Don't you . . . Rupert?"

Rupert nodded. "You and many others, Gerald."

"So. Exactly how long *did* you know?"

"That Lional was . . . unstable?" Rupert steepled his fingers. It was profoundly disconcerting, such an un-Rupert-like pose. "Since I was six."

"What happened when you were six?"

A flicker of pain twisted Rupert's face. "Lional killed someone I cared for. Our nanny. He was ten."

*Ten*? "How?"

"A toy left carelessly on top of a staircase," said Rupert. His gaze was unfocussed, lost in memory. "Of course everyone said it was an *accident*. Lional wept. But as she lay dying Nanny asked to see me. Held me close to her poor broken body and whispered, *"It was murder. Never turn your back on your brother, lovey. Never let him see your true face. This poor kingdom will need you one day."* Rupert shrugged. "Nanny never lied to me. I believed her."

Gerald felt a cold shiver run through him. "And so you invented . . . the other Rupert."

"Not all at once," said Rupert, nodding. "I didn't wish to arouse suspicions. Just day by day . . . one mannerism, one eccentricity at a time . . . until my true face was hidden, not just from Lional but from Melissande too. From the whole world." He grimaced. "From myself, in the end."

He tried to imagine it and couldn't. "But you were only six. You were a *child*."

"A child?" Rupert laughed; a dreadful sound. "With Lional as my older brother? Oh, Gerald. I was *never* a child."

"But what about your parents?"

"What about them? They doted on their kingdom's heir. Lional was . . . a beautiful boy. It was only later, as his nature refined itself, that they began to worry.

I think, perhaps, to suspect. But by then it was far too late."

Reg cleared her throat. "Silly buggers."

Rupert did a double take then smiled. "I'm sorry. I confess I still find you a trifle hard to believe . . ."

"Ha," said Reg. "*This* from the man with a pet butterfly named Esmerelda." She sniffed. "How's the little Dumb Cluck doing, anyway?"

"You mean she's not dead?" said Gerald. And why that would sting him with tears he couldn't begin to say . . .

Rupert smiled sadly. "No. She's the only survivor, though. I found her hiding under a rose bush. With Boris."

It was ridiculous but he felt comforted by the news. "I'm glad."

"Believe it or not, so am I," said Rupert. "She really is very sweet." His expression darkened. "And after seeing the carnage at the stables . . . and elsewhere in the kingdom . . . I needed cheering up."

"I'm sorry," Gerald said at last. His throat was hot and tight: it was hard to get the words out.

"Not your fault," said Rupert heavily. He looked ill. Years older.

Did he believe that or just say it because it was expected? Because the wizard was half-blind now and needed careful handling? Gerald couldn't tell. But in staring at Rupert, trying to decide, he discovered a rising resentment.

"You should've told me what you knew." The criticism came out more sharply than he intended, than perhaps was wise. But he was tired and newly aching and blind in one eye. "Maybe if you'd *told* me—"

"I couldn't!" said Rupert just as sharply. Then he sighed. "It was too risky. I couldn't trust you'd not give me away. Not on purpose, perhaps, but even so. Lional was very . . . astute."

Astute. That was one word. "He was mad, Rupert."

"Oh yes," said Rupert softly. "Above all else, he was mad." He hesitated, then added, "And of course it seemed for a while there you were in his pocket."

"Except I wasn't! I was only pretending so I could find out what the hell was going on! Melissande *asked* me to—"

"I know," said Rupert, placating. "It seems all of us were wearing masks, Gerald. Trying to protect each other or ourselves. I did the best I could, you know. I tried to put you on your guard. Steer you in the right direction. I just couldn't afford to be explicit. If I had been, you can be sure I'd have met with an accident too."

Although resentment lingered he had to smile. "You should've been an actor, Rupert. I never *dreamed* there was a brain inside that ninny head of yours."

Rupert grinned. "Thank you. I think."

He winced. "Sorry."

"Don't be," said Rupert, amusement fading. "I'm the one who should be apologising. I've hardly slept since . . ." He cleared his throat. "Hindsight is an unkind thing. Could I have stopped him? One minute I'm convinced I couldn't, the next I'm sure if I'd just confided in you or Greenfeather, if I'd gone for help, persuaded Melissande to leave, raised the alarm, fled to Zazoor—"

"It seems to *me*," said Reg, hopping onto the bedrail and fixing them with a stern dark gaze, "there's not one of us not wishing right now we'd done something different. That's called second-guessing yourself, that is, and if you ask me it's a load of mouldy old bollocks. *If only—I wish—what if—*" She snorted. "I'm telling you, Rupert, and you too, Gerald, and you can pass it along to Princess Pushy when she gets back: you'll drive yourselves as mad as that mad bugger Lional if you start down that road. We can't undo what's happened. The dead are buried and we can't unbury them. All we can do is live what's left of our lives in a way that won't shame their memories. And make sure nothing like this *ever happens again.*"

"Indeed," said Rupert after a prickly silence.

Gerald nodded. "I suppose." He just had no idea how. "So. What happens now?"

"Now?" Rupert frowned, considering. "Now I appoint a new privy council and get on with the business of governing the kingdom. New Ottosland is hurt, and as her king it's my job to heal her wounds."

"And what about the Kallarapi? Are they still hanging around, or have you sent them packing?"

Rupert's face was lit by a sudden smile. Achingly, fleetingly, it held an echo of Lional. "No, they've gone home. But their visit proved *most* agreeable. The army, you know, pitched in and helped all over the place, picking up the pieces that dragon left behind. Wonderful chaps. Not very talkative but good God, their stamina! And I had a *wonderful* meeting with Sultan Zazoor. Everything I remembered about him from boarding school was right. He was an excellent cricket captain and I'm sure he'll do an equally fine job as sultan. We've worked out a schedule for repayments of the outstanding debt and there are some ideas for a possible renegotiation of the original treaty, as well as future collaborative enterprises. It's very exciting."

Certainly Rupert looked excited; the shadows were chased from his eyes and he looked young again. "That sounds great, Rupert. But . . . what about Shugat?"

"Ah. Yes," said Rupert thoughtfully. "Well of course he saved your life, so I'm bound to look on him favourably. But you know, Gerald, just between you and me and the window . . . I wasn't sorry to wave him goodbye. A most . . . *uncomfortable* . . . fellow."

Uncomfortable was one word. "You're sure there are no hard feelings after everything Lional tried to do?"

Rupert shrugged. "Apparently not. So it's full steam ahead. Tradition with a capital T is about to make way for Progress with a capital P. And *not* before time."

"And what about Melissande? Is she going to remain your prime minister?"

"Dear Melly." Rupert smiled. "No. It's time my sister had a life of her own. I've had a good long talk with your Department of Thaumaturgy, and with Markham, and since she appears to have some thaumaturgical aptitude she's to be enrolled in Madam Olliphant's Witches' Academie. I understand Markham's sister Emmerabiblia was very happy there."

Good for Melissande. At last she had the brother she deserved. "Oh, yes, Monk's sister had a great time at the academie. Really enjoyed it. Well. Except for the uniform." When Rupert looked at him, puzzled, he added: "Bibbie's very tall and thin and the academie uniform is green and silver. She says it made her look like a frostbitten asparagus."

Reg chortled. "Saint Snodgrass alone knows what Miss Ex-Prime Minister's going to look like. Frozen squashed cabbage probably."

"*Reg* . . ."

"And as for the poor bloody staff, they're going to go bonkers trying to unteach her everything she's learned from that charlatan Madam Rinky Tinky! Poor buggers."

Rupert eyed Reg askance. "I'm sure it'll all work out fine. I mean, I know Mel doesn't wear her heart on her sleeve but I'm her brother and I can tell: inside, she's very excited."

"That's nothing to what the academie's going to be when it finds out madam can't tell the difference between an etheretic transductor and her own right foot!"

Gerald gave up and shoved her under the blankets. "Well, Rupert," he said. "Is that it? We just . . . go on?"

Rupert ignored the strangled squawking emanating from under the bedclothes and nodded gently. "Yes. We do. After all, my friend . . . what other choice is there?"

He stared at the foot of the bed, feeling . . . suspended. As though he was waiting for the other shoe to drop. "So," he said, almost to himself. "It's over."

Rupert stood. "Ah . . . well . . . I wouldn't precisely say *over*, Gerald. Not quite yet."

He crossed to the bedroom door and opened it. On the other side stood a man. Average height.

Average build. Average hair of an unremarkable brown. His nose was neither thin nor fat, straight nor aquiline. It merely occupied the centre of his face. His eyes were a nondescript shade of grey. His suit was plain. His shirt was cotton. He was bland. Ordinary. *Average*. He looked like a shopkeeper.

"Good morning, Mr Dunwoody," he said in a clipped, precise voice. "My name is Sir Alec . . . and we need to talk."

# CHAPTER
# TWENTY-NINE

As the mysterious Sir Alec entered and Rupert left, closing the bedroom door behind him, Reg erupted shrieking from under the blankets.

"Gerald Dunwoody! Just what do you think you're—" She saw the stranger and stopped. "Oh for the love of Saint Snodgrass. Not *you* again. I thought we'd ditched you back at the Department."

Gerald could've wrung her neck. "Would Polly like a cracker, then?" he said, teeth gritted.

"It's all right. Mr Dunwoody," Sir Alec said calmly. "Reg and I have met."

"Yes we have, more's the pity," said Reg, glowering. "Gerald, pay no attention to him. He's nothing but a stooge."

Ignoring Reg, he looked at Sir Alec. "You work for the Ottosland Department of Thaumaturgy?"

Sir Alec nodded. "I do."

Something about the man's beige blandness was

getting on his nerves. Thinking of Monk and his un-deserved disgrace; of himself, and how Scunthorpe's cowardice had started all this; and no longer caring about his career, he sneered. "As a stooge?"

Sir Alec's expression underwent a slow alchemy. Grew older. Colder. The nondescript blandness melted like wax, revealing the true face beneath. Hard, with lines suggesting experiences beyond those found in an ordinary life.

Staring at the man with his one good eye Gerald felt an answering chill. Felt his own face remould and reveal, starkly, the fingerprints left behind by the last few weeks.

So long as he lived, he would *never* be bullied again.

Sir Alec nodded, a salute like the one fencing op-ponents gave each other before crossing swords, and the air around him crackled with a ferocious leashed power.

So. The man was a First Grade wizard. And a sneaky one to boot.

*Well, I can be sneaky too, Sir Alec from the Department. I can do a lot of things. I think I might surprise you.*

With a blink, Sir Alec calmed his thaumic aura. "As I said, Mr Dunwoody, we need to talk. It won't take long, I do realise you're convalescent . . . and in any case I am needed elsewhere. You've kicked up some dust both at home and abroad; ruffled feathers require tactful soothing."

Gerald considered him. "Maybe they wouldn't if you lot had been doing your jobs. Five minutes after I made Lional his dragon you and your counterparts from the UMN should've been crawling all over New Ottosland. Why weren't you?"

Sir Alec's pale eyes were cold and calculating, the brain behind them summing him up . . . "I'm sorry if you felt . . . abandoned, but I'm afraid politics both domestic and international raised their ugly heads at precisely the wrong moment. Valuable resources were . . . diverted. May I sit down?"

"If you must," said Reg, before he could answer, and relocated to the bedrail behind the pillows. "But don't get too comfy. Gerald's been through a terrible ordeal so talk fast and leave faster, sunshine, because—"

One hand raised, Sir Alec moved towards the bed, a thin smile curving his lips. "Yes, yes, Reg. Or should I say: *Your Majesty*? Seeing as you are, beneath that quaint disguise, Queen Dulcetta of Lalapinda, born in the year 1216, only daughter of King Treve and Queen Amyrl, who ascended the Lalapindian throne in 1234, foolishly married the warlock Vertain in 1235 and apparently drowned soon thereafter. In reality Vertain ensorcelled you, trapping your soul in the body of a bird and dooming you to wander the world ever after . . . provided the enchantment placed upon you is not touched." He cleared his throat. "Did I leave anything out?"

Reg closed her gaping beak with a click. "You *nosey* bugger! How did you find out?"

Another sardonic smile. "It's part of my job description."

"And what job is that?" said Gerald. He wasn't at all sure he liked where this was heading . . .

Sir Alec seated himself in the armchair by the bed. "All in good time, Mister Dunwoody."

So. Here was the other shoe dropping with a

vengeance. Gerald scowled. "That's *Professor* Dunwoody to you."

Sir Alec nodded. "Certainly. At least for the moment."

"All right, all right," said Reg, rallying. "That's enough with the cut glass repartee, sunshine. Why are you here?"

"Why do you think, Reg? He wants to find out how I did it," he said tiredly. "How I made the dragons and all the rest of it."

"On the contrary," said Sir Alec. "I know precisely how you did it."

"So?"

"So the question is: what are we going to do with you as a result?"

He made himself meet Sir Alec's cold, grey gaze. *Here we go.* "You're saying I'm dangerous."

Sir Alec smiled. "Everyone is dangerous, Mister Dunwoody. In their own way, in their own time. All it takes is the right catalyst, the right circumstances. The perfect confluence of events."

He shook his head, rejecting the cynicism. "No. Not—"

"Everyone, Mister Dunwoody." Sir Alec flicked a speck of dust from his knee. "Shall I tell you how you're feeling, sir? Yes, I think I shall. You're feeling . . . betrayed. As though the world has betrayed you. And do you know why you feel like that? It's because you've lost your innocence. Like the vast majority of people, Mister Dunwoody, until New Ottosland came into your life, you bumped along happily enough. Oh, you had dreams that didn't seem likely to come true, but they were comforting and you dreamed them.

You'd had career disappointments, yes, but you trusted they were temporary. Your faith was a little battered, perhaps, but you still believed. You looked upon the world with a benevolent eye. Oh yes, of course you knew there were scoundrels among us, certain gentlemen whose company you preferred to avoid, but on the whole you found the world good. And then you came here. With the best of intentions—eager and anxious and so terribly naive. Without ever meaning to, you kicked over the rock of New Ottosland . . . and from under it crawled Lional."

Deep inside, Gerald felt himself shiver. "You make me sound like a fool."

"A fool?" said Sir Alec thoughtfully. "Not at all. Before this . . . adventure . . . you were no more foolish than any other ordinary man. You saw the sunlight, not the shadows. The trouble is, Mister Dunwoody, the shadows exist. And if we're not very careful, very vigilant, they will swallow us. And our good world will be plunged into darkness."

Gerald watched his fingers clench, his knuckles whiten. Sir Alec was right. *And I hate it. I never, ever wanted to know this.* "All right. Say I agree with you. So what? What has any of that to do with me?"

Another flick of manicured fingers, banishing dust. "In the time that's passed since the incident with the two dragons and the late King Lional," said Sir Alec, "certain of my colleagues have been conducting an exhaustive search into your ancestry. Also your medical, educational and various employment records, the results of your original Thaumaturgical Aptitude test and several eyewitness accounts of what happened at Stuttley's."

"You really *are* a nosey bugger," Reg grumbled.

Sir Alec rested his elbows on the arms of his chair, apparently quite at ease. But a dynamo of tension hummed inside him, thrumming the invisible air. "The technical term for your condition is 'thaumaturgical distillation'. The slang term is 'rogue'. In metaphysical parlance, Mister Dunwoody, it means you're a sport. An anomaly. It means you are irregular." He sniffed. "*Highly* irregular, if you must know. And as I said, it's causing no end of a stir in certain circles."

Gerald breathed out slowly. *How did this happen? My dad's a tailor* . . . "That sounds inconvenient."

"Let's just say you've added a new level of complexity to my already complicated life," said Sir Alec, his tone extremely dry.

"All right. So I'm thaumaturgically distilled. Is it fatal?"

Sir Alec's smile was wintry. "Only to other people."

"You miserable *shit*!" snapped Reg. "That's not funny!"

Sir Alec considered her for an arctic moment then nodded. "Point taken. Forgive me, Mister Dunwoody. A macabre sense of humour is an unfortunate side effect in my line of work."

*Ninety-seven dead. Twelve of them children.* "How does it happen?" said Gerald, when he could trust his voice again. "This . . . distillation?"

Sir Alec shrugged. "Nobody's certain. We believe it's the result of no wizards being born to a particular bloodline for three or more generations. In your case, however, it appears to be more like fifteen."

*Fifteen.* That sounded . . . impressive. *Or maybe inconvenient.* "Is the condition common?"

"Quite the contrary. Many experts consider it something of a myth. No rogue has been born in the modern era."

"That you know of," he pointed out. "I mean I was tested, wasn't I, and classified Third Grade."

Sir Alec frowned. "It would appear the condition remains dormant until something triggers it."

Ah. And that would be the sound of the *third* shoe dropping. "You mean something like Stuttley's?"

"Exactly."

Meanly, viciously, he felt vindicated. "So if that prig Scunthorpe hadn't—"

"Mr Scunthorpe," said Sir Alec repressively, "is no longer your concern, Dunwoody. I'm here to discuss your aberrant *potentia*, not the decisions, prudent or otherwise, of your past supervisors."

*Aberrant.* It was as good a word as any. Gerald thought about that for some time. About the implications of this aberrant, inconvenient condition. Its ramifications for himself and everyone who knew him.

At last he looked up. Sir Alec was watching him, still coiled inside like an overwound spring. "All right, Sir Alec. We know what I am. But what does it *mean*?"

"Don't ask him," Reg said sourly, as Sir Alec hesitated. "He hasn't got a bloody clue. Accidents like you are so rare you're nothing more than a footnote in a mouldering textbook in the back room of the Department's basement library. Isn't that right, mate?"

Incredibly Sir Alec looked faintly discomfited. "I'm afraid so."

A *footnote*? He was a *footnote*? Practically a *myth*? "Then . . . what's going to happen to me? Is there some way of switching off this—this—aberrant *potentia*? Can I go back to being a common or garden variety Third Grade wizard?"

The question appeared to take Sir Alec by surprise. "You'd do that? Surrender all your power? Mister Dunwoody, do you know what you're saying? Do you have any idea how *strong* you are?"

*I'm strong enough to make two dragons. Strong enough to survive the sympathetico. Strong enough to get ninety-seven innocent souls killed.*

But not strong enough to stop any of it happening.

Sir Alec leaned forward. "Princess Melissande tells me her brother tortured you for many days. With curses from texts listed on the *Internationally Proscribed Index*. One of them was *Grummen's Lexicon* which I'm pleased to say is now safely dismembered and under lock and key." Again, that grimness in Sir Alec's face. "Mister Dunwoody, I'm not sure you understand. No other wizard I know—or have ever heard of—could have survived an ordeal like that. If the physical stresses of such brutality didn't prove fatal then prior evidence indicates the mind of the tortured wizard would simply . . . snap. But you didn't die and your mind appears intact. And then of course there's the matter of Lional being unable to steal your *potentia*. Don't you see? At the risk of sounding melodramatic . . . you are something of a *miracle*."

He made himself meet Sir Alec's gaze. "I don't want to be a miracle."

Sir Alec snorted. "What sane man would?"

"Then can't you—"

"No," said Sir Alec. "I'm afraid that's not possible. I'm aware of no incant or potion capable of undoing whatever the accident at Stuttley's did to you. You are what you've become, Professor, and will remain like that till the day you die. I am very sorry, but there's no going back."

Was that pity in Sir Alec's grey eyes? If so he didn't want it. Above him on the bedrail he could feel Reg's consternation. She'd been unnaturally quiet through all of this; he wasn't sure what that meant.

"Then I'll stay here," he said. "As a private citizen. I'm sure King Rupert will have no objections. I'll dedicate the rest of my life to making up for the damage I did to his people."

Sir Alec sighed. "Again, I'm sorry, but no. That's not possible either."

"You're not leaving him too many options, sunshine," said Reg. "There's wheels and wheels turning behind your eyes. What is it you're thinking? What have you got planned for Gerald?"

He lifted his hand to touch fingertips to her wing. "I already know what he's thinking, Reg," he said, not taking his gaze from Sir Alec's watchful waiting face. "He's thinking I'm a problem. He's thinking how best to . . . *resolve* me. Aren't you, Sir Alec? Isn't that your plan?"

Reg let out a furious squawk. "Resolve? You mean *assassinate*! Over my dead body, mate! Raise so much as an eyebrow to this boy and I'll be wearing your eyeballs for earrings! Gerald, we're leaving. All of a sudden the décor in here is getting right up my sinuses. When

I give the word, you head for the door. I'll keep Sir Stooge here occupied while you—"

"*Really*, Dulcetta," Sir Alec said, bored. "*Now* who's being melodramatic? Mister Dunwoody, please. I'm not here to assassinate you. Or coerce you. Or do anything contrary to the oath I took, as you did, when I became a wizard."

Bleakly, Gerald looked at him. "Yes, but oaths are more fragile than you might think, Sir Alec. I broke mine and people died. Perhaps you *should* . . . resolve . . . me. Perhaps the world would be a better place if you did."

Sir Alec nodded. "It's certainly one solution. And I won't deny it was suggested. It was. Quite vigorously, in some quarters."

How odd to know that people he'd never met had argued for his murder. He felt almost . . . academic. As though he were a student again, discussing hypotheticals in a classroom.

"Suggested by you?"

"No," said Sir Alec. "Although I certainly considered the notion. In the end I decided eliminating you would be . . . wasteful."

*Wasteful.* He didn't know which was more outrageous . . . the word or the idea that Sir Alec would calmly admit he'd contemplated killing him.

"Might I ask what you *do* want to do with me?"

Sir Alec sat back in the armchair. Steepled his fingers and considered him thoughtfully. "Offer you a job, I think."

And he hadn't been expecting *that*. "A job," he repeated blankly.

"*Work*, Mister Dunwoody. Gainful employment.

You've already had four positions, you must be familiar with the concept by now."

"Bloody hell," said Reg. "Whatever it is don't take it, Gerald."

He eased himself against his pillows. *So. This must be what Monk was hinting at.* "A job where? Doing what?"

A faint crease appeared between Sir Alec's pale brown eyebrows. "In the Department, of course. Working for me. As a janitor."

"A *what*?" Images of buckets and mops danced across his inner eye. "Look, all this cryptic crap might be meat and drink to you, Sir Alec, but I'm tired and in case you hadn't noticed, I'm also blind in one eye. So why don't you stop playing your stupid bloody games and tell me what you mean, straight out, no riddles."

Sir Alec smiled, his gaze intent. "Certainly. Janitors are very important people, Mister Dunwoody. They go about their business with a dustpan and brush, sweeping up all the little messes other people leave behind. Nobody notices them. All that's noticed is the world is kept clean and tidy with a minimum of inconvenience to the ordinary man."

"And woman," said Reg, glaring.

Gerald frowned. "Messes."

"Yes."

"Messes like, say, for example . . . murdered wizards, stolen *potentias*, illegal grimoires, the attempted inciting of international religious conflicts . . . those kinds of messes?"

Sir Alec's smiled widened. "Precisely."

Gerald nodded. *And now I understand.* Because of

Sir Alec, and men like him, the world at large would never learn of the recent events in New Ottosland. Lional's death would appear as three lines on the bottom of the back page of the few newspapers who'd even heard of New Ottosland's king or cared at all that the poor man died young. History would record that Lional perished choking on a fish bone, perhaps. Or falling down some stairs. Certainly there'd be no mention of dragons . . .

"You do appreciate it's often . . . better . . . that way."

"I can appreciate," said Gerald quietly, "that some people might be inclined to take that view."

"Also," Sir Alec added, refusing to pick up the conversational gauntlet, "janitors are occasionally called upon to perform certain maintenance tasks as well."

*Maintenance?* "As in fixing faulty wiring before it burns the whole house down?" he suggested. "That kind of maintenance?"

"Exactly. Mister Dunwoody, you catch on fast."

Gerald pulled his knees up to his chest, rucking the blankets, and rested his chin. Considered his visitor in a new, more cautious light. "And are you a janitor by any chance?"

Sir Alec shook his head. "I used to be. Before I retired from fieldwork." Some unbidden, unpleasant memory skated the chilly surface of his face, so swiftly it might have been imagined. Then again, looking at Sir Alec's eyes . . . maybe not. "Don't be fooled by the prosaic euphemism, Mister Dunwoody," he said sharply. "This is not a job for the faint-hearted. Surgeons can't afford to be squeamish."

"So you want me to be a surgeon now? What happened to my dustpan and brush?"

Sir Alec shrugged. "Dustpan. Scalpel. Blunt instrument. You'll find there's a wide range of implements at your disposal. Some have more finesse than others, but they all have their uses."

Ha. It was Shugat all over again. Gerald felt himself contracting like a snail into its shell. "So that's what I am to you? Just another hammer?"

"Of course," said Sir Alec. "And so am I. So is everyone with a gift that can be exploited. We are at *war*, sir. With all the forces of darkness who desire to use magic to serve their own nefarious purposes. My organisation, and a few others like it around the world, are all that stands between what passes for tranquility, and utter chaos. You've had a lucky escape, Mister Dunwoody. An evil man sought to use you as *his* instrument . . . and he failed."

He made himself meet Sir Alec's unforgiving gaze. "Not completely. I did make the dragon. People died."

"In war there are always innocent casualties. It's regrettable but unavoidable. The sooner you come to terms with that the better, because the alternative, doing nothing while evil flourishes, is not an option I care to explore." Abruptly, unexpectedly, Sir Alec's severe demeanour softened. "You did the best you could with the resources you had, Gerald. I've known experienced janitors to do far worse with more."

Not pity this time, but understanding. Even . . . absolution. And coming from this man, this cold and calculating *frightening* man . . .

Gerald wrapped his arms around his knees. "How long do I have to make a decision?"

"Now."

"And if I decline your generous offer?"

"I'd advise against that," Sir Alec said gently.

He smiled, unamused. "So this is a once-in-a-lifetime kind of deal?"

Sir Alec's lips tightened. "Abandon your obsession with death. It's unhealthy. If you decline my offer, terms will be reached. I'd prefer, however, that you accept it."

*I'll bet you would. The clever Sir Alec and his very own myth.* "What's going to happen to Monk?"

"Your friend Mister Markham knew perfectly well he was breaking the rules," said Sir Alec, eyebrows raised. "I'm afraid there's nothing I can do for him."

Gerald leaned forward, fury kindling beneath his fatigue and sorrow. "Well I suggest you find something, Sir Alec. I never would've beaten Lional without Monk. So he bent—broke—all right, *disintegrated* a few rules. By all means rap his knuckles. Rap them twice if that'll make you feel better. But Monk Markham's a bloody genius and you'd be a fool to throw him away. You say we're at war? Then we need as many weapons as we can lay our hands on. You won't find a better one than Monk."

After a long moment Sir Alec nodded. "Is that a condition of your accepting my offer?"

He sat back. "Say it is."

Sir Alec examined his manicured fingernails. "It so happens I share your opinion of Mister Markham. As I'm sure you can appreciate, we are obliged to rap his knuckles. We may even be forced to spank him slightly. But once he can sit down again we'll certainly find a use for him. You have my word, Mister Dunwoody: Monk Markham's unorthodox career is safe."

There was a violent pounding behind his eyes. The effort of focusing now that he was half-blind, most likely. He pushed the pain aside. "This job. Your organisation. What aren't you telling me?"

"A great deal," said Sir Alec. "Most of it is . . . irrelevant. At least for now."

"Then tell me what you wish *you'd* known when your Sir Alec made you the same offer."

Reg rattled her tail feathers. "Gerald . . ."

He flicked her a severe glance. "I need to know, Reg."

She subsided, grumbling under her breath.

Sir Alec's expression was guarded, as though he were afraid of revealing too much. "It's a lonely life. You can never tell anybody outside the inner circle what it is you really do. That includes your family and friends. Acquaintances of the female persuasion. In effect you'll be living a lie. And you'll be placing your life at risk on a fairly regular basis. We swim in murky waters and we take as few people with us as possible. To the outside world you'll be plain Gerald Dunwoody, Wizard Third Class. A passably competent, never more than adequate locum who drifts from job to job, never settling down, and certainly never making a name for himself getting rich, or being noticed."

He pulled a face. "It sounds irresistible."

"I never said it would be easy," Sir Alec said curtly. "But it is worthwhile. And with your unique talents

I believe you'll make a contribution that will save many lives. I happen to think that's worth a little personal sacrifice. Perhaps you don't. Only you can say."

Gerald looked at Reg. Held out an arm, waited for her to jump on it, then set her on his upraised knees. "What do you think?"

She rolled her eyes. "Don't look at me, sunshine. It's your decision."

He turned to Sir Alec. "Can I keep Reg? I won't do it if I can't keep Reg."

Sir Alec sighed. "In principle, yes. But there will be wrinkles we'll have to iron out."

"Wrinkles?"

"She may make you . . . conspicuous. Janitors often disguise their appearance when they enter a new . . . situation. Reg could compromise your anonymity. She may even cost you your life."

"That'll be the day," Reg snorted. "Trust me, Sir Alec, or whatever your real name is, I've *forgotten* more about stealth than you'll learn in three lifetimes. Whatever else you've got to worry about, you won't need to worry about *me*."

Sir Alec smiled faintly. "Yes. Well. That remains to be seen, doesn't it? But as I say, Mister Dunwoody is welcome to keep you with him. For the time being, at least."

Gerald closed his eyes and pinched the bridge of his nose. "I don't know. I'm so bloody *tired . . .*" His eyelids felt like lead. He dragged them open and squinted at Reg. "What *do* you think? Honestly. I want to hear it."

"Honestly?" she echoed. "Honestly, Gerald . . .

what've you got to lose? Except your life. And everybody dies sooner or later. Even me, I expect. It's not how *long* you live that counts. What's important is *how* you live."

He let his eyelids slam closed again, retreating into welcome darkness. He really was tired. No. Exhausted. Hollow. All used up. Changed, on some fundamental level having nothing to do with his *potentia* or the fact that he was a miraculous *rogue*.

Whoever Gerald Dunwoody had been the day he arrived in New Ottosland . . . that man was gone. In his place stood a new Gerald Dunwoody, with one working eye and blood on his hands and a power that nobody living seemed to understand. Least of all himself. A man who understood pain and sorrow, though, in ways he'd never dreamed were possible.

Sir Alec was right. There was no going back. Too much had happened. Too much had been done to him. By him. The memories were raw now. Brutal. And although they'd fade in time, they'd never disappear completely. Forever and always, till the day he drew his last breath, he'd be the Gerald Dunwoody who'd made Lional that dragon.

If he wasn't careful he knew that could destroy him.

Mysterious Sir Alec was offering him a new life. The chance to make a difference. Put a stop to all the other Lionals in the world, wherever they were, before their greed and madness and cruelty, their lust for power in all its forms, destroyed the lives of innocent people. Dangerous work, but necessary. Perhaps even vital.

And in doing it he might eventually atone for the

ninety-seven souls who'd died because of him. Killed by the dragon he'd made.

Knowing the debt he owed them, how could he refuse?

He took a deep breath and let it out slowly. Opened his eyes. Looked at Reg as he answered Sir Alec.

"All right. I'll do it."

"Excellent!" said Sir Alec and stood. "I'll get the paperwork started immediately. I understand from that *singular* Kallarapi holy man you've a few more days in bed ahead of you. Just as a precaution." He sniffed. "I'm sure he's an admirable fellow but of course you'll be receiving a full physical from our own medical staff once you return to Ottosland. As soon as you're feeling up to the journey, call me at this vibration." He produced a business card from an inside jacket pocket. "You'll portal directly into the Department."

Gerald took the card. "Actually I want to go home first." His parents weren't there but he had a key. He needed to go home, to sleep in his childhood bed and breathe in memories of love and laughter.

"Yes. Of course. Family business. Friends. Two days grace, then. But only two." From the look on Sir Alec's face and the tone of his voice it was clear the man didn't have a family of his own. No close friends either.

Gerald promised himself he'd never let his new job do that to *him*. No matter how hard it tried.

"Naturally," Sir Alec continued, "you won't be going into the field right away. We'll need to get a proper idea of what you can do. Test you inside out and back to front to get a handle on the extent of your *potentia*. Then of course there'll be training. Lots and lots of training." He started towards the bedroom door. "You've a great deal of hard work ahead of you, Dunwoody. But you won't regret this decision, I'm sure of it." At the door he turned back, lips curved in that thin, sardonic smile. "Although there'll be times when you'll come very close."

The bedroom door shut behind him with a decisive thud. Groaning, Gerald collapsed onto his bank of pillows. Well, he'd done it now. For better or worse, for richer or poorer, in sickness and most probably excruciatingly dangerous and imminently life-threatening situations . . . he was cryptic Sir Alec's newest secret janitor.

With a sniff, Reg hopped onto his chest. Stared down her beak at him, pinning him to the bed with her bright and brilliant gaze.

"Well, well, well," she said, and balanced on one precarious foot to scratch the side of her head. "*This* is going to be interesting, sunshine!"

# ACKNOWLEDGMENTS

Linda Funnell, who rescued this brain dead author and came up with the spiffiest title. Thanks a million, Linda!

Tim Holman, a champion among champions.

Glenda, for being such a great beta reader and support in those authorly moments of woe.

Elaine and Pete, whose friendship means the world.

Steve Stone, for the great cover art. And Peter Cotton for the wonderful design.

The entire Orbit team, for their tireless efforts.

The readers and booksellers, who make this adventure possible.

cally deaf, not exactly. But he was most definitely compromised. No wonder he couldn't get past the hexed gates. He hated the shield, and had said so, forcibly, but nobody would listen. In the end he'd taken his complaints to Sir Alec. Grey-eyed, softly-spoken and blandly nondescript, the man lurked in the shadows of every conversation. As though he could see through walls. Read thoughts from a distance. Even when he was absent, his presence at janitorial headquarters was inescapable. He was the absolute, ultimate authority.

But Sir Alec hadn't had any sympathy either.

"Mister Dunwoody," he'd said, his pale grey eyes severe, "stop wasting my time. You're wearing the shield whether you wish to or not. Your identity must remain obscure, and so far this is the best way we can contrive that. So you'll not put one toe in public without first activating your shield-incant, any more than you'd leave the house stark naked. The last thing we need is anybody . . . noticing . . . you."

And of course, Sir Alec was right. Janitorial agent Gerald Dunwoody couldn't afford to stand out in any way. Which was also why Monk had devised a nifty little incant that turned his silver eye brown again. The change wasn't permanent; even with Monk's best efforts it wore off after five hours or so, but it was easily reapplied. And with both incants activated he could pass muster as the old Gerald Dunwoody, with two normal-looking eyes and a lousy Third Grade thaumic signature.

*The good old days.*

With the shield-incant cancelled, he could feel his wakened senses coming alive again. Feel the ebb and flow of the ether, fluctuations in the thaumic cur-

challenge. Reg would never forgive him if he tucked his tail between his legs and ran.

*So all right. I'm here. I'm ready to be tested. But first I need to find a way in.*

The gates were hexed shut, and he couldn't pin down the incant. The moss-covered wall they were hinged to was high and slippery, impossible to climb over, and there was no kind of crystal ball or mundane telephone set into the stonework, or anywhere else he could see, that would allow him to call up to the house and tell whoever was in charge that janitorial trainee Gerald Dunwoody had arrived.

He blew out a short, frustrated breath. Damn. He *really* wanted Reg. If she'd been here she could've flown over the stone wall up to the house. Bellowed at the front door. Bashed on a window. Attracted someone's attention before he was completely waterlogged, or took root in the driveway like some exotic weed.

*But she's not here, so just get over it, Dunnywood. What kind of a janitor are you going to make if you can't get through a pair of gates without help? And anyway, this is probably your first test. Any use of Reg would be counted as cheating.*

Feeling ever-so-slightly petulant, he took hold of the gates' wrought-iron bars and shook them. "Come on! Let me in! I'm catching pewmonia out here!"

Nothing. The gates' locking incant buzzed fuzzily through his gloves. *Fuzzily . . .*

"Oh!" he exclaimed. "You *idiot*, Gerald."

With a fingersnap and a single command he deactivated the anti-etheretic shield that muffled his unique thaumic imprint. Wearing the wretched thing was a bit like wearing faulty earplugs. He wasn't thaumaturgi-

pots and a vague hint of higgledy-piggledy gables. No luck. But whether that was because he was blind in one eye, or because the mist was just too thick, or because the house was protected by some kind of deflection incant, he couldn't tell.

The towering oak trees on either side of the gates dripped moisture like a leaking tap, *plink plink plink* on his hatless head and coated shoulders. The water trickled nastily between skin and shirt-collar, all the way down his spine to the waistband of his trousers. The gravel beneath his feet was muddy and rutted. Fading into the distance, the muffled clip-clop of hooves and the creak of wooden wheels, as the cart that had deposited him here returned to the railway station.

Otherwise, the surrounding countryside was quiet. Too quiet. Not a cock-crow, not a bleating lamb. No dog barked. No milch cow lowed. He could hear his heart thudding sullenly against his ribs. Nerves. Because here he was, in far-flung, bucolic Finkley Meadows, and the last tumultuous, exhausting, un-expected six months of his life had come down to this.

*Testing time.*

Tucked beneath his overcoat, in the pocket of his jacket, was a single folded sheet of paper, decorated with precise, spiky writing in plain black ink. *Time to pay the piper, Mister Dunwoody. Finkley Meadows. The 8th, at dawn. Someone will meet you on the platform. Sir Alec.* A one-way railway token had accompanied the missive.

He remembered thinking: *So is the Department merely being fiscally responsible, or should I take the hint and give up while I still can?*

But of course he'd accepted the invitation. The

he understood . . . but theory and practice were two very different things.

Anyway, there was no point working himself into a state over it. *No pining.* He'd chosen this new life. This new direction. This . . . penance. Looking over his shoulder at who and what he'd left behind would do nothing but give him a stiff neck. He had to look ahead. Focus on the job at hand.

Which right here, right now, was surviving till supper. Because one of Sir Alec's senior janitors, a pale, bruised-looking chap by the name of Dalby— well, this week, anyway—had confided over a mug of stewed tea that the property's name-tag designation had a habit of changing. Whenever, rumour whispered, the house claimed a new victim. Today it was tagged Entwhistle. Tomorrow it could be . . . well, it could be Dunwoody. You never know, eh?

Gerald tucked his cold-nipped fingers into his armpits, and bounced on his toes to keep his blood moving. *That's right. You never know. Life is full of surprises.*

Some of them, it turned out, more palatable than others.

Frowning at himself, he shook his head. Close on the heels of Rule One: *No pining,* came Rule Two: *No dwelling on the past.* Especially when the past contained his kind of memories. Memories that more than six months later still woke him sweating in the night, shaking and sick.

So instead of dwelling, he peered through the impassable, imposing wrought-iron gates before him, up the long, straight driveway to the house, trying to make out more than a few haphazard chimney

take? Without question. But not, *really* not, in the mood for a giggle.

*I wish Reg was here. Or Monk. Melissande, even. At this point I'd probably throw my arms around Rupert, butterflies and all.*

But he squashed the thought almost as soon as it formed. The first rule he'd made for himself upon entering janitorial training was *No pining.* Yes, he missed his friends, but they'd stay his friends no matter how long he was away. And anyway, he'd see them again sooner or later. He'd already seen Monk once. And they knew why he had to ignore them for a while.

He just wished his parents could understand. Back from gallivanting around the world, they were so hurt, so disappointed, that he kept putting off a visit. And was so—so *vague* about his new employment . . . and why he'd given up on his last position as a royal court wizard. So grand. So prestigious. What had gone wrong *this* time? And when are we going to *see* you, son?

*"Sorry,"* he kept saying in his letters. He'd phoned them once, but couldn't bear to do that again. His mother's tearful voice was enough to break him. *"I'll tell you all about it soon, I promise. Just a bit busy now. You know how it is."*

Except they didn't know. And they never would. The first lie he told about his new life would be to his parents. It was a lie he'd put off for as long as he could. Because once he told it . . . once he crossed that line . . . he knew he could never go back. And something precious would be irreparably broken. Sir Alec had warned him how it would be. And he'd said

According to Department records, the property was known as *Establishment 743-865-928/Entwhistle*.

Gathered in smoky mess-hall corners, inhaling a quick fag—or a pipe, if they were particular—Sir Alec's senior janitors, his most hard-bitten secret agents, called it *the haunted house*. Rolling their eyes when they said it. Sort of joking. But mostly not. Never elaborating; why should they? Nobody had warned *them*. Nobody gave *them* a heads-up the day before they faced final assessment. They'd sunk or swum, no half-measures. And no help. What do you reckon, Dunwoody? You reckon you deserve any different, just because someone's told you you're the bees' thaumaturgical knees? Sink or swim, mate. That's how it gets done. That's how the pretenders are shuffled out of the pack. If you're as good as they say you are, well . . . you'll be laughing, won't you?

Shrouded in a damp early morning mist, deep in the wilds of rural Ottosland, Gerald wasn't feeling particularly amused. Cold? Yes. Apprehensive? Certainly. Beginning to wonder if he'd made a mis-

# introducing

If you enjoyed
**THE ACCIDENTAL SORCERER,**
look out for

# WITCHES INCORPORATED

Book 2 of the Rogue Agent series
*by K. E. Mills*

# meet the author

K. E. Mills is the pseudonym for Karen Miller. She was born in Vancouver, Canada, and moved to Australia with her family when she was two. She started writing stories while still in primary school, where she fell in love with speculative fiction after reading *The Lion, the Witch and the Wardrobe*. Over the years she has held down a wide variety of jobs, including horse stud groom in Buckingham, England. She is working on several new novels. Visit the official Karen Miller Web site at www.karenmiller.net.

# extras

orbit